HITCH-HIKERS

A TALE OF BOATS, GIRLS AND SEVERELY TWISTED INDIVIDUALS

IAN DOLBY

BOOK ONE OF THE FIREBIRD SERIES

DISCLAIMER:

This is a work of fiction. While names, characters, businesses, events and incidents are the products of the author's warped imagination, places and locales are as correct as possible, but are used in an entirely fictitious manner. Some characters are a composite of several personalities the author has encountered in his travels across Australia as such richness of true-life character could not be ignored. However, any resemblance to actual persons, living or dead, or actual events is unintended, accidental and purely coincidental.

The opinions expressed by the various characters in this story are deemed appropriate for their role and should not be assumed to be those of the author. I ride bikes and embrace the right to freedom of the open road on two wheels for everybody.

Published in Australia by Sid Harta Publishers Pty Ltd,
ABN: 46 119 415 842
23 Stirling Crescent, Glen Waverley, Victoria 3150 Australia
Telephone: +61 3 9560 9920, Facsimile: +61 3 9545 1742
E-mail: author@sidharta.com.au

First published in Australia 2019
This edition published 2019
Copyright © Ian Dolby 2019
Cover design, typesetting: WorkingType (www.workingtype.com.au)

The right of Ian Dolby to be identified as the Author of the Work has been asserted in accordance with the Copyright, Designs and Patents Act 1988.

Dolby, Ian
Hitch-Hikers: A tale of boats, girls and severely twisted individuals
ISBN: 978-1-925230-63-5
500pp

ABOUT THE AUTHOR

I was born and raised on the Gold Coast, Queensland and my love of boats was instilled by the family before I could walk, as indicated by an early photo that shows me crawling around the deck of the family boat in nappies. The love of sailing developed through a series of ever-larger racing catamarans and led to the purchase, at the age of 21, of an old 47-foot wooden, engineless, monohull cutter-rigged yacht that had been built in Ireland in 1905 and taken part in the WWII Dunkirk evacuation. I lived on this boat at a marina in Rushcutters Bay, Sydney Harbour for several years and my engine-free adventures on this wonderful old boat may one day appear in writing.

The love of flying dragged me away from the boating scene, commencing with gliding, which in turn led to the establishment of a commercial gliding school at Narromine, NSW. After six years of gaining valuable flight experience in this successful enterprise, I sold out and undertook the necessary study and flight training to gain both Aeroplane and Helicopter Commercial Licences. After some 38 years and 16,000 hours of mixed Aeroplane and Helicopter flying, I have retired to a country town in New South Wales with my partner and two young cats where I am now relishing the new challenge of full-time writing.

To my late Mother who insisted that I learn to
speak, spell and write properly.

To Jenny, for your endless support, love, and suggestions;
the brainstorming sessions and putting up with the all
the (very) early morning writing sessions, not to mention
the revisions and mugs of tea.

To Liz, thanks for the rough draft editing. It made Barbara's job
easier. Thanks also for your advice and hard work and for getting
me in the right dinghy.

To all those who gave the greatest encouragement of all by
reading the rough draft and saying they actually liked it.

Thanks to Smokie and The Bandit for your
furry company in the wee small hours.

Thank you, Mark, for the loan of your character.
You have more appearances to make.

Thank you, Sue, for the early years.
And to Ali for providing the inspiration that started the process.

*'Sometimes the snowball grows as it rolls downhill, but sometimes the
blowtorch of public opinion merely creates another wet spot!'*
Musings from The Cat

Ian Dolby, 2019

CONTENTS

With the warmth of a late-summer day setting the sex-starved male cicadas frantically buzzing in the trees, inside the classic old Victorian house was quiet, and would have been superbly peaceful, if it weren't for the all-pervading, but subtle air of menace that hung over it like a noxious gas. The slow, metronomic ticking of the grandfather clock in the entry hall, once so comforting, was by far the loudest noise.

That was until Janice loudly and very forcibly said, 'Fuck it!' as she cursed her aching wrist and the stiffness in her hands caused by numerous, week-old bruises on her arms and shoulders. She found that typing on her computer was a lot more difficult than she'd imagined, but nevertheless, she was determined to finally set down a timetable of the catalogue of violence that had befallen her over the past 18 months.

Oh, she'd started to write all this down several times before, but had either given up in sheer despair at the relentless tide of insane violence directed at her by her outwardly charming and quietly-spoken husband Luke Emery, or had her writings discovered and been forced to abandon the project by yet another particularly savage beating that left few visible marks, but often confined her to bed for days at a time.

However, one thing that she did was take photos of the injuries with her phone. She'd either take them herself or get Jill, their pretty 22-year-old housekeeper, to do so when she helped Janice clean herself after a particularly bad beating.

Despite her injuries, by far her greatest concern was for the safety of her beautiful twin girls, soon to turn 19. Luckily, they had not seen any of the insane rages of which their father was capable, but she felt that day was coming. They still thought the sun shone out of his fundamental orifice, and it appeared that he tried very hard to help maintain their delusions for as long as possible. For their sake, Janice also worked hard to conceal her injuries from them where she could, assisted by the hopelessly intimidated Jill.

However, Janice felt that a breaking point wasn't far off and before it happened, she wanted the girls, Jill and herself as far away as possible from this raving lunatic she'd mistakenly married.

Although she had a comfortable private income, courtesy of a benevolent and doting grandfather, her husband was a very well connected, multi-millionaire. He'd made his money primarily in the earth-moving business, but more lately, he had branched out into property development.

He'd hit on the relatively simple, but apparently highly lucrative scheme of buying up old inner-city industrial sites, warehouses and factories cheaply from suspiciously near-bankrupt owners. He then used his earth-moving business to tear everything down and build upmarket, trendy housing for the seemingly endless supply of yuppies, anxious to move in from the unsophisticated outer suburbs and join the bullshit-sprouting latte set, happily buried in the concrete canyons of CBD Melbourne.

(The fact that they saved themselves ridiculously long commutes to and from the daily inner-city grind was the only real positive to the scheme).

Still, for some time, both her accountancy training and the small amount of information she gleaned from various sources, told her that Luke's income from these projects was well short of his very extravagant outgoings.

She shared her concerns about apparent financial discrepancies with her father, a well-respected Melbourne barrister, whom she'd grown much closer to since her mother had died eight years ago from cancer. So far, she'd managed (or so she thought) to hide the domestic violence from him. His advice had been that there were plenty of rumours circulating about Luke's dodgy dealings, stand-over tactics with stubborn prime-site building owners, as well as kickbacks to politicians and Council planning department heads. However, she would have to try to find some actual proof of wrongdoing or face the near-impossible task of proving her word against a person of Luke's sterling reputation in the community. Not to mention his connections with nearly everyone in high places!

Janice had a small, but pretty room on the ground floor, where she kept her computer and collection of books and which had a lovely view out over the extensive gardens. At one time, it had been her pleasure to curl up in a comfortable chair and read, with the beautifully tended garden to gaze at occasionally.

Now, she had to keep her door open all the time, with Luke's private study just two rooms away. His door was always kept locked with a massive thumbprint-operated deadlock, whether he was in there or not.

This particular day, the silence was broken again by a hammering on the front door, which was next to Luke's study, and as usual, he allowed Jill to see who it was.

Janice heard the door open, but before Jill could say anything, a loud male voice demanded to see Luke.

'Mr Luke is busy, sir', Janice heard Jill say in a frightened tone, 'he can't be disturbed.'

'I'll bloody well disturb him all right,' the voice yelled, 'get the stupid fucker out here now. We've got some things to discuss!'

Before Jill had a chance to reply, Luke had ripped his door open and stormed out, pulling it to behind him.

'What the fuck is going on out here?' he demanded loudly, glaring at a terrified Jill and the belligerent visitor in turn, 'What part of 'I'm busy' don't you fuck-wits understand!'

Jill started stammering an apology but was violently swept aside by Luke's arm as he charged through the front door, barrelling his visitor out in front of him. Before the massive door crashed closed, Janice heard him yelling, 'How dare you come to my house, you stupid prick! I've told everyone that there's never to be...'

Janice quickly walked up the hall, gave a trembling Jill a quick hug and sent her back to what she had been doing. Shaking her head at yet another example of her husband's temper and odd business dealings, she was walking slowly back to her sitting room, when she noticed that the door to Luke's study hadn't properly latched closed. With a quick look over her shoulder, she pushed the door open and took a quick look inside. Nothing seemed out of the ordinary, but her gaze locked onto his computer sitting on his desk, switched on and apparently in the middle of a letter.

With a flash of inspiration and a heady dose of daring, she darted back to her room, grabbed a 2TB portable HDD from her drawer, and returned to Luke's study. She glanced out the window, which overlooked the driveway, and was reassured when saw the two of them, still shouting and poking each other in the chest, beside the stranger's car. With trembling hands, she plugged her HDD into a spare USB port, minimised the open document while it booted up, and started a copy of all the desktop folders and documents, then a copy of the Documents folder itself. Even with the super-fast USB3 transfer protocol, it seemed to take a very long time to make the copies, although she kept a close eye on the continuing drama out front, ready to stop the copy and run if it came to a premature conclusion.

Her mind boggled at the thought of Luke's reaction if he even just caught her in here, let alone copying his private files.

Finally, a soft chime announced that the process was completed. Hastily, she closed the open folders, ejected the drive, enlarged the document that he'd been working on and left the room, leaving the door almost closed, but not locked, just as she'd found it.

She also figured that Luke would be less than happy when he came back inside, and even more so when he found that he'd left his study door unsecured. As he hadn't seen her when he charged out of his office, she thought that she might be able to get away with pretending to have been absent for the whole time, and therefore not a suspect for having been in his study.

Accordingly, she went down to their private dock, and took the rowing boat upriver.

An hour later, pleasantly sweaty, she returned, tied the dinghy up and went to her room to shower and change.

That was where Luke found her.

What followed was the mother of all beatings, at which time he didn't bother to give her a chance to confirm or deny any wrongdoing; instead, he blamed her for the bloke who came unannounced to the door and for making him forget to lock his study door. Along the way, she was accused of breaking into his private study to spy on his business. As usual, he became very sexually excited during a beating and as he got ready to have sex with her again, she kicked out and landed a perfect blow right on his nuts.

He limped away, threatening all sorts of retaliation, leaving her naked and bleeding on the floor of her bathroom. As they'd been living in separate quarters for quite some time and hadn't had consensual sex for years, his fumbling attempts at penetration became the final act in the more severe beatings. On this occasion, it was up to Jill to take more photos of Janice's injuries, help clean her up before the girls came home, and to concoct the story that she'd tripped over the vacuum cleaner that Jill had carelessly left at the top of the stairs and fallen all the way to the bottom.

Luke left her alone for several days, so she had time to partially recover and to plan for her and the girls' escape from his reign of terror. Finally, she told the incredulous girls the whole sordid story, waited until Luke was away for the day on business, withdrew a large bundle of cash from her bank account, packed their bags and had Jill drive them in her SUV to the train station.

Janice advised Jill to take her car and disappear as well although she didn't think that Jill was bright enough to predict the extent of Luke's meltdown when he discovered his wife and daughters had fled the scene.

That evening, when he returned from visiting a construction site, Luke's meltdown was of truly epic proportions! From some misplaced sense of loyalty, Jill hadn't had the sense to leave as Janice had suggested, so she was the number one target. Luke hadn't bashed her up before, apart from pushing her roughly about sometimes when he was in a rage, but this time he really lashed out.

She copped the same treatment he would have lavished on Janice, including ripping off all her clothes and attempting to have sex with her. That part she found to be a bit of a joke as he proved to be so short-changed in the erection department that she could barely feel him, yet alone be hurt by his grunting efforts! It was his weight on her and the gusts of bad breath washing over her face that were much worse than what she could barely feel further down. The beatings were a totally different matter however, and she was thankful that he didn't break any bones.

After letting Jill clean herself up, he produced a pair of handcuffs and secured her hands, then tied a rope to the linking chain before leading her, still naked, after him wherever he went. When he stopped in one place for a while, he'd tie the rope to any handy, heavy piece of furniture, making her sit awkwardly on the floor.

Her requests to visit the toilet were met with a curt, 'Piss on yourself, you stupid bitch!' Inevitably, after a while, she had to, after which he made her clean it up.

THE OFFER

She was also present, later that evening, when Luke received a phone call, just after he had finished arranging for his head foreman, Jimmy Fitzroy, to mobilise some men to apply pressure on the owner of a derelict building in the old docks area that Luke had been trying to buy for a pittance. The problem was that the old guy knew what Luke was up to and just wanted a fair price for his property, a concept that Luke found quite ridiculous. Hence the call to Jimmy to pay a friendly visit to the old man's daughter and her husband in the middle of the night.

His advice that they all should wear condoms this time fell on deaf ears!

Luke was busy calculating what the imminent acquisition of the building would mean to his grand plan for converting a series of old warehouses into inner-city apartments for Melbourne's upwardly mobile set, when the phone rang.

'Hello? Who's this?'

'Mr Emery, I presume?'

'Speak up, for Christ's sake! You sound like Darth Vader! Ha, Ha. What've you got a cold or something?'

'Never mind what I've got, Mr Emery. You may call me Darth if that appeals to your warped sense of humour. Can you confirm that you have two blonde, 18-year-old daughters?'

'Yes, I have. I guess that's common knowledge. But what's the age of my daughters got to do with you?'

'Listen carefully, Mr Emery. I have a proposition that could be worth a lot of money to you.'

That grabbed Luke's attention like nothing else.

'OK but go slow! I've got to take notes. You're still very hard to understand and I don't have one of those robot translator things. Ha, ha!'

'*Very droll, Mr Emery. Now pay attention. I represent a gentleman who resides in another part of the world, and who is offering a large sum of money for two blonde, Caucasian, virgin females under the age of 20. He has seen photos of two such girls on your, ah...group's website, and wishes to know if these girls can be made available for a suitable price.*'

'Holy crap! Are you offering to buy my daughters?'

'*Not precisely, Mr Emery. I am merely the agent, if you will. It is my client who is offering to do just that.*'

Luke was quiet for a minute, thoughts whirling around his head. It was one thing to trade nude photos of his daughters, but a huge step up to actually selling them! Where would he find another pair like them? Blonde, beautiful and who loved to be photographed naked! Even with all his resources, it would be a difficult search.

Naturally, the concept of being concerned for the safety and future of his offspring didn't enter into Luke's calculations for one moment. However, the dangled prospect of converting the girls into some serious money was of far greater interest. And so, the negotiations began.

'Just how seriously are we talking here, Mr Vader? I mean they are my daughters!'

'*From what I hear, you couldn't care less about them, except as a source of naked photos for a bunch of twisted old men to masturbate over!*'

Luke made a show of spluttering indignantly, 'Listen you fucking robot! You watch what you say! '

'*No! You watch what you say, Mr Emery. You're the one who needs the money, teetering on the verge of bankruptcy as you are. In this instance, you are simply the most convenient and amoral source of these items, but by no means the only source! So be very careful or the offer of all that lovely money will disappear from in front of you like a grain of sand in the desert!*'

That shut Luke up immediately. 'OK, OK! Let's presume that for the moment I'm interested! What's the deal?'

'That's better. Upon production of the two girls, in perfect health, with no marks or bruises from handling, and with their virginity physically intact, at a place and time to be advised, I am authorised to offer the sum of one million US dollars.

The money will be transferred to your bank account upon hand-over of the items and medical verification that the agreed specifications have been met.'

Luke thought quickly. One million US translated to about $1.4 Australian and would go a long way to bailing him out of the mounting mass of debt that was piling up daily.

'Very well. That's agreeable. But when is this transaction to take place?'

'I will contact you shortly, once I have had communications with my client, but expect my call within 10 days.'

'Ah...Look. The ah...items have gone away for a few days.'

'I don't see a problem with that, Mr Emery. But it would be wise if you were to be ready to produce the items within the 10-day time frame I suggested. Do you have any problem with that?'

'Ah...No. No, I'm sure that'll be fine. I'll be ready.'

'Excellent, Mr Emery. I'd like to say that it's been a pleasure doing business with you, despite my natural dislike of persons of your peculiar persuasion! Still, business is business, as the saying goes, and we can't always chose who we do business with.'

There was a definite 'click' as the Darth Vader voice hung up, leaving Luke sitting slightly stunned, as the import of the deal he'd just made sunk in. There was still no remorse over the morality of the 'deal', just that a million dollar plus payday was sufficiently rare in Luke's world to warrant serious thought about what it would mean to his personal welfare.

Now he just had to get the mobile moneybags back from wherever that bitch Janice had dragged them off to! His next action was to hit a speed dial number on his phone.

'Jimmy. I've got a job for you.'

'...Yes, I know you're on a job. This is different.'

'...I don't care what time of night it is! Don't argue with me, you fucking idiot! Who pays your exorbitant salary? And who makes sure you've always got plenty of girls — and the right sort of guys as well? Don't forget because I won't.'

'...Okay. That's better. Now, I want you to put a team together and find my family.'

'...No, of course they're not here! Would I be asking you to find them if they were here? Christ! What a moron! Get your thumb outa your bum and zip your fly! You've got work to do!'

With that, Luke passed on details of Janice and the girls' disappearance and authorised spending as required to find the three of them.

CHAPTER 1

Around 15:00 Monday afternoon and the summer sun was starting to lose its heat as I wandered up from the wharf landing where I'd tied up my dinghy, a Rigid Inflatable Boat, or RIB. I bought a paper from the newsagent, chatted briefly with the owner, a very pleasant and friendly lady who always asked after my cat, Jasper, before stepping next door to the small bar and grill. Most afternoons, I met up with Johnny, the boat refueller and harbourmaster, for a beer or two. I also ate there often as, although I quite enjoyed cooking, I rarely bothered doing it just for myself. The only other eat-out alternative was a walk up the steep hill into the town to other eateries like the excellent Eden Fisherman's Club.

I'd been in Eden for 4 weeks now, taking my time cleaning up my 60 ft catamaran, as well as resting myself and Jasper, my 2-year-old, 25kg, black, male Chausie-cross cat. We'd taken a battering from an un-forecast storm that developed from a small cut-off low off the coast of NSW.

The parachute anchor got a good work-out in the 30 to 40ft seas whipped up by 50 to 60 kts winds and although the boat sustained no real damage, a few annoying leaks appeared in the deckhouse where they shouldn't, and the rear deck hardtop had been cracked by something very heavy landing on it.

That something had long disappeared by the time I'd carefully ventured out into the cockpit, but it had broken a solar panel and left a smear of blood and some very large scales that didn't look like any scale I'd seen before or wanted to see again. By the time the wind had settled down and the waves dropped to a less intimidating height, Eden was both the nearest decent port to lie up and recover, as well as a very pretty place.

Jasper appreciated the rest as well, having retired to his bed on a spare bunk in my dressing room for the duration of the blow, and regularly voiced his displeasure with the conditions by a series of mournful yowls.

Now that I'd been here in Eden a while, I quite fancied staying longer, although my original goal was to explore the West coast of Tassie while the weather was suitable before winter set in. Macquarie Harbour and the fascinating remote wilderness expanse of Port Davey further to the south attracted me like few other places.

This Monday afternoon, as Johnny was already waiting, it wasn't long before we were sitting at our usual window ledge, sipping cold schooners of beer and perving at and rating the surprising number of wandering female tourists.

'How's that mini black panther cat of yours?' Johnny asked, 'You haven't brought him ashore for a few days.'

'Nah,' I said, 'after that silly bloody Dutch woman freaked out the last time I was walking him around the wharves, and wanted to report me to the cops for keeping a dangerous animal, I decided to walk him at night.

Johnny laughed, 'Yeah. That was real funny. She was screaming and yelling, but Jasper just sat and looked at her. Tell you what, though' Jasper's scored a big hit with Molly at the newsagency. She reckons he's the duck's guts!' He gave me a grin, 'She reckons you're OK too.'

'Ah, come on,' I chuckled, 'she's a really nice lady, but I think you're stretching things a bit. Still, she's pretty and very nicely built! She looks like she works out.'

Johnny gave me a flat look. 'Yeah, and of course you hadn't noticed that she's got great tits, too!'

I didn't encourage him with a reply to that one, and got back to Jasper's exercise program, a much safer subject.

'Anyway, to keep Jasper happy, I've been taking him over to Aslings Beach in the RIB and letting him have a good run around that sand spit. He really likes the sand and it's a safe place for him to have a swim. I'm not too keen on him swimming off the boat. There are too many bitey things in this particular bay!'

He nodded and after a few moments and a few sips of beer, Johnny said,

'Did that woman and her daughters come to see you yet?'

I looked at him blankly, 'What woman and what daughters would that be, Johnny?'

Johnny looked annoyed with himself. 'Oh. Sorry, I guess I forgot to tell you.'

Sometimes Johnny can be so vague, I don't know how he stays in business.

'Well, last Saturday, this woman, who's a pretty good sort by the way, with two chicky-babes in tow, comes by the office and asks if there are any yachties heading out in the next few days that might be willing to take on some crew. So, I mentioned the Yanks as a long shot, but they seem to travel just as a family with their three kids, plus the fact that they only just arrived.

Then there's the Danish couple, but as she seems to like running around naked most of the time, they probably wouldn't want anybody else around. Their boat's a bit small for another three, anyway, although Henk would probably love to have more females aboard!

Course there's Doris and Albert, but I doubt they're going anywhere in the near future and although they'll need crew when they do go, they probably wouldn't take amateurs.

Then, when I mentioned that you were heading off to the Tasmanian West coast sometime soon, she just said thanks and wandered off. So, I guess that she hasn't been to see you yet?'

Like most re-fuelling persons in ports, Johnny is a chronic gossip and busybody, so he was always trying to get some information.

'No, mate. I haven't seen or heard from them.'

'Oh. Okay.' We drank and chitchatted for a while, then as we started our second round, he suddenly pointed past me and quietly said, 'Hey! There they are! The three of them! That's mum in front.'

I slowly turned my head and saw a woman, medium height, about 30 to 35, dressed in baggy shorts and a loose top, walking along the footpath, followed by two tall, lanky teenage girls wearing the obligatory just-sprayed-on short-shorts and short tops with lots of bare, tanned skin in between.

'Yeah. That's them,' Johnny repeated. 'See. I told you that mum wasn't bad looking! The daughters are a bit of alright too!'

He was right. She wasn't bad looking at all — rather pretty really, with short, blonde hair and with a pleasantly rounded body in welcome defiance of the current anorexic standard of attractiveness. She had really nice legs and moved with a grace that the baggy clothes failed to hide. Her daughters were also very blonde and pretty.

Due to the dark fly screen over the open window in front of us, we were able to watch without getting sprung, but then they conveniently stopped at a café table just a couple of meters from our window vantage point, where the two girls sat while mum went in to order.

They were close enough for us to hear some of what they were saying.

One said, unhappily, 'I'm glad Mum finally told us why we've been dragging our arses around from motel to motel these last three weeks or so, although it's hard to believe that Dad could have been so cruel to her. We never saw him do anything like that!'

Her sister replied in a carefully reasoned tone,

'No, we didn't. But thinking back, remember all the bruises that she said were just her being clumsy? She's never been clumsy in her life! Not a former tennis and surfing champion! And remember that broken wrist that she said was caused by a baking-pan falling on it? Bullshit!'

'But Dad was always so good to us,' her sister said softly, 'I know what you're saying, Angie, but I still have trouble believing that he could do those things and we didn't even suspect there was a problem.'

'I know, I know,' apparently-Angie comforted her, 'but it seems like he's really got the shits now that we've left, by the way, he's sicced his goons onto us. I just hope that we *can* keep away from them and I guess that's why she's looking for a boat ride somewhere. It might just be a good place to hide for a while. But I reckon Dad's not going to just let us slip away too easily, and with all his money he can pull as many strings as is necessary to search for us, so this might be our only chance.'

'Yeah. I know,' her sister replied, 'but I'm not sure about just jumping on a boat! I mean, it's not like catching a bus or something.'

'True,' Angie replied, 'and this place doesn't seem to be overrun with yachts heading out of town on the hour! Ha, ha!'

'Yeah. But now I'm starting to really miss our friends and being able to hang out at the mall, and it's only been three weeks! I'll especially miss Jason. He's such a nice guy, although he seems terribly shy, but I've nearly got him convinced to play "show me yours and I'll show you mine". Tricia says that he's really well hung! I can't wait to see it, although I did wonder that if he's so shy, how does Trish know?'

Angie giggled. 'I know what you mean. Boys can be so stupid about that stuff. I read in Cleo that boys are several years behind girls in the maturity stakes, so that might explain it.'

Her sister laughed, 'Maybe we can stay in one place long enough to get to know a couple of boys well enough to be able to mess around with! I'm a bit tired of us being the only two virgins in our group! Real sex sounds interesting! Not that I'm unhappy with our Big John! He's great fun!'

'Yeah!' Angie giggled, 'He sure is, but I'm sure the real thing will be better. I'd just like us to have the chance to find out!' Which started them both giggling, but they quietened down when their mum returned, followed by a waitress carrying a tray of drinks.

'So,' Mum said, eyeing them both, 'I'm glad to see that you can still laugh.'

'Yeah, sorry we've been a bit down lately, Mum,' Angie said after Mum was seated and the waitress left. 'It's just all this travelling and shifting motels every two or three days. We're really glad you told us why though, but you should've told us earlier.'

'I know and I'm really sorry that things happened like this but running away seemed to be the best and only thing to do!'

'We think so too now that we know what's been happening, but what's the plan from here?'

'Well, Angie,' Mum replied to the first girl, 'To be honest, I've pretty well run out of ideas, so the only other way I can think of to break our trail is to jump on a boat and disappear until things settle down a bit. Then, maybe we can deal with the legal stuff to stop your dad chasing us.'

'Okay, Mum,' Angie replied, 'but I don't think it's going to be like catching a plane or bus or something. How does one just hitchhike a ride on a boat? Or more importantly, how do we convince the skipper to help us? I mean, he or she would have to know what's going on, surely?'

Mum grinned, 'No. I'm sure it's not just like catching a bus, but otherwise I don't know. I did ask around the wharves to see if there was anybody willing to take on three novice crewmembers, even though we do have some boating experience.'

The second girl replied, 'Get a grip, Mum, that was just around the Bay in Dad's power boat. There's nothing like that here apart from the fishing boats and I'm sure they won't take us anywhere. They live here! Everything else that floats seems to have bloody great masts poking up, and that means sails and stuff which we know nothing about!'

'Oh, Zoe! Of course the fishermen won't take us,' Mum replied, 'but someone might help us if we keep trying. If not here, then maybe at another port that has more private yachts! We really need to break our trail for a while.'

'Yeah. I know, Mum,' Zoe replied, 'I'm sorry and we do understand. It's just so frustrating, but we're with you!'

Mum smiled. 'Thanks girls, I know you are. I just want to try to make the best of this insane, crazy situation!'

They sipped their drinks in silence for a while, before Angie said, 'So who have you asked about a boat?'

'Well,' she replied, 'several of the trawler guys, but the best one seems to be the refueller fella down on the main wharf. He said he'd ask around for us, but out of several possible, he did suggest that there's a single guy with a catamaran who's maybe leaving in a few days.'

CHAPTER 2

I looked at Johnny and raised my eyebrows.

'How does all that sound to you?' I asked quietly.

He frowned. 'I don't know. Sounds true, but, jeeze, they're carrying a lot of baggage. You may find yourself in the middle of a real mess if some angry husband is chasing them!'

I grinned back. 'True. But I'm a sucker for helping damsels in distress!'

'Yeah,' he smirked, 'especially if they've got nice tits and look good!'

I scowled at him. 'How can you say such a thing? My intentions are pure!'

'Yeah! Sure. Purely depraved!'

I stood and drained the last of my beer. 'Ok, enough of your insults. Come and introduce me and I'll see if they can be my new crew.'

'But,' I looked carefully at him, 'if I do take them on, you have to keep quiet. You can't tell anybody where we've gone. It sounds like somebody may come around asking questions, especially as she's spread the story of wanting a boat ride, so you just have to say that nobody wanted to take them on and they'd left town on a bus or something. Okay?'

Johnny looked thoughtful, which maybe was a bit of a stretch for him.

'Yeah. You're right, that's what I'll have to say. No problem, mate, I'll handle it.'

I clapped him on the shoulder and said, 'Good man. Let's go talk to my new crew then.'

As we walked outside, I hung back a bit so that hopefully Johnny was recognised.

Luckily he was and the mother's face lit up.

'There's Johnny now!' she said to Angie and Zoe, 'Hi, Johnny!' She called out as he pretended to walk past their table, 'Remember me? Janice. I was asking you about boats leaving Eden.'

Although Johnny's acting wasn't too good, he did a passable double-take and pasted a sappy smile on his dial as he stopped and said, 'Oh, yeah. Sure, Janice. I remember. In fact, I was just having a beer with my mate, Harry here. He's the one I mentioned.'

Three sets of assessing female eyes swivelled like cannons in my direction. They saw an above average height guy, about 5'11' or so in the old measure, in his late 30s, clean-shaven, with pleasant but un-remarkable features (or so I've been told), vivid blue eyes and shaggy, sandy hair. The lean body was thanks to good genes and the lifestyle of living on a boat. Not wanting to scare them too soon, I hoped that they'd missed the hard, sometimes haunted look that I've been told lurks further back rather than the slightly vacant look of a dedicated boat-bum I normally liked to show the world.

Janice jumped to her feet with a huge smile on her face, and stuck out her slim hand, unadorned by any jewellery.

'Hi. I'm Janice Emery and these are my daughters, Angie and Zoe.'

I shook hands with all of them, pleased that the girls responded immediately and had genuine smiles and firm grips the same as Janice.

'Hi, I'm Harry Stevens and Johnny says that you're looking to make a boat trip.'

Janice sat down and waved to the fourth chair at the table. 'Well. It's a bit more complicated than that, but please join us if you would and I'll explain. Johnny, do you want to sit as well?'

Johnny shook his head. 'No thanks Janice. I've got to get back to the wharf. I've got three trawlers coming in the next hour or so to refuel. I'll see you later, Harry. Bye girls.'

He sketched a wave to everyone and headed for the wharf across the road as I pulled out a chair and sat. Up close, Janice was still pretty, but her very bright green eyes were almost mesmerising and fixed me with an intense gaze, as I suppose was natural under the circumstances. I thought it best to pretend that I had heard nothing of their previous conversation for now, to see if the story stayed straight.

I also reminded myself that I shouldn't let my current lengthy drought of female company unduly influence my decision to take on crew — something I normally avoided with a passion!

After ten minutes of Janice talking and the girls listening carefully and watching for my reactions, I accepted that she wasn't trying to snow me with some bullshit. She told it like I'd heard before, although with a lot more useful info. Like, her husband Luke Emery, was a very wealthy man with connections at all levels of industry and government. He had mobilised a search with his own thugs to comb the country looking for the three. She and the girls were all puzzled as to why her husband was trying so incredibly hard to find them.

Although her mother had died of cancer eight years ago, Janice still had her father and other family and friends, who just needed time to put together the case against Luke and present it to the Police to get a Domestic Violence Order and file for divorce. Meanwhile, she and the girls were trying to stay off the radar and out of the clutches of Luke's 'investigators'.

'So,' she said, staring at me with an intense gaze from her bright green eyes, 'Do you think you can help us? I do have money, cash, which friends have been posting to me so that I don't have to use plastic and leave a trail, but it's getting harder to find motels that will take cash only. Still, I want to pay our way. The main thing is we've been here too many days already and really need to leave as soon as possible.'

I sat back and thought while I looked at each in turn. Janice radiated a mix of impatience and fear. The girls seemed more interested in the new environment they were possibly getting into and were carefully checking out the bloke in charge of that environment.

I had no problem with that scrutiny.

Despite my earlier comments to Johnny, I did have a lot of concerns about the size of the mess I was potentially getting into. Still, I could always bail out and sail away if things got too hot. Whether I kept the ladies with me or not depended quite a lot on how well they fitted in and behaved.

I was far from being a saint, and as Johnny suggested, if it was pretty and had tits, I'd prefer to have all three girls close by than not! The opportunity to get to know Janice better had a lot going for it, since she seemed very bright, very attractive and it'd been quite a while since I had a female crew member sharing my bed.

All this heavy thinking must have taken longer than Janice was prepared to sit still for, as she kicked me in the shin. Not too hard, mind, but still not the behaviour I'd expected.

'Oy!' I said, more in surprise than for pain, as the girls giggled at my reaction, 'What's that's for?'

'For taking so long to answer me,' she said in exasperation, 'Can or will you help or not?'

'Bloody hell, woman, you're impatient, aren't you?' I snapped in annoyance. 'You'd better not do that when we're at sea! I'm supposed to be the Skipper!'

It took a few moments for that comment to sink in, but then her face suddenly softened and a tear or two glittered greenly in her eyes.

'So, you will help?'

'Yes. But it's got to be done my way or not at all. That's the first and main thing. OK?'

They nodded, waiting for the other shoe to drop. 'In that case, this is what we have to do.' I looked at the girls in particular. 'If there really are some serious guys looking for you, your trail has to end here and now. You all have to do exactly what I say at all times and without argument. I wasn't totally joking about kicking the Skipper.'

They nodded nervously, hopefully impressed by my newfound intensity that matched Janice's. While I had their total attention, I held up my hand, fingers spread and ticked off the list.

'There must not be any contact with family or friends by phone or anything else until we can do so without too much concern about being traced.'

I looked at the girls again, 'I'd like you to turn off your mobile phones now and give them to your Mother. That part of your trail has to break now!

There can't be any last-minute chat with your best friends either, I'm afraid. These people can track you by your phones. And your friends won't be able to keep it secret that you called, so don't call. As I just said, you either do this properly or not at all, in which case, you might as well go back home and save everyone's time and money. Especially mine! You've got to agree to abide by those terms without reservation or I say goodbye right now!'

Janice nodded immediately, and after a moment the girls did too, although they were very unhappy at the 'no phones' rule.

'As long as that's settled, please go back to wherever you're staying and check out. Tell them that you've just spoken to friends who are driving to the Gold Coast and will be passing through town this evening. You've decided to go with them and they're going to pick you up from the Fisho's Club, so you'd like to check out now. You might have to pay for the extra day — if so, do it without arguing.

Collect all your gear and go to the Eden Fisherman's Club. It's in the main street toward the harbour from the motel.'

Janice nodded, 'We've passed it many times.'

'Good,' I replied, 'you get to wait there. The receptionist will let you park your gear if you say that you're waiting for friends to pick you up and that you'd like some drinks and a meal first. The restaurant opens at 17:30 and is really good! '

'That sounds good,' Janice nodded, 'It's been a long day and we are hungry!'

'Have a good feed,' I advised, 'cause we don't want to be messing around making meals later. It won't be dark for a while, so play the pokies or something. You girls look old enough for that.'

They nodded, 'Yes. We're 18, nearly 19.'

'Okay, good. Then at 20:30, but not before so it's properly dark, get your gear, leave reception and walk around to the carpark, .'

'Excuse me, Harry. But what's 20:30?'

I felt a slight surge of exasperation, before smiling. 'Sorry. Old Service habits. It's the 24-hour clock system and means 8.30 PM.'

She nodded thanks, so I continued. 'Wait by the East wall of the Club well back from the main street and try to look as though you're waiting for someone to arrive to pick you up. Don't hide or you'll look suspicious. Just try to blend in since you want to keep the lowest profile possible so people don't remember you.

If someone in the carpark asks if you need help, just stick with the story that your friends are on their way to pick you up, and how excited you are to be going to the Gold Coast. When you see an old blue Holden Commodore come in, be ready to get in with as little fuss and delay as possible. You can trust the person driving the car.'

Janice nodded again.

'Now, it's important that you follow these instructions exactly. Is there anything so far that any of you don't understand or have a problem with?'

All three shook their heads, which was a real advance. I was serious in wanting to stop their trail dead and supply a little misdirection.

'Ok. I'll see you later and we'll plan further from there. Alright?'

'Thanks for helping us, Harry. We really appreciate your efforts,' Janice said quietly, 'we'll do what you ask. It's so good to at last have a plan to follow that has a chance of working.'

'Yeah, thanks, Harry,' Angie echoed, 'You're being great.'

I smiled at them. 'That's OK. You may regret taking the boat option later if you aren't used to small boats.'

'Ah. Speaking of that, how small is your boat?' Janice asked with some trepidation in her voice, 'I mean, is it really big enough for four people?'

I grinned, unable to resist the temptation of a bit of a wind-up, 'Yeah, just. We should be able to squeeze in, although things will be pretty tight. But you don't have a lot of choice at the moment, do you?'

'No,' Janice looked downcast, 'we really don't.'

'OK. Don't worry too much,' I offered, 'things will work out.'

At that we parted, the ladies to walk back up the hill, and me to organise a quick re-provision, refuel and plan. My first job was to see Johnny, and then to make out some provisioning lists.

CHAPTER 3

EDEN, MONDAY, EARLY EVENING

I managed to beat the trawlers to the fuel dock, although it didn't take long as the tanks were about 60% full to start with, then I moved back out to the mooring. I figured that boarding passengers out there would attract less attention than tying up at the main wharf for a few hours and loading supplies and passengers. What people didn't see, they couldn't gossip about.

I decided to shop for supplies myself to avoid the attention a delivery would attract and borrowed Johnny's old car. It didn't take too long as the boat was already quite well stocked.

With twilight deepening and 20:30 approaching, *Firebird* and I were ready. Johnny had agreed to stay back after dark to let me use his old car again. He offered to make the pickup, but I preferred to keep his involvement to a minimum. Trusting him to say the right thing to the investigators when they arrived was a big enough worry.

Once full dark settled in, I went ashore in the RIB and tied up at the fuelling wharf. Johnny was still refuelling the last trawler, so I hadn't delayed him with my plan.

'Keys on the desk, Harry,' he called out from the trawler's deck, where he was wrestling with a fuel hose the size of a Queensland Scrub python. I waved and kept moving, and five minutes later wheeled into the Fisho's Club carpark. I drove slowly around to see who might be coming or going, but as it was quiet at the moment, I headed for the rear corner where I'd told Janice to be waiting.

I didn't see them at first, but then she appeared out of the shadows and bent down to peer through the passenger side window.

'Oh. Hi, Harry,' she said nervously. 'You were right. I guess I can trust the person driving this old car, can't I?'

I grinned as I hopped out, 'Yup. Sure can.'

They had what seemed to be a large pile of bags holding their stuff.

'Bloody hell!' I exclaimed, 'You've brought enough!'

'Well. We had to,' Janice burred up defensively with a catch in her voice, 'this is all we have left. There's only two suitcases plus a small carry bag each!'

That made me remember how she must be feeling, on the run and having to put all her trust in a total stranger who appeared to be a boat bum as well!

'Sorry, Janice,' I apologised as I helped the girls stow the bags in the boot and back seat, 'I didn't mean to be rude. That was uncalled for.'

She nodded acceptance, but in the dim carpark lights, I saw a gleam of unshed tears in her eyes.

'Come on. We'll all squeeze in. It's not far.'

'Bloody sight further when you're walking uphill,' Angie panted, heaving a final suitcase into the back seat since the boot was full.

I chuckled. 'Yep. I know all about that. I can't always borrow Johnny's car, so I've nearly worn a track up that hill. Still, you won't have to do that again.'

'Halle-bloody-lujah!' Zoe said.

As the last small bag was stuffed in, I said, 'Ok. Let's get going before somebody recognises Johnny's car with strangers in it.'

The girls had a brief argument about who sat where, but Angie prevailed, grabbing the only rear seat space left with Zoe on her lap.

'Why do I always have the last choice?' she muttered.

'Because Mum popped me out before you, so I'm older,' Angie triumphantly returned.

'Yeah. By what, about 10 seconds?' grumped Zoe.

'Actually, it was about 60 seconds, as I remember,' Janice said with a chuckle that raised a general laugh as I swung quietly out of the car park and headed for the highway. 'Aren't we going the wrong way?' she asked.

'Sure,' I replied, 'but just in case someone does notice that you were picked up, I'd like to reinforce the idea that you're heading for Queensland. By the way, did you have any trouble at the motel or in the club?'

'No,' Janice said, sounding pleased with herself, 'it went just like you said. The motel people didn't mind at all, and since the room had been fully serviced that morning and we'd been hanging around the wharves all day, they didn't charge for the extra day. They were just pleased for us that we'd found a lift with friends. The club people were great, especially when we said we wanted to eat. They looked after our gear and wished us a safe trip to the Gold Coast.'

'Well done,' I said, 'that's just what we wanted them to think. It should help throw your investigators off the track, at least for a while.'

'I certainly hope so,' Janice replied quietly, 'I'm sick of having to peer over our shoulders all the time.'

I glanced over at her, sitting scrunched up in the corner against the door, 'Well, you certainly won't have to do that for a while, at least. And, if your friends can sort out the charges and court stuff, maybe never again.'

The rest of the ride was in silence as I looped around off the highway on the northern outskirts of town at Barclay St. I took the first street on the right and followed it right to the end, then turned left for the run down the hill to the wharves. I parked Johnny's car in its usual spot.

'Unload everything as quickly as you can and double-check that nothing is left behind.'

Then I pointed to the wharf almost in front of us, 'Carry your stuff out to the first little landing on the left of the wharf there. There's a black Rigid Inflatable Boat tied up there, hopefully with a Mercury outboard still screwed to the stern, but wait until I've seen Johnny before you load up.'

I left the ladies to get on with it, while I found Johnny in the office, writing up the fuel accounts for the trawlers. Thankfully, nobody else was around to see the activity.

I tossed the keys on the desk. 'Thanks for that, Johnny, and thanks for everything else you've done. You've got my phone number, so let me know if anything unusual happens or if strangers turn up asking the wrong questions.'

He stood to shake my hand and gave a big wink.

'No problem, mate. Hope you enjoy the sail up to the Whitsunday's. The chicks should be flashing their boobies and waggling their bums when you get there.'

We'd become good friends, and both laughed as I left him to his paperwork. Being also the Harbourmaster, my harbour clearance for the Whitsunday's was on record and had the stamp of official approval. Of course, there was nothing to stop me from changing my mind about my destination once I sailed.

I quickly checked Johnny's car, making sure it was totally empty.

'Don't trust me?' asked Janice, drifting out of the darkness.

'Yes, I do,' I replied, 'but from here on, we have to double-check each other. We can't afford any slipups.'

'Fair enough,' she replied quietly. 'I presume that's your RIB, but where's your boat?'

'It's out on a mooring away from curious eyes. I'll take Angie and your gear with me, then come back for you and Zoe.'

She just nodded as we made our way to the little side jetty. They'd stacked everything neatly on the platform beside the RIB, ready to go.

'Good job, guys,' I said, 'Angie, if you get in the boat, we'll start passing stuff to you. There shouldn't be any water in the bottom but check the floor's not wet before you put anything down.'

Loading went smoothly and shortly Angie and I were motoring quietly across the calm water toward my darkened boat. It wasn't until we were almost at the port stern platform that Angie realised this was the one.

'Oh, wow! Fuck! Is this it?' she squealed.

'Sure,' I replied with a chuckle, 'but keep it quiet, if you would. We still don't want to attract attention.'

'Oh. Yeah. Sorry, Harry. I just got a bit of a shock. I mean, like this thing is freaking huge! I was looking for something maybe twice the size of this dinghy!'

I stopped the motor and climbed out taking the bow rope with me. 'Well, just so you know, it's a catamaran called *'Firebird'* and it's 60ft long and 26ft wide. There are three dedicated sleeping cabins and a saloon with tables and chairs that holds the galley and navigation station as well. The cockpit just forward from here has the steering station, a table and seats and a king-sized daybed just above us, with the dinghy stowage under it. Up the sharp ends are more seating spots and a large trampoline for sleeping or sunbaking or whatever takes your fancy. It's a very cool spot to sleep on a hot night and fun to lie on while we're sailing to watch the water rush past!'

By now I'd hopped out and tied the RIB off and held out my hand to help her out as she still looked a bit gobsmacked and was trying to look everywhere at once, so I reached out to a waterproof touch panel and turned on the dim, blue boarding lights.

'Far out!' Angie exclaimed again, as a series of blue LED's lit up the stern boarding platform and the day bed jutting out beside it, 'Everything just looks fucking fantastic!'

'I presume that your mother doesn't approve of you swearing,' I commented drily.

'What? Oh, no, she doesn't. But what the! We're old enough and heaps more mature than she likes to think and she needs to adjust. I mean, this whole thing with Dad bashing her up and us having to run away has been really bad for all of us, but Mum's had the worst of it.'

I let that go without comment, but said, 'While you're there, if you'll pass your gear out, I'll carry it up top. We'll just leave things up in the cockpit for now until we get everything and everyone aboard.'

'Ok,' she replied, stepping gracefully back into the RIB and starting to pass bags and suitcases out. Before long, I had everything stacked in the cockpit out of the way, although I deliberately left the cabin locked until I had the others on board.

'OK,' I said to Angie as she climbed out again, 'I'm going back in to get your Mum and Zoe. I'd like you to sit and wait quietly until I get back. Please don't explore, or leave the cockpit, or turn on any more lights until we get back. I have a cat around here somewhere and he'll get a bit spooked by having a stranger aboard without me being here as well.'

I chuckled to myself at the thought of Jasper being spooked. I also knew precisely where he was at this moment; in his favourite spot on top of the cockpit roof, peering over the edge at Angie, his black coat blending perfectly in with the night, with only his large, bright green eyes to give him away.

She looked around as she perched on the comfortable cockpit lounge cushions, but didn't see anything and nodded at me in the blue dimness,

'OK. I'll just sit here and behave. I won't scare him.'

I had another chuckle when I thought of the fun to be had later when they all got introduced to my big pussycat.

'Thanks Angie, I appreciate that. I won't be long.'

'Oh,' I added, 'and please turn off your mobile phone! They can be tracked very easily.'

I chuckled aloud when I saw her hand slide back into the top of her carry bag.

After loading the other two, we made it out to the boat without attracting any attention and Angie was there to help them out. They were just as surprised with the boat as Angie had been but were more restrained with their language.

Janice chuckled, 'You really pulled my chain on this, didn't you Harry? So much for, 'we should be able to squeeze in'!'

I chuckled, 'Yeah! I guess I did, but I didn't like to brag, you being a wealthy Melbourne socialite and all! You might have thought I was a tosser!'

'I was a good girl, Harry,' Angie said smugly, once the others were safely up in the cockpit, 'I didn't move around, but I haven't seen your cat.'

'Thanks, Angie,' I smiled, 'He'll come around now that I'm back.'

'Oh! Have you got a cat?' cried Zoe, obviously the principal cat person of the trio. 'That's really cool! A real ship's cat!'

'Yeah,' Angie drawled, 'but he's hiding from us, so he sounds like a real pussy!'

The girls broke into giggles at the lame joke and I smiled but held my tongue.

'OK,' I said to them, 'Just let me unlock the doors, de-activate the alarms then I'll give you the standard housekeeping briefing and a quick tour of the boat. You can choose your cabins before we move all your stuff inside and get it stowed.'

The three nodded and waited until I'd unlocked the main doors but left the dim cockpit lighting as it was.

'I won't turn on all the lights yet as it might be too obvious that I've got guests. We don't want to advertise that fact if possible.'

'No problem,' murmured Janice, as I led them into the spacious saloon and turned on two small white down lights that still lit the area well enough to see everything.

I pointed them to the dining table seating, 'Ok, grab a seat for a minute or two while I play tour guide, but first up: Yes, I have a cat, so I hope that none of you are allergic, although he hardly seems to shed fur, so long as I brush him occasionally. His name is Jasper, and he's very protective of the boat and me, and acts as a guard cat. I'll need to introduce you properly so you don't have any problems.'

The girls giggled and Janice looked amused with my description, so I called, 'Jasper. Here boy.'

There was a soft thump from the cockpit and a very large, jet-black cat, as long and tall as a Labrador dog, but much leaner and weighing a lot less at 25 kg, stalked silently into the dimly lit saloon and parked himself beside me, leaning his considerable mass possessively against my leg so that I was forced to brace myself on the dining table. Sitting down like that, his head was level with the top of the table.

'Holy crap!' Angie exclaimed, 'Is that what you said was watching me when you went back for Mum and Zoe?'

I grinned at her discomfort.

'Yep. That's why I told you not to explore. He wouldn't have hurt you because I brought you aboard, but he wouldn't have taken his eyes off you. He allowed you to be on board without me there, but he might have become a bit upset if you'd wandered away from the cockpit.'

Angie frowned with the daunting thought of Jasper being 'a bit upset' about anything, but Janice asked, 'What breed is he?'

'He's supposed to be a Chausie, which is a cross between a jungle cat and a domestic breed, and that's what's on his registration papers. I acquired him as a kitten from a Korean cook on a cargo ship I happened to be on briefly, but, for some reason, a vet thinks that some of his breeding got a bit buggered up since he's grown a lot bigger than he's supposed to. He's only 18 months old, weighs 25 kg and seems to be still growing, although that might be just because he eats so much.'

'He'll be fuckin' enormous I reckon, if he does keep growing,' Angie said very respectfully, slowly getting over her initial concern, although Jasper kept his startling green-eyed gaze on her.

Under the circumstances, Janice even forgot to chip her about her language.

'Will he be friendly with us?' asked Zoe, way too fascinated with him to be too apprehensive.

'Oh yes, of course. I'll introduce you one by one and he'll be fine. Just treat him like a normal cat, with the benefit that he'll defend you just the same as he would me, once he knows that you're special friends and staying aboard to share his home.'

So, I called them each by name and got them to come forward and let Jasper sniff their hands, and then stroke his head. Disconcertingly, he then proceeded to shove his nose into their crutches for even better identification, so I found myself apologising for his rather intimate ID check. Fortunately, none of them was offended.

Angie was the most hesitant, but once she'd stroked the soft, black fur on his head and he immediately purred loudly at her touch, her concern turned to total delight.

'His fur feels absolutely beautiful,' she exclaimed, 'and he seems happy with me as well!'

I waited until Zoe and Janice had gone through the same routine, before I said,

'Now that he's noted your scent, you won't have any trouble with him, whether I'm here or not. You're all part of his family now.'

I noted that Jasper had padded over and parked himself beside Zoe, to her obvious delight and Janice's mild concern.

'Anyway, back to what's where. To the right of us is the nav station and what's generally my work desk. It holds the computer, nav displays, radar, sonar, engine instruments and the radio stack that includes HF, marine and air-band VHF, CB-UHF and several other special VHF and UHF comms. We also have a satellite phone and full-time Internet connection.'

That finally got the girls interest, until I added with a grin, 'But it's not for Facebook! That application isn't downloaded and is banned on board. Also, satellite bandwidth can be a bit limited at times, so there won't be any big downloads either.' The girls grimaced, even more so when I said,

'I don't want you using the boat's phone, either, unless I say so. Phones are too easy to track, particularly mobiles, which is why you've had to turn them off.'

Janice nodded and spoke for all of them, while giving the girls a hard look. 'I promise that we'll do what you say. This really does seem the perfect way to lay low for a while, so we don't want to do anything to jeopardise it!'

'So,' I continued, 'back to the tour. Behind the Nav desk is the electrical switch panel for the whole boat and the gauges for the fuel, water and holding tanks. Remember it well, since that's where we can turn anything on or off, especially in an emergency.

The galley is to the left and is completely electric with an induction cooktop. There's no oven as such, but for toasted sandwiches or small grills, there's an electric griller stowed in the locker near the sinks. Plates, cutlery, etc. are in the usual places, same as at home, except that here they're in fixed racks to stop noise and breakages at sea. Mugs and glasses are in the overhead racks underneath the overhead lockers. Please stow everything back where it was immediately after you use it or put it in the sink in case the boat moves unexpectedly. It won't always stay calm like this, even on a mooring in harbour if a big boat goes past at speed.'

'I use the gas BBQ outside for simple grilling as well as for baking, so that keeps all gas outlets outside the boat in case of leaks.'

I waved at the small dining area where we sat. 'You can see what this is, and it has fold-out leaves for extra guests should we have any, and we can bring in extra chairs from the cockpit, which obviously is the main living area in good weather.

There are two companionways or stairs down to the hulls from here, plus access through any of the deck hatches when they're unlocked.

In the left hull, we have two separate cabins, one forward with a decent queen bed and one right aft that's a large double.'

'The forward queen cabin has a large dressing and storage cabin further forward again, while the aft cabin has much more restricted storage under the berth, with a small hanging space as well. Whoever has that cabin may be able to stow and hang some gear in the forward dressing room.

I have the whole right hull as my sleeping and sometimes work area, but if you need the laundry or urgently need another toilet, you can use mine in the bathroom right aft.'

'Now, before we go further, there are some house rules. You must follow them, or the boat systems may be badly affected or even fail, and that will affect us even more so!'

They looked at me silently and intently.

'This boat is set up as almost a stand-alone eco-system which means that we really only need the engines for getting in and out of port safely and not always then. So as long as the wind blows, we sail. I don't mind running the engines when it's calm, but not if we can sail.

Apart from the BBQ, everything is electric, with power coming from solar panels on the cabin top and rear wing, wind generators and, if necessary, water turbines when we're sailing on dull days. A large, light-weight battery bank stores that power.'

'We make our own, very pure water with dual systems, that are both electric and engine-powered and can make a lot of water, but the storage tanks aren't big, to save weight and space, since water is very heavy. So even though we can make plenty of fresh water, we can't store much, so you still can't waste it! Showers must be short, toilet flushes minimal, and don't even think about leaving the tap running while you brush your teeth!'

I paused to look at each in turn. 'Although you are very welcome on board, please remember that you are guests and this boat is Jasper's and my home. The boat also keeps us alive and well in a potentially very hostile environment. Treat it with respect and there won't be any problems. With the boat or me!' I threw in the last as a bit of a joke, but they chose to take it very seriously.

'Nearly done,' I continued, noticing some yawns, 'However, I must mention the toilet system. Even though I've installed proper flushing toilets instead of the usual electric ones that can clog very easily, the golden rule is that nothing goes in the toilet that hasn't passed through your body first! No hair trimmings, no tampons, no pads, no cotton-buds, no makeup stuff or tissues. No cigarettes or matches either for that matter, since this is very strictly a non-smoking boat! Only body waste and the supplied toilet paper & bum wipes go in the toilet! If you clog one, you may find that you get to help unclog it!'

'There are two inside toilets, one amidships in the left hull, just beside us here, with a shower and wash basin, and the other in the bathroom just aft of the laundry, toward the stern in the right hull, which is mine as I've said, but if you need to, use it. My shower is there as well. There's another hand-held shower, outside on the right-hand stern steps. It's stowed in a locker just under the second step, which is also the location of the outside toilet.'

Noting their blank looks at that, I continued,

'Hanging over the side to go to the toilet is traditional on any small boat where space and water can be limited, although it's not recommended in most public harbours, or under way if the sea is rough.'

I saw all three girls poking faces at the thought of hanging their bare bums over the stern, but they'd learn.

'Nevertheless,' I continued, 'it's a very useful alternative and there are good handrails to help and a roll of toilet paper in the dry locker where the shower head stows.'

I could see that it would be quite a while before any of them relieved themselves over the stern, but time would tell.

I also noted their looks of surprise at mention of the laundry. 'Yes. We have a washing machine and you can use it when you need to, but you really must minimise how often you wash stuff. Hourly or daily clothes changes are definitely out! You don't have to wait until you get really smelly but be sensible. Water and power resources are limited!

It's best to hang stuff up to dry either under the boom, on the lifelines, or under the cockpit canopy if it's raining. There are plenty of lines to hang stuff on but use the big pegs you'll find under the kitchen sink and secure them tightly or your stuff will blow overboard.'

'Underwear is best washed in the shower with you each day. I just drop mine on the shower floor and stomp on it a few times. Other items can last for several days before a wash happens.'

'Clothing can also be as minimal as you like in the warmer weather and that'll help you stay cool and cut down on the washing bit. Bear in mind that no matter what you are used to, it's very difficult to preserve modesty while living in such a close environment.'

I grinned to lighten up the talk, although the girls were already grinning happily at each other and even Janice wasn't looking upset at the thought that I might be trying to incite her and her daughters to wear less clothing. 'I'll try to remember to wear something, most of the time, but you'll have to make up your own mind about what level of modesty you're comfortable with. There are no rules on that one.'

As I give this briefing to each new guest, I'm never sure how it will be received, although as most single guests are ladies who are planning to share my bed, it isn't an issue. This was the first time I'd delivered it to three strangers, particularly a mother with her two teenage daughters.

'Please use the stern hand shower to wash sand and salt off if you've been to the beach or swimming. The right-hand stern platform is the swimming platform as it has a fold-down ladder firmly bolted to the rear edge to make it easy to get out of the water. A dip over the side and a quick outdoor shower is a good alternative to using the ones down below, as the wastewater doesn't go in the holding tanks.

However, please don't go swimming without letting someone else know that you are. It's too easy to get swept away by the currents that can be deceptively strong.'

'When we're at a marina, we'll have shore power and water unless we're at a mooring. We will call into different ports occasionally to collect supplies, but only briefly. For general appearances, it will be best if we can appear to be a normal boat family — if that thought doesn't offend you too much, and it only has to be while we are around other people.

This is a very different environment to what you've been used to, and you must adapt your normal habits to fit in with it as quickly as you can. I won't make any apologies for that, since you asked me for the ride, but nevertheless, I'm still pleased to have your company.

Also, bear in mind that we don't know how long we'll be living together like this, so we must make the best of it. I'm used to this life and really love it. Most visitors don't have a problem adjusting to the changes, so long as they keep an open mind that things are very different afloat.'

Janice nodded and said, 'We understand and appreciate what you're doing, Harry. We're partially familiar with boats, as my husband has a 45-foot power cruiser and in earlier, happier times, we spent several holidays afloat.'

'Great,' I smiled, 'that's definitely a help. Does anyone get sea-sick?'

Three heads shook.

'Good. But a cat's movement on the water is different to a mono-hull, especially a powerboat that's usually very top heavy. Cats sit on top of the water and react to waves with a lively, dancing motion, even though they stay flat. They don't roll very much and don't lean over like a monohull sailing boat does, but you must hang on if you are moving around. I'll talk about safety matters tomorrow when we head to sea.'

I felt all talked out, and the ladies were drooping, so I led the way below and showed them where their quarters and facilities were. I'd made up the two beds with fresh sheets and doonas earlier before I'd picked them up.

'If anyone uses my facilities, just close the connecting door so I know it's occupied. Otherwise, please leave all bathroom, cabin and other doors open to maintain ventilation and for safety.'

As I suspected, the two girls decided to share the forward queen cabin, while Janice chose the smaller aft double. They envied the amount of room I had all to myself in the starboard hull.

'After you've unpacked what you need and you've got suitcases and gear that you can't fit into the forward dressing room, I can stow some in my dressing room,' I offered, 'I don't have that much gear and have plenty of space. But for now, you should plan on settling in and getting some sleep. Tomorrow we'll be sailing at dawn and you've got a lot to learn about travelling on and operating big cats.'

With the three of them fading fast, I handed out towels and washers, showed them where extra blankets were stowed, requested that all lights be turned off when they were ready, except for the few dim blue LED night-lights that showed the way to the toilet and saloon, and left them to sort things out. Janice took over directing operations, so I locked the main cabin doors from the inside, made sure that Jasper's access door was working, set the outer perimeter alarm, showered quickly and went to bed.

I heard some giggling on and off for a short while, but as no alarms went off and nothing seemed to blow up, I presumed that my instructions were being followed and went to sleep.

CHAPTER 5

I was up, washed and nursing a mug of tea before dawn the next morning. There'd been no excitement during the night when I'd checked twice in the small hours. My new 'crew' slept dead to the world, experiencing the peaceful sleep a boat at anchor usually generates, and perhaps feeling safe and relaxed for the first time in weeks.

They were still asleep when the sun poked its golden rim above the eastern horizon just as I dropped the mooring line, allowing the buoy to surge away. With the dawn, a light westerly land breeze had sprung up, making *Firebird* lie to the mooring pointing west. I'd made the inner staysail ready for unfurling and unrolled it as soon as we were free. We drifted backwards with the breeze, so I swung the wheel to the right, which swung the bows left, and watched as the breeze filled the staysail from the right side and we smoothly and silently gathered way.

This always was a thrill for me: leaving a mooring or dock, in silence with no engine noise. Not often possible, but highly satisfying when it was.

Even with a light breeze and a single sail, we still moved at 2 to 3 knots, which gave enough steering to avoid the other boats around us. I steered close by the only other occupied yacht in the bay, a 50ft steel ketch owned by an elderly and delightfully dysfunctional couple, Doris and Albert from the UK. They were both real characters and as usual, I could see Doris sitting in the cockpit sipping her morning coffee.

'Good Morning, Doris,' I called cheerfully as we approached, 'looks like a lovely day.'

'Bound to be,' she called back. 'Where are you heading?'

'Up to the Whitsunday's,' I replied, adding another piece to the general misdirection, 'even though it's still a bit warm, there's a Sail Carnival on that should be interesting. I'll probably join up with another couple of boats at Brisbane and we'll head up together.'

'Ah. You just want to look at some bare tits and bums, that's what you're going to do. In fact, what you should do is get a few bare-bummed girls to help you sail that great thing. Do you the world of good. You spend too much time alone.'

I spoke more quietly, since we were ghosting past just a couple of metres away from her boat's side, 'Actually, Doris, that's not a bad idea at all. I might just take your advice and go live a little!'

'Good boy,' she replied with a cheeky grin, 'I'd volunteer, but Bert won't let me. Reckons that if I took my bra off, I'd trip over my tits and fall overboard!'

I chuckled dutifully, but she cackled so hard, she slopped her coffee over the deck.

'Bugger it! Look what I've done. Anyway, keep moving, dear boy, and look after yourself. We'll see you again.'

I waved. 'Cheers, Doris, take care of each other,' pressing the button that made the mainsail rise magically out of its hibernation home in the boom and started yanking the appropriate ropes that made it useful.

I heard a giggle and looked down to see a tousled, blonde mop of hair poking out of the saloon doorway down at cat level, wearing the same baggy clothes as yesterday.

'I heard all that,' Janice grinned, crouched down on hands and knees to avoid being seen. 'The cheeky old tart! Just where does she think you're going to get these crew members flashing their tits and bums?'

I grinned back, 'You heard Doris. Up at the Whitsunday's, of course. But it's a pity we're not going there, I could set you up with a good mate of mine! He's a real stud! But for me, well, you know how it is, a single bloke with a boat has to beat the ladies back with a big stick, or so I've heard.'

Janice reached out and whacked me on the calf,

'Behave!' she grinned, 'I'm an happily, almost-not-married woman!'

I chuckled with her for a moment, then said, 'Thanks for staying down like that. Doris wouldn't be able to hold back from telling half the world if she saw me with three live, attractive females aboard!'

Janice sat on the floor looking up with a grin. 'You say the nicest things sometimes, but do you mean that it's been so long since you had a girl on board that the neighbours would find it remarkable?'

I shrugged, 'You know how it is, or maybe you don't, you being an unhappily sort-of-married old stick. It's always feast or famine for us sailors.'

She gave me an odd look and poked her tongue out, but didn't elaborate, so I continued with the task of making our conveyance get a move on in the light breeze.

Once past the last moorings, I laid a course for the North headland and reached over to turn George the Autopilot on, which he did with a click, a hum and a whirr of the toothed drive belt that turned the wheel.

'What's that you just turned on?' Janice asked, 'I can see the wheel moving!'

'That's George the Autopilot. He does most of the steering in open water. Never wanders off course, never complains and never gets tired.'

She looked intrigued. 'Can you trust him to keep the boat off the rocks?'

'Sure,' I said, 'so long as where I tell him to go, doesn't have any hard bits too close to the surface. George has built-in dual redundancy, interfaces with the Chart plotter for details of where to go, and if there's a problem, an alarm sounds.'

'But what if another boat gets in the way?' she wanted to know.

'Ahh! That's when George talks to his other mate, the radar. If an object, moving or otherwise is on a course to hit us, or vice-versa, another alarm sounds in plenty of time for me to do something about it.'

She smiled, 'I'm reassured, but what's that rope you're pulling on now?' she asked.

'This one with the red stripes is the mainsail sheet, it controls the position of the sail depending on the wind direction. I used a powered winch with an endless loop to raise and lower the mainsail because of its weight. When it's down, it's rolled up in the boom out of the weather and I can roll up as little or as much as I want very easily and quickly. I'll be showing you and the girls how to do all this stuff in the coming days, just in case I'm busy with something else.'

She looked a bit alarmed by that, so I added, 'Not that I'm planning to be, but redundancy on the water is always prudent.'

'You seem to take safety and the sea very seriously,' She said.

'Yes, I do,' I replied, 'Fifteen years in the SAS and Afghanistan taught me to take everything seriously that's trying to hurt or kill me. I do try to have as much fun as I can along the way, however,' I added to lighten the mood, making note-to-self to try to lighten up around the crew.

Janice nodded. 'I guess that explains a few things. What exit rank?'

'Major,' I replied.

She nodded approvingly, 'Well. I'm very glad that we happened to meet up with you and I feel that we're in good hands. I'll let the girls know your background as it might make them follow your instructions a little more carefully if they know that.'

'Well. I'm not really so much of a soldier anymore, but I've had the training and 'been there and done that', as the saying goes, so old habits don't go away.'

'But,' I added in a serious tone, 'I must warn you, I'm not really a very nice person. I mean — I'm no knight in shining armour charging to the rescue of damsels in distress. I'm more likely to be the one ravishing the damsels in the first place! I just don't like to see nice ladies being hurt by bad guys.'

'That's very complex, Harry, but doesn't it add up to the same thing?' she asked innocently. A comment I wisely chose to ignore.

She sat and watched while the main winched itself up and I sheeted it to suit the course I'd plotted. I then let the huge screecher unfurl from its rolled-up position on the head stay. It was an enormous sail, purple with a horizontal lemon band, and always gave the boat a real speed boost, especially in light winds.

By now, we were well away from prying eyes, so I said to Janice, 'You can get up and move around the saloon and cockpit now, if you want, but don't go up on deck until we're well out to sea.'

'Ok,' she said, standing and stretching, 'that's better. Can I get you a mug of tea?'

'That would be great,' I replied, 'Standard NATO — Milk and two, please,' and she ducked back into the galley.

As we made our rather stately way across one of the finest harbours in Australia, the light westerly land breeze barely ruffling the sparkling water, pleasant domestic sounds came out of the galley.

One of the twins stuck her head out of the doorway, careful not to show herself too much, 'Good morning, Harry. Mum wants to know if you'd like some Vegemite toast with your tea?'

I smiled at her, 'Yes please. That'd be excellent! And you're all allowed out into the cockpit for now.'

She grinned and disappeared back inside. Shortly, the lovely smell of fresh toast drifted out, followed by what I think was the other twin, since she also wished me good morning, bearing a mug of tea and a plate of toast.

'Now that's service,' I said as I took the offerings, 'Do you want to sit out here? It's safe for now and you can share the driver's seat with me if you want.'

She grinned, 'Yes, please! I'll just grab my cuppa.' Soon she was happily seated, copying my habit of propping my feet up on the expensive instrument panel, but with her long, bare, tanned legs, she looked a lot more graceful and attractive about it.

'How do I tell you two apart?' I asked.

'Easy,' she replied with a big grin, 'I'm Zoe, the one without any freckles. Angie has a spray of them just under her eyes. They darken a bit if she's out in the sun a lot, but even if she stays indoors, they're still there.'

She blushed a bit, 'I've got a small birthmark on my left bum cheek, but very few people get to see that in person!'

I chuckled at that, 'I look forward to the pleasure of that, if I'm so honoured.'

Zoe blushed a bit, but grinned back. 'We'll see,' she said, as Janice and Angie brought their breakfast out, and sat around the cockpit table.

'This is very pleasant travelling, Harry,' Janice said, 'but I presume that at sea it's a bit different.'

I smiled, 'Yes, usually it is, although even the ocean can be pretty flat at times. But we're heading out into one of the roughest areas of water on the planet, the Tasman Sea. But before you get worried, the forecast is for light to moderate northerlies and a low swell, so we'll move a bit faster and the boat will move around a bit more than this, but it will still be very comfortable running with the swell.'

Angie chipped in. 'On Dad's 45ft power boat, we didn't leave Port Phillip Bay, but it still got a bit choppy at times and the boat rolled a lot.'

'Yes, most power boats will do that,' I replied, twisting the knob controlling George's heading bug to make a small adjustment to our course, 'but as cats sit flat on top of the water, they hardly roll at all. It's an unusual motion being quite lively, but it rarely seems to make anyone sick.'

She nodded and continued looking around the boat and the beautiful area we were sailing through.

Soon, we were approaching the North Head of Eden with the usual cluster of small fishing boats taking advantage of the rough bottom and swirling currents that attracted so many fish to the area.

'You'd all better get back inside now,' I suggested, 'I'll be expected to pass quite close to some of these boats to have a quick chat as I know some of the owners quite well. You'll be OK in the saloon, so long as you sit still and don't move around. It won't be for long, maybe 20 minutes at most until we are well clear of them and heading out to sea.'

They all nodded, gathered up our plates & mugs and trooped inside where the reflective UV/IR tinting on the cabin windows made seeing inside impossible in the daytime.

I furled the screecher and let out the main and staysail to slow down and five minutes later, we eased close by a 25ft half-cabin tinny with a pair of 150hp Mercury outboards strapped to its stern.

'Where're you off to now, Harry?' called Brian.

'I got a call from a mate in Brisbane,' I replied easily, as we were only a couple of meters apart by now, 'He wanted me to join him in a run up to the Whitsunday's. There's some sort of Sail rally going on soon. It sounded like fun. Girls, booze, sailing. All the usual crap.' What I told him was perfectly true, but I didn't add that I had no intention of heading north.

He laughed as we swept past, 'Good on you mate. Are you coming back soon?'

'Count on it, Brian,' I replied, 'I want to get amongst more of those beaut snapper.'

He waved as I re-set the screecher and adjusted the other two sails and our course to clear the other boats and head up to the east-northeast. I needed to make it obvious that we were heading north, but we had to head seawards first to clear the wind-shadow of the headland.

The offshore breeze stayed light for a while until we cleared the wind shadow, then it started to back around nicely to the north and freshen a little as forecast, although the water stayed fairly smooth. Within the promised time, I was able to call the ladies out of their confinement, as the fishing boats were small dots astern.

'Ok, ladies,' I announced, 'welcome to the Tasman Sea. We'll hold this course for a while longer then we'll turn south and run for about 60 km or 29 nautical miles until we pass Gabo Island. Once clear of that, we can turn southwest to head straight for Flinders Island.

That way we'll miss hitting the Aussie mainland, the Bass Strait gas and oil platforms and the boat traffic around them. We can be off Flinders Island by tomorrow morning.'

'Are we going to stop there?' asked Angie.

'Yes, we will,' I replied, 'but it won't be at a town. We'll anchor up for a day or so in a quiet cove, probably the north end of Marshall Bay and I can make sure that my repairs are all OK. There's no real hurry now, so there's time for you three to adjust to boat life and we can push on from there when we're ready and in mostly day-sailing stages.'

Janice looked a bit concerned. 'Will it be ok sailing across there at night? I mean, we won't be much help to you yet. We don't even know which strings to pull to make things happen.'

I chuckled at her description. 'We'll be fine. I'll do the whole watch to Flinders Island, but it would help if one of you, perhaps in three hourly rotations, can share the watch with me through the night stretch. That'll make it easier to keep a lookout although we still have radar looking out as well, plus George does the steering for us.'

The girls looked excited by the adventure, but Janice asked, 'So what's the plan from Flinders Island onwards? Is there somewhere that we're actually going, or are we just wandering?'

'Sorry,' I smiled, 'I do have a sailing plan — I just haven't got around to telling you yet.'

She smiled acceptance of the apology.

'I'd like to go down the west coast of Tasmania and explore Macquarie Harbour, where Strahan is, then Port Davey, a bit further south, which is a very remote and protected harbour on the south-west coast. It's a few hundred kilometres south of Strahan and not as big as Macquarie harbour, but it's much more remote. There're only a few isolated farms there and certainly no towns or even villages.

I've always wanted to explore the area and was planning on

going there after Eden but then you guys came along, so it's no real change, except now I have delightful and attractive company. Being remote is a bonus, of course, under the new circumstances. We may even hear or see a Tasmanian tiger!'

That drew some smiles and Janice looked pleased at my compliments and that they weren't being a burden.

'We'll probably call in at Strahan on the way to get supplies,' I added, 'since there's nothing at Port Davey, except maybe another yacht or two. We have to be totally self-sufficient.

So, with that in mind, I looked at Janice, 'I'd like you all to go through your own stuff, as well as what supplies I have aboard, fresh & frozen, to see if there's any additional things you need, or would like, or think that we should have. I've got a small stock of wine, beer and some rum, but you can list whatever you'd like. Just remember that there's no corner store to pop out to and get some milk and bread.'

'Speaking of that, what *do* we do about milk and bread?' asked Angie, who seemed to be the practical twin.

'I sometimes freeze some fresh bread and milk, although they take up a lot of freezer space, but what's much better is to make our own bread. I have a bread-maker with all the ingredients, so without much extra work, we always have beautiful, fresh bread. Milk is the long-life variety that I keep in sealed plastic bags in the bottom of the bilges, below the waterline. It stays quite cool there, even in summer and lasts a very long time.

When we spend time in Macquarie Harbour, you'll see that it's a huge and fascinating place to explore and has several rivers we can get a fair way up with the boat, including the famous Gordon and King Rivers. If we do spend any time in the pretty village of Strahan, we'll get to enjoy a few shore-side luxuries like cafes, restaurants and pubs. The local fish and chip shop has grilled scallops that you'd crawl over hot coals for. Thirteen or fourteen to the dozen at least, providing you smile nicely at the lovely lady. Works for me anyway!'

While the girls mulled over those thoughts, I decided that we were far enough away from land that a course alteration to the south, rather than the north wouldn't be noticed. Therefore, I dialled George's heading bug around to 180° and set about resetting sails while George took care of the course.

Obligingly, the breeze had picked up and backed even further to the northeast, so we didn't have to jibe, merely ease all sails out until our speed and the apparent wind stabilised.

Our speed picked up to around 10-12kts, with a low swell out of the north and small wind waves. Perfect sailing conditions to settle newbies down.

'So, what happens now?' asked Janice.

'We stay like this until we reach the south-east corner of Australia at Gabo Island around 15:00,' I replied, 'easy travelling.'

She smiled, which was a much more pleasant look than her usual worried frown.

'Ok, I might go below and finish cleaning up. It's been a busy morning so far.'

'Goodo. But, before you do, just a word about safety now we're at sea. If conditions are light like this, there's very little danger of falling overboard, but please remember that the boat can still lurch unexpectedly and make you lose your balance. When you're moving around out of the cockpit, please hold onto something solid with one hand. There are plenty of handrails or the rigging for just that purpose. But when the weather gets rough, we all must wear a lifejacket with a safety line, even in the cockpit. They are the auto-inflatable kind with built-in harness and are quite comfortable.

But for now, you're welcome to go forward. The trampoline is a great place to lie and watch the water rush past.'

'Sounds great,' said Angie, 'We'll do that, but I'll clean up first as well.'

With that, the three girls went below, while I played with sail trim and checked the radar, while contemplating what human-generated storms might be heading our way that didn't show on even the best radar.

The morning passed peacefully and attractively, as the twins appeared in bikinis and headed for the foredeck. It always amused me that the cost of women's swimwear seemed to be in inverse proportion to its size.

Based on that theory, I guessed that the twin's bikinis were very expensive indeed!

Janice reappeared in a T-shirt that would be cooler than the baggy shirt she had on earlier, but more importantly from my perspective, was also pleasantly tight across her chest.

She joined me on the steering station chair and we watched the girls have a heap of fun laying on or bouncing around on the trampoline and sitting on the little seats right up on each bow, squealing when the bows dipped deeper into the trough between waves and showered them with cooling spray. They ended up sprawled out on the tramp, soaking up some sun.

I chuckled and said to Janice, 'They're very pretty girls in those bikinis that they're almost wearing; the trampoline has never been so well decorated!'

Janice jammed an elbow into my ribs and said with a giggle, 'You're just a dirty old man, but they are over 18 and much more mature and sensible than most that age, but don't tell them I said that.'

'Yeah. Well, they do look younger, but hey, steady on with the 'old man' bit. I'm a few years short of earning that title. But seriously, they really do seem like great girls,' I added, 'and this bit of nonsense with your about-to-be-ex hubby doesn't seem to have affected them too much.'

Janice said proudly, 'Yes. They seem to be doing quite well in the circumstances. In fact, this is the most fun they've had since this whole mess started. They've been very unhappy about it and leaving home and friends. But hopefully, it's not forever and they're being very supportive of my wild scheme to run around until my family can get some restraining orders and divorce proceedings in place.'

I nodded. 'Yes. I see that. Unfortunately, it seems the only thing you can do for now. Who's looking after your DVO application and all that legal stuff??'

'That'd be my Dad,' she replied, 'He's a barrister, so he's looking after all of that, but my husband is playing all sorts of dirty tricks to prevent the divorce and naturally he wants the girls.'

'That'd be a bloody disaster! I mean, that's a no-brainer, isn't it?' I asked, 'Like a history of him bashing you like that! What's he got to argue against?'

She didn't answer for a few moments. 'Quite apart from losing face among his peer group, there might be some other issues that I'm not sure about yet, but since you're directly involved, perhaps you should be aware of them, as I really need some help and advice.'

I shifted around on the seat to look directly at her, instead of looking at her reflection in the cabin window in front of us.

'OK. Yes, I should be aware of anything that's likely to affect us, 'cause that in turn will affect where we go, what we do and what we're going to be up against. So, tell me!'

'Well,' she said, hesitantly, 'there's not a lot I know for sure, except that for some time now, my father and I have been increasingly unsure of how Luke makes so much money. I mean, he has a very successful earth-moving business, and is now into property development, but Dad reckons that he's spending many times what the business could possibly be earning.'

'Yes, that sounds a bit suss,' I commented, 'but you need more than that if you want to nail him with something criminal.'

She looked a bit uncomfortable for a moment as if she was going to hold something back, but then she said, 'Luke has a study in our house that he usually keeps locked. The housekeeper isn't even allowed in there to clean.'

'But one day, someone came to the front door to see him and he rushed out without closing it properly. They went out to this guy's car in the driveway and were arguing for ages, so I took a chance and went in. His desktop computer was still on and open, so on impulse, I grabbed an empty 2TB portable HDD from my work station in the next room and copied all the files on the Desktop and in the Documents folder.

Luckily everything was USB3, so the download was fast, but it still took a while. There's an awful lot of stuff on it.'

'Wow!' I said, 'That was taking a risk!'

'Yes. I suppose it was, but I was desperate to find anything that I could to hold against him.'

'OK. That's understandable, but what was in the files?'

She shrugged, 'I don't know. I haven't had a chance to look at them yet. Based on his rather extreme reaction to finding the door open, I got the feeling that he also knew or at least suspected that the files had been opened, but because I left the house before he came back in, he couldn't accuse me directly of going in the room. It still didn't stop him from giving me a bit of a work-over that night.'

I shuddered to think what her 'bit of a work-over' entailed, and the casual way she said it made the episode even more bizarre.

'So, you've left the drive in a safe place, I hope?' I asked.

'Ahhh…Well, I think so. I've got it with me,' she said quietly.

I closed my eyes. 'Oh shit! This could up the ante a bit if your boof-headed husband thinks you've pinched his precious files. So, do you want me to go through them?'

'Yes, please. I was hoping you would. Whenever you want.'

'Not now,' I replied hastily, 'and not with the girls around in case we find something a bit nasty. Let's start going through them tonight when you share a watch with me and the girls are asleep. Maybe you take the first watch. That way I'll be more awake.'

'Okay, thanks,' Janice nodded, 'that's a plan.'

We were about halfway to Gabo Island when I commented to Janice, still companionably perched next to me at the steering station, 'The girls have a good tan but they're copping the reflection off the water as well, and as much as I like seeing them up there enjoying themselves, perhaps they should get under cover for a while.'

Janice had been half-dozing. 'Hmmm. Yes. Good idea.' Raising her voice, she called to them to come aft out of the sun.

After a bit of good-natured grumbling, they complied, and were soon contentedly sitting around the cockpit table, chatting with us. They were good company, smart, and articulate.

Shortly after, Janice offered the girls' services to organise some lunch, a suggestion I didn't mind at all.

'There's fresh bread and ham, tomatoes and cheese for sandwiches,' I hopefully informed the cooks, 'and you know where the tea & coffee stuff is.'

'Yes, Skipper,' Angie said, with a cheeky grin, 'that'd be ham, cheese and tomato sandwiches with a NATO tea for the boss coming right up.'

They were quick and efficient, obviously having done this before, but showing that they were adapting quickly to their new environment.

Shortly after the very tasty lunch was cleared away, Gabo Island reared out of the slight sea mist to starboard, right where it was supposed to be, allowing us to make a course adjustment to the SSW on track for Flinders Island. This time, I set our destination of Marshall Bay, Flinders Island on the chart plotter and slaved George to it. Pressing the Engage button, the wheel turned smoothly, and we swung right onto our new course.

As a precaution, I set a guard range of 10 nm on the radar, with an audio alarm.

'If you hear that alarm go off,' I explained to Janice and Zoe who were in the cockpit at the time, it means that another boat or very solid object is within 10 nautical miles or about 19kms of us. It could be something in front, or a fast container ship charging down on us from behind. Either way, we need to get as much warning as possible of its approach, particularly with the big ships. They're fast and don't keep a very good lookout!'

While the ladies did their own thing and Jasper hung about with them, I wandered around the boat checking on things like the tightness of shackles and fittings, no dangling ropes that could foul a prop, and re-trimming the sails. The breeze had picked up a little more, but was steady out of the northeast, so we were able to hold a port tack with the sails quite loose on a very broad reach.

All gear and sails were in perfect condition, so there wasn't much to do, and I found myself slipping into my usual at-sea routine, except that there were three relatively inexperienced crew to watch out for and to fit into the routine.

Teatime came and went with little fuss and the crew showed signs of settling in more, each doing a job, generally directed by Janice. I was content to let them do things their own way, so long as the boat or systems weren't affected. Evening showers were thankfully brief, even though the batteries and the water tanks were full. I'd pumped the holding tanks once we were clear of the shore, so that wasn't a problem. I'd have to remember to pump them more often with the extra bodies aboard.

I set the watch roster to be Janice until midnight, then Angie 00:00 to 03:00, then Zoe 03:00 to 06:00 and I didn't expect to make Flinders until 08:00 or so.

'By the way,' I said while they were all together, 'when we are travelling at night, those on watch need to preserve their night vision. The way we do that is to have only red lights in the saloon and cockpit and I've flipped a switch so that happens automatically. No white lights at all, except in the cabins, the stern nav light and for the searchlight in emergencies.

Please remember this rule as our safety can depend on it, so don't come into the saloon with a white torch or we'll be effectively blind for 15 minutes.'

They all nodded their understanding, so I let the girls watch some TV until 21:00 when Janice chased them off the bed.

'No talking half the night again,' she admonished, 'Angie has to be up again at midnight to relieve me, so get some sleep!'

'Yes, Mum,' was the stern reply as they trooped down below to their cabin.

We gave them 15 minutes and then Janice went quietly down to check on them.

'Fast asleep, both of them,' she reported with a grin. 'They didn't realise how much being at sea takes it out of you. I'm surprised how much the body works, just moving around.'

I smiled, 'Yeah. It's a good workout all right. Now, would you like to fetch the drive?'

She gave a weak smile and went below.

CHAPTER 7

We sat at the nav station, Janice perched on a stool pulled over from the lounge space.

'I'm going to make two copies of this stuff,' I told Janice, tucked pleasantly close in beside me, 'I'll put the files on another portable HDD for backup, as well as downloading them to my computer.'

She nodded agreement as the progress bars swiftly moved across the screen, and I had a swift image of Janice doing this in her husband's forbidden study, while he argued with a confederate just outside the window.

Despite the 1.5 TB combined size of the two folders on the drive, the copying went quite quickly, thanks to USB 3.

'Damn!' I commented, half to myself, 'Most of these Documents folder files are very big. They can't just be written documents. They must be jpeg or data files to be this big.'

When it was finished, I unplugged and set Janice's original HDD in front of her. 'I'd like you to keep this in a safe place, but not necessarily with your gear, just in case we get searched — willingly or not!'

She looked a bit alarmed. 'I'm just being careful,' I said soothingly, 'I have a bad feeling about this stuff — I mean the way he kept everything locked up.'

In fact, I had a very strong suspicion as to the content of the folders, but kept my mouth zipped for now.

'I'm also going to put this third copy HDD in a waterproof zip-lock plastic bag, then in a manila envelope and seal it. We'll both sign across the flap and I'll tuck it away at the back of the chart table drawer right here.'

She nodded and did as I asked. With the third copy tucked away and Janice's hopefully well hidden, at least one should be safe if we were burgled. Of course, there was always Jasper for any intruder to get past!

She nodded as I opened the Desktop folder, which appeared at first glance to be fairly innocuous. They seemed to be just documents and spreadsheets relating to the earthmoving and property development business, although one contract finalisation with a prominent Real Estate company caught my eye. It was the figure of $12m that really made it stand out, as well as the brief property description that seemed to describe an old mansion situated on prime land in one of Melbourne's oldest and most prestigious suburbs.

It was dated some five years previously and a quick look at other documents around that time turned up an invoice from Luke's development company for the sum of $1.25M in what was loosely described as 'renovations as required by the owner' at the same address.

'But the owner is Luke himself,' Janice said softly, 'the seller is XYZ Investments and I think they're Chinese, while the purchaser is shown as L.E. Investments P/L, and that's Luke's personal company. I helped him set it up and there aren't any partners, not even me.'

'Ok,' I said slowly, my mind trying to connect a set of well-separated and at the moment, fuzzy dots, 'So why would he buy a very expensive mansion in his own name and pay himself to do it up? Then what is he doing with it?'

Janice looked equally puzzled, 'I don't know. But unless there's a sales record, it would seem that he still owns it and that's a lot of spare change he doesn't have just to keep tied up in a property that apparently doesn't make any income. He can't afford that!'

She nudged me aside, 'Can I get online. I'd like to have a look at where this mansion is.'

'How about Google Earth,' I replied, and quickly hooked up to the Internet via the satellite system, then slid the laptop over to her.

'Yeah. That'll do it. Thanks.'

Moments later, she had zoomed in on the prime suburb she wanted.

'Ahh,' breathed Janice in satisfaction, 'It is an old mansion, but look, it's surrounded by office blocks. Of course, being heritage-listed, it can't just be bulldozed. It has to remain completely as is. All it could be used for is a private residence, an up-scale guest house or a corporate entertainment centre.'

She looked at me with a predatory glint in her eye. 'I'm betting that it's neither of the first two choices. Now if you were setting up 'Corporate Entertainment', what might you do to make the place pay its very money-hungry way?'

I looked at her and grinned, 'I'd set it up a very high-class brothel! Particularly with the area pretty well deserted after hours'

She leaned forward and, in her excitement, kissed my cheek. 'Good man! It's got to be something like that to be lucrative enough. There's no sense otherwise. Perhaps we can search for the current listed owner through the Land Office records.'

I agreed, but said, 'You can chase that up later. For now, I want to have a look at those big files in the Document folder.'

She nodded, so soon we were looking at the list of sub-folders and files, where we quickly noticed that there were mostly .jpg and .mp4 files. The sub-folders simply had a year as a name, and they went back 13 years.

'To shortcut the process, I'm going to dive into one of these .jpg files,' I said quietly, 'I think that this is where the answer is to all this aggro.'

Janice nodded, as I opened the first one that was also the earliest, which showed a naked girl of Indian appearance, about 7, with a scared look on her face, standing square on to the camera.

'Oh, shit!' I breathed.

'Oh fuck!' was Janice's succinct comment. 'Kiddy porn!'

We had stumbled onto a paedophile ring!

Very reluctantly, we scanned through random files and while

most were Asian or Indian children, male and female, a number were Caucasian. They seemed to range in age from 5 or 6 up to teenagers of 13 or 14.

Suddenly, Janice gave a soft scream and slumped down on her stool. 'That's Zoe. I recognise the birthmark on her bum cheek and that's the kids' bathroom!'

Compared to the others we'd looked at, the photo was a fairly innocent one, of a young girl standing up in a bath. She had a cheeky grin on her face and was turned slightly to the side, showing the left side of her bum cheek where there was a small, pale red mark.

'Oh, the rotten, filthy, depraved arsehole!' Janice fumed, 'That bastard has sold photos of his own daughters!'

That photo, and I was sure there were more of Zoe as well as of Angie, would seem to tie Luke well and truly into a paedophile ring and confirmed that we held dynamite in our hands. His position in the ring was the question that we urgently needed answered.

A quick look at some of the later collections, as well as boys and girls alone, had mostly men with the kids, boys and girls, but surprisingly, there were a couple of women who repeatedly showed up in the same sort of environment as did many of the men, and in most cases had their faces visible. Even I, who was generally ignorant of Australian politicians and celebrities, recognised a few faces.

Janice was devastated and could go no further. 'I can't look at any more,' she sobbed softly.

'I understand,' I replied, 'Go sit out in the cockpit and I'll make a cup of tea and bring it out.'

She did, and shortly, I joined her, a mug of hot tea, enhanced with a very healthy dollop of Mr Jameson's finest.

Before sitting down, I checked our course, conditions and the radar, but we were proceeding very nicely on track at a fairly steady 12 to 14kts, and the Chart plotter politely suggested that we should be at our waypoint off the top end of Flinders Island by 06:41.

I joined Janice on the cockpit settee, and as she wanted or needed to snuggle, I let her scrunch down against me and put an arm around her. Once she was comfortable, she sipped her Irish Tea.

'Would you mind seeing if there are any more of Angie or Zoe?' she asked.

'Of course not,' I replied, giving her a gentle squeeze, 'but I'll wait until the girls are busy elsewhere. I also have a contact in the Federal coppers who might be very interested in Luke's activities, but we'll talk about this tomorrow.'

She just nodded against my side and I felt the wetness of her tears soaking my shirt.

After a while, she said in a more settled voice, 'A lot of those later photos showed a similar, rather old-fashioned background. Could we use that to find out where they were taken? I mean logically, it should be that old mansion Luke owns.'

I thought about that for a few moments, 'That's a very good point. I should have thought of that sooner. But when I get the chance to go through them more carefully, I'll see if anything is identifiable. In the meantime, are you happy for me to make contact with my friend at the Australian Commonwealth Police?'

Janice nodded against my chest, 'Sure. It'll be interesting to hear what they say.'

I thought that I'd leave that contact until the boat was clear of ears.

'Tomorrow morning,' I said to a sleepy Janice, 'I'd like you to take the girls and Jasper for a long walk on the beach or explore the top end of Marshall Bay.'

She squirmed around and sat up. 'Will Jasper go with us?'

'Oh, sure,' I replied, smiling, 'he loves a ride in the dinghy and will probably have a swim. But most of all, he loves a run along the beach, chasing the seagulls.'

'Okay,' she said with a bit more life in her voice, 'that sounds like fun. The girls will love it.'

'I doubt that you'll see anybody else,' I added, 'but there is a road paralleling the beach and an occasional farm along that stretch, so somebody may stop when they see the boat, but I certainly don't expect any problems with bad guys at this stage. If you do meet locals, say that we're just passing through on the way to Geraldton. That should muddy the waters a bit more should Luke's goons get this far.'

She nodded, and then stood up to check the time on the saloon clock.

'It's just about midnight. I might go and wake Angie. She takes a while to get her mind functioning after just waking up. Are you OK?'

'I'm fine, 'I said. 'Thanks for the company. Go get some sleep if you can after you've got Angie functioning.'

She leant over and gently kissed my cheek again. 'Thanks for what you're doing and for just being here, I feel much better already having someone competent on our side,' she said softly. 'Goodnight.'

FIREBIRD...TUESDAY, AT SEA – AM

The rest of the night passed quite quickly, with Angie, sleepy at first, then increasingly animated and chatty, followed at 03:00 by Zoe, who fairly bounced out into the cockpit where I was ensconced, fizzing with excitement at sailing and living on a boat. As well as giving me a lot more information about their daily lives, it was obvious that they'd had no idea what their father was up to. He'd rarely even raised his voice to them, let alone his hand, so it was a bit puzzling how he could have been so violent with Janice. Still, that was a question for the shrinks at a later date.

She was very keen to pet and play with Jasper, who always kept me company on night watch. Mind you, he didn't always stay awake, in fact he usually slept, which made his company a token gesture only. Still, he could be awake and alert in a moment if trouble happened.

Zoe regarded Jasper's apparently slumbering form, draped untidily across the steering station seat.

'Will he wake up soon?' she asked softly, 'I'd love to pat him for a while if he'll let me.'

I chuckled and called softly, 'Jasper! Get your lazy arse over here. Somehow you've got an admirer.'

Instantly, he lifted his head, eyed Zoe and me sitting on the cockpit settee, and slithered silently off the raised steering station seat, to pad over to Zoe. To her utter delight, he hopped up onto the seat beside her and rested his sleek, slender head in her lap.

'Does he like being scratched?' she asked, 'We've got cats at home, but Jasper's three times their size and looks a bit different.'

'Try him at your own risk,' I said dryly, 'but he may not ever let you stop!'

So, she gingerly scratched him behind the ears, and stroked the soft, black fur on his muscular neck.

She jumped when he started purring, a sound which some have likened to a 4-stroke generator running under heavy load. He also brought one of his massive paws forward and laid it across her lap as well.

'Wow!' she exclaimed, still scratching and stroking. 'He likes it — he's beautiful!'

I agreed, 'Yes. He's pretty special. But I'm seriously concerned about my ability to feed him if he does keep growing!' She laughed as Jasper rolled half onto his back so she could rub his belly.

'So much for the killer cat image.' I leaned forward to say *sotto voce* in his ear, 'A pretty girl scratches your belly and you instantly turn to mush!'

Jasper made a huffing sound and stretched his head back as an invitation for Zoe to scratch his throat.

'Now that's really yanking your chain,' I commented dryly. 'He's really the perfect conman.'

Jasper looked at me and yawned dismissively, showing his large, sharp and gleaming white teeth.

'Cheeky big puss!' I said good-naturedly, 'Go on. Soak it up while you can, bozo. You'll get none of that namby-pamby stuff from me!'

'But he's just a young cat,' Zoe said. 'He needs a bit of a scratch and some petting now and then.'

'Wait 'till he decides to sleep on your bed and ends up pushing you out of it,' I growled at him. 'Just a young cat! Ha!'

The rest of the watch passed peacefully, as Zoe was totally smitten with Jasper and kept petting him and asking about *Firebird*. We stayed nicely on course as the breeze picked up a little more, but as we were sailing on a broad reach, it was very un-dramatic and easy with the waves almost behind us; even surfing at times at 15 to 17kts. The occasional wave-top broke quietly, the softly-hissing white necklace of foam showing briefly against the black water, before fading into streaks down the wave's back as they were left astern.

Like Angie, Zoe gave me more background on the family and, inadvertently, some valuable insight into Luke's character. It seemed that Zoe had been Luke's favourite and he'd told her more about his business than he'd told Angie.

First light was at 06:22, so 06:00 came and went in the dark, but when I mentioned it to Zoe, she waved her free hand dismissively, the other one still engaged with scratching Jasper. 'I'm fine. I'm awake now and this is more fun and exciting than lounging about in bed, as comfortable as it is.'

I smiled at her enthusiasm. 'I'm sorry that you had to share with Angie, but when I had the boat built, I only wanted three cabins so there would be more space overall. The daybed or the trampolines are good for sleeping on a hot night, but they're not exactly a separate cabin.'

'Oh, no!' she exclaimed. 'We don't mind sharing at all. In fact, it's quite fun and even if you had a spare cabin, we'd probably share anyway!'

'Okay. That's good to hear. But in the meantime, if that great, black lump of fur will let you up, how about you make the Skipper a mug of tea?'

'Oh. Sure,' she replied happily, 'coming right up.'

She was back with two steaming mugs of tea just before first light and then experienced her first dawn at sea, a rather magical experience as fingers of golden light poured slowly up from the horizon, steadily brightening just before the glaringly bright orange edge of the sun itself heaved up out of the gently rolling ocean.

'That's so beautiful,' she breathed in awe at nature's casual display of grandeur.

'It is rather special,' I confirmed, 'I'm glad you got to see it like this.'

She grinned, 'I can't wait to tell Mum and Angie what they've missed. We owe you so much for getting us away like this and giving us the chance to have an adventure on your lovely boat with your fabulous cat!

We've been so worried about Mum, now that we know how incredibly badly Dad has treated her.'

'She does seem a very nice lady,' I commented lamely.

'Oh, yes. She is. She's been a great Mum to us. But while she tries so hard to look after us, she really needs support herself. Someone she can really lean on. Pops is great and hopefully, he can make legal things happen, but we don't know how long this is going to go on, do we?'

'No, we don't, I'm afraid,' I replied, 'We'll just have to keep moving and maintain a low profile.'

She grinned, excitement dancing in her eyes, 'The keeping moving part is the fun bit. We've never lived on a boat before. Have you had it very long?'

'About three years,' I replied, 'I liked the basic design and talked with the designer about what I wanted in terms of layout and equipment. Normally a cat of this size needs a crew, but I found that needing casual crew is risky since they are too unreliable. They always seem to want to bail out in some port where you can't easily get a replacement, so it seemed far better to design the layout of the boat so that I didn't need a crew in the first place!'

She nodded, 'Well, that makes sense. If you don't need them, then no problem, and if you have them, like now, you don't need to depend on them.'

I smiled at her very acute observation.

'But,' she added, 'we might be with you for a while and we'd really like to be able to properly help out with things. Mum wants to give you some money to at least cover our expenses, but what we really want is to be proper crew. It all looks so interesting. Angie and I certainly want to learn, and I'm sure Mum does as well.'

I nodded, remembering Janice's earlier comment about 'pulling the correct bits of string', 'OK. You can start learning right now.'

She looked excited, 'Can I? What can I do?'

I pointed to the steering station. 'Hop up there, get comfortable and find the compass.'

She untangled herself from Jasper and re-positioned to the steering station.

'OK. I found it. It's this big ball-shaped thing in the middle of the panel with white letters and numbers.'

'That's it,' I replied, 'there's a vertical white line standing up called the lubber's line. That represents the centreline of the boat, or where we're pointing. What number is it lined up against?'

She peered at the compass. 'It keeps moving a bit, but it seems to be mostly around 220.'

'OK. That's 220 degrees magnetic, which is southwest. That's the course we need to steer to safely pass between the Sister Islands and Craggy Island. They're all off the north Coast of Flinders Island, so we need to reach a point where we can safely turn south for Marshall Bay.'

'OK. I've got that,' she replied. 'What's next?'

'Next you look over on the left side of the instrument panel for a dial with a knob under it and a switch beside it that's marked A/P 1.'

She looked and said, 'Found it. The dial looks like the compass, except that it's just a flat circle with the numbers right around it, and there's another one that looks the same right beside it. But it's marked A/P 2.'

'Good,' I replied, liking her enthusiasm, 'because I sail alone most of the time, I need the autopilot steering most of the time, so I have two. The second one is the backup autopilot and I run them alternately to keep them working smoothly. If you move that switch for A/P 1 up to the OFF position, you turn George off and you can steer manually with the wheel.'

As if expecting something dramatic to happen, she gingerly reached out and turned the switch off. Naturally, nothing appeared to happen.

'There's a red light showing above the switch,' Zoe reported.

'Good. That means that the autopilot is turned off. Now you

have to steer with the wheel, and you'll have to hold a steady course of 220°, or we'll run into Flinders Island!'

She gave me a brief, worried glance, saw that I was only half-joking, but quickly turned her attention back to the compass, grasping the wheel in a white-knuckled death-grip, so I gave her some tips about watching the way the boat was being pushed around by the waves and how to counteract that, without moving the wheel too much.

After about 10 minutes, our wake had straightened out considerably and Zoe had relaxed enough to look over at me in triumph.

'How's that, Skipper?' she grinned.

'Pretty good,' I conceded. 'Keep checking your course and look out ahead from time to time as well… just in case that freighter off our right bow decides to speed up or slow down. As it is, he'll pass well in front of us.'

Zoe gave a horrified look over the right bow and was appalled to see how close the ship was and how big it seemed.

'Oh, fuck!' she said, very succinctly. 'How did I miss that?'

'You were concentrating on just one thing, like keeping on course, but as you now see, you have to keep your eyes moving all around. Remember that a big ship is usually faster than us and can come up from behind. Use the radar as well to assist your lookout.'

I showed her how to read the radar display and the chart plotter and all was quiet for a while after that, as Zoe got on with the concentration thing. By the time first Janice, and then Angie wandered sleepily out to the cockpit, Zoe was doing pretty well with her scan around the horizon and frequently checking the radar and chart plotter.

'Meet the first mate,' I said with a wink to Janice, 'hand-steering as well. Only had one near-collision with a freighter bound for Hobart, so things are looking up.'

'Oh, you dobber! You weren't supposed to say anything about that,' she exclaimed indignantly.

I smiled at her to show that I wasn't criticising and said, 'Seeing as the boat is in safe hands, I'm going below to have a shower, then I might have some breakfast.'

Zoe suddenly looked a bit worried about being left in charge, until I leant over and whispered, 'You'll be fine. Just keep on course and look around occasionally. I've set a radar alarm so that if something does sneak up on us, even from behind, it'll let you know. Besides, I'm not far away. If you need me, send your Mum down to get me!'

She grinned nervously and returned to concentrating on her job. Janice and Angie looked a bit concerned, but showing my trust in Zoe, I casually wandered below, leaving Zoe in charge.

In the comfort of his now family and maid-deficient home, Luke hit a speed dial number, and moments later a gruff voice said, *'Yeah, Boss?'*

'Progress Jimmy! What's happening? You're not calling me!'

'Ahh...Well, at the moment, we've sort of lost the trail.'

Luke felt the familiar red rage rising but fought it down.

'You're not supposed to 'lose the trail', Jimmy. I'm paying out a great deal of money to supposed experts who aren't supposed to 'lose the trail!'

'Yes, Boss,' Jimmy, muttered miserably, knowing he was in for a tongue-lashing, if not worse and wishing he'd never taken this job on in the first place. Fuck the money! It wasn't worth it!

'So just where did you lose the trail, Jimmy?' Luke asked in a quiet and dangerously mild tone.

'Ah...Well. We sort of lost them in Coffs Harbour, Boss.'

Luke took another deep breath. 'Lost them in Coffs Harbour! Gee whizz. That's a pretty long way from Melbourne, Jimmy. What were they doing in Coffs fucking Harbour, Jimmy? Can you at least tell me that?'

'Yeah! I can, boss. They were staying at a cheap little motel on the highway, close to the centre of town.'

'And then what happened, Jimmy?'

'Ah...That's where we lost them, Boss!'

'I know that, Jimmy. Now how do I know that? Because you fucking-well just told me that, you useless fucking moron!' Luke roared. 'What I want to know, you useless sheep-fucking idiot, is HOW did you manage to lose my dim-witted little wife and two pretty, air-headed daughters from that cheap, little motel in Coffs Harbour?'

'*Oh. Yeah. I see what you mean. Well, one of the guys spotted them leaving the train station, so we tracked them to the Motel and took turns to watch, 'cause they paid for three nights.*'

'That's funny, Jimmy. I don't recall the 'phone call from you telling me that you found them staying in Coffs Harbour. Can you refresh my failing memory as to just WHEN you called to pass on that rather important fact?'

'*Ah...Well. Maybe I didn't actually call you straight away, Boss. You see, when we checked that they'd booked for three nights, I figured that there was plenty of time for you to get up here and grab them. But then they left after the first night. They just took all their gear with them, left the room on foot before dawn and disappeared!*'

'Really, Jimmy. Is that what you figured? You didn't think to call me straight away when your three targets were literally right in front of your dopey bloody eyes? Didn't it occur to you that they just might leave before the convenient three days booking was up? And didn't it occur to you that just maybe, you useless, clumsy, flat-footed morons might have been spotted hanging around a cheap motel perving on three females?'

'*No, Boss,' Jimmy whispered miserably.*

'I don't suppose that you thought to ask the taxi drivers who were on duty that morning if they'd picked them up?'

'*We did that, Boss, but nobody picked them up.*'

'Wow! Maybe you can think occasionally. It's a pity you don't when it counts!'

Jimmy knew when to keep his mouth shut.

'Well, how about the train or bus? There's also an airport there, if I remember correctly.'

'*We checked the airport and showed those fake ACP ID papers you gave us, but they weren't listed. You said that the airlines have to see proper ID before someone can buy a ticket.*'

'OK. So they didn't fly. How about the bus or the train? Jesus

Christ, Jimmy! This is like getting blood out of a stone. Do I have to do all the thinking for you?'

'*No, Boss. But the bus and train people sell tickets to anyone who can pay. They don't need personal ID like the airline people, so we don't know if they used either one. They could've hitched a ride instead.*'

'I don't suppose that any of you mental giants, who, I might add, are letting three dopey females run rings around you, thought to ask around the bus and train stations in case somebody noticed three attractive blonde females with a pile of Gucci luggage catching a ride?'

'*Yes, we did that, Boss,*' Jimmy was grateful to be able to report something positive, '*but nobody remembered them. I mean, they'd certainly stand out, but nobody has seen them.*'

'Okay Jimmy, then tell me their trail so far.'

'*But I already did that, Boss,*' whined Jimmy.

Luke lost it, big time lost it. He crashed the handset against the desk over and over, and when Mr Telstra's finest product refused to break, he calmed slightly before raising it to his ear again and saying quietly,

'Then tell me again, Jimmy. Humour me! For what I'm paying you, I'm allowed to have a lapse in memory. Just tell me before I crawl down this fucking phone line and strangle you with my bare hands!'

'*Sorry, Boss. After they left your place, they somehow got to Southern Cross Station*' that's in the city, '*then went to Albury by train then took the train back to Wangaratta the same day. They spent two nights in a motel in Wangaratta, and then jumped on a bus up to Wagga Wagga. What's with these double names, boss? Isn't one enough?*'

'Obviously not, Jimmy. They're all over the place up there. Get on with it!'

'*Oh. Sorry boss. Anyway, they spent three nights in Wagga Wagga, and then took the train again to Sydney. We lost them in Sydney but had a really lucky break when one of the northern crew spotted them in Coffs Harbour. You know the rest.*'

'Ok, Jimmy. Split everyone up. I want half the boys working back toward Melbourne and the other half can work toward Queensland. Check every little town as you go. I presume that she's stopped using her credit cards?'

'Yeah. That's how we lost her in Sydney. She must have a wad of cash now.'

'Yeah,' Luke replied, 'she does, and can get more. I think her arse-hole barrister father is sticking his nose into it as well and that makes me very unhappy. I'm trying to get him shut down, but he's very high profile and that makes him a little bit bulletproof.

Anyway, move the boys out ASAP and try to pick up a sniff of their trail. I've got a very big deal riding on this, and I need them back in my control now!'

'Ok, boss. I'm on it'

CHAPTER 10

FIREBIRD...AT SEA – FLINDERS ISLAND, WEDNESDAY MORNING

The next few hours went smoothly. I tried to relieve Zoe at the wheel, but she begged to be allowed to stay on watch, so after she batted her baby blue eyes a few times, I relented and left her there while I took Janice and Angie on an upper-deck tour, showing them how to check for chafing or damage. It was something that I did on a daily basis, which helped avoid breakages at bad times when gear was under extreme stress. I also explained about how the sails worked and what ropes did what, although learning the functions of all the cordage on a modern yacht was a daunting task that would take time.

We were accompanied, as usual, by Jasper who had become very happy with the girls and even let them feed him, which was a major step. I showed them his toilet; a section of artificial grass that was attached to the deck by Velcro straps that made it easy to either tip his doings overboard, or just hose the whole thing off with the deck-wash hose.

At one point, I called out to Zoe, her head sticking up through the hatch in the cockpit canopy as she watched and listened to as much as she could of my commentary. 'How far to run to our waypoint?'

'Two miles,' she replied after a quick check of the chart plotter.

'Goodo,' I replied, 'at the waypoint, hit the Cancel button to stop the alarm, then turn onto a course of 123° for 10 miles. That should take us between four small islands, right into Marshall Bay.'

'OK.'

I was ready to re-trim the sails at the course change and was pleased when she smartly cancelled the waypoint alarm when it sounded and smoothly turned to the southeast. Our wake wobbled a bit until Zoe got used to the different handling of the boat with the waves hitting us broadside on, but she quickly adjusted. We picked up speed on the beam reach and it wasn't long before the string of small islands protecting the northern part of Marshall Bay lifted out of the soft sea haze directly ahead.

I sat beside her at the wheel. 'Aim right for the middle of the gap between the two islands on the left and what looks like two on the right. If you look at the chart plotter, you will see that there are actually three islands to the right side, but from this angle, two merge into one.'

'I can see the gap you mean.'

'Good, but make sure we go right through the middle where there's plenty of water. I'll drop the sails in a moment and start the engines. It'll be safer and make us more manoeuvrable.'

Shortly, I did just that, raised the dagger-boards, and with the engines running at 50% RPM, Zoe steered us neatly between the tiny islets and into Marshall Bay.

'Come left a little and steer east,' I said, 'Can you see that cluster of rocky islets poking up over there near the shore?'

She nodded, 'Yep.'

'Ok. Aim just to the right of them. We want to anchor about 200 meters to the right of those rocks, and only about 30 metres or so off the beach.'

I let her take us most of the way in, but she was glad to hand over as the hard bits got closer. The water was very clear and the uneven bottom, a mixture of sand, weed and rock was clearly visible.

The girls got a bit nervous to see the bottom so clearly, until I pointed out the reading of the depth-sounder showed 8 to 10 meters beneath us, while at our deepest point we drew just 0.6m or two feet.

By mid-morning, we were lying peacefully at anchor, 30 metres or so off a deserted sandy beach, the nor 'easterly breeze gently sending little patches of ruffles over the surface of the otherwise calm bay that stretched in a smooth curve into the far distance to the south of us. The land beyond the beach to the east of us was a band of green, open pasture, rising gently to low, green hills. To our north, the hills were considerably higher, covered in scrub and trees, while the cluster of rocky islets we'd dodged around on the way in, were about 200 metres off our left side.

'Harry, this is absolutely beautiful!' Janice exclaimed, visibly drinking in the peace and tranquillity of the scene.

'Yeah, really, really great,' echoed the twins, 'we love the look of the beach. Is it safe to go swimming?'

I looked around. 'Sure. But maybe just between the boat and the shore for now; until we suss out the fish life around here.'

They sparked up immediately and raced off to change, while I looked at Janice, still sitting and patting Jasper.

'Not swimming?' I enquired, raising my eyebrows.

'Not for the moment, I might just sit up top and watch,' she smiled.

'Ok. I'll lower the RIB into the water. Later, maybe after lunch, you can take the girls over to those rocky outcrops if you like to have a look around. There should be good fishing there as well if you want to try your hand at catching dinner.'

'That'd be great!' she replied, 'Fresh fish for dinner. Yum!'

I had just dropped the RIB in and tied it up to the left stern platform, when Angie called out, 'Harry!'

I looked up, appreciating the sight of her in a different, but still tiny bikini that was delightfully, barely decent.

'Yo!'

'Oh, there you are. Jasper is acting like he wants to come with us. Is that okay? I mean, does he really like swimming?'

'He likes swimming with people he wants to be with, so yes, he'll go with you. He might even give you a tow if you hang onto his tail.'

'Yay!' she cried out. 'Come on Zoe. Jasper can come with us.'

I watched as the pair of them and their furry black sidekick, slid into the water off the right stern platform, gasping at the initial shock of the cool temperature, but then both immediately set off for shore with a strong stroke, Jasper trailing only slightly.

I went over and lowered the swim boarding ladder for their return, took the hand-held shower out of its locker and laid it out ready for all three of them, then joined Janice on the foredeck where she was watching the girls.

'That went well,' she commented, 'I didn't think that Jasper would be so keen to go swimming.'

'Yeah. He's funny like that. Normally he won't, unless I throw him in, but with me or someone else he likes in the water first, he seems quite happy.'

By now the girls were on the beach, running up and down chasing Jasper who behaved more like a medium-to-large very frisky dog, dodging the girls' lunges with ease, until he spotted some seagulls along the beach and raced off to chase them instead. With shrill cries, the girls set off in pursuit.

'Bloody hell he's fast!' she said, as Jasper stretched his stride and left the girls far behind. 'He won't run off, will he?'

'No way!' I said, 'He'll stop and wait for them any moment now. See how he turns his head a little even while he's running? He's making sure they're alright.'

'Good guard dog,' she said with a smile.

'For those he considers are under his protection, he's the best,' I said proudly.

'Well. They're certainly having a great time at the moment. They deserve better than having to be on the run from my insane, vengeful husband. None of this was their fault!'

'From what I've learned so far,' I commented mildly, 'it wasn't really yours either!'

She frowned. 'That's something you're never sure about. You think back to see if there was something that you could have done better, or some incident that might have triggered the change, but so far, I can't think of anything.'

To keep her talking, I asked, 'How were things in the early days of your marriage?'

'Oh, great,' she replied with a trace of enthusiasm, 'We were both very happy and very busy. Luke was always driven by his dreams of what he wanted to achieve and worked very hard at developing his earthmoving business while I looked after the home. I'd been a bookkeeper before we married, so to be of more help, I studied accountancy. We used to talk about his business all the time. I was more like a partner than just a wife.'

'But when the girls arrived, I was kept busy with them, of course, but Luke just stopped discussing his business like he used to. He went through a big expansion phase and spent a lot of time away with business meetings and trips. He got to know most of the important people in Victorian politics and business and brought many of them home for dinner at various times.

Luckily, we had a maid by then which helped a lot, but he didn't want to discuss his plans and what he was doing any more, so that level of contact faded away very quickly. He became very secretive and started doing all his work in his study that he kept always locked.'

'Looking after the girls kept me busy and fully occupied, so for a long time I didn't notice how far we'd drifted apart. He had his businesses, friends and colleagues, while I had the house and the girls. Some of my girlfriends told me stories about the business trips, because their husbands were on them as well, but I didn't really register for a long time that he wasn't interested in me anymore, except as a trophy wife and very occasional sex toy.'

She looked a bit embarrassed, 'I mean, we'd had a reasonable sex life up to then and I'd tried to teach the girls that nudity and sex were healthy and normal, not something bad and dirty, to be hidden away like what some of their moronic school teachers were trying to tell them. Anyway, it seemed to work well for them, and they have what I think is a very healthy attitude toward sex and nudity.'

She giggled unexpectedly, 'That's why I almost laughed yesterday when you gave your housekeeping speech. They weren't embarrassed by what you said, quite the opposite!'

I kept silent, surprised by the fact she was revealing intimate details to a person she'd only known two and a half days.

'Anyway,' she resumed, 'to cut a long and horribly sordid story short, we quickly became two strangers sharing a house. It was about that time that he brought some workmen in and built separate quarters for each of us.

He still seemed to dote on the girls, though, and I have to admit that he's always done the right thing by them, even making sure they didn't know he was beating me. Those also became the only times we had sex, if that's the name for it.

It all quickly degenerated when I realised that he couldn't get an erection unless he fantasised that he was raping me, but then he seemed to have more and more difficulty developing even that fantasy, so he discovered that if he beat me until I struggled, the more I struggled, the more excited he became!'

'He'd actually froth at the mouth and could only grunt like an ape until he finished, which thankfully never did take long.

Anyway, even when I saw that photo of Zoe last night, I wasn't upset by the fact that he took it. We both took photos of the girls all the time and they were often naked or partly so, especially in and around the pool in summer.

What really upset me was that the rotten bastard had posted it on-line for all his sicko mates to look at! That's unhealthy as far as I'm concerned, and now I don't think that he's truly cared about the girls for a long time! It's like he's got some other agenda for the future concerning us. There's no way he should be reacting this strongly just because we ran away! And it's not just to have us back in the house, either!'

She thought a moment, before adding, 'I'm also really puzzled as to why he's gone to so much trouble to keep the dark side of his nature away from the girls, but to then go and sell or trade the photos of them on-line? What's the point of having just a few more photos of naked girls to share amongst his sicko friends? That's why I feel there's more to this that we can't see yet!'

She was silent for some time after those revelations and I respected that by not commenting on the tragic saga that had set the three of them on the run from his insane rages. I carefully considered the question her final statement raised, and also contemplated the implications of the paedophile ring, combined with the acquisition of the old mansion and didn't like the hazy, foul picture that was starting to form. Particularly as the main, unhealthy focus of his attention seemed to be on the two girls and not so much on Janice. Or maybe she was included?

I needed to look at a few more of those folders from Luke's computer, as well as make a very private call or email to certain high-ranking persons in the ACP in Canberra. However, a small voice alarm sounded softly in my head urging extreme caution as to which person I contacted.

The reason I felt painfully impaled on the horns of a dilemma was that although we'd only looked at a few photos in some of the file folders, among the prominent faces that I did recognise, two most unfortunately belonged to very senior members of the ACP, an organisation that I was required to report to on occasion.

If Luke was prepared to turn over every rock around Melbourne and Interstate looking for his family, whether or not they had a copy of his files, I shuddered to think of the hellfire and damnation that would descend on one Harry Stevens should I talk to the wrong person at ACP HQ!

This meant that the web of corruption and filth had spread even wider than just the upper business, social, law enforcement and political arena!

While I watched the girls chasing Jasper again, in and out of the water with shrieks of delight, and Janice stared into the distance, lost in her own private hell of memories, a name popped into my head.

Greg James. He was a Queensland Police Inspector on the Gold Coast, whom I'd been involved with not long ago on another operation. I'd gotten to know Greg well enough on a personal level to know that he was very firmly heterosexual and apparently had no leanings toward kiddie porn or paedophilia. He also maybe held enough rank to be able to make the right contacts for me and keep my name out of the discussion until I knew whom to trust.

I moved closer to Janice and gave her a hug. She didn't respond at first, but then briefly returned the hug with surprising force.

Sitting back, she smiled bravely through eyes sparkling with unshed tears.

'You're a good listener, Harry, and a good person,' she said. 'I've only known you a couple of days and already I'm telling you all my intimate secrets!'

'I appreciate your trust,' I smiled, 'and I'll do all that I can to help you sort out this mess. But I do have a request.'

She raised her eyebrows.

'Would you mind taking the RIB ashore and go for a walk with the girls? You probably need their company more than you do mine.'

She smiled, 'That's not quite true, Harry. But I'll do as you ask, and we'll deal with the other stuff later. I know how to work the outboard. We had a similar one with the cruiser. I'll get going now.'

With that she went below, and after a few minutes, reappeared in a lovely little bikini that gave me a funny feeling in the pit of my stomach. Well, maybe the feeling was a bit further south of that, but it was enough to remind me that my last live-aboard lady was many long-months gone.

Janice grabbed a towel, waved, then competently untied the RIB, pushed off and motored sedately to shore.

The girls gave her a big welcome, and their happy chatter seemed to lift Janice's depression almost immediately. Even Jasper got in on the welcome act and capered around them like a frisky puppy.

Eventually, they set off along the beach, so I went below and fired up the sat-phone.

'*Southport Police Station. May I help you?*' said a polite female voice.

'Good morning,' I replied, 'Detective Greg James please.'

There was a slight pause, then, 'Ah, yes, he's in. Putting you through.'

A few clicks and a buzz later, Greg's gravelly voice sounded very officially, 'Detective James, may I help you?'

'I bloody well hope so, Greg. It's Harry Stevens.'

'Harry!' came a delighted cry. 'How are you cobber? I haven't heard from you for yonks. What're you up to?'

I chuckled at his dramatic change of manner. 'Oh, a bit of this and a bit of that, old mate,' I replied, 'I've been trying to stay out of trouble.'

'Ah,' he said, 'that sounds like you've recently failed to avoid trouble and I'll bet there are some lovelies involved! Am I right?'

'Well. I hate to admit it, but yes, you are right, Greg. In fact, I need some help.'

'No problem is too great for the best bad-guy busting team afloat,' he replied cheerily. 'What's going on and what can I do?'

I took a deep breath. 'First up, do you have access to an encrypted phone?'

There was a few moments silence before he replied more slowly and seriously. 'Yes, oddly enough I do. We have a Tactical Response Group stationed here now, with the Commonwealth Games only a month away, and they have a thing called a Thuraya SG-2520 that's supposed to be pretty secure. Is that what you mean?'

'Yeah. I know that one. I can set my gear to mate with it. Look, this is a kinda sensitive and I can't say any more like this, but can you get one of those things and call me soon as?'

'Yeah. I can do that,' he replied, a million questions hovering in the tone of his voice. 'Do you remember Sandy, the comms tech we had on our last job? Well, she's just been trained on them and has a couple of units on trial for our own use. If things are that sensitive, I'd like to bring her in on this: as in, in case I need back-up!'

I thought quickly and did indeed remember Sandy, a pretty and very shapely, auburn-haired, General Duties Constable, with a bubbly personality, who did wonders for Service recruitment anytime she appeared in a bikini!

Despite that, she was a very competent communications specialist and maybe it would be a good thing if Greg had another person who knew what was going on.

'Yeah. OK, mate. Bring her in, but you'd both better get out of the office before you call. Go to a coffee shop or something where you can't be overheard.'

He replied dryly, 'Yes, mum! I think we can handle that!'

I chuckled, 'Sorry, mate. Old habits! I'll tell you more soon.'

I gave him my number before hanging up, made some changes to my all-the-bells-and whistles sat phone courtesy of the Feds and sat back to wait.

Surprisingly, it was only about 10 minutes before my phone trilled, a sound that always sounded like a castrated galah having a coughing fit.

I snatched it up, crossed my fingers and pushed the 'Auto-encrypt' button.

There was a small delay while a series of clicks, pops and buzzes sounded that were designed, I'm sure, to make the owner happy about the ridiculous cost of the things, then a tentative female voice, crystal-clear over the high-fidelity console speakers said, *'Hello?'*

FIREBIRD...FLINDERS ISLAND, WEDNESDAY

'Good Morning, Sandy,' I said in my suavest James Bond voice, 'Stevens. Harry Stevens. I have you loud and clear.'

She giggled. 'Oh. Hi Harry, I'm glad that you're still an idiot, but you're clear as well. Greg's here and we have earpieces in and are in a park down on the waterfront. Say hi, Greg.'

'Hi Harry,' he said, 'that all seems to work well, although I'm glad Sandy's here. I'm hopeless with these things!'

I chuckled. Some things never change, and Greg's lack of affinity with even the most basic electronic device was legendary.

'So, Compadre,' he went on, 'what's the rattle this time that we need to sneak around with encrypted sat-phones, pretending to have a lunchtime nookie date?'

They had, in fact, had a bit of a temporary fling together on my boat during the last operation, so it followed that I heard Sandy giggle and with the superb clarity of the system, what sounded like Greg getting smacked on the arm.

I took a deep breath. 'Just a quick question, no offence intended please, but what do you guys think about Kiddy-porn?'

There was a stunned silence from the other end, before Greg cleared his throat. 'I presume that you have a very good reason for that question, but for both of us, we emphatically despise it!'

'Good,' I replied apologetically. 'Sorry to ask, but I thought I'd best do so.

Now, this is what we've found has been going on.'

I explained to them as quickly as possible what had been happening, what I'd learned from Janice and what I'd deduced from the scanty information I had. I made sure they understood the implications of me identifying at least two high-level ACP guys. When I finished, there was a low whistle from Greg, while Sandy just said, '*Oh, fuck! What a mess!*'

'Yeah!' I agreed. 'It is that.'

'*Okay, Harry,*' Greg said, '*we've got that part and it sounds like real dynamite, buddy, even with just the dudes you're identified so far, but what do you need us to do?*'

'Well. Obviously, I don't want to draw direct attention to our movements, or myself, by maybe asking questions of the wrong person at the ACP. So, what if you were to initiate a routine enquiry to the ACP, based perhaps on a tip-off from a trusted source, that a rock-spider has been trying to flog some very high-grade kiddie-porn so he could score some dope?

But tiptoe with this 'cause I don't want you to draw down too much attention either, but it might be very informative to know who responds, how quickly, and how much interest they show in your enquiry.'

The Queensland crew were silent for a few moments, and then Sandy said, speaking to Greg as well as myself, 'That could work if we tied the enquiry into one of our on-going paedophile investigations. We've got a couple of those and there was a small bust just last week. Now there's a case file, we could make it seem like the tip-off came out of that!'

'*Good thinking, Sandy,*' said Greg. '*OK, Harry, you're on! We'll work something out and see what shakes down from on high.*'

'Thanks guys,' I said with obvious relief, 'that'll be a great help. I really didn't know who to trust over this.'

'*No problem mate, we'll get on it right away. Can we call you anytime on this number?*'

'Yes, you can. But if the girls are around, I may not be able to say too much, but I can take your progress reports.'

'*No problem. We'll call again soon.*' There was a series of clicks and odd tones as the devices decoupled from each other, before the call terminated. I left it in standby mode, with a coded lock so only I could answer it.

It was the better part of an hour before Janice, the girls and a wet, sandy Jasper tied up to the right boarding platform. In their absence, I'd used the time productively to scan through more of Luke's happy holiday snaps, and had indeed found more pics of Zoe, getting progressively older, as well as a series of Angie at various ages. All of them showed the girls naked, but were, thankfully, totally innocent shots, either taken in the bathroom or, as they became older, in or by the pool. In most of them, the girls knew they were being photographed and were smiling or laughing. Some candid ones were obviously in places around the house, but none appeared deliberately posed, or could in any way be classed as pornographic. They were just happy photos of pretty girls, who happened to be naked and enjoyed being that way.

I would freely admit that I enjoyed looking at their photos, particularly as they became older, but then I always enjoyed looking at naked ladies. On the contrary, I took absolutely no pleasure at all in looking at all the other photos of the other ones or what was going on with them.

After sorting through the masses of photos, I slowly realised that the later ones of Angie and Zoe were the only ones of kids over the age of about 12. All the nasty ones were of younger kids, sometimes much younger and most were Asian or Indian appearance.

I did identify several more prominent figures in State and Federal politics, quite a few social celebrities and a number of business leaders. Against my better judgement, I wrote down, on a scrap of paper, a list of the names of every person I could identify, then hid it in plain sight by clipping it in with a bunch more just like it, and left it in the drawer under the chart drawer with other old shopping lists, radio messages, etc.

One of the folders I came across contained a number of short videos, apparently made professionally, all set in the same ornate, old-fashioned bedroom. It was difficult to identify anything about the room, except that the furnishings, pictures and wallpaper looked old or old-style. The wall-to-ceiling cornices, in particular, were also very old-fashioned and elaborate, and might be identifiable in a future investigation.

About then, I heard the outboard coming and went aft to greet the troops with the freshwater shower. Janice was driving and made a tidy job of bringing the dingy alongside. Zoe hopped out and tied up neatly. The girls and Jasper were covered in sand and dried salt, but as Janice hadn't been swimming, she just rinsed her feet and went up to the cockpit. Zoe held Jasper still, while I rinsed him off thoroughly. He was pretty good about being hosed off and it was only at the end when he shook himself like a dog that I got wet.

I retreated to the top of the steps to dry Jasper off properly with a towel before he soaked everything in sight, and as much as I would have enjoyed it, I left the girls to mess around washing each other off.

While I dried Jasper, I kept an eye on them, but they didn't waste water and were soon drying off in the cockpit as well. They were all, including Jasper, in a very upbeat mood, so the long walk and play had been good therapy.

I raised an eyebrow to Janice and scored a smile in return. When the girls went below to change out of wet bikinis, Janice asked, 'Did you get any more done on the files?'

'Yep,' I smiled, 'nothing bad on either Angie or Zoe, though. There were plenty more photos up to about 8 or 9 months ago, but all innocent-looking stuff. Just normal, naked happy-snaps of healthy teenagers.'

She looked very relieved. 'Oh, thank goodness for small mercies! Thanks for checking that for me.'

I grinned, 'No problem, although I have to say to you, as much as I disliked wading through all the other photos, I really enjoyed seeing the girls' photos. They were happy photos, they're really lovely and so much like you. I'm very glad that they aren't intentionally involved in this foulness!'

She almost teared up, but instead, stepped over Jasper, never an easy task, and gave me a hard, full-body contact hug that felt really good. Especially as she still had that little bikini on, it was like, *really* good!

Janice must have liked it too, since she stayed there some considerable time, even after Jasper eased himself out from between us. I've no doubt that she definitely felt how happy it made me and I was glad the girls didn't suddenly appear, or I'd have had to sit down in a hurry.

Finally, she looked up at me, a strange grin on her face, 'I don't mind that you appreciated the girls,' she said softly, 'I take it as a compliment and they would too, if they knew. I'm also sure that you'll always look after them.'

'Yep,' I replied, hoping that the tightness in my shorts would hurry up and go away, 'I will.'

She smiled, glanced pointedly at my somewhat distended shorts and giggled. 'You either need the next size up in shorts, Harry, or to do something about that thing. You can do damage if you restrain yourself so tightly like that!' She giggled again and went inside to put the kettle on.

I joined her when I decently could and while we could hear the girls still chattering in their cabin, I patted her lightly on the bum, and said softly, 'You're a very cheeky young lady!' She grinned, until I added, 'Anyway, I made contact with an old friend with the Queensland Police, and passed on the whole story. He's going to make some discrete enquiries in a way that will protect our identities. I'll give you the full story later this evening when the girls have gone to bed.'

Janice looked thoughtful but smiled. 'Okay, that's really good that someone else in an official position knows the story. So long as you can trust him.'

'Yeah, we can.' I said.

'OK,' Janice replied, 'tell me the rest later.'

'I'll do that,' I replied, 'but as a by-the-way, you don't happen to have your passports, do you?'

She looked a bit surprised, 'Well, yes as a matter of fact, we do, and I've got them with me. Along with all our Birth and my Marriage certificates! But why would we need them?'

'Oh. Just in case we had to run further afield,' I suggested lightly. 'We are on a boat after all!'

Janice looked thoughtful at that. 'I see. So, if necessary, we could go to, say, New Zealand, or the Pacific Islands?'

'Yep! Sure could!'

I left her looking thoughtful and we ended up having a late lunch while the girls regaled me with stories about Jasper playing with them and chasing seagulls.

'He's just like a dog at times,' Zoe enthused.

'Yeah. And he really seems to like splashing around in the water,' added Angie.

As it turned out, Janice and I didn't have to wait until that evening to discuss my contact with Greg James. After lunch, Angie asked if they could borrow the RIB to go explore around the little rocky islets just to seaward of us.

'Mum showed us how to work the outboard,' she said seriously, 'and we know not to get into shallow water with the engine running. We've got the oars for that.'

I looked at Janice for her approval and when she nodded, I said, 'OK. But please be very careful!'

Angie smiled, 'Thanks Harry. We'll be good. Can Jasper come too?'

I looked at the big lump, discretely being fed some cheese by Zoe. 'Sure. Go ahead. But maybe keep him out of the water this time.'

'No problem,' she replied, 'we weren't going in again anyway.'

So, equipped with hats, towels, sunscreen and the cat, they puttered away, chattering non-stop.

With a contented sigh, Janice snuggled up against me on the cockpit lounge, forcing me to wrap an arm around her. 'Thanks, Harry. They really seem to be relaxing properly at last. Jasper especially is turning out to be a real help.'

I grinned, 'He's enjoying himself. He's not had much company other than me for a while, and certainly not active, attentive young ladies!'

'Anyway,' I said with a grin, 'I know that they're okay, but is their Mother relaxing yet?'

She looked up at me, scrunched down against my chest. 'Not yet,' she replied frankly, 'but it might help if I felt a bit more of what I felt in that hug we had before lunch!'

I grinned, 'Really? Now?'

'Sure,' she said with a cheeky grin. 'Plenty of time, they'll be a while.'

So, we hugged and kissed a bit, and although we'd only known each other a few days, one thing led to another, and before long, items of clothing were scattered around the cockpit.

She was a very active little bundle of firm, delightfully female flesh, and although the first coupling between strangers was often not perfect, on this occasion, everything seemed to fit properly and work as advertised.

It was a good thing that we didn't have to be particularly quiet on account of the girls, as despite, or perhaps because of the circumstances, it was a very intense and supremely satisfying encounter for both of us. Afterwards, I was happy and relaxed, and Janice looked and acted even more so.

With the knowledge that the girls could return at any time, we reluctantly decided to make ourselves decent, consoled by the knowledge that now that particular personal hurdle had been overcome, we could and would indulge again at the next opportunity that offered some privacy.

It wasn't long before the purr of the outboard was heard and the RIB could be seen swinging safely wide around the nearest islet and heading for the boat.

Displaying a commendable degree of competency, Zoe turned the dingy hard at the last moment and cut the motor. With hardly a bump, the RIB parked alongside the boarding platform. Angie hopped out and securely tied off the painter.

Jasper jumped out, with what looked like a grin on his face and trotted up the steps, followed by the girls.

'Hi guys,' Janice said casually. 'Was that fun?'

The girls looked at her, looked at me, then at each other, before bursting out into giggles.

Janice just looked at them until their mirth settled a bit, then asked, 'Are you two OK?'

That set them off again and it wasn't until that died down that Angie said, between more giggles, 'You did it! You really did. We were so hoping you would sooner or later, but you did it sooner! Oh, Mum. We're so happy for you! We want to know all about it!'

With that, they both went and hugged Janice who at least had the grace to blush a little.

I looked at Janice, raised an eyebrow, and waved a finger to indicate the two girls and then both of us.

She just nodded in reply.

'Well,' I said to Jasper, 'so much for keeping things a secret.'

Zoe looked at me. 'Oh, come on Harry. There was no way Mum was going to hide the fact that you two had been having nookie while we were gone. It's so obvious, but we think it's great! You both looked like you needed a tension release and that's seems to be the perfect way.'

I held my hands up in mock surrender and grinned, 'Ok. I give up. Yes, we did the deed and it was great!'

The girls laughed with delight and I scored a big hug from each of them.

Angie grinned at my slight discomfort. 'You don't have to say any more, Harry. We'll get a moment-by-moment description out of Mum before long.'

She rolled her eyes and put on an awful foreign accent, 'Ve have ze need to know ze most in-ti-mate secrets off your affair! Zarefore, you vill tell ze virgin sisters efferysink!'

I didn't know whether to laugh or look horrified, but Janice just said, 'Stop it you two teases! Poor Harry doesn't know what he's got himself into.'

'Ha!' crowed Angie, 'He'll soon find out!'

So, I did what any red-blooded male would do in the face of such a challenge; I retreated inside the saloon, where I pretended to be busy checking a chart and measuring important things, leaving the three females in the cockpit.

As I snuck the occasional glance outside, I saw that they already had their heads together, the girls listening to Janice with rapt attention and giggling excitedly. To make sure I couldn't hear what they were discussing, I decided to go down and check the oil level in the starboard engine, which is where Janice found me 20 minutes later.

'You can come out now,' she taunted with a chuckle, 'I talked them into leaving you alone, so they'll behave, for a while.'

'Did you really tell them what we did?' I asked apprehensively.

Janice looked a bit uncomfortable, but only for a moment. 'Well, yes, I did. I've always been totally open with the girls about everything, and I've found that's been the best way to earn and keep their trust. They might not have any sexual experience, but they know how everything works and they always want to know more. So instead of hiding it like so many parents do, I tell them.'

She gave a sigh of frustration at my apparent lack of understanding.

'When they were younger and Luke and I still had a halfway normal sex life, we got sprung a couple of times. It was just by accident each time, but while we definitely didn't try to give them a practical demonstration, we didn't try to pretend that we were just kissing and cuddling either. I explained to them that this is the way that males and females who really care about each other show their love and affection, and that it was totally natural. It seems that my method has worked, as they seem well-balanced to me.'

I nodded. 'I agree. I guess that I've had very little experience with teenage girls, but your explanation makes total sense and from what I've seen, the girls do seem very well balanced with a healthy outlook on life.'

I grinned. 'Obviously, I've spent my time around the wrong sort of females!'

Janice giggled and gave me a hug and a kiss. 'Just go with the flow on this one and trust the girls and me. Relax and enjoy what good times we can manage to have; maybe they'll help balance out all the bad stuff that's going on right now.'

I kissed her back. 'OK. I will, I promise.'

FIREBIRD...FLINDERS ISLAND, WEDNESDAY EVENING

Even though Angie had told me that she loved cooking and was perfectly happy to take over the galley, I cooked a bunch of sausages on the Weber BBQ, leaving Angie to organise vegies or a salad. We had vegies.

After tea was eaten and washed up, we had a fun evening, with all three girls in a funny, upbeat mood and even played a game of Monopoly, with much blatant cheating and laughter.

Finally, the girls went to bed, Jasper tagging along with his new best buddies, leaving Janice and I alone to catch up on news.

A quick kiss and a cuddle, then I sent her to the cockpit while I made two Irish coffees.

'Do you really trust your Queensland copper mate?' Janice asked as I set the wonderfully aromatic coffees down on the table and sat beside her.

'Yes. I do. He's a very straight and down-to-earth copper. Plus, he has developed some good contacts in the Service and the ACP. He also understands the need to keep us isolated from involvement in the initial investigation.'

'Ok, so long as you're happy. I'd hate to bring Luke's goons down on us now.'

'I'm actually more concerned with the senior guys in the ACP that are part of this filth,' I replied, sipping at the tasty brew. 'If they, or someone high up tries to stifle or shut-down Greg's line of enquiry, we'll know that it crossed the wrong desk and maybe the corruption has spread lower down!'

She nodded, taking a large sip herself, 'I guess that it's as good a red flag as anything else.'

'That's the idea, but I believe that Greg was going to run another, less public query via one of his very discrete contacts, a lady called Annette DeSilva who's the Human Trafficking deputy head. She's a 52yo divorcee who Greg has worked with before, and although he's told her the whole story about the paedophile ring, he's left out your involvement with the files and photos for now, so there shouldn't be any chance of us getting named.

She's been told not to ask questions, but to search for the specific names and addresses that Greg has given her. Even if there's a bad reaction from up top, she may still be able to feed back what's really happening.'

Janice smiled around the rim of her mug. 'That sounds like an excellent backup system. Almost like having a spy in the enemy camp, except that these guys are supposed to be the good guys.'

'Well. Nearly all of them are,' I pointed out. 'It's just that we don't know who we can trust, apart from Annette.'

'Yeah. I know,' she sighed, 'It's all getting rather twisted when we can't tell good from bad!'

I finished my coffee and put my mug down and slid my arm around her shoulders. She'd already finished hers, and happily snuggled into my side, as we stared out across the calm waters of the bay, a low-set moon casting a low, silvery finger of light toward us. A light breeze took away any lingering heat from the boat and the mosquitos were, for once, totally absent.

She had a hand resting on my thigh, and when my thoughts returned from afar, I realised that I was absently stroking the side of her firm right breast. The small sounds of pleasure she made alerted me, but as I couldn't find a good reason to stop, I didn't. Moments later, she was gently rubbing the front of my shorts.

'Goodness, me, Harry,' she sounded surprised. 'Is that really you? You seem to have recovered magnificently!'

I chuckled. 'Well, in fact I've been 'recovered' for quite a while, but I didn't think it appropriate straight after dinner, to ask the girls to clear the table, then clear out themselves, so I could share my recovery with their mother!'

She laughed. 'Very interesting! But you're right, it would have been a bit unseemly!'

So, without much further messing around, we shed clothes again and retired to the huge daybed, which was open to the stars and cantilevered out over the water with the dingy stowed beneath it. We took our time getting to know each other much better. During a short break in what turned out to be quite lengthy proceedings, I thought I heard some faint noises from the saloon, but it was probably just Jasper having a late snack of dry food. We were not in any rush, so the end result, when it arrived, was as good, or better than the first time.

After finally separating, we collected clothes, decided not to wear them, but did decide to sleep in our own beds that night, and tenderly parted company in the saloon.

THURSDAY

I was up early, as usual, to feed Jasper before he helped himself to the fridge, and have a mug of tea while I checked the upper decks over. Janice must have slept in, as it was Zoe who joined me as I was eyeballing the anchor chain and scope. Nothing had changed, and with the clear water we could see the chain stretched out along on the sandy bottom right up to where the anchor was dug in well out of sight.

'Sleep well?' I asked her.

She gave me a grin, 'Yes, thanks. That's a very comfortable bed, but Jasper takes up an awful amount of room!'

I smiled, 'I did warn you. I usually make him sleep in his own bed up in the forepeak. Even though my bed is more than big enough for two, he still insists on sleeping on my side.'

'Yeah. That's exactly what he did to us. He wasn't content to sleep in the middle, it was either all over Angie or all over me. Still he's a real darling, I love him heaps!'

Then she looked directly at me and asked, 'Is Mum going to move in to your cabin to sleep with you?'

I answered her directly, 'I don't know. I'll leave that up to her.'

'But would *you* like to share with her?' she insisted on knowing.

I smiled, 'I certainly would, but only if that's what she wants.'

Zoe grinned happily, 'Excellent! She will, trust me. This is really good!'

Still grinning, she bounced away across the trampoline and headed down below.

I was about to go below, when Janice wandered forward, a gentle smile on her face. 'Hello,' she said, half shyly, 'or good morning.'

I gave her a kiss, 'Good morning to you, too.'

'Has Zoe been talking to you?' Janice asked.

'Yeah. She has. Why? Did she front you as well?'

'Yes. About sleeping together?'

I nodded and chuckled, 'Yes. That's the question we both seem to have been asked.'

She shook her head. 'The little minx!'

'They both seem very keen to push us together,' I commented, 'although I thought we were doing pretty well by ourselves!'

Janice laughed. 'We're doing extremely well together, thanks very much! Best ever, in my opinion!'

I laughed at her enthusiasm. 'Well. I must admit that it's been rather special for me too, but do you want us to share a bed?'

She spoke frankly, 'Yes, I would! But what do you think? I mean, you've had these three quirky, female runaways foisted on you out of nowhere, who've taken over your boat, are spoiling your cat and now messing with your privacy!'

I smiled at her. 'You can mess with my privacy any time you fancy, but since we've become rather intimate over the last 24 hours and seem to both enjoy it, sharing a bed each night is hardly going to ruin my independent lifestyle. So, move on in!'

That earned me a very big hug. The girls appeared and were

obviously very happy for us and when they'd untangled themselves, headed off to make a special breakfast to celebrate.

It was an excellent meal and afterwards, they chased Janice away to move her gear into my cabin. Having a lot of extra space, she could hang up more tops and had more drawers to stow things, so she needed to raid the suitcase pile. Having a private dressing room and a much bigger bathroom was an extra bonus.

At one point, she said, a little shyly, 'I haven't actually shared a bed with anyone for a very long time, but I'll try to be good.'

'Don't worry,' I said, trying to reassure her, 'It'll work out just fine.'

During the morning, Angie and Zoe decided to sunbake on the vast daybed, which stretched like an awning between the two hulls, just above deck level. Zoe climbed up first and was about to spread out her towel, when she called back to Angie,

'Can you get a paper towel from the galley? There's a big puddle of something sticky on the bed!'

Angie came out with a single sheet of towel, but when that wasn't enough, Zoe sent her back for several more. At this point, Janice came up from cabin-shifting duties and stood beside me.

'What's going on?'

I whispered in her ear, 'I think they found the remains of our fun session last night that I forgot to clean up!'

Janice giggled a few times, then burst out laughing as Angie brought three more sheets of towelling before Zoe got it all cleaned up to her satisfaction.

They looked at us standing there laughing, with strange looks on their faces.

'What's with you guys?' demanded Angie. 'We don't know what that stuff is! It's slippery, but it doesn't smell or anything like that.'

That was enough to send Janice off again, tears streaming down her cheeks at the expression on the girls' faces.

Angie looked at Zoe, realisation slowly dawning. 'You don't mean...was that really...I mean, that's a hell of a lot of...stuff!'

I just nodded at her, a big grin on my face, but Zoe was a bit slower to pick up on Angie's deduction. Finally, she did catch on as to what that stuff was she'd been cleaning up, and the disgusted response I was expecting didn't happen as she was more fascinated by the revelation and asked a whole lot of embarrassingly direct questions that I totally deferred to Janice.

With all this going on, I decided that we'd stay in Marshall's Bay for the rest of the day and night, but plan on heading across the top of Tasmania to Three Hummock Island first thing next morning. It was about a 140nm run, so the first thing was to check the weather. Zoe wandered past and stopped to see what I was up to, so I explained the process of deciding how, when and where to go to avoid being caught out in bad weather.

A moderate strength cold front was approaching from the south-west and would probably pass through the area Friday night or Saturday morning.

Therefore, our present anchorage would be blown out, so we had to move tomorrow, Friday anyway. The approaching front would generate moderate northwest winds, which would give us a very fast run across the top of Tassie to Three Hummocks Island, with a beautiful anchorage on its east coast called East Telegraph Bay. Right up at the north end looked to be a good spot in case the nor 'wester kept blowing, or alternately, there was a narrow inlet just north of the big bay that looked to provide even better shelter.

I allowed for the fact that the southwest winds behind the front could last a few days, so we might have to stay at Three Hummocks for a while. We had plenty of supplies so that wasn't an issue.

Based on the forecast wind, I figured that we could make the run there in about 12 hours, but it could be a bit wild and wet.

With all this worked out, I called the crew into the saloon, interrupting Janice moving her gear with the girls and Jasper getting underfoot.

I briefed them on the weather and the sailing plan I'd just worked out.

'We have to move out of here by tomorrow anyway, as it will become a bit uncomfortable with the northwest wind blowing in, so we might as well be making progress to our goal of Tassie's west coast,' I explained. 'But, as we've got something like 15 hours of light tomorrow, that should be plenty of time to get to a safe anchorage before dark. I'd rather be anchored in daylight if at all possible, just for safety, as I haven't been into East Telegraph Bay before and the sailing directions are a bit sketchy, although it looks okay on Google Earth.'

Janice nodded thoughtfully, 'Okay. That sounds like a good plan, especially if this spot won't be so nice by Saturday.'

'That's about it,' I replied, 'but we should get going at first light tomorrow, which is just before 06:00. That means actually ready to go at 06:00! However,' I smiled at Angie, who looked unhappy about having to get up early, 'Unlike on land where you have to get up and pack your gear, we've got everything with us, so I'll do most of the work. Those who insist on sleeping in, can, if they want, but there'll be a fair bit of noise once we get moving! With a strong beam wind, we'll be moving fast, so it'll be wet up top as well! Not much sunbaking probably!'

I added, 'It'll also mean wearing lifejackets if you move outside the cabin, and all hatches and portholes will be closed and fastened.'

I'd already shown them the lifejackets, the Crewfit 180N with the auto-inflate function and are worn like a vest with an integrated harness. I left them to digest all that, because the phone rang. It was the sat-phone and a blinking light told me that it was an encrypted call, so I shooed everyone away.

'Private stuff,' I said with a grin, so Janice took the girls back down into the right hull again to continue messing up my cabin, while I quickly fitted a small headset and hit the answer encrypt button.

There was the usual series of squeaks and squawks, and then Sandy said, 'Hi, Harry.'

'Hi, Sandy and Greg too, I presume?' I replied, happy to be back in contact with my trusted friends.

There was a moment's hesitation, before Sandy spoke again, 'Actually, no, Harry. Greg's not here and I'm doing this by myself.'

'Ok,' I said, 'what's happened?'

'We forwarded the enquiry to the ACP like we discussed, under Greg's name and authorisation, and first thing this morning, our boss came down and delivered the message personally to Greg, that he was not to take any action or request any further info from the ACP on paedophile rings until further notice, since he may, 'compromise an on-going Commonwealth Police investigation'. He also told Greg that he was under orders from the highest level, to pack a bag as he was transferred on temporary duty to the Commonwealth Games Security Detail!'

She started to sound a bit agitated. 'I mean, that's just so much bullshit! The organisers have private companies handling all the Games security, with Brisbane coppers providing a few uniforms for show. No other Local Area Commands are involved at all and certainly not Southport!'

'Ok,' I replied, trying to calm her down, 'where are you now?'

'I'm out in the carpark, hanging half out my car window so this stupid sat-phone gets a good look at the satellites and trying to look as though I'm chatting with my Mum!'

I chuckled at her imagery. 'OK. This is the red flag we were half expecting but I didn't expect such a strong reaction so quickly.'

'This means that those two top dogs in the ACP are monitoring this whole thing very closely,' Sandy said in a very subdued tone.

'Yes, it does, or that they have some others placed to report any unusual activity or requests to them ASAP,' I commented, 'but Greg will be fine and so will you, so long as you keep your head down. Did Greg leave you the contact details for his friend at the ACP?'

'Oh, yes. He did,' Sandy sounded calmer.

'Great! I'd like you to contact Annette by whatever means seems safest — land-line phone is probably the best, and tell her that there is now a red alert on this and she's not to ask anybody any direct questions about paedophile activity, unless it's something that she'd routinely ask as part of her job and even then, she should do it through one of her staff.

'It's very important, however, that she looks up the records for human trafficking, both into and out of Australia. Since it's not a direct paedophile activity, the files may not be monitored as closely as the paedophile ones.

'She should be looking for Indian and Thai children coming into the country and possibly Caucasian girls out, maybe to the Middle East. We need to have an idea of where the kids go when they come in; particularly if they are sent to Melbourne.

'Also ask her to consider if there is a reasonably senior person in the ACP who she knows we could trust. I haven't really got the time or inclination to scan through the thousands of photos on the files looking for more ACP brass, and really, I don't know that many of them anyway. I only got lucky with those other two!'

A nasty thought suddenly popped into my head as we were talking. There were a few disconnected things that had been said and some stuff we'd talked about previously suddenly joined up to create this nasty thought.

I carefully said to Sandy,

'Another thought. We also need to know if there have been any intercepted enquiries, like emails, text messages or Skype calls directed to Luke, particularly from the Middle East, about the availability of teenage, blonde Caucasian girls in Australia. The enquiries may be in a basic code, but she'd be across that type of communication. It would make things a lot easier to build a case if we could come up with something that tied Luke directly to the ring.'

'That sounds like you have some situation in mind,' she probed.

I couldn't discuss this too much with Janice, so Sandy was the only other one I could trust.

'Yeah,' I replied hesitantly, 'I just connected a few dots and something even worse presented itself as a strong possibility.'

'Go on,' she said impatiently, 'spit it out!'

'Ok, let's play the Wotif game!

What if Luke's good behaviour toward the girls has been a sham all along?...

What if he just wanted them relaxed, on his side and happy with wonderful Daddy, so as to keep them close?...

What if these photos of the girls have been going out to their circle for years, although that's very likely anyway!...

What if he's been cultivating a market for two teenage, blonde, blue-eyed Caucasian virgins?...

What if that market was in the Middle East where they can afford to pay top dollar for fresh, unblemished white goods?...

What if his rage and very expensive manhunt is so intense because perhaps there's an auction happening and the huge offer he's been hanging out for is about to come in...?'

Sandy was silent a few moments, 'Ah shit! That's really a very nasty thought you've had, but I admit that your reasoning makes some sense! Of course, you realise that this puts you and the ladies in even more danger?'

'Yes, I do.'

'And that you'll need to keep moving even more often than you have been and maybe visit more remote areas?'

'Yes, Mum!' I chuckled.

'*Fuck it, Harry!*' *she cracked up a bit, 'I really wish you'd take this more seriously! You've got a mess of Luke's bad-guys hot on your trail chasing the girls. And, if your latest theory is correct, some Middle-Eastern billionaire with a penchant for having his share of the 72 promised virgins while he's still alive, is about to chuck a right royal wobbly, wholly directed at the person standing between his royally diseased groin and twin overhead virgin pussies!*'

'Ah...yes. I actually do appreciate your concern Sandy, especially when it's expressed so eloquently.'

She had the grace to laugh at that feeble reply, but that was something at least.

'Ok. Let me go and get this other ball rolling with Annette. I'll call you when I get something new. OK?

'Ok, Sandy, and thanks for your work!'

'*Cheers for now. Keep your head down and stay dry!*'

When I had a chance, I told Janice that I'd bring her up to speed later, so the rest of the day passed pleasantly. The ladies fluffed around with girly stuff, made morning tea and lunch, while I checked the boat and made ready for a heavy sail. There wasn't really much to do as we'd only been at anchor for a few days.

We all went ashore for a walk and let Jasper have a good run. While the girls were off hunting for shells, I managed to tell Janice most of Sandy's phone call but held back my idea about Luke selling the girls. That would be way too much for her still fragile mental state.

Back on board, I hoisted the dingy and double-secured it in its protected slot under the day bed with a heavy webbing strap around the middle. I removed the outboard and stowed it in one of the cockpit lockers.

Janice and the girls did some sunbaking on the foredeck, taking advantage of the comfort of the trampoline. I joined them with a beer later in the arvo and offered to fetch drinks as required. Janice went for a white wine, while the girls asked if they could have a Lemon Ruski. Janice approved, so I fetched. I realised with a start that it was a very domesticated scene, and to my even greater surprise, I found myself enjoying it!

Tea was a happy affair and we followed it with another hilarious game of Monopoly. It was an easy decision not to stay up late, given the active day and early departure in the morning. It would also be, of course, the first night Janice and I would sleep together. She seemed a bit nervous and the girls were excited for some reason, which made for a different retiring routine. We sorted out the 'who-sleeps-on-which-side' bit; I said I always slept naked, so after some indecision, she gamely said that she would too.

I made a circuit of the topsides, to check that all was secure. The breeze had picked up a little, and backed slightly into the north, but we were still in a sheltered position, the anchor was well set, so it should be a comfortable night.

With the boat secured, I told Jasper that he was confined to either his or the girls' bed, then stripped in my/our dressing room and climbed into bed. Watching a naked Janice wander back and forth between dressing room and bathroom several times was a particularly stirring sight, and I said so, several times, but when the girls came in to say goodnight to both of us, I had to quickly pull the doona up and try to keep them from getting too close to that particular portion of my anatomy. I was only partially successful in that, raising a few eyebrows and a lot of giggles, Janice included, who thought that my efforts to remain as modest as possible around the girls were a hoot!

Their choice of sleeping attire didn't help my condition either, being just longish T-shirts with obviously nothing underneath. Apparently, I was the only one somewhat disconcerted by the display of jiggling breasts and the bare flesh being indiscriminately flashed. After a round of goodnight hugs and kisses, which now included me, they were finally persuaded to go to their bed in the other hull, and hopefully take the great lump of cat with them! Janice had discretely pointed out that as only 2 or 3 meters of deck-locker space separated the two forward cabins horizontally, and that there was a large, full-opening deck hatch above each bed for ventilation and quick egress purposes, we needed to be careful what we discussed in bed. Or any other incidental sounds we might make for that matter!

Finally, we were alone, and I turned out the light, the open hatch above us letting in a gentle, cooling draft of air. Janice cuddled up beside me and wanted to be kissed. So, we did for a short time, until the action of her naked body wriggling provocatively against mine caused rather more basic instincts to take over. Finally sated, satisfied and whatever else, we lay back with the sheet pushed to the bottom of the bed and let the breeze wafting in through the overhead hatch cool our perspiration. We drifted off to sleep like that and I was only dimly aware of Janice pulling the sheet up in the wee small hours as the night air cooled.

FIREBIRD...IN TRANSIT FLINDERS ISLAND
TO THREE HUMMOCK ISLAND

FRIDAY MORNING

My internal alarm clock woke me around 05:00 and Janice stirred too as we were again wrapped around each other. The feel of her warm bare skin almost tempted me into a repeat last night's performance, but I reluctantly settled for a cuddle and a few rubs of her firm bum.

'You can stay here, if you want,' I said softly, 'but things will get noisy when the anchor gets raised. The chain stows just beyond where our pillows are, I think I forgot to tell the girls about that!'

She giggled, 'It'll do them good to get up early, but I'll get up anyway and make some tea.'

I offered to let her use the bathroom first, but her response was, 'Don't be silly! I only need to pee and have a quick wash, there's plenty of room and it'll be quicker if we go together.' She was right, it was, but I wasn't quite used to sharing a toilet with a female, even if it was just peeing. The female washing process was a bit different as well and went beyond just a face and hand wash, but she was unconcerned, so I was determined not to show that I might be! I guess I could get used to anything!

That piece of intimacy over, we dressed and headed up top, Janice to the galley, while I unlocked and opened the cockpit doors. Given our location and the darkness, I decided to initially motor out of the bay, so I started the engines to let them warm up, then went on deck to check the weather. The wind had increased and backed a little further, now NNW, at 12 to 15 kts, and significantly warmer than last night. Apparently, the front was definitely approaching and as we were getting out just in time, we were in for a great sail!

By the time I'd hauled in some anchor chain, disconnected the mooring bridle that kept us stable at anchor, then winched in the rest of the chain, the girls were up and dressed and I was presented with a steaming mug of tea. With the anchor stowed and security-pinned in place, and with the twin 75hp Yanmar diesels just above idle, I turned *Firebird* away from the beach and with constant reference to the chart plotter, carefully picked our way out of the bay.

It wasn't long before the rocky islets and other hazards were clear astern and I could shut down the engines. As she had already steered the boat, I parked Zoe on the wheel, while I set about raising, then setting sails and lowering the lee dagger board. With the way I'd set the systems up, it didn't take long and I had Angie and Janice watch as I explained each move. I eased off the main sheet a little to give the boom some slack, before activating the main halyard winch, and watched the sail carefully as it slowly unrolled out of its stowage place in the boom. I thought it wise to only raise the main to the 75% mark, and just set the inner staysail until I saw how the boat behaved in the rising breeze.

Once clear of the land, the wind rose to 25kts, with some gusts to over 30kts. After some sail trimming to balance the helm, we were soon making a comfortable and exhilarating 18 to 22 knots, with a moderate beam swell.

The windward bow flicked some light spray across the deck, but as we weren't punching into the swell, the ride was more like a smooth series of swoops over the swells. My three crew were initially a bit concerned as the rising wind made some weird whistling and howling noises around the carbon mast but were reassured once they saw how flat the cat was riding and felt the totally exhilarating feeling of a big cat at speed in a strong breeze!

To Zoe's disgust, I talked Janice into taking the wheel for a spell and after a bit of coaching, she too was feeling the excitement of hand-steering a cat at speed. As the sun made its slow climb up into the cloudless sky, the breeze steadied at Force 6, a strong breeze with some higher gusts, but *Firebird* only heeled slightly, and I felt comfortable with the sail settings.

Nevertheless, I didn't stray too far from the mainsheet quick-release and instructed the crew in its use.

Despite the jiggling, swoopy ride, Angie managed to boil the kettle safely and served another round of tea with toasted crumpets and honey for breakfast. Two of us were in the cockpit at all times, and I relaxed the rule about lifejackets, so long as everyone stayed well within the cockpit confines.

After breakfast, with Janice on the wheel again, the girls, wearing lifejackets over their bikinis and tethered to the lifelines at all times, went forward to the bows.

There they had an incredibly wet and wild experience, being pelted with a constant stream of spray from the windward bow, although the thrill of laying on the trampoline in these conditions was extreme! Just hanging on with the bows swooping up and down was a task, and by the time they returned, they were exhausted, but fizzing with excitement.

'Mum! Mum!' squealed Zoe, 'you've got to try it! That's the best thrill ride I've ever been on!' Janice looked very dubious, until Angie joined in.

'Come on, Mum! We'll come back up with you! You've got to try it! It's so much fun!'

So, Janice went inside the saloon and to my surprise, just stripped down to just her brief panties and put her lifejacket back on over bare skin. She made a delightful sight and the girls applauded her choice of gear.

'We should have done that!' lamented Angie. 'Then we wouldn't have wet our bikinis!'

I checked that all three were clipped onto the lifelines as they made their careful way forward. Soon Janice was squealing with delight, along with her daughters as she alternated between the two bow seats and the trampoline netting. After about 15 minutes, they'd all had enough and groped their way back to the cockpit. The stiff breeze was warm to hot, blowing off the mainland, but as they were wet, they cooled down quickly, so I sent them below to rinse off and change to dry clothes.

Janice was back first, looking highly desirable wearing only fresh panties, as she'd left her shorts and T-shirt draped over the nav station. Gracefully, she slipped them back on, before joining me in the cockpit.

I grinned my best evil smirk at her,

'If you keep running around dressed like that, I'm going to have to park the girls on the wheel and take you below!'

She giggled, 'Can we? I'm game if you are!'

I looked at her again and saw a look in her eyes similar to what I thought must be in mine. Adrenaline does that every time and beats the hell out of artificial drugs!

I sent her below and five minutes later, the girls re-appeared and were pleased to be told that they were to take the wheel, one to steer and the other to watch the mainsheet release.

'I've got to go below for a few minutes,' I said, 'but I've eased both the mainsheet as well as the staysail a little, so gusts won't be a problem. The breeze is pretty steady, so just keep it pointing on course and keep a lookout for ships. Call if there's a problem.'

'OK,' Angie said with a knowing grin, wriggling into position. 'Don't worry about us, we'll be fine! Enjoy!'

Zoe giggled as I beat a hasty and slightly embarrassed retreat inside.

Janice was waiting for me, naked, perched up on the end of the bed in our cabin and laughed when I related the girls' parting comments.

'Cheeky minxes!' she said. 'They're too mature for us! I don't know what they'll come up with next!'

I leered at her, 'You may not know what they'll come up with next, but I know what we will!' And proceeded to demonstrate the point, with Janice obliging twice before we finished, then as quickly as we decently could, we cleaned up, dressed and went back up top.

'Really!' Angie made a Freudian slip in mock disgust, 'I don't know what's got into you two!'

'I can tell you exactly what has!' Janice replied in her best dry drawl. 'Or me, at least!' This absolutely cracked the girls up, so much so that their laughter left a wiggle in our wake.

As all was going well with the current watch on deck, I sheeted the sails in slightly for better speed, checked that it was still safe for inexperienced hands, then took Janice to sit together on the cockpit lounge and enjoy the ride.

The rest of the run proceeded uneventfully, with the stiff breeze holding steady out of the NNW. The swell rose a little more but didn't cause any problems apart from helping the bows to toss a bit more spray and green water around.

Due to our higher speed, the lumpy green line of Three Hummock Island rose out of the mist and spray just on 18:00. By then everyone had had their share of hand steering and were happy to turn the duty over to George. There was only one isolated rocky outcropping to watch for on our approach, but as it was off-track to the north of our landfall on the north end of East Telegraph Bay, it wouldn't be a problem in the good visibility.

Fifteen minutes later, having sailed right into position, the anchor rattled down into four meters of the clearest water I'd seen, and just 10 meters off the beach. *Firebird* was safely tucked right up into a little hook of shallow water at the north end of the mile-long stretch of pure white sand that comprised the magnificent beach. It was so white it rivalled Whitehaven Beach in the Whitsunday's, and that's world-class!

With the shelter afforded by the low hills bordering the bay, the stiff breeze had dropped away just enough to keep the heat tolerable.

Janice looked around at the glorious scene. 'Oh dear, Harry. You've done it again! I thought that Marshall Bay was beautiful, but this is so much better! Just look at that beach!'

I bowed and replied, 'Yes Ma'am. As your humble skipper, it's the least I could do!'

She whacked me on the arm and laughed, 'You're an idiot!'

'Harry,' Angie spoke up, 'is it safe to swim here? We'd love to go in. It's very hot!'

I looked around and decided that as we were so close to shore, there was little or no danger of nasties coming into such shallow water.

'Yeah, sure. But don't swim out past the boat, OK? Just toward the shore.'

With a screech of delight, they disappeared below to change, and I looked at Janice.

'Going in?'

'Yes,' she said, 'I will. It looks so inviting. How about you?'

'I'll think about it,' I replied.

The splashing, shrieks and growls from just past the bows told of the girls and Jasper having fun and cooling down. 'I might join them,' Janice said, casually slipping off her top and shorts and clad in just her brief panties, she dived in.

I decided to stay and watch out from the bows, just in case of uninvited visitors, so I perched on the padded seat in the right bow and looked at the carrying-on just below me. The topless Janice was greeted with a cheer and within moments, two tiny bundles of wet cloth hit me in the chest, accompanied by shrieks of laughter at my surprised reaction. Even Jasper got into the water play, ducking and swirling around.

I must confess that I greatly enjoyed watching the three of them splashing around topless, looking remarkably similar with their short, blonde hair with only Janice's bigger boobs showing who was who. I declined their invitations to join them and waited until they headed for the stern before walking aft to get the shower ready. I'd almost reached the cockpit when another wet bundle hit me square in the middle of my back. I stumbled to more shrieks of laughter as they gathered around the stern, waiting for me to get the shower ready.

Jasper got hoisted up first, and I quickly hosed the salt water out of his fur. There was no sand this time, so the job went more easily.

Sending him up to the cockpit to shake water everywhere, I stood with a grin as the three naked nymphs emerged. Janice was first, gave me a kiss and let me spray fresh water all over her. I tried to pass the shower nozzle to her, but she shook her head and grinned, 'No way. This is crew's privilege. You've got to do the twins as well!'

I swallowed to free up a suddenly dry throat as the first delightfully naked twin climbed the ladder. Trying to only look at her face, I saw it was Angie, and she was desperately trying to stifle a fit of giggles!

'Oh, Harry,' she giggled, 'you should see your face. It's okay to look at us. We actually like it, dummy! Really, it's natural!'

I shut her up by spraying water in her face and over her head, snatching a glance down her lovely body as I did, suddenly conscious of the fact that I only wore damp jockey briefs. Her wash-down was therefore very brief, and I sent her up the steps with a quick smack on the bum.

I heard a quiet exclamation from Janice, and then in an amused tone, she said

'What's this, young lady? Have you been practicing your hairdressing skills?'

Angie giggled again. 'Zoe and I thought we'd try a bit of trimming on each other to see how it looks and feels! I mean, you haven't got much fur there either, and we love the way you look, so we thought we'd do the same!'

'You realise that if you stop, it'll itch like buggery!' Janice warned.

'Yes. But we wanted to try, anyway. I tried leaving this little line just above, but Zoe's got a tiny triangle!'

'Ok,' Janice replied, 'but be careful when you re-trim,'

'Yes, Mum, we will,' Angie replied happily.

By now I'd guessed what they were talking about and surreptitiously took a quick look at Zoe when she turned around. Sure enough, she had a tiny, but decorative little triangle positioned just above her otherwise bare and smooth interesting bits.

Zoe received the same treatment, except that she didn't stop giggling. By the time I'd replaced the shower in its locker, Janice had the twins sort of wrapped in towels, drying off.

I had a quick look down to make sure I was almost decent before climbing up to the cockpit and was relieved to see that I was in merely a 'very swollen state' rather than 'fully erect' which would have been quite excusable under the very trying, yet delightful circumstances. Nevertheless, I retrieved my shorts as soon as I could, but not before seeing the twins checking the shape of my jocks way too carefully.

Finally, they hung their towels up to dry on the cockpit lines and went below, still giggling, while Janice, happily standing around still naked, was no help at all, bursting out laughing as she looked at my crutch.

'It's not that funny!' I said, desperately trying to stand upon my shattered dignity. 'I didn't know that was coming at me!'

'Oh yes, it really was that funny, Harry,' she laughed, 'especially as I did warn you. The girls aren't showing off, or not much anyway, and they really like getting around like that and do consider it natural and they're obviously really comfortable with you. But the funniest thing was that lovely bulge in your jocks that you were desperately trying to hide or make go away!'

I tried to glare at her, but it was impossible to be mad, so I chuckled ruefully.

'Well. I guess you're right. If you, the girls' mother is happy with the situation, I guess I'll have to be!'

She kissed me softly. 'That's the spirit. You're a good man. Stay like that!'

Once again, dinner that evening, courtesy of Angie displaying her considerable culinary skills, was a very happy occasion, although I remained the main source of hilarity. As always, I found it impossible to take offence with these three irrepressible females, one of whom I found that I was becoming quite attached to. It was a very new sensation for me, and I tried to view it objectively, but gave up and just enjoyed things moment by moment.

For a change, we played Scrabble, a game that apparently lent itself to even more cheating than Monopoly.

I checked the weather before we all went to bed and discovered that the front had slowed a little and wasn't expected to pass through the King Island area, which applied to us as well, until mid-morning tomorrow, Saturday. Therefore, the winds were expected to stay blowing from the same direction and strength overnight and *Firebird* wouldn't require any extra ground tackle.

Despite the pressures of business and his missing family, Luke headed for his favourite place for some much-needed relaxation. Although the $12M initial cost plus another $1.2M for the 'special renovations' took most of his available capital, the payback had been well worth the trouble he'd had to go through to raise the money. Even though two 18 y/o, blonde-headed chunks of the security for the special low-interest loans were currently running around loose somewhere in the country!

This night, some Interstate members of The Circle were in town, and Luke was keen to play the gracious host in the converted mansion. None of the Principals of the Circle had questioned the weekly fees he was charging just so he could pay off the interest! As extra spice to look forward to, Luke knew that there had been a delivery from Vietnam, and according to the Inventory, there were some items that were exactly what appealed to his particular, perverted taste.

Just the thought of checking the Inventory made his groin tingle in anticipation!

Already living the pleasure ahead of him, his reverie was rudely interrupted by the trill of the mobile phone.

'Yeah. What is it?' he barked, in his endearingly polite manner.

Jimmy here, Boss. I've got some good news!

'About fucking time! Ten grand a day to keep you clowns running around the country tripping over each other's dicks! None of you could find your own fat arses with both hands! So, what's the good news?'

'We got a break and we think they went to Eden, Boss.'

'Excellent, Jimmy! Are we about to have another session where

I get high blood-pressure trying to drag the story out of you word by word, or is there any chance that you might actually tell me this momentous news?'

'Ah...Yes, Boss!'

'Great! Which 'Yes' would that be, Jimmy. The 'Yes, I'm going to tell you the good news story and make you a happy Boss?' or the 'I'm going to prove once and for all what a moron I am and make the Boss put a Contract out on me?' Now which one is it going to be? Jimmy!'

'Ah...I think the first one, Boss.'

'Great, Jimmy. So, go ahead and tell me, before I drive to wherever your worthless hide is at the moment and turn you into a new bonnet ornament! I think I need a new one, don't you, Jimmy?'

'No, Boss. You don't need to do that. Anyway, we had one of the girls phoning all the motels in every town on the main highways. I'm afraid the phone bill is going to be very high, Boss. Is that alright?'

'Yes, Jimmy. If you produced a result, I don't give a flying fuck about the phone bill!'

'Oh, good, then. Well, our girl finally found a motel in Eden on the south coast of NSW that had three females staying for two nights. It was a mother and two daughters, they shared a room that they'd booked for four nights, but checked out suddenly last Monday, late in the afternoon.'

'Oh, well done, Jimmy. You can do it! Think that is! Anyway, where are they now?'

'Well, according to the Motel owner, they were being picked up by some friends that evening and were going to the Gold Coast. I'm in Eden now, and we're asking around to see if they really did get picked up.'

'Good work, Jimmy. I'll cancel that contract on you if you keep doing the right thing! Now you will remember to call me when you find out more, won't you?'

'Yes, Boss. Thanks, Boss!'

'Good dog, Jimmy! Now fuck off and get on with it!'

Luke continued his journey to The Circle's Pleasure Centre in a much better frame of mind. He could even imagine the net he'd cast for his family, closing tighter and tighter, and became quite excited at the thought of his lovely blonde virgin daughters standing naked in front of him, while he conducted a world-wide video 'Sale of the Century', live and in full colour.

CHAPTER 16

FIREBIRD...THREE HUMMOCK ISLAND, BASS STRAIT, SATURDAY MORNING

It was 06:30 the next morning when the phone rang. Luckily, Janice and I had just finished a delightfully extended round of getting-to-know-you-very-well, so it wasn't too embarrassing to head for the saloon without waiting to put some clothes on.

It was a secure call, so I pressed the appropriate buttons and waited for the devices to agree to talk to each other. Finally, a long beep and a green light indicated that an effective agreement had been reached.

'Hello,' I said hopefully, 'Sandy?'

'Hi, Harry,' she sounded despondent, 'how're things with you?'

'Really good so far, thanks Sandy. But it sounds like things aren't so good at your end. Is Greg Ok?'

'Yes, he's Ok, but only just. Some thugs beat him up last night, on his way back to the Hotel after work. It could have been much worse, but he's pretty good at defending himself, and gave better than he got! Despite that, they had to keep him in hospital overnight with a busted rib, mild concussion and facial contusions!'

'Bloody hell! How could that happen?'

'That's what we'd like to know. The local coppers he's working with are a decent bunch and they reckon it's a weird attack! It wasn't just a routine mugging, as nothing was asked for or taken, even though Greg nailed two of them and the third bailed out. Greg went through the usual mug shots, but nobody stood out! The locals reckon it looks like an organised hit!'

She broke down for a few moments.

'I'm sorry, Harry. It's getting a bit too serious when the good guys can get beaten up so easily!'

'Yeah, I know,' I commiserated, 'but he knew the risks and there really is some bad shit going down!'

'Yes, I know he did! But apart from that initial enquiry, he's not made any follow-up that I know of. And I'm supposed to be his partner!'

'Ok, Sandy. How about you speak to him again and make sure that he didn't make any follow-up calls! We both know what he's like when he gets his teeth into something, so he just might have slipped up. This bashing could just be a warning to 'butt out or else'!'

'I'd really like to think that's all it is. But I will call and ask him. Is there any other message you want me to give him?'

'No. Not really. Just to keep his silly head down, mouth shut and stay cool.'

'Ok. I've already done that in less polite language, but I'll pass your version on,' she replied.

'Oh yes! There is one more thing. Can you call Annette at the ACP and see if there's any action on the Human Trafficking emails or text messages that we asked about earlier? And perhaps ask her if the ACP has Luke Emery listed as a Person-of-Interest? If he is, they might already have a tap on his phones and emails. It would be great if we could get a handle on what's going on with the search for the ladies, as well as what's planned for the twins!'

'Yeah. No problem, Harry. I'll do all that and get back to you ASAP!'

'Thanks, Sandy, take care yourself. Low profile now!'

'Yes, Dad!' she chuckled softly, *'I'll be a good girl!'*

The unit beeped and squawked like it was going to chuck a hissy fit as it went through its usual sign-off procedures. I sat there a bit longer, digesting what she'd said, and planning what our best moves would be.

Finally, I convinced myself that we were doing all we could to stay under the radar and that we should just stick with the plan for now. That was mainly because I hadn't come up with a 'Plan B' yet!

I must have been thinking too long, because Zoe suddenly appeared giggling and asked if I wanted a mug of tea. Belatedly, I realised that I was still naked and probably smelling a bit musky, so I muttered, 'Yes, please!' before, under her intense and somewhat critical gaze, I abandoned the shelter of the chart table with as much grace as I could muster, ducked out into the cockpit, and accompanied by her peals of joyful laughter, dived over the stern into the crystal-clear water.

Almost immediately, the water performed its usual magic by cleansing both body and mind, so in a far more composed condition, I re-boarded, quickly rinsed off with the shower and snagged one of the towels still hanging up from yesterday. While I dried off, I scanned the clear sky, noting that the warm North wind was blowing a lot harder than last night.

There was nowhere to safely hide, without looking like modesty personified, so it was only slightly mortifying to see that Angie had now joined her sister in the galley, both evil twins grinning as they intently watched my quick-dry antics. Finally, with the towel safely wrapped around my nether regions, I marched without a word through the saloon and to my delightfully shared quarters where Janice laughed herself into hiccups when I told her.

I'd barely re-gained the bed, when Angie appeared with two teas and a bunch more giggles, which made me realise that the ladies were laughing a lot more than they probably had for a long time, even if it was at my expense.

After Angie had departed to join Zoe at breakfast, I told Janice the details of the phone call. Once again, I felt no remorse that I held back any reference to the notion that Luke might be in the process of auctioning the girls.

Twenty minutes later, I was still reading in bed, when Zoe poked her head around the cabin door.

'Sorry to disturb your peace, Harry, but there's some dirty-looking cloud coming up from the west!'

I'd noticed that the wind was making a lot more noise in the rigging than it had earlier when I was on the phone, so I scrambled out from under the sheet and ducked into the dressing room to drag on a pair of shorts. I noticed that Zoe waited by the door, a smirk on her face.

'Be nice to Harry,' Janice feebly offered with a chuckle.

'Yes, Mum,' Zoe grinned as she followed me up top.

Her warning was spot on and none too soon! A large mass of angry, black cloud was already well above the western horizon, spears of jagged lightning making an awe-inspiring, but potentially dangerous display along the leading edge. The hot, gusting northerly was still moaning through the rigging, but I knew that would change shortly to a howling, cold southwest gale when the front arrived.

'What do you have to do?' Angie asked, all previous frivolity forgotten, 'and what can we do to help?'

'We need to get a second anchor out over the bow to make sure we stay put,' I replied, keeping one eye on the storm edge to gauge how quickly it was moving. And it was moving very quickly; I thought we might have less than an hour to prepare.

I turned to the control panel and started the engines so we could move forward to lay the second anchor.

It was the work of about ten minutes to move forward with the crew helping handle the second anchor, until we ended up with the two bow anchors firmly buried in less than 1.5 metres of water so the anchor chain pull on them was nearly flat, which was ideal for maximum holding power.

Once I was happy with the set of the bow anchors, I fitted claws to each chain, not trusting the winch locks alone. I also added extra ties on the long boathook stowed on deck beside the coach house handrails and added more lashing on the tightly rolled sausage of the inner staysail.

Re-assessing the time before the squall line hit, I decided to drop the screecher completely, to reduce windage and the risk of it coming loose. Therefore, I called the girls forward to help, even though it wasn't a difficult job, but with the hot and now-howling north wind, extra hands made it much safer.

I released the screecher halyard, which neatly dropped the long, rolled up tube of sail onto the trampoline, disconnected all attachment points, then directed my helpers to bundle the fat, purple sausage into a spare locker beside the centre chain locker.

Despite the low humidity of the north wind, we were all sweating heavily with exertion and the high temperature of the air.

The ladies were much too excited to go below, so we remained on deck to watch the approaching monster.

The Storm

The upper edge of the cloud mass was now a razor-straight line of pure, malignant blackness, arching from the far south to the far north horizon, even with the morning sun shining brightly on it. The sun also accentuated the menacing colour of the cloud mass, relieved only by the almost-continual flashes of lightning. Fortunately, for a boat with a carbon mast-top poking 24 meters above the water, they were mostly cloud-to-cloud, but enough were ground strikes to prompt me to lower the copper grounding plate that was connected to the base of the mast with a thick, gleaming braid of woven copper.

While most of the lightning activity was further away, lower down toward the western horizon, there was still an almost continual rumble of thunder, a lot of it sub-sonic that was felt with the whole body rather than the ears.

As a final check, I went below and got on-line to the BOM radar site for NW Tasmania at West Takone. It had an excellent view of the approaching frontal squall line and showed a rather ominous picture!

The cloud band was much deeper than expected and showed a huge number of lightning strikes. It was also moving quite quickly, a fact that I'd already worked out!

I went through my usual pre-storm routine, by shutting everything electronic down, disconnecting antennas and stowing small electronic items in both the microwave and a Faraday Cage locker I'd had constructed. They would protect sensitive electronic gear from the incredibly destructive effects of a lightning strike that would generate massive voltages, current and electro-magnetic radiation.

After a final check, I re-joined the ladies on deck, who were still making awed comments over the appearance of the storm and its attendant light show!

'How much longer before it gets here, Harry?' asked Angie.

I looked at the speed of advance of the cloud band that was nearly overhead, swallowing the pale-blue morning sky like a rampaging blue-black monster.

'Definitely time for a cuppa,' I said, hoping to calm the apprehension showing in their eyes.

'Oh, Okay,' Angie replied, heading for the galley.

We enjoyed watching the final approach as we sipped tea and munched vegemite toast, but as we were nearly finished, the leading edge of rain and wind, came sweeping over the crest of the low hills just west of us, with a rapidly building roar like an on-coming freight train.

'Ok,' I said, 'this is it! We'd better get inside right now!'

There was a semi-dignified rush along the side decks and down into the cockpit, where I started both engines.

'What's that for?' Janice asked.

'The first gust will probably be very strong,' I replied, keeping an eye on the cloud of suddenly airborne sand off the beautiful beach, 'so I'll use the engines to take some load off the anchors. It won't last long, then I can shut them down.'

Seconds later, the water around us turned into a seething mass of white foam, as with a screeching howl, the gust front hit. I shoved the throttles into drive and advanced them to 50% power, but the wind just pressed us back and down like a giant hand. The ladies were suddenly very scared when their world went from fairly serene to utter mayhem in seconds, as we felt the anchor lines jerk *Firebird* to a halt. I could feel the immense strain they were under but had confidence in the tackle and the fittings to which they were attached.

I gave the engines more power, and then leant over to yell in Janice's ear; she was hanging onto the helm seat with considerable strength.

'Take the girls into the saloon and sit down. This won't last long, but it'll still be pretty breezy for a few hours!'

She nodded her understanding and carefully groped her way to the girls who were hanging on just as hard and shepherded them into the saloon. She returned to my side, however, after closing the heavy weatherproof sliding door that would cut some of the howling noise.

I saved my breath going crook at her, admitting to myself that it was comforting to have her presence beside me. The morning had turned almost full dark, so I turned on the forward-facing spotlights that I usually only used for groping around a strange harbour at night.

The view, however, wasn't very encouraging as torrents of rain lashed the boat, bringing with them truckloads of leaves, branches, sand and sea foam.

'This isn't exactly like storms ashore,' Janice yelled into my ear, and I grinned at her levity. The anemometer on the masthead was flicking madly between 50 and 75 knots, but the anchors were holding well, and the anchor watch GPS showed no rearward movement that would indicate that we were dragging. I was very thankful, as I really didn't fancy getting blown seaward into the maw of this monster.

Oddly enough, it was only another ten minutes, before the insanely-gusting wind started to ease and the massively thick cloud mass that had been streaming overhead, just above the mast top and had turned bright daylight into almost pitch black, started to lift as well. Mind you, 'ease' was only a relative term as the actual wind speed was still well up in the gale force range of 40 to 45 knots, but I was comfortable enough to shut down the engines, and let *Firebird* look after herself.

Janice looked at me, her eyes a bit wild.

'Is that it?' she asked, a shake in her voice.

'Not quite,' I replied with a smile, 'it'll still blow hard for a while, but that's the worst of it!'

'Thank the Lord for that,' she said, and I noticed that she was shaking a bit, so I gave her a hug.

'Thanks for staying out here with me. I really intended for you to go in and look after the girls, but it was nice to have you here.'

'No problem,' Janice smiled, 'it looked like a situation where you might have needed an extra hand in a hurry if something went wrong.'

'Yes, you're right,' I reflected, 'I've learned to never take those frontal squalls for granted! Too many unpredictable things can happen!'

We stayed out in the cockpit for a while longer to see how *Firebird* was handling, but now the worst was over, she sat quietly to the twin anchors, although the wind still howled through the rigging and kept up that eerie moan from the mast.

The girls were glad to see us when we went inside and shut the door, creating an almost snug little oasis from the continuing fury of the storm.

I put the kettle on, which got Angie moving as she now regarded the galley as her domain, a task I was delighted to relinquish!

Janice was the first to notice that the air temperature had dropped dramatically, which, seeing as we were all damp, if not wet, from rain and spray being swirled by the wind around the cockpit, felt very uncomfortable.

'Ok,' she said briskly to the girls, 'go dry off and change into dry clothes. Put something warmer on. Harry thinks it'll stay cool for a few days.'

There were no arguments, so we all split to change into trakkie-daks and jerseys that were much warmer and more comfortable. Being inside and warm lifted everyone's mood considerably as did the hot chocolate and toasted sandwiches Angie whipped up.

'How long will the storm last, Harry?' Zoe asked.

'Hard to say, but from the look of the satellite photos, maybe a day or two. These winds will drop to something more reasonable in a few hours, but the rain will probably hang about into tomorrow. At least the boat is getting a good fresh water wash!' I chuckled.

'So, I guess we'll stay here until the weather settles?' Janice asked.

I eyed my crew, 'Yep. A High will eventually move in, but there may be a couple more fronts sweep through before it takes over, hopefully not as savage as this one! Anyway, we'll stay here for a few days at least as there's no need to rush off.'

'I'm happy about that!' Angie said, 'it's been very interesting, but scary!'

'I agree. Running into a storm like that at sea is very uncomfortable and potentially dangerous, which is why I usually hole up somewhere safe until the good weather and favourable winds resume.'

'So, what's the best wind for us to get down to Strahan?' Janice asked.

'A north to north-easterly would be best,' I replied, 'just like what we came south from Eden to Flinders with, and like what we'll probably get if this next High moves over Tasmania. It'll knock the swells down a lot as well! There'll be a full day's sail to reach Strahan. Anyway, for now, we're safe and comfortable and we have the time to wait until conditions improve.'

CHAPTER 17

FIREBIRD...THREE HUMMOCK ISLAND – BASS STRAIT, TUESDAY AFTERNOON

The next few days in our new anchorage went quietly. The wind blew from the southwest, quite strongly at first, but it slowly diminished; the rain spattered down in brief squalls from fat, swollen clouds that scudded low across the scrubby hills to the west of our sheltered bay. They looked threatening enough for the first day and a half to discourage outdoor activity, and the temperature was cool enough to make staying in bed in the morning just snuggling, an unusual but strangely pleasant experience for me!

Janice and I became closer and the girls seemed to thoroughly approve of our bonding. They were as frisky and uninhibited as always, but it was always in fun and high spirits.

They brought us breakfast in bed on two occasions, and had their own with us as well, so the bed became littered with crumbs when we'd all finished. When Jasper nosed in to scrounge any unattended food, things became crowded, yet highly entertaining!

It wasn't the first time that I caught myself wondering what could have driven Luke to destroy his relationship with such a wonderful wife and kids.

I still didn't see myself as a surrogate husband/father, despite the relationship appearing to be headed that way. I really didn't want that level of long-term domesticity. Nor did I think that if push came to shove, Janice would trade a comfortable lifestyle on shore, with all the trappings her money could provide, for a decidedly nomadic sea-borne existence!

It was a dark and windy Tuesday evening when the sat-phone rang again. We'd finished dinner and were just sitting around;

Janice and I reading, a pastime that we enjoyed as an alternative to fooling around in bed, while the girls watched a movie on the TV, selected from my very extensive library stored on portable HDDs. I still had their phones in lock-down, so they couldn't inadvertently give our position away, which fortunately eliminated texting and the insidious Facebook as a diversion.

They had all realised that when the encrypted sat-phone rang, it was serious and affected their future, so there was no argument when Janice paused the movie, then gathered them up and took them to our cabin.

'Hello? Harry's Homeless Shelter!' I tried to enliven the usual dumb response that's almost part of our genetic programming.

'Hi, Harry, It's Sandy,' came her more cheerful voice.

'Good evening, Sandy,' I replied, 'it sounds like things are looking a bit brighter up there?'

'Yes, things are better. Greg's recovering well, although his ribs are giving him heaps of trouble and will be for a lot longer, but his concussion has subsided quickly and the rest of his injuries are just uncomfortable, rather than painful.'

'Great news. Did you get a chance to ask him those questions?'

'I did, and although I had to drag it out of him, the sod finally admitted that he did put in another request for information and it wasn't through Annette! It was some turkey he'd met on one of those Inter-Force conference things that passes for an excuse for the boys to strut around comparing dick sizes while they booze it up for a few days at taxpayer expense! Do you think that might have triggered the beating?'

'I'm sure of it!' I replied, 'There's no other reason for them to want to try to put a scare into Greg! Frankly, I think they've panicked and made a big mistake by doing this, especially if, as you say, the local coppers are suspicious about the motive. I mean, they can't possibly hope to silence a State Police Force and stop coppers investigating odd-looking crimes, can they?'

'No, you're right, and I've tried to push that as much as I can. I've got some good contacts in the Central Brisbane Local Area Command that's

got the case, and I've suggested to some mates that there might be a lot more to this than they're being told, plus there's some deliberate high-level interference happening. That's really got the detectives stirred up, they hate political shit getting into investigations and now they're asking the questions!'

'Please be very careful!' I cautioned.

'I have been and still am. The guys who I laid some of this stuff on already had doubts about this incident, so they're making all the enquiries now as part of their own investigation. I've just supplied a little bit of behind-the-scenes information.'

'Ok. With a bit of luck then, this thing might start to unravel all by itself!'

'Yeah. I was thinking that too. But look, the other thing I needed to tell you, was that I contacted ACP's Annette, and the way she's taken this whole mess on board, we might have got a real break!'

'Tell me, tell me!'

'I'm trying to, you goose! Belt up! She'd already made a legitimate Human Trafficking enquiry into activity in the Melbourne area, as part of an on-going H.T. investigation. To cut her long story short, what triggered that enquiry was that a rubbish collection crew in St Kilda, found a 12-year-old Thai girl at 3am one morning, around a month ago. She was very dirty and wearing only torn, grubby panties. She was also very traumatised, mentally and physically, and only spoke some strange tribal dialect.

It took a while for the hospital to find someone who could understand her story, but finally a Doctor on exchange from Thailand managed to talk to her and that was the breakthrough! It seemed that she and her sister had been sold by her parents to human traffickers, and then smuggled into Melbourne in a container with a bunch of other young kids and teenagers, both boys and girls. She managed to escape from a very fancy old house with high, ornate ceilings and lots of polished wood panelling, by hiding in a rubbish bin, which was how the Garbos found her! Interestingly, the only fancy, old house in the area she described is the old mansion that Luke Emery owns, although at this stage, that's the only connection to him! At least for the moment!'

'Wow!' I said getting excited, 'that's a stunning break!'

'Yes, it is. But wait, there's more! The fact of an illegal immigrant girl escaping from a house that Luke owned and apparently visited fairly regularly, has established enough of a connection to support an application to a judge for an intercept on both his phones and email service. And the very best part of that is that those taps were put in place four weeks ago and Annette has all the transcripts since Janice and the girls bugged out! She's also managed to keep the on-going feed from the taps under her direct control, as well as to hide the fact that Luke's under audio surveillance!'

'Oh, this just gets better and better! But tell me, has Annette checked through all the transcripts yet?'

'No, not all of them and she hasn't been through any of the emails yet; there are thousands! But what she has discovered so far is a series of calls Luke's had with one of his employees, a thug called Jimmy. She thinks that his full name is James Fitzroy and he's got a record of arrests and convictions as long as your arm for intimidation, break and enter, and assault occasioning actual bodily harm. He's spent some time in prison on account of those minor character flaws, but it apparently hasn't done any good reforming him!

Anyway, it would appear that this Jimmy is in charge of the whole bunch of hired thugs looking for Janice and the girls. The calls detail the progress they've made as they tracked them around, and it seems that Janice initially used her credit card to pay for travel and accommodation, as well as to get as much cash as she could, spread over several days, maybe deliberately, because they jumped all over the place, staying a few nights here, a few nights there, with a lot of backtracking, but it wasn't until they hit Sydney that she stopped using her plastic and Jimmy and his crew lost track.'

'Is there any hint that they were tracking them via mobile phones?' I asked, dreading the answer.

'Yes, they have been, so it looks like they have the technology. It's concerning just how much money Luke's spending on this search; it's huge!'

'Yeah, well that sort of fits in with my theory that he's hoping for a big payday selling the girls!'

'*Yeah. I agree, as nasty as it is. Nothing else makes sense of the amount of money he's laying out! It must be a huge deal to justify all this fuss and expense!*'

I asked again, 'I don't suppose that there's any hint of when it might be coming up? I'm sure the answer will be in the emails, so I hope she can get to them soon.'

'*I'll call her again if you like, just to try to hurry that along, but I do think she's trying as hard as she can. She's paranoid about trusting the wrong person too, but she did say that there's at least two or three of her staff that she can trust implicitly!*'

'OK, that's a good call. We'll leave her to get on with it then. We seem to be under the radar for now, so we'll try to stay that way.'

'*It sounds like a real holiday cruise, Harry! I'm due some leave, I could come down and join you.*'

'I'd love to see you, and I just happen to have a spare cabin at the moment, but I think you'll be a lot safer staying away from any contact with me for now. Plus, you're doing such a great job keeping all us good guys in touch. We badly need that to keep going.'

'*Yeah, yeah! Got that, Harry. I'll stay here for now while you cuddle up to our star witness! Don't you worry about me, I'll be alright!*'

I chuckled, 'Yeah, righto. That's impressively pathetic, but don't give up your day job just yet! I'll think about your proposition and you call when you get more news.'

She laughed and cancelled the call.

Over the next three days the south wind kept blowing, and according to the maritime reports, the rather large southwest swells kept marching up from the Southern Ocean in their endless ranks and pounding on the west Tasmanian coast. The sun shone brightly from a nearly cloudless sky that had been turned a faintly washed-out blue by a very thin, high cirrus cloud cover. After updating Janice on the latest news, I told the troops that I could see no point in uncomfortably bashing our way further south, while we could remain tucked up safe and secure in a beautiful bay.

The ladies were very happy with that decision, since they loved our latest hidey-hole and there were plenty of places to explore around the rocky inlet immediately north of our anchored position.

They also became quite good at fishing, landing some beautiful snapper, as well as the large and very tasty King George whiting and a few flathead. It was a delicious way to extend our pantry stocks!

I used some of the time to check *Firebird* over carefully for storm damage but found none. I also retrieved the second anchor, as we were totally secure on the main Excel anchor in anything up to and including a whole gale. I'd just been very cautious by putting a second anchor out ahead of the storm, but I'd developed a healthy respect for squall fronts, especially when there was the weight of a fast-moving cold front behind it!

There was plenty of time for long walks and runs on the amazingly white beach to keep our fitness levels up and we even ventured inland a little way through the dense scrub, although when I casually mentioned that Tiger snakes were present on the island in large numbers, enthusiasm waned dramatically for any more bush walks.

Nevertheless, we did see kangaroos on the beach, and even Jasper, who was delighted to be taken on at least two walks a day, couldn't get close to them, although it wasn't for want of trying! I had to very firmly tell him not to chase them off the beach!

I carefully didn't report to the girls that I'd spotted a snake on the beach one afternoon. It was quite rare for them to venture into the open as they became easy prey to eagles and ospreys, and it was very unlikely that one would pose a problem to humans or Jasper.

As the days warmed up and the cool south winds eased, the girls took to running around naked again, including going for beach walks sans clothing. Janice also joined the undress movement, and they badgered me to join them. I resisted for a while, and only gave in when I thought I could keep my body at least partly under control while surrounded by their bare, tanned bodies! Most times it worked, but I had to be very careful where I looked, to the endless amusement of my fair companions!

'It's really not fair!' I exclaimed to Janice one afternoon, attempting to act dismayed as I tried, but failed to control my body's response to the girls' mock wrestling bout on the soft, white sand just in front of us. 'When you females get aroused, everything is still tucked away, mostly out of sight even, while a male, who has everything hanging out in the breeze to start with, ends up with a mini flagpole that can be seen 100 meters away!'

Janice giggled as she made an overly exaggerated inspection of the source of my complaint.

'Golly gee, Harry! I suppose I could say that if you weren't so big, it'd be less of a problem, but then I'm definitely not going to make any complaint about size! Particularly after what I'd been used to!'

I raised my eyebrows and looked at her. 'Oh, yeah! Please explain?'

She avoided my gaze for a few moments, before replying. 'Luke has always been small, even when he could get it up! Thin and short was the best he could do on a really good day, which is why his forced attentions didn't hurt at all, just the beatings! I even needed artificial insemination to get pregnant! Apparently, the little guys just couldn't swim that far without help!'

She suddenly giggled, 'Yesterday, I heard the girls making a comparison. You would have been very flattered if you'd heard them!'

There didn't seem much I could or should say to that, so I didn't, and we walked on in comfortable silence. After that, however, I was less concerned about my occasional erection in front of the girls, although I still felt a bit uncomfortable when they paid such close attention to it!

The generally happy demeanour of the girls remained a real pleasure to both Janice and I, although they had down times when they missed their close friends back home. Still, the adventure of the boat trip always won through any depression and having Jasper to cuddle and play with was a great distraction and a guaranteed mood lifter!

SANDY, SOUTHPORT, FRIDAY 8AM

Sandy had the midnight to 09:00 shift on Friday and was back at her desk finishing up writing another interminable report before she knocked off, when her boss, Superintendent Bob Casey called on the intercom and asked for her presence in his office.

With a feeling of dread, she tidied her hair, straightened her uniform and beat feet upstairs. He had a corner office with a charming view of a traffic-choked street in downtown Southport.

'Good morning, sir,' she stated from the open doorway after knocking politely, 'you wanted to see me?'

He looked up from a pile of reports he'd been ploughing through; a thickset man in his late 40s, thick hair well speckled with grey and muscles slowly turning to fat from too much beer, too much time behind a desk and too little exercise.

He smiled, stood and waved the pretty, curvaceous, auburn-haired Senior Constable to the chair opposite his desk.

'Come in, please Senior, and take a seat. Thanks for coming up, there's just a couple of small matters, then you can go back to generating more of these things to choke my desk!' he said, smiling genially, while waving disdainfully at the pile in front of him.

'Thank you, sir,' Sandy sat primly in the attention position.

'Now, firstly,' he stated, 'I believe that you've got one of the TRG's sat-phones?'

Sandy nodded, 'Yes, sir. I'd been running some tests as it was a new model and we don't have those even in our budget. It does seem very good though, much better signal quality than the old model we sometimes use and no encryption dropouts. We should be getting them!'

'Ah good, good. However, the records show that you've been using it several times to make quite lengthy calls to the same number. Can you explain?'

Sandy swallowed and prepared to lie. 'I'm sorry about that, sir, but I'd wanted to see how well the new encryption algorithm holds up during a lengthy call, to make sure there was no degradation of signal quality or strength, so I called a friend of mine in the ACP. Our old ones sometimes drop the encryption partway through the call, so the user had to start all over again.'

Superintendent Casey held up his hands in mock horror.

'Enough! I sometimes think you tech specialists speak a different language to the rest of us normal mortals. Anyway, I presume that you've done all the endurance testing necessary?'

Sandy tried to smile, 'Yes sir. That's enough for me!'

'Good, very good, because the TRG need that one urgently! It seems that one of their brightest managed to drop his from a hotel balcony and it went into the main pool 20 stories below. Very nearly hit some old duck on the head, so of course she's suing the hotel for a case of advanced palpitations and in turn, they're suing the TRG!'

He chuckled, 'I've gotta tell you, it turns out, the incident was spotted by some religious cult leader having lunch with his secretary on the balcony of his room that was just across from the TRG chappie, who it seemed was making a call with the sat-phone while standing there stark naked, and according to the secretary, quite aroused!! It was about then that he dropped the bloody thing! Hotel security were already on the way in response to the outraged call from the religious dude, where they found that it wasn't a TRG room at all and the two young ladies in there with him were also naked, with one of them tied to the bed with the TRG guy's handcuffs! What a clusterfuck!'

He looked quite cheerful about the much-vaunted TRG cocking something up so publicly!

'Anyway, if you wouldn't mind boxing it up and calling a courier to collect it. Here's the address,' as he passed her a post-it note.

'OK, sir. I can do that,' she replied, 'Was there anything else?'

He looked a bit discomforted for a moment. 'Yes, yes there is. It's that bloody paedophile business again. I just took a call from that nosy, condescending little prick from the ACP, Alistair Swinford is his name! Rotten little arsehole! The same one who ripped into me about Greg's enquiry last week.'

Sandy just nodded, not trusting herself to speak.

'Anyway, he asked if anyone else had been making further enquiries into the investigation, and naturally, I had to say NO! But then I thought I'd better talk to you since you were Greg's partner on this thing.'

Sandy opened her mouth to speak, but he held a hand up for silence.

'Sandy, you've done truly excellent work since you've been here and I've got no complaints, but I really get upset when a Commonwealth copper gives me a serve because my people are just doing their jobs! And the smarmy little prick not only refused to tell me what was going on, but also said it was on a 'need to know basis' and I didn't need to know! Bullshit! If it affects this station and/or my staff, 'I need to know'!

Now, what I need from you is any information that might shed some light on this mess. I feel like I'm trying to fight a bunch of clowns in a dark room with my hands tied behind my back!'

Sandy thought for a long few moments, then looked him in the eye and said, 'Sir, I can honestly say that I have no idea what the ACP are investigating that might affect this station. Like you, I'm not privy to that info and I'm sure Greg wasn't either.'

He patted the air between them wearily, 'I know. I know. I've already spoken to Greg and he said the same. Alright, if you don't know, all we can do is wait for their Lordships to let us little people know what their high and mighty plans and machinations have revealed! If they bother!'

Sandy tried desperately not to show relief on her face, but seized the opportunity to ask, 'With all this fuss going on, may I please put in a request for some leave? I've got more than 4 weeks banked up and HR wants me to clear it. I really feel like a break from it all!'

He looked concerned and frowned. 'Of course, of course! Send it through the usual channel, but make sure it gets sent to me! I suppose you want to start straight away?'

Sandy smiled, 'Yes sir, I really would. This whole mess of being under suspicion of I-don't-know-what, has been preying on my mind!'

'Understood! Say no more. Go fill out your paperwork and bring it straight up for my signature!'

Sandy stood. 'Thank you, sir, for being understanding.'

She paused, having one of those rare epiphany moments where a bright light suddenly reveals the solution to the puzzle, then she gave him what she hoped was a sufficiently meaningful look, 'Look, sir. If there should be anything I remember that might help you, or if, by some chance I do come across some pertinent information from, let's say an informed friend, may I call you directly, perhaps on your personal mobile phone if I can have the number?'

Superintendent Casey frowned briefly as he considered the import of her words, then smiled.

'Oh! Oh, I see. Yes indeed! That might be a very, very good idea, Senior. Here's the number and you can call at any time, day or night!'

'Yes sir and thanks again, sir. I'll really try to remember as much as I can and let you know what I find…that is remember!'

'Good work, Senior. I look forward to hearing from you before long…!'

He stopped as obviously some dots connected and a thought struck him. 'Oh, now here's another thought! How about we don't worry about that leave application. And how about I assign you to work plain clothes, solo, investigating the connections to the National paedophile ring that we were told about by that local rock spider we snagged last month! If I were to leave the investigation area to your discretion, you can do what you consider appropriate, but remember that you're reporting only and directly to me! A reasonable expense account goes with that, but don't go crazy with it! And keep all receipts otherwise Accounting will go nuts!

Do you think that Interstate travel would be involved?'

Sandy couldn't help but break out into her trademark, beaming smile.

'Oh, sir. That's fantastic! I know exactly where and what to investigate, especially under the terms you laid down, so that we can comply with the 'no interference' edict by the ACP.

And yes, there will be some Interstate flying, but I'll report as I go, rather than in advance. Based on what I think I might possibly know, I must ask, respectfully, that you don't communicate any of the information that it's possible that I might pass on to you in the course of my legitimate enquiries to anybody else! At least for now.'

Superintendent Casey beamed at her, like a father might look at his favourite daughter.

'I can work with that,' he smiled. 'Just be careful. I still don't like the way these ACP clowns seem to be running around the country deflecting enquiries into investigations! Makes me very suspicious!'

Sandy left and hurried downstairs to wrap up her work. With her normal partner, Greg laid up for many weeks to come, she wasn't working with anybody else in particular at the moment, and so her absence wasn't going to be noticed. Officers were transferred in and out all the time on temporary duty. She was about to pack up the sat-phone, when a thought struck her.

Checking the battery charge, she went out to the carpark, found her car and dialled the number she'd almost learned by heart.

CHAPTER 19

FIREBIRD...THREE HUMMOCK ISLAND - BASS STRAIT, FRIDAY 09:00

We'd just come back from a beach-walk when the sat-phone trilled its distinctive 'secure call' tone. Janice rolled her eyes and shooed the girls up for'rard to sit around the bows. They'd been really good about my private calls, Janice having told them that it was to do with evading the search for them.

'Yo!' I answered for a change.

'Hi, Harry,' came Sandy's voice, 'I only have a minute, so listen up! The ACP has been sniffing around again, not looking for anything in particular, just flashing their dicks, basically. Nevertheless, it's made my position very awkward and rendered me almost useless sitting here, as the sat-phone has to go back to the TRG. Anyway, the big news is that my boss, Superintendent Casey, has picked up on some of what's happening and is right royally pissed off at being jerked around by the ACP investigator who's been doing this local cover-up job.

I've managed to drop enough hints that I know more than I can say, so the darling man has assigned me to my own, solo, plain-clothes investigation of the information the paedophile we have up here has given us. I'm all on my own, have an expense account and almost unlimited scope of operation. I just have to report direct to him every so often!

How do you like that?'

I was trying to absorb all that she had said, then replied, 'That's terrific, to have that support. But I presume that you've not told the boss very much and that you do trust him?'

'That's right. I just inferred that if I could get away from under the gaze of nosy ACP investigators, I'd be able to find out more. And, yes, I do trust him. There's no way he could be involved with these creeps!'

I thought a bit more, then quickly logged onto the 'net and called up airline schedules. 'OK Sandy, then I presume that you want another boating holiday?"

'Yes please, Harry. I won't have this phone any more as soon as we hang up, I've got my boss covering my back, and I can help with contacts wherever I am. You've got every form of communication known to man on that lovely boat, so I think we can stay in touch with those who matter just as well!'

'Ok. Come on down. You know what to pack but bring enough for at least a month. It's quite warm to hot at the moment, but plan for very chilly as well! Any of your special gadgets you've got laying around might come in handy as well, but you really need to cover your movements, so here's a plan. Got a pen?'

'Go ahead.'

'Don't make any more phone calls after this, and don't tell anybody about your movements. On the way, but as soon as you can, buy four or five pre-paid mobiles. Just the basic type; no bells and whistles needed. You'll only use those from here on. You can buy them on your credit card, but that'll be the last use for it for a while.

Withdraw as much cash as you can from your account, so you don't have to use any plastic from now on!

Book the first flight to Melbourne, with a connection through to Adelaide, but only book your checked bag as far as Melbourne. Make up some story about not trusting the transfer system as to why you don't want it to be booked through.

You're going to be a no-show on the Adelaide flight unfortunately, so you'd better let the Service pick up the tab for the flights!

At Tullamarine, get your bags and go to the King counter and try for a one-way to Burnie, Tasmania. Pay cash only!

There are flights today at 12:30, 14:50 and 18:55, getting in respectively at 13:40, 16:00 and 20:05. Got that so far?'

'Copy that.'

'OK. At Burnie airport, you're actually right beside the town of

Wynyard! Don't ask, it must be a Tasmanian thing, 'cause Burnie is actually 18 km or so down the road! Take a taxi into town, and have the cabbie take you to the Jetty Hotel. It's a rather neat little pub on the waterfront, and they have accommodation, but you're not going to check in. If the cabbie wonders why a pretty chicky-babe wants to stay there, just say that you're going to hook up with a bunch of biker mates, tonight or tomorrow. That should make him lose interest. Naturally, don't mention boats! OK?'

'*Copy that.*'

'Make your bookings now and let me know via one of those pre-paid burners which flight to Burnie you'll be on. We've got about a four-hour run to Wynyard from here, so let me know ASAP about the flight. At this stage, I don't think that we should spend too much time in Wynyard, but we'll make that decision after we see what the local situation is like!'

'*OK, Harry. I've got all that. I'll call back shortly with flight details.*'

The phone went through its usual cacophony of squeals and warbles to indicate it was disengaged as I mentally reviewed the new arrangements, before waving Janice and the girls back down from the trampoline.

'Things have changed, yet again,' I started with once they were inside, and then explained what was happening. The mention of the search-net slowly tightening, reminded the girls that as fun as the trip was, it had a very serious purpose.

'So, we're going to have another companion joining us later today,' I concluded, mainly to the girls, since Janice was privy to most of my info from Queensland. 'Sandy is a lovely, very smart lady and a lot of fun! She's also a Senior Constable with the Queensland Police, a comms tech, Instructor in hand-to-hand combat so she knows how to handle herself and most weapons.'

'She's going to call again soon to tell us what flight she's got to Wynyard. I'd like to try to time our run so that we get there about the same time as she does. I don't think we should spend too much time there, but it'll depend on the reaction we cause when we arrive.

It's a very small port and we'll certainly be noticed. We'll wait and see how it looks at the time.'

'How long will it take us to get there?' Janice asked.

'It's an almost straight run of 48 nautical miles, so with the wind as it is, we'll be on a beam to broad reach and will be quite fast. We should do it in about 4 hours or less. I hope!'

'What happens after we pick up Sandy?' Janice asked again.

'Well. The wind is still from the south, so there's no reason to be uncomfortable. We might as well return to here, at least for a few days. There are also a couple of beautiful-looking bays on the east side of Hunter Island, which is the next island just to the west of this one. We could go there for a couple of days if the southerly keeps on. Regardless, we have plenty of choices in that area, so long as the food holds out.'

I looked at Angie. 'Speaking of that, Chef! How is the pantry holding up?'

She grinned and answered confidently, 'Pretty good, so far, Skipper. Frozen meat and veges are okay, although bread supplies are good only for about another week. Fruit juice and Long-Life milk stocks are good, but everything will need to be built up if we're going remote again, especially with an extra mouth to feed!'

'OK. That'll be enough. The southerly will turn before that, so we'll be able to head for Strahan. And you guys can catch more fish! Those spicy Thai fishcakes you made last night were terrific!'

Angie beamed with the praise, which was genuine, as she really was good in the galley. It was, however, still a little disconcerting for me to see their bare little breasts bobbing around up close and personal! By unspoken agreement, Janice and the twins always wore panties of some sort when inside or sitting in the cockpit. Needless to say, I at least pulled shorts on once back aboard.

'Ok, boss,' she grinned, 'your trusty crew will fire up the fishing lines again! Should we toss a line over now?'

I looked at my watch. 'Yeah, you can, although as soon as Sandy calls with a time, we may have to set sail immediately.'

'No problem,' she replied, as she and Zoe moved as a well-practised team, baiting lines that were ready and casting over the stern. The fish life in this beautiful bay was amazing, so it was only moments before Zoe was hauling in a 2.5kg snapper! On its own it would feed two of us, but by the time the boat-phone rang 15 minutes later, they had eight more, even bigger!'

As expected, and although the calling number was strange, it was Sandy, sounding quite excited at the prospect of the trip and getting more closely involved in the action!

I didn't bother to chase the girls away as they needed to hear most things from here on, except stuff about their dear Daddy's ultimate plans for them!

'Hi again, Harry,' she said, 'I've got the times for you.'

'Go ahead.'

'Although I had heaps of choices, the flight to Melbourne was the most difficult since it's the longest and I've still got to pack and get to the airport. I've conned a Code 3 ride with Highway Patrol, which should save some time getting to the airport, but I still couldn't make the early Burnie flight, but I will be on the 14:50 that gets in at 16:00. Will that be okay?'

'Great! That'll work out fine. We won't have to rush so much in that case, although we might have some night sailing if we want to get back to our lovely little hidey-hole tonight! By the way, I see that you've got the burners already!'

'Yep! There's a shop just across the street, so that saved a bit of time, although the battery needs charging.'

'Okay. Only call if your schedule changes, otherwise get cracking and stick to the plan!'

'Roger boss! See you this arvo!'

I terminated the call and checked the time, before informing the crew.

'It's 10:00 now, and Sandy's on track with flights, but she won't lob in Burnie/Wynyard until 16:00. That gives us plenty of time to make the run if this breeze hold. If we leave about 12:00, we should time it about right, by the time she clears the airport and gets a cab. The airport's just on the edge of town, so that bit won't take long.'

'Is there anything we need to do to get ready?' Janice asked.

'Nah! Not really. *Firebird*'s ready, the second anchor is in and stowed, the RIB is stowed and no loose gear on deck! Just the usual stowing of loose stuff in the galley and around the saloon, but we should be in quite sheltered water all the way there and back, so I reckon it'll be a fast, fun sail!'

That pleased the crew, although Jasper had only had one romp on the beach today, having been used to at least two! Still, I was appreciative that all the extra exercise meant that he slept most of the night through, and when he wanted a human to snuggle, he usually chose to bunk with the girls. Although their favourite wee-small-hours saying seemed to be a sleepy grumble of 'move your fat arse, cat!" I noticed, however, that they didn't shut him out of their cabin at night!

So, we had a leisurely morning tea, while the twins hauled in a few more fish. As we had plenty of fresh fish in the 'fridge, they'd planned to fillet, then freeze some, but Angie was also very keen to try smoking some on the Weber. To that end, she'd braved the Tiger snakes in the scrub and collected what she reckoned would be a bundle of nice-smelling wood to do the job and had it stowed in a bag in the corner of my otherwise pristine cockpit! Nevertheless, I was delighted by the way they had fitted in to the boat routine and cheerfully taken on their share of jobs, whereas most teenagers would have been content to lie back playing with their phone or iPad without lifting a finger to help. For about the twentieth time, I reminded Janice what a terrific pair of girls she had!

THREE HUMMOCK ISLAND TO WYNYARD, FRIDAY 12:00

Promptly at 12:00, with Zoe on the wheel and me pulling the appropriate strings, we raised the anchor. I retracted the mainsail cover, slacked off the mainsheet and electrically started the main hoisting, before I unfurled the inner staysail and sheeted it in to help blow the bow around. Three minutes later, we had all sails up and set, a stiff 25 knot breeze out of the southwest sending *Firebird* scooting along at 15 to 18 knots, with a low swell alternately lifting the bows, then the sterns in a gentle, almost soothing rhythm. The breeze was too much for the big screecher, so for safety, I rolled some of the huge sail onto the bow furler. Our speed didn't noticeable decrease, but the boat felt more comfortable as the bows weren't being depressed so much.

As I had hoped, the swells stayed quite low, as there was insufficient fetch to let them build too much, while the breeze picked up a bit more once we were clear of the islands.

It turned out to be a great sail, with *Firebird* only heeling a few degrees and slicing cleanly through the backs of the swells with an easy, loping motion. Zoe let out a whoop when the speedo touched 20 knots and stayed there for minutes on end.

'This is brilliant!' she enthused, a beaming smile on her face. 'Even better than coming across from Flinders! The swells are smaller!'

We all smiled at her infectious happiness, as I mentally revised our landfall time downwards.

Angie had no trouble making and serving sandwiches for lunch, the motion was so easy that no tea was spilled either. So, it became a very pleasant, comfortable and fast run to Wynyard, the 50 nautical miles straight leg to 2 miles seaward of the river mouth, completed in 3 hours flat for an average speed of 16 knots. We then wasted a bit of time buggerising around trying to beat inshore against the almost direct offshore wind, before I got jack of the short, sharp tacks and fired up the engines for the last leg into port.

With sails neatly furled, *Firebird* motored easily and quietly towards the river entrance. The offshore breeze completely flattened the swell in close, so there were no significant waves on the shallows either side of the entrance to worry us as we followed the lead triangles to stay in the channel.

I supervised Zoe carefully, but she picked up the idea quickly and kept us safe. We were ahead of time anyway, so we didn't rush but were still anchored across from the Wynyard wharf by 15:30.

As I shut down the engines after setting the anchor firmly, I said to the ladies, 'I've had a brilliant thought. Let's go ashore and have a beer or two while we wait for Sandy!'

'I thought you didn't want to hang around?' Janice asked, 'I mean I'd love to go join normal civilisation for a while, however short, but is there any risk?'

I looked around at the peaceful, pretty little harbour with the neat white-painted Jetty Hotel overlooking the water.

'No, I think it's worth a looksee. Don't dress up, we're only going to the pub!'

That raised a laugh as everyone rushed below to chuck something half-decent on, which really didn't take more than a couple of minutes. I just changed my shirt and splashed some anti-stink under the armpits, then went aft to lower the RIB into the water. Leaving the boat unlocked and with Jasper left on guard watch and looking slightly forlorn about it, five minutes later saw us puttering quietly ashore.

I noticed that there was a security fence along the wharf's inner edge, so we went around the end of the short berthing fingers of the tiny marina and tied up right beside the carpark.

A brief stroll through a pretty little park, then over the road and we plonked down at an outside table on the veranda looking out at *Firebird*. Jasper's black head could just be seen peering wistfully over the cockpit surround, his eyes firmly on us. Over the last week and a bit, I reckoned he'd become way too used to constant company and attention and thought that he'd have a rough time when the ladies went back to their shore-side life and we resumed wandering. 'So will I, for that matter!' a random thought flashed across my mind as I went into the bar to order.

'Gidday, love,' called the cheery barmaid, 'wot'll you have?'

'Two schooners of Cascade and two Lemon Ruskies, please.'

'Coming right up!' she answered. 'You lot off that bloody big cat?'

'Yeah. 'Fraid so,' I grinned.

'Jeez, don't be afraid!' she said laughing, 'I'd be on it with you in a flash. Trouble is, this place is just starting to turn a profit so I can't leave.'

'No bloody wonder you're making a profit!' called out one of the grizzled old regulars from down the bar. 'The prices you charge a poor old fisherman, it fair makes me eyes water!'

'Oh, bullshit, Ernie!' she scolded, placing the drinks in front of me and accepting the $50 note in return. 'The only thing that makes your eyes water is too much of that bloody cheap rum you buy from the Bottlo up town! Now if you got off your skinny arse and went fishing a bit more often, you'd appreciate the good stuff I serve here!'

With Ernie grumping in his beer and with that battle won for the moment, she smilingly handed over my change and went to top up some others, while I carried the drinks out to the ladies.

We clinked glasses, the twins eagerly sucking down their cold Ruskies. I'd discovered that Janice enjoyed the odd beer on a hot day, so we relaxed as we drank, soaking up the peace and tranquillity of the harbour.

'Can we get some chips?' Zoe asked.

'Sure,' said Janice, looking at me helplessly, 'but I didn't bring money ashore!'

I smiled and gave Zoe $15. 'Better get a couple of bags,' I said, 'this is so nice, we might just stay a bit longer!'

The old fisherman, who'd joshed with the owner before, wandered out, beer in hand and looked the ladies over, looked over at *Firebird*, then looked at me.

'Bloody hell, Skipper, that's a good-looking crew you've got there. Why can't I pull glamour like that? Surely pretty girls would rather work at sea covered in fish scales and come home stinkin' of fish guts, than lounge around on that bit of luxurious fluff!'

The ladies looked up then giggled at his comments.

He looked a bit put out for a moment, but then laughed.

'You can take a joke, I reckon that maybe you lot are okay!' he declared, 'We get a few wankers from across the strait, drift in here with their bloody great gin palaces, poncing around like they've just crossed the Tasman, but that looks a half-decent boat! Can she handle a good blow?'

'Yeah,' I replied, taking a pull of beer, 'she is at that, and yes, she can handle a blow. Been through several in the Tasman.'

'Good thing you've got a dog aboard,' he commented, squinting his rheumy eyes at Jasper's head, still poking above the cockpit coaming, 'helps with security in strange ports, I reckon. He looks a bit like a Rottie from here, is he?'

'Yeah. He's actually a Rottie/Doberman cross. That gives him the narrower head shape.' I didn't bother to correct him. A cat that was close to the size of a Rottweiler/Doberman cross would attract way too much attention in the sleepy little port of Wyndham.

'Anyway, folks, didn't mean to butt in, but I just wanted to let you know that if you wanted to stay a while, where you're parked is just fine.'

'Thanks, mate,' I said as he turned to amble back inside, 'we might just do that. Or at least stay for a feed. Is it okay here?'

'My bloody oath,' he enthused, turning back with a gap-toothed grin, 'old Mavis in there puts on the best feed in town, bar none!'

'Goodo! That'll do us!'

'Are we really staying for tea?' Janice asked quietly, after he left. 'Isn't that a bit risky?'

'Maybe, but I'm getting a good feeling about this place. The biggest risk was coming here in the first place, but I wanted Sandy out of circulation ASAP. Now that we are here, I think it might arouse more curiosity if we just grabbed her and ran, rather than to stay a while, then wander off after dark.'

She thought about that for a few moments then nodded. 'Okay. That makes sense, and I think we'd all like a night out. It's just a bit unexpected; delightfully so, I might add!'

So we drank, chatted and generally just soaked up the normal shore-side routine we'd been missing. I went in to get another round of drinks and asked about tea for later on. My new best friend, Mavis, slid a menu across and said we could eat anytime and just let her know.

'Nah! No rush, thanks, Mavis. We'll suck up a couple more of these lovely beers first!'

'Good on you, Jimmy,' she said, pouring the next round. I didn't think that using my right name would've been the best idea under the circumstances.

We'd almost finished the second round of drinks and another couple of packets of chips, when a battered old taxi pulled up out front.

By now I had a slight glow on, and Janice definitely had rosy cheeks and looked looser.

'Ah. This looks promising,' I announced cheerfully, and the ladies looked on with interest as their new crewmember dragged herself and a couple of bags out of the cab and paid off the driver. Her shoulder-length, auburn hair glowed with health in the late afternoon sun while the pale-blue denim jacket over a white T-shirt did little to hide her well-developed chest. Likewise, the rest of her, encased in tight jeans, wasn't hard to look at either. Obviously, since I'd last seen Sandy, she hadn't let herself go at all!

'Wow!' exclaimed Angie, rather reverently. 'That's Sandy?'

'She doesn't look like a copper,' Zoe threw in.

'You can check her badge later,' I joked, getting up to greet her, as she climbed the steps and stopped at our table, dumping her bags on the ground with a thump.

She looked sternly at us, then at the empty beer glasses clustered in the middle of the table.

'I hope you don't intend trying to drive that overgrown Hobie-cat out there while partly under the influence, Mr Stevens? Especially with untrained passengers aboard,' she asked sternly.

'Wouldn't dream of it, Constable, oops, that is, Senior Constable!' I replied cheerfully, flashing a highly derogatory two-fingered salute. 'I'd probably wait until I was properly pissed, then let the semi-pissed First Mate here do it!'

'Oh! Well, that's all right then. I was afraid I'd come to the wrong pub and found the wrong Harry!'

With Janice and the twins looking on with puzzled expressions, Sandy dropped the 'Smart-arse Cop' routine and beamed with pleasure, the smile transforming her face, as she grabbed me in a tight hug and kissed me soundly. I couldn't help but notice that Janice had a somewhat ordinary expression on her face when we finally separated, the feeling of Sandy's lovely chest pressed firmly against mine still lingering.

I turned to introduce the others, but Sandy beat me to it, grabbing Janice's hand and leaning down to kiss her as well.

'Hi Janice,' she said softly, 'please excuse me taking liberties with Harry. We go back a way and been through some tough times together. I tend to get very fond of people who save my life!'

Not giving Janice a chance to speak, she turned to the girls.

'I know one of you is Angie and the other is Zoe, but I'm buggered if I can pick which is which!'

A tanned, freckled Angie slowly stuck her hand up. 'Hi. I'm Angie with the freckles. This is Zoe, my sister, sans freckles.'

Each promptly received a hug and a kiss from Sandy, who then rounded on me.

'And where the hell's my beer, Harry? Jeez, the service is rat-shit around here! Have I got to get my own or what?'

I sketched another mock salute and smiling with pleasure at seeing my dear friend again, hustled inside to order another round and was promptly set upon by Ernie the fisherman.

'Bloody hell, Skipper. Now you've snagged another one! Where'd you pull her? Fair dinkum, you gotta teach me how you do that. I mean, she'd just arrived and was giving you what for, when wham! She's all over you like a bloody octopus! I mean, how the hell do you do it?'

I couldn't help jerking his chain, as I replied with a helpless shrug, 'Buggered if I know either, Ernie. I mean, there we were, just sitting minding our own business when she rocks up and demands a beer! Says she was supposed to meet up with some bikie mates this evening, but then changes her mind and says she'd rather go on the boat than sit on the back of a bike! Bloody hell! I mean, what's a guy to do? I'll have to put her to work to pay her keep, I suppose. And if I do take her, I'll have 50 rabid bikies chasing me for pinching their main Momma! If you know what I mean!'

'Yeah, well. You could always sling her my way,' Ernie sniggered, 'instead of being a greedy bugger! As if three aren't enough, when I'm stuck with a moron for a son-in-law who's got two left feet and doesn't know starboard from the hole in his bum! Tell her that if she likes boats so much, I'll keep her busy and the bikie blokes won't find her!'

'Oh, turn it up, you old goat!' Mavis laughed at him. 'You wouldn't know what to do with a lovely young lady like that! Now you leave the nice gentleman alone. And while I'm at it, it wouldn't hurt if you learned a few manners. Might get you a lot further with females!'

'Does that mean that if I learn some of those fancy poncy manner things, I might finally score with you?'

'You'll never know if you don't try it,' she said cryptically, with a wink at me, as I loaded the drinks onto a tray and beat a hasty retreat back outside.

Sandy quickly won Janice and the twins over completely and soon they were giggling and laughing like old mates, particularly when I told them of my exchange with Ernie.

'So now I'm a bikie moll who's abandoned the pack to go off as part of a boatie's harem! Is that the picture, Harry?'

I shrugged carelessly, 'Yeah. That's about it, Sandy! I mean, what else can I say? Ernie did make you a serious offer, though!'

That earned me a serious smack on the arm.

Zoe looked at her, 'Harry says that you're an instructor in hand-to-hand combat. Can you teach Angie and I some moves?'

Sandy chuckled, 'Yes. I am and sure I can. Some of the more basic self-defence ones are quite easy. We can have a session each morning up on the trampoline mat.'

Zoe's eyes gleamed, 'That'd be great. Thanks!'

After another round, I could see that we were all getting a bit pissy, so decided it was late enough to order tea. I wrote down the decisions and went in to see Mavis.

'No problem, dearie!' she chortled, taking my money and still highly amused by my taking the piss out of Ernie who still looked a bit bemused by the whole exchange. 'I'll bring it all out to you just as soon as it's ready!'

Shortly after, Sandy went in to the toilet and I saw her stop by Ernie on the way back. She whispered in his ear, and then gave him a big kiss on the cheek.

'What was that about?' I asked when she sat down.

'Oh, nothing much. I just told him that taking on a gang of bikies was great fun, but because the blonde ladies told me that they'd stayed around because you were hung like a 15-hand horse, I just had to find out for myself! I mean, normally, once you've been had by a gang of bikies, everything else is pretty boring!'

That really cracked Janice and the girls up as I nodded ruefully that I'd been paid out big-time. Just before our dinner arrived, Ernie wobbled past and threw me a salute.

'I'm glad I found out your secret, Skipper,' he slurred, 'I can sleep well now knowing that I can't compete with what nature provides some and not others! Calm seas and fair winds to you!'

To a chorus of 'Good-nights', he stumbled down the steps and steered an erratic course down the road towards home.

'Ernie's a nice old bloke,' Janice said to Mavis as she and a young girl handed our meals around.

'Yeah! He is. You never guess it, but he's also filthy rich, although he's worked his arse off all his life to earn it! He's become the un-official town mayor. '

She noted our raised eyebrows and shrugged.

'He doesn't like to show it, but that's just his way and there's quite a few more very un-assuming rich folk just like Ernie in town. It's that sort of a place, so they stay here because, unlike most small towns, people here really do mind their own business. For instance, there won't be any talk about your visit. Ernie liked you and really appreciated that bit of fun. That was enough for him to accept you. Anyway, enjoy your meals!'

She left and we tucked in and really did enjoy our meals. Ernie was right, the food was terrific, with decent size serves. None of that prissy little blob of something unidentifiable in the middle of a huge, white plate with some artistic scribbling with a fancy sauce to make it look good! The party was getting happily raucous and being Friday night, the pub was as well, with a wide selection of customers. The young girl who'd helped with serving our meals, appeared with a guitar, and perched beside an open window not far from us.

She sang several Irish ballads in a beautiful, clear voice, loud enough to be heard over the ceaseless chatter, but without any microphone. She was a pleasure to hear and more than a few drinkers stopped chattering to listen and sing along, our group included.

However, by 21:00, yawns were appearing around our table; it'd been a big day for all of us so we decided to pull the pin.

I ducked inside to say goodbye to Mavis and thank her for her hospitality.

'No problem, lovie!' she said. 'It's been a pleasure to have you here and have a bit of fun with Ernie! Come back soon if you can.'

'Thanks Mavis. After what you said earlier about curiosity, we just might do that! It seems a beaut little place.'

'Oh, it is, darlin'. Bye now,' as she bustled off to satisfy some more thirsty drinkers. I re-joined the crew, who were standing, waiting, Sandy shouldering one bag while Zoe hefted the other.

'Well, troops,' I said, 'I don't think that we should even think about going anywhere tonight, except straight to bed. We might get going early tomorrow though and head back to Three Hummock Island; what do you think?'

'Yea!' was Zoe's comment, and that seemed to sum up the others as well.

We crammed into the RIB and puttered quietly out to *Firebird*.

As we approached, Sandy asked me, 'I don't suppose you've still got that beautiful little black kitten that Korean cook gave you?'

I chuckled, 'Still got him, but he's not exactly a kitten anymore!'

'Oh, yeah. I suppose he wouldn't be,' she said, 'it's been a while.'

'Yep! About 18 months,' as Zoe swung neatly against the stern.

'*Firebird* looks good,' she noted as she carefully stepped out and we handed her bags up.

'Better than ever,' I smiled, 'we've had a couple of really cracking runs lately. Huge fun!'

Sandy was looking casually around when I turned on the dim, blue courtesy lights, so she jumped back and nearly fell overboard when saw a huge, black form silently stepping toward her across the cockpit.

'Oh, shit! Harry, what the hell's that?'

Luckily Janice grabbed her arm before she disappeared over the rail, while the twins dissolved into giggles.

'Ahh...This is the kitten. I called him Jasper,' I announced to a still shocked Sandy.

'Bullshit! That can't be that little kitten! Can it? I held him in the palm of my hand!'

'One and the same,' I smiled, 'but let's see if he remembers you. Just stand still. He has an odd routine for this, but you only have to suffer it once.'

'Jasper,' I called clearly, 'this is Sandy and you should remember her. She's going to stay with us.'

My beautiful big cat drifted silently up to a clearly apprehensive Sandy and gently nuzzled her hand, then poked his nose firmly into her crutch, rocking her back on her heels! As unexpected as that was, it probably bothered Sandy more that he didn't have to stretch up to do it! After a few moments of nuzzling, he stepped back, sat, and then raised his right paw to her.

Hesitantly, she took it, marvelling at the softness of his fur, but noting the steel-hardness of his razor-sharp claws, carefully sheathed.

'That's amazing,' she said as she automatically stroked his head, only slightly startled by the loud, rumbling purr that vibrated up from his chest, 'he's absolutely beautiful.'

'He does remember you,' I said softly, 'he hasn't done that with anybody else!'

'He certainly didn't do that with us,' Zoe confirmed, 'that was incredible. Cats aren't supposed to do stuff like that!'

FIREBIRD...WYNYARD, FRIDAY 21:00

With introductions over and Jasper having done his usual trick of taking over the party, we got on with settling Sandy in. It turned out that Janice and Angie had made up Sandy's bed in the left rear cabin on the way yesterday, and as she'd been on *Firebird* before and knew the routine, I was able to dispense with the briefing. She was familiar with the restrictions applying to baggage on a boat, so there was plenty of drawer and hanging space for her gear.

The twins were tired and more than a bit wobbly, so we did the kissy-huggy routine and sent them off, Jasper in tow, while, even though the rest of us were tired, we decided to have a quick cuppa and chat about the future. The three of us settled in the cockpit with steaming mugs of NQ tea in front of each.

'What's this NQ tea?' Janice asked, peering at the highly aromatic black brew.

'It's black tea with a very healthy dollop of black rum added. They make something very similar in Western Austria around Salzburg called *Jagertee!*' I added as the day's bit of trivia.

She tentatively sipped the brew and smiled with delight.

'Yum! Very tasty! It'll be even better on a cold day.'

Sandy took another big sip of hers and settled back into the cushions with a smile and a sigh, 'You don't know how good this feels to be with you guys and away from that bloody Southport station with that creepy ACP goose, Alistair Swinford sniffing around, trying to find someone poking into his precious investigation!'

She looked at me and asked, 'So, what's the go from here?'

'Well. Unless we come up with a better plan, I think we should head back to Three Hummock Island first thing and lay up again.'

She looked at Janice and me. 'Yes. That's a plan, but very soon, I think we need to meet with Janice's Dad to get him a copy of that HDD! I mean, that's going to be his main prosecution weapon!'

We looked at Janice and I asked, 'Sandy's right! What do you think? Is that something that we should do now or very soon?'

She nodded, 'Yes. Sooner, not later. We haven't had contact for a couple of weeks and even then, he thought his phones might be tapped, so I really don't know what's happening on the legal front!'

'Ok. So, we need to set up a safe meet so there's no chance that he could be traced to our location! Is that about it?'

Sandy grinned, 'Tall order! How do we contact him in the first place if his comms are tapped?'

'I've got a germ of an idea for that, so let's think about where we should meet!' .

Janice shrugged,' What about here?'

Sandy nodded, 'Tempting, but wouldn't that be making us look even more obvious?'

Janice shrugged again, 'Yes, it would, but it'll be so much easier with the airport handy and some friends ashore watching our backs.'

I nodded acceptance, 'True. I was keen to get away from here, but the pros probably outweigh the cons in favour of meeting him here, so long as our plans put a few safeguards in place.'

Janice looked pleased, then Sandy asked, 'How are you going to make contact with Robert in the first place, without alerting the bad guys?'

'Good question!' I thought a few moments, before looking at Janice; 'I think that certainly Robert's and most likely his shared secretary's phones might be bugged, but if we could contact one of the other barristers there, that might be safe. I don't suppose that you know one of the other guys or girls there?'

She thought a few moments. 'There is a female barrister whom I met at Dad's place a couple of times. I thought that they might hit it off, but unfortunately it didn't work out which was a pity since she's a really nice, fun lady! I think that I still have her mobile number in my address book. I'll just go look.'

While she was gone, I said quietly to Sandy, 'I'm avoiding any mention of our suspicions about the girls' sale for now!

'Yeah, you're right. No way! But we'll have to pass those thoughts on to Robert after they go shopping! And at some stage, you'll have to tell Janice. She'll kill you, or worse, if you don't!'

Janice returned, address book in hand. 'Yep! Here it is. Jacky Holt is her name.' She'd scribbled Jacky's number on a scrap of paper and handed it to me.

'Ok. I'll call her in the morning. But she doesn't know me, so she's very unlikely to do anything I say!'

I looked at Janice. 'Is there a phrase, or saying, or perhaps a reference to something that only you and her would know about? I just need something to convince her that I'm calling on your behalf. I'd get you to do it, but just in case, I don't want your voice going over a phone!'

Janice thought a few moments, then her face brightened, 'Yes! Once Dad had to go to Court at Geelong and was in such a hurry, he forgot his wig. Their secretary and Jacky were in a business meeting at the time, so the secretary called me to come in and pick it up from the office and chase after him. I didn't catch him until he got to the Courthouse, but it was in time! Jacky would remember that 'cause she really payed him out over that one!'

'Ok. That'll do. I'll say something about a wig to Geelong and hope she's happy with that! So! If I get her attention, I'll ask her to get Robert to go buy a burner phone and call me so I can pass on the contact plan.'

'Can I say hello too?' Janice asked wistfully.

'Yeah, yeah! You can. But jumping ahead, once Robert's aboard and everybody's said hello, you'll need to take the girls ashore for a while to get some supplies, while we show Robert the files and give him the copy we made.'

She nodded acceptance. 'Ok. I understand. But I'd like to be able to tell the girls the full story as soon as we can!'

I nodded agreement, then continued, 'Before he gets here, you'll have to write a Stat Dec to say that the original copy you made of Luke's computer drive has stayed under your secure control at all times since leaving the house, and that when I made the next three copies, your drive didn't leave your sight at any time. Then say that the extra copies we made were sealed in two brown manila envelopes with both our signatures across the flaps! That should satisfy the chain of evidence, with a bit of luck! One's for Robert and one for Annette.

After that, Robert has to see what we've seen on the drive, then we'll discuss the best way to get things happening to nullify Luke's search.'

Once more, I carefully refrained from mentioning in front of Janice the nasty bit about Luke selling the girls!

'The other concern is that those rock-spiders at the top of the ACP have a lot of pull and getting an investigation going will be difficult. Anyway, until we have Robert in front of us, we're only guessing, so what do you both think of that plan?'

Both ladies were agreeable, but as Sandy was yawning, Janice and I were tired and we'd covered things pretty well, we pulled the pin, turned off the lights, locked the doors and went to bed.

CHAPTER 22

FIREBIRD...WYNYARD TO THREE HUMMOCK IS, SATURDAY – EARLY MORNING

My usual built-in alarm clock woke me at 06:00, after a deep and dreamless sleep, so I felt more relaxed than I had for weeks. Janice snored softly on beside me and I almost felt guilty that shortly I'd have to wake the whole crew to get under way, but then decided to have a mug of tea up topside first and soak up more of the peace and tranquillity of the beautiful little harbour. There wasn't a breath of wind, and while the early morning sun glittered off the unruffled sheet of glass that was the river's surface, the outgoing tide made little swirls around the moored boats, then promptly disappeared as though they'd never been. The scattered trees on the shore bordering the small golf course opposite the wharf, stood bathed in soft, golden light.

I hadn't long sat in a bow seat and taken the first few sips of the hot, sweet liquid, when Sandy appeared, also with a mug of tea, and sat on the deck close by, leaning back against the life-lines.

'Sleep well?' I enquired.

'Like a log!' she grinned, 'I always did sleep well on *Firebird*! Spending the day travelling was a bit tiring as well, I suppose.'

'Well, you can kick back a bit now,' I said, 'Angie does the cooking, she and Zoe do the fishing, and Zoe does all the steering duty! All I do is navigate and yank a few strings occasionally!'

She laughed and I was very grateful that circumstances let her join us. Despite the bond I felt with Janice, I realised that sooner or later she and the girls would want to establish a new life for themselves and that would be that! In the meantime, I greatly enjoyed Sandy's company, so different to Janice in experience and outlook.

The fact that she was delightful to look at didn't hurt either!

'Just for the record,' she said, bringing my thoughts back to earth, 'I brought some hardware! I have my Glock 22 Service pistol and a bunch of extra magazines. Plus the usual handcuffs, capsicum spray and flick-extendable baton!'

I raised my eyebrows, 'That's a great collection to bring! Well done! Isn't your Glock in .40 S&W?'

She smiled, 'Yes, it is, but I've got a decent supply of ammunition. Have you still got those pump-action shotguns?'

'Yeah! One tucked away inside the cockpit table's seat back, and the other inside the helm seat back. You'd never find them if you didn't know where to look! There's a pile of ammo for them, in a hidden locker behind the main switchboard, mostly SG, but there are some Brenneke rounds as well, in case some longer range deterrence is needed!'

'Good choice, but let's hope we don't need to use them!'

'Amen to that.'

'When do we leave?' she asked.

'Probably very soon. I held off 'cause everyone was so tired, but you and I are up, so the rest can be too!'

Suiting action to the words, I took our empty mugs and headed for the cockpit.

'Can I do anything?' Sandy called.

'Nah! With no wind in here, we'll have to motor out a way until we can pick up some. There's no real hurry, but thanks anyway. Kick back and enjoy life on the bounding main!'

I rinsed our mugs and started the engines one after the other. Checking that oil pressure came up and charging current was flowing, I hit the anchor winch button, making sure that the chain washing jets came on as well. Watching the chain counter, I slowed the retrieval then stopped it neatly when the anchor snugged firmly into its security socket.

Engaging forward drive on both engines, *Firebird* slowly gathered way and slipped almost silently toward the open sea. A faint farewell floated across the pellucid water, and I saw old Ernie waving from the jetty. I returned the gesture, before returning my attention to tracking by the shore leads to stay in the channel.

It was 07:30 by the time we'd cleared the breakwater at the mouth of the river, and Janice had dragged herself out of bed to make an appearance. The twins followed close behind, and I scored a kiss from all three, but then there was a great bustle in the galley as they all wanted tea and breakfast together. With Bass Strait so flat calm, Angie started cooking a hot brekkie, a rare treat at sea, even though catamarans sail so flat. Before long, another mug of hot tea was parked in front of me and a large bacon, egg and cheese toasted sanger was handed across.

Sandy came aft to retrieve hers, but then went up for'rard again, to be joined by Janice with her food. I stayed on the wheel for a short while, watching the interaction between the two ladies, but although they talked a great deal, everything seemed very amicable.

We maintained our most economical motoring speed of 8knots and I let Zoe take the wheel while we waited for the breeze to arrive. Actually, she more or less pushed me off the helm seat to make room for Jasper, so I gave in gracefully and went for'rard to sit with the ladies.

'What time would Jackie normally be at the office?' I asked Janice.

'Normally 09:00 to 09:30.'

'So, if I called her now, would she still be at home?'

'Oh yes. For sure!'

I went aft and found *Firebird's* mobile in the nav station charger, before re-joining the ladies up front, the piece of paper with the number on it clutched firmly in my hand.

I carefully dialled the number, and finally heard the ring tone.

'Hello?' came a professional-sounding female voice,

'Good morning, Jackie. You don't know me, and I apologise in advance for being devious, but I'd like you to hear me out. This is not a telemarketer call.'

There was a silence that I took to be positive, so I quickly continued,

'I'm calling on behalf of a person you know and may have been concerned about recently. I don't want to say too much, but this person was a key player in the Geelong wig chase. Does that help?'

She was silent for a few moments, and then chuckled, a warm, throaty sound that raised a tingle down my spine. 'Oh, most certainly yes, it does help! Is our friend alright?'

'Yes. The whole package is well, and with me now.'

'I presume that you want a message passed to someone else?'

'You can presume that, and in turn, how secure can we consider your phone?'

'Reasonably so. But the office phone system seems to have been infested with bugs lately. We have an exterminator coming in today. So, we should keep it short and cryptic!'

'That's my intention. Now, would you ask our friend to buy several pre-paid mobile phones, a very basic version, and use one to call this number ASAP, but from somewhere away from the office!'

'Copy that! Take extreme care and pass on my best to the package!'

With a click, she was gone. I checked the phone log and saw we'd been connected just 30 seconds!

'That was usefully short and sweet,' Sandy commented.

'Yes. Now we wait for Robert, but I've just realised that I've made a mistake!'

The ladies raised their eyebrows at me and smirked at each other. 'Really!' Sandy commented sarcastically. 'Can this be the real Harry, admitting a mistake?'

I poked my tongue out at her, while Janice giggled.

'Yes. I buggered up! I called Jacky on the boat's cell phone, but if we get too far out to sea, we won't get reception! I should've used the sat-phone. Still, too late now, but there's a work-around, we'll just have to stay inshore, although it won't make any difference since were not in a hurry and I can pass the sat-phone number to Robert directly!'

By now the breeze was starting to kick in from the southwest, so I shut down the engines and set about hoisting sails, while directing Zoe to steer a course that would keep us within a mile of the shore. Fortunately, there weren't any hard bits sticking out of the water for her to dodge, so I left it to her to steer a suitable course.

Two hours later, we were 0.75nm ENE of Stanley, of 'The Nut' fame, when the phone rang, and I answered.

'Hello?'

…'Excellent, Robert. I'm Harry and I have a lot of information and questions for you, but first, for verification, you might like to very briefly say hello to someone!'

I handed the phone to Janice who was already tearing up.

…'Hi, Dad! It's so good to hear your voice, but we can't talk much at the moment.'

…'Yes, we're all very well. In fact, never better and being looked after and protected by two wonderful people!'

…'I can't say where we are, please Dad! Just in case, you know?'

…'Yes. We need to do that ASAP and Harry has a plan to achieve that and to protect us at the same time. He needs to talk to you right now! I'll see you soon Dad. Bye now.'

With tears leaking down her cheeks, she handed the phone back to me and turned to bury her face in Sandy's chest. I tried to feel only slightly envious as I spoke to Robert.

'Hi, Robert, Harry back.'

…'It's a very long story, Robert, that'll have to wait a little while.'

…'It's water, Robert. Moving wet stuff.'

…'Sorry, I get that way sometimes…No. You can assume what you like, but I can't tell you that at this time and you should stop voicing your assumptions, big ears and all that!

…As Janice said, they are all very well and safe at the moment. How long that happy state of affairs lasts could very well depend on you and your actions!'

…'Yes, I am!

… No, you can't now, but I really need for you to stop asking questions that can wait and pull that very expensive pen out of your pocket and start writing what I tell you on your legal pad!'

...'Yes, I do know who you are, you're Janice's father firstly and a well-connected barrister secondly! That's all I need to know, and all you need to remember right now, apart from the fact that you're wasting my time and increasing the chances we can be overheard!'

...'Thank you. That's better! OK, OK. Accepted! Now, here's the plan and you should make the bookings several days in advance, just to be sure, but do so yourself on one of these phones and away from the office. Have you ever been followed by bad guys before?'

...'Excellent! So, I don't have to explain, because you certainly are now!'

...'Completely serious! Look around on your way back to the office and I bet you'll see two or more faces that you don't recognise but think that you've seen before. They'll be pretending not to look at you. Once you start really looking, they'll stand out like tits on a bull!'

...'Yes. I know you are; and so are we, so we must move on or we'll never get this situation fixed and like it or not, you're now a key player.'

Now that he'd stopped blustering about being a father and grandfather with his daughter and granddaughters in danger, he reverted to his barrister persona and became very efficient, so I laid out the plan quickly and concisely.

...'Yep! That's the plan. We need at least three or four hours to bring you up to date, but it could be longer. As outlined, you'd better plan to stay overnight. You'll understand the secrecy better after you hear what we have to say and show you.'

...'Yes, it is very messy and involves a lot of VIPs in high places, which is why there's such a hunt going on! To put it into perspective, it could turn out to be a Government toppler!'

...'Yes, sir. That's exactly what I said, and you really need to bear that in mind!'

...'So that you might understand just how serious this really is!

To say that these people will stop at nothing to keep the lid on this is an understatement!'

...'Yes, I did mean that. Nothing is sacred to them except their rotten hides!'

...'Look Robert. Of course, we need to meet, but it can't be until Tuesday. We have to let the movement of another piece of the puzzle settle down.'

...'Sorry to be so cryptic, but we'll explain everything when we talk and you'll understand it all, but it has to be face-to-face.'

...'Yes, we'll be there. I'll 99% guarantee it, even though there will always be some factors outside our control. In the meantime, think the plan through and refine your end if you want, but keep all the safeguards in place and let me know immediately if you can't do as we've planned. I don't want to expose us unnecessarily. Have you got all that for now? We really must get off the phone.'

...'Ok, great, Robert. I'll give them a hug from you. Call this other number if you need to and to let me know that the plan is on track!'

I read out the boat's sat-phone number and checked as he crisply read it back.

...'Terrific! You're welcome, cheers for now. Bye!'

'Wow! That was a marathon,' Sandy commented, as I gave Zoe and Angie the promised hug from their Granddad.

'It certainly was.' I looked at Janice then cuddled her close. 'He can be a bit stubborn at times, your Dad.'

'I'm afraid so, but is he going to follow the plan?'

'Yes, I'm pretty sure he will. He saw the sense in it finally.'

I leant past them to call to back my first mate. 'Steer a direct course for Three Hummock Island, please, Zoe!'

She only had a minor correction to make and as it was a little more off the wind, I left the sails alone and let *Firebird* romp on.

I relieved Zoe at the wheel while Janice and Angie brought her up to date and had a brief family discussion, then let her take over again, as the miles swooshed past and Sandy got her first taste of effortless passage-making, at least on a minor scale.

The look of delight permanently on her pretty face was a pleasure to see.

Despite the slight diversion, we were dropping anchor back in the same spot in the north end of the pristine and deserted East Telegraph Bay well before midday.

As we all were at the time of our first visit, Sandy was absolutely entranced with the beauty and serenity of the place with the stark white sand beach and the barely-rippling clear water surrounding us.

'No wonder you wanted to come back here,' she breathed, taking in the near-silence once I'd shut off the engines, with just a gentle breeze blowing woody scents off the scrubby land.

Now the breeze had dropped in the lee of the land, we noticed that the air was warmer than at Wynyard, which prompted the girls to whoop with delight, and, forgetting that Sandy wasn't used to their antics, drop their clothes on the daybed and dive in off the stern. Jasper didn't hesitate to jump in with them and swam ashore for a brief romp on the sand, before returning to play with the girls.

Sandy's reaction was to laugh at their delightful lack of inhibition, express wonder at Jasper's apparent love of swimming and carry on helping Janice make sandwiches for lunch. We'd grabbed a few fresh loaves of bread from Mavis at the Jetty Hotel last night, so that would extend our stocks of sandwich-making ingredients a little longer.

We ate while the girls frolicked around and under the boat, then they climbed out, showered salt off each other and Jasper, who promptly bounded up to the cockpit to shake himself over the three of us, while the girls grabbed the last few sandwiches. They didn't bother dressing and I could see by Sandy's half-smile that she was happily re-assessing the situation, as I hadn't gone into details of all the finer points of life afloat with two uninhibited 18 year olds.

The rest of the day we just lounged, Sandy visibly relaxing, although we all went for a long beach walk in the afternoon. Only the girls went naked this time, and Jasper clearly loved having an extra person to play around.

Once back aboard, Janice, Sandy and I sat round to have a bit of a planning session. I invited the girls to sit in, but they said they were happy just messing about with Jasper and watching a movie.

'I'll catch them up later on just the stuff they need to know,' she offered, 'they are very interested in seeing Pop again, of course, but they get bored with adult planning sessions. They've not been told of the photos and the Ring, of course!'

I nodded approval, as we started to pick our way through the actions we'd hopefully put in place to make contact with Robert, to see if we could find any flaws or loopholes. It was hard to find a glaring fault, because so much depended on the actions of others, but we still talked it through and that seemed to help ease the feeling of mounting pressure. I had a nasty feeling in the back of my mind that something was about to come unstuck, and at this stage there was little we could do about it!

'I think we should hear from Annette at ACP,' I said looking at Sandy, 'what's the arrangement for contacting her?'

'I call her on her personal mobile,' she replied, 'do you want to check in so soon?'

'Yeah. I think we should.' I looked at both ladies, thoughts tumbling through my mind, like leaves blowing in a wind, and just about as chaotic!

'But just thinking ahead for a moment, I reckon that after Robert gets to review all the files, documents and photos, Annette should see all that evidence as well!'

I looked at Sandy. 'And we mustn't forget that you haven't seen the evidence yet either, so we'd better get you to view that soon as.'

'Yes, please. Can we perhaps do it this evening after the girls have gone to bed?'

'Sure,' I replied, 'It'll take a long time to go through the lot, but you could do what I did the first time and just skim a cross-section. That'll at least give you an idea of the scope of this thing.'

'Okay. That'll do.'

Janice nodded, 'Are you thinking of trying to get Annette down here to see us, or could we get dear old Dad to go to see her?'

I smiled appreciation, 'Yeah! I was tossing around both ideas. If your Dad went to Canberra to see her, he'd have to be very careful to cover his tracks otherwise he'd make a direct connection to Annette for the bad guys to maybe follow and act on!'

Sandy chipped in, 'But if Annette were to come down to Wynyard to see us, although it's more trouble to do so, it's maybe safer for her?'

'It might be safer, but she'd have to travel on her own time,' Janice played devil's advocate, 'There'd be two flights to connect and catch each way, and there won't be the convenient excuse of a client visit for her!'

'That's right,' I put in, 'so I'm more inclined to ask Robert to visit her. They don't have to meet in Canberra, it could be somewhere not far away like Cooma or Yass;, it's only a 40 minutes drive out of Canberra, but maybe we should wait until after we've spoken with Robert and laid this stuff on him, 'cause at the moment, he doesn't know anything about the rock-spider ring!'

'Yeah! You're right,' Sandy sighed, 'we keep forgetting that we're the only ones who know about Luke's secret life and the real reason he's chasing Janice and the girls!'

I didn't comment on that, so she looked at me and said, 'Oh dear. Janice, we have to take care when Harry goes quiet. It usually means he's thinking and that's very dangerous!'

Janice giggled, something she'd become prone to do a lot.

'Ok, smart arse,' I grinned, 'I *was* thinking, but even further ahead! So even after we let Robert and Annette know the scope of this thing, that still just makes five of us who know the story! Earlier, to impress Robert, I used the term 'Government toppling'! The more I think about it, the more I believe that that's exactly what this thing could be! In which case, there would be some very heavy hitters lined up against us.

We'd have to hope that when it blows up, there are a few Supreme Court Judges who *don't* like playing around with little kids!'

Now it was Sandy's turn to go thoughtful. 'Just carrying on with that thought. What we're talking about is maybe some form of Insurance!'

'Yes,' Janice came back with, 'so what if we went to the press? Pick a reputable newspaper and a reporter with solid credentials. A paper and reporter known to be impartial to Government policy or influence, and with a record of digging out dirt!'

'I like that,' I said, 'but what paper and which reporter?'

It was Sandy's turn to look thoughtful. 'I did read the other day that Hillary Jones received an award for being the most objective investigative journalist in Australia. She's freelance, but the Age in Melbourne and the Sydney Morning Herald print a lot of her stuff. She was or is, a professor at Sydney UT and has received a Walkley Award for articles about Police corruption. She also claims that her writing is "for those who resist abuses of power and seek social justice, rather than to support existing political power structures". She says "people should be encouraged to do what is necessary to oppose injustice."'

I blinked. 'Wow! That's heavy stuff. But can she back it up?'

'Oh, yes,' Sandy came back, 'she's become somewhat of a reluctant celebrity figure in media circles for her outspoken attitudes, but she's so high profile, none of the bad guys she exposes dare touch her!'

'Well, isn't that exactly who we should be taking to?' Janice demanded.

'Yes,' I said, thoughtfully 'you're absolutely right. She sounds exactly the right person. But how are we going to manage it? We can't just dump this whole mess in her lap! I mean, if even a hint of this leaks, there'd be bad guys ducking for cover and getting rid of a whole bunch of kids in five minutes flat, just to protect their arses!'

Sandy commented, 'Let's wait until we've seen Robert, but in the meantime, we, that is Harry, should come up with a plan to contact and meet with Miss Jones ASAP. Harry, you come up with the contact plan!'

We decided to stop about then and conned the girls into making afternoon tea, which they did so quite happily, and joined us in the cockpit to enjoy it.

'Do we have a plan of action for the next few days?' Janice looked at me.

'Yes, as a matter of fact,' I was happy to reply, 'tomorrow, Sunday, in case anyone is losing track, I'd like to drag *Firebird* into the shallows a bit more, and scrub her bottom. If we all go over the side with scrubbing brushes and Scotch-Brite pads, it won't take long. If you four do the sides from just above the waterline down as far as you can reach, I'll put on the Hookah gear and get right underneath where you can't reach.'

That plan seemed to meet with general approval, so I continued. 'Then on Monday, we'll make the run to Wynyard in the afternoon, aiming to get in around 16:30 or so. The winds are forecast to back around at least to the North by then, so we should get a good run, although there will still be a fairly heavy southerly swell, but that won't bother us at all. We'll stay the night and Tuesday morning at 09:55, Robert should lob into town and that's when the fun starts.'

They all looked excited by the thought of some water fun followed by a half-day of action sailing, with, hopefully, a meeting with dear Daddy/Pop at the end!

Somehow, using the Weber BBQ, Angie managed a roast lamb dinner for us, with real roast vegies and greens, and it was a huge success!

Afterwards, we introduced Sandy to what had become a staple evening entertainment, cheating at Scrabble! Finally, the girls were yawning so much they announced they were going to bed, taking the ever faithful and spoiled Jasper with them. With the three adults left alone, I brought the laptop with the files on it out into the cockpit and set it up in front of Sandy so that even if one of the girls came out, the screen wouldn't be immediately visible. After showing her where the folders were, Janice and I chatted about nothing much, while Sandy's muttered curses grew more and more foul!

Finally, she clicked her way out of everything and flipped the lid closed.

'I could do with something to drink after that lot!' she exclaimed. 'What an incredible collection of absolute depravity and as you said, I recognised quite a few faces! Why didn't the idiots wear masks at least? Like, how stupid were they to think that those files would never be seen by anyone outside the circle?'

I retired to the galley to make my speciality, NQ tea.

When Sandy took her first sip of the steaming, black aromatic liquid, her eyes lit up.

'Yum! You didn't serve this last time,' she commented.

I smiled, 'It didn't seem appropriate last time, but it seems to be so here!'

Both ladies seemed to agree with that thought, and even Sandy's anger quickly subsided as a second round went down almost as quickly as the first. I was amused when they lined up for a third, since I was using a double nip of OP Bundy rum in each serve, but finally the OP kicked in and they slowed a lot on the third and both showed signs of being quite pissed! Giggly pissed which was healthy and funny for me! So, when that one was finished, we agreed to head for bed, but not before Janice and I were soundly hugged and kissed by a now very relaxed Sandy.

The feel of her firm breasts jammed tightly against my chest was impossible to ignore and my loins reacted all too quickly, which Janice noticed to her very vocal amusement. Sandy pretended not to notice, while I was just glad that Janice didn't seem jealous in any way!

As was my habit, I headed straight for our dressing room and peeled off my clothes.

Janice took one look and started giggling again. 'Oh dear! It really doesn't take much to set you off, does it?'

I pretended to glare at her. 'Well if you were a male and got hugged like that by a very well-built young lady, you just might have a reaction too!'

She got as close as she could without getting poked too hard and hugged me.

'That's alright. I'm female and I enjoyed it too!'

I looked at her in surprise, 'Really?'

She gave one of those enigmatic smiles that ladies seem to produce at the most maddening moments, instead of a proper verbal explanation and headed for the bathroom. I followed and we had a brief shower together, too mindful of water conservation to fool around too much in the confined space. Well, maybe just a tiny bit!

We weren't long with the bathroom routine, and soon were snuggled up in bed, my arm around Janice, gently stroking her left breast. She occupied herself by playing with the appendage that had caused her so much mirth earlier. We were just fooling around quietly and enjoying it immensely, when there was a knock at the open cabin door and Sandy said softly, 'Are you guys decent?'

Janice giggled and replied, 'I sort of am, but perhaps Harry isn't, although that probably depends on how you define decent! But come in anyway and we'll discuss the definition!'

Sandy chuckled and came in, perching on the end of the bed. She wore just a long T-shirt like the girls did, although in Sandy's case, it had a bit more to cover and although it was having a tough job keeping things decent, Sandy didn't try to help. She smiled at Janice, sitting up with the sheet down around her waist and erect nipples on display, then looked across at where I was trying, but failing to disguise my rampant erection with artfully arranged folds of sheet!

'Is he like this all the time?' she asked, making herself comfortable.

Janice grinned and looked fondly at the tangled mess I'd made of the sheet in my lap.

'Yeah! Pretty much! He's a bit smaller sometimes, but that's not often!'

'Hang on!' I retorted indignantly, 'I hang down most of the time!'

Janice smiled gently, 'Yeah. But even pointing down, it's not exactly shrivelled up, now is it? And the only time it's like that is when the girls and I aren't in sight and you're concentrating of some boat stuff, maybe! But just one flash of a bare female bum, tit or pussy and you're off!'

Sandy broke down laughing, so all I could do was sit there, abstractly noting that the object of their attention was not subsiding at all! That obvious fact hadn't gone un-noticed by the ladies either!

Sandy finally settled and said, 'Despite the fun we're having with Harry's erection, I actually came in to see if you had any anti-itch cream. I scraped my back up near my shoulder-blade this afternoon and now that I've showered, it's itchy and I can't really get at it.'

'Oh, sure,' Janice said, sliding gracefully out of bed and down to the lower floor, 'I've got some great analgesic & antiseptic cream that's really good on scratches.'

I noted Sandy paying close attention to her as she padded unconcernedly naked through to the dressing cabin, scrabbled through a drawer and returned with the appropriate medication.

'Here we are. Now, where's the problem?'

In answer, Sandy stood so she could drag the T-shirt out from under her bum, and then dragged it right up to her neck which had the disturbing effect of baring her entire side, neck to knee including the delightfully full profile of her left breast and a firm and shapely bum. She looked over her left shoulder.

'Just inside my left shoulder blade. It feels like a torn area of skin.'

Janice looked, 'Yup! Just a bit abraded. This'll fix it,' as she rubbed the cream in gently.

Within a minute, Sandy sighed, 'Oh, that's better!' She tugged her T-shirt down and turned to go with a cheeky grin. 'I'll leave you in peace now. Have fun!'

So we did and as Janice was considerably more amorous than usual, I was unsure if it was due to the Jamaican Tea or the interaction we'd had with Sandy. On reflection later, I felt that it was more likely to be the latter. I was also thankful that the genteel snoring from the girls' cabin, drifting through the open overhead hatches, suggested that they had been fast asleep throughout.

EAST TELEGRAPH BAY TO THREE HUMMOCK ISLAND, SUNDAY MORNING

Sunday dawned clear, with a soft, warm breeze drifting off the scrubby land and along the beach from the Northwest. I sipped my morning cuppa, perched as usual on the foredeck bow seat and was joined by Jasper, wanting head and back scratches, after he'd performed his usual morning toilet routine without the fuss most cats carry on with. I wasn't surprised to be joined soon after I'd cleaned his toilet mat, by Sandy looking terrific wearing a bikini top and a pair of loose shorts with her mug of tea. The subtle change in our relationship that I'd drowsily decided last night was unlikely, became reality when I received a very warm kiss in greeting, before she parked herself on the deck at my feet.

'Good sleep?' I enquired softly.

'Oh, yes!' she smiled, 'really good. I didn't stir all night and feel really refreshed! Must be the sea air!'

I grinned back, 'Yep! That can do it! Janice and the girls are still asleep. They can sleep-in this morning and tomorrow for that matter. There's no rush.'

'How so?'

'We only have a four-hour sail to get to Wynyard. So we don't have to leave until midday or so.'

'Oh, okay. That makes it very relaxed.'

'Yeah. It would've been a lot more rushed and uncomfortable for us to get to Macquarie Harbour! Plus, it's got a very dangerous and narrow entrance that we'd have had to run at just the right time. So, all in all, going to Wynyard is a much easier choice.'

She nodded understanding as we sipped out tea in companionable silence, just soaking up the unspoiled beauty of the place.

After a while she asked, 'What's the area like if we do get to go down there?'

I smiled. 'Very different to this; beautiful in its own right, being very wild and rugged! For a start, there's so much rainfall, the water in Macquarie Harbour is part fresh and both there and to a lesser extent in Port Davey, it's stained a brown or tan colour due to the tannin from the heavy forests that cover the whole landscape. It's a true wilderness, although Macquarie Harbour has a fair amount of traffic with salmon fisheries, tourist boats and fishermen. Port Davey has fewer visitors, being very remote with no towns and only a couple of isolated farms. There are a few 4WD tracks for the adventurous souls and of course boaties and charter boats visit in the summer months. Winter weather is usually bad with an almost continuous series of cold fronts delivering lots of rain and keeping the sea rough.'

Sandy gave a shudder as she looked around. 'So we might have to leave this idyllic paradise to go hang out in a remote hellhole?'

'No. It's definitely not a hellhole! At least not in summer! You'll like it if we go, wait and see. It's just different! Besides, we don't have to stay down there if we decide that we can remain safely below Luke's radar by continuing to hang around here! Apart from this bay, there're others on the other side of the island and on the next island west, Hunter Island. White sand beaches and crystal-clear water!'

Sandy smiled, 'That's sounds more like my idea of a place to hang about and hide out!'

'True. I didn't know how good this place was going to be. It really is beautiful! Anyway, at least we don't have to rush off there anytime soon, but let's talk about it over breakfast. Plans can be changed if necessary!'

Just then, a plaintive, slightly croaky voice floated up from the master cabin hatch.

'Any chance of a mug of tea?'

Sandy and I laughed as I called back, 'Coming dear!' I went to get up, but Sandy waved me back down.

'Stay there. I'll get it. I want to have a girl talk with Janice. Do you want another tea?'

I nodded, slightly puzzled, but resigned to the fact that the females aboard did do odd things for even odder reasons that a mere male couldn't fathom.

I admired the slight swing of her shapely hips and the bounce of her breasts as she rose and took both mugs below, leaning back with a contented sigh as I thought that even in a fairly dire situation, life was still rather pleasant!

Despite the distractions, I applied my thinking to our various meeting schedules coming up to make sure that we were still staying low-profile enough by using Wynyard as a pickup point instead of making the long run down to Strahan, which carried the risk of having bad weather cut us off.

Access by air to Wynyard was obviously much easier, and although the others could make the drive to Strahan without too much trouble, it would be a lot more difficult for us! I was still mulling over options when Sandy re-appeared with a fresh tea for me which she handed over with just one of those enigmatic female smiles, before she turned to go below for her 'girl talk' with Janice.

The very pleasant view of her coming and going did stir things in my groin, just as Janice had stated last night, but I didn't see a problem with lusting after one lovely lady while sharing a bed with another! Angie and Zoe wandered up to me about then, mugs in hand, which helped divert my attention from thinking about Janice and Sandy. At least they were dressed.

The girls parked themselves and inquired about what they called '*Firebird's* arse-cleaning' exercise coming up later. We chatted back and forth until Zoe asked, 'Where's Mum and Sandy?'

I grinned at her. 'They're down below having a girl's talk. What-ever that is!'

'Oh. One of those! Mum and Dad used to have those all the time. Right before he walloped her again!'

I nodded in sympathy, but there wasn't much to say about that.

JANICE:

She woke slowly, her mind still a bit muzzy from what was for her, the excessive number of Jamaican Tea's consumed the previous evening. After padding aft to pee and wash her face and other bits, she returned to bed and called through the hatch overhead for a mug of hot tea. She expected to be told to get it herself, but decided to wait a while, just in case. It was then that her memory caught up and she blushed a little as she remembered the almost animal passion that had overcome her as she wrestled with Harry the previous evening. He was at least partly to blame, she recalled, if the residual soreness in her groin was anything to go by.

As she lay propped up on the pillows, she ran her hands up and down her bare body but couldn't feel any bruises. She also recalled, with pleasure, Sandy's very provocative visit and the fun they'd had laughing at Harry's efforts to disguise his erection! Her thoughts drifted over what was said and perhaps not said and wondered where that was all leading.

It was just as some thoughts were starting to gel, when Sandy herself waltzed in, looking disgustingly bright and cheerful, but at least bearing the life-saving mug of hot tea.

'Here you are sleepy-head!' she chuckled, 'it's a lovely day outside, warming up nicely, so a swim after breakfast will be just the thing to get you going!'

Her breezy attitude needed to be absorbed slowly, so Janice sipped her tea in silence, until she felt the hot liquid working its usual magic. She grinned at Sandy.

'We played up a bit last night, didn't we?'

Sandy smirked back. 'Just a little! But it was fun, wasn't it?'

Janice had to giggle. 'Yes, it was. I enjoyed it heaps! But you were an awful tease to poor Harry! His erection wouldn't go down for ages!'

Sandy tried to look contrite but failed! 'I'd say sorry, but I'm not! Especially as you got all the benefit from my efforts! Although I suspect that when you did your little naked parade to get that excellent cream, it might have helped!'

Janice grinned, 'We both were more vigorous than usual, so I suppose I did get the benefits and I'm still feeling a bit sore to prove it. But very nicely so!'

Sandy chuckled again, 'That's alright. I'm just jealous! Don't worry about me.'

Janice looked pensive. 'Oh, of course. I hadn't thought of it that way, but I do understand.'

Sandy shrugged. 'So, what do you intend when all this nonsense is over? Have you thought that far?'

Janice hitched herself up in the bed, the sheet pushed down to mid-thigh, and tossed Harry's pillows to Sandy so she could prop them behind herself. Sandy got comfortable with her back against the aft bulkhead on Harry's side of the bed.

'I'm not sure, exactly. I mean, the girls have to finish Uni sooner or later and I'd like to be able to provide a stable home life for that! Then presuming that Luke gets locked up for a very long time, which is the least he deserves, I'll have to sell the house, although the big turd's probably got it mortgaged to cover that den of iniquity he bought! Anyway, I could never live in it again! There are way too many bad memories and to me, it'll always be tainted by evil!'

Sandy nodded understanding, before gently probing, 'So based on that, how serious are things with Harry, if you don't mind my asking?'

Janice smiled, 'Of course I don't mind anything you ask! After all you've done and are still doing, I could never repay you properly! But to answer your question, so far, I think that Harry and I are just having a great time, without getting serious! I desperately needed someone I could trust and relax with and he met that need! He's been caring, funny and very protective of the girls and me and of course, the sex is great; it's lovely to feel a real man inside me again! And of course, since he treats the girls really well and respects them, they love him like a favourite Uncle, and he loves them back!'

Sandy butted in with, 'But how did the girls take to you and Harry sharing a bed?'

Janice giggled, 'Oh, there never was a problem with that! They actually wanted me to and were concerned that I'd waited so long, even though it took less than three days from the time we met before we first got it off!'

'So, they weren't upset?'

'Good grief, no! Like I said, they were delighted, they love Harry and were just waiting for us to get together.'

Sandy shook her head. 'They certainly are amazing girls. So, what started them running around naked in front of Harry?'

'Oh, they've always done that at home, which is where those photos that Harry's told you about came from, so they were very comfortable and used to doing that. But with Harry, that took about two days, I think.'

Sandy smiled, 'Sorry to interrupt, I just wondered about those points and what the girls' attitude was like, but obviously there's no worries there. Please go on.'

So, Janice resumed, 'I was going to say that of course there's Jasper, who's almost done as much to help stabilise the girls as anything else. I mean, they were getting very edgy with the constant running from Luke's goons, but there's something almost mystical about that beautiful cat, he seems to really understand people and know what they need. And he certainly does understand Harry and most of what he says! I don't know what it is, but he's a big part of the soothing magic this whole boat seems to lay on troubled souls!'

She looked a bit embarrassed. 'Sorry for the philosophical observations. I guess I've been one of those troubled souls for way too long!'

She paused a moment to gather her thoughts, before resuming.

'However, I just don't know how I could work being a full-time mother to the girls, as well as sailing around with Harry. As much fun as that would be! But I'm a bit uneasy about the dark and very serious side to him that I can't see into. On the surface he's great, funny and caring, but deep down, he doesn't talk about his previous life at all except to say where and what he was. Do you think it goes back to Afghanistan?'

Sandy nodded. 'Yes. From what I've gathered and been told, he had a very rough time there and lost most of his sub-unit in a very nasty fight with the Taliban.'

'I don't know much about how the SAS work, but a Major doesn't normally lead a unit, does he?'

'Well, no. Definitely not! That's a Lieutenant's job! But at the time, there was some cock-up with the Intel for a scouting party and their Lieutenant was sent elsewhere playing nursemaid to a bunch of Aussie pollies on a junket, while a bunch of his guys were caught in an ambush by some bad guys. Harry was just doing his thing in HQ, some distance away from the firefight and found out about the ambush just in time to quickly form a small squad from a few of the guys who were hanging around Base and went to get them out.

He saved most of those that were left, by running back and forth in the open with a machine gun, attracting the bad guys' fire to himself long enough for his troops to break out of where they were pinned down. While he was spraying bullets around and attracting fire, he managed to take out quite a few bad guys, including two of the senior tribal leaders they'd been chasing for months! He was hit a couple of times, lost most of the small unit he'd scraped together, carried one wounded squaddie out over his shoulder while under fire, and eight of his original unit survived. Nevertheless, he felt really bad about losing most of the scratch unit, but he scored the Victoria Cross for Australia for his actions!'

'Wow!' Janice's eyes were wide. 'I had no idea!'

'Yeah, well, no one does really! He keeps all that war stuff locked away – which isn't healthy! Maybe that's why he needs stress relief and focuses on sex rather than hitting the bottle or drugs like many others!'

Janice giggled, and then added seriously, 'But that hasn't worked very well until now. I heard that he hadn't had a girl aboard for months, before the girls and I lobbed on his doorstep!'

Sandy gave a lecherous grin. 'So, he's choosy, and correct me if I'm wrong, but my guess is that he's been making up for that drought ever since?'

Janice had the grace to blush a bit, the colour of which spread in an intriguing manner down to her bare chest, Sandy couldn't help but note, feeling some interesting sensations of her own as she gazed at Janice's well-toned body, most of which was revealed by the sheet slipping lower and lower as Janice wriggled about.

'Yes, you're right. In fact, that might explain why he's so...very demanding, active and recovers very quickly.'

'That's handy,' Sandy commented with a grin, 'it's always good to have a guy who doesn't need a day or so to recover.'

'So, what are your plans?' Janice asked, 'I can see how much you like Harry, he obviously likes you and that's totally fine by me. I mean, I don't mind sharing his affections if that's what you'd like! I'd be very happy to do so, but I suppose it could be a little bit awkward since Harry and I fell in lust very quickly and now we're sharing a bed, but there's no way I'm going to be jealous about anything you and he want to do! Bearing in mind that one day, when this bad stuff is settled, the girls and I will have to be moving on! But also remember that the girls sort of expect that he and I will share a bed for now and as I said, they've been really happy for me now that I've been having very regular sex!'

She giggled at Sandy's questioning look. 'Before Harry, sex for me has been a highly irregular and totally unsatisfying occurrence! My former husband was sexually challenged in just about every possible way you could think of, although he did just manage to produce enough sperm to help create the twins, but even a Doctor had to insert that! The useless shit couldn't even manage to get that far enough into me for it to take!'

She looked thoughtfully at Sandy. 'You know, the girls have really taken to you too, so I'm sure there won't be any problems if they see you and Harry being rather more affectionate than might be usual! I mean they've always been very open and relaxed about sex and nudity! If necessary, I'll have a word to them that we aren't really lifetime commitment-type serious and they'll understand.'

Sandy blinked at Janice's unexpected candour and took a few moments to reply.

'I've felt close to Harry ever since we last worked together and found that we got on very well, but as much as I wanted to, there wasn't really an opportunity to develop that level of friendship any further.

Honestly, I'd very much like to do so now that we're in this very interesting environment and perhaps have the opportunity, but maybe because of the girls, and since you're being so open and relaxed about this, can we just be discrete about what we do? Would that work?'

Janice smiled happily and felt compelled to crawl over to kiss Sandy full on the lips and hug her as best she could. She was surprised by the intensity with which her affection was returned and what was to be a quick hug and kiss, lasted a lot longer and started to turn into something rather deeper.

'Of course, we can make it work! It'll be great fun! We just need to get Harry to play the game. I mean, he can be very uptight and way too proper for his own good sometimes. For instance, it took days before he'd even look at the girls when they first stripped off! And he was even worse when they got bored one day and experimented with shaving each other! It was hilarious, they asked him to admire their handiwork, while he was trying desperately not to look at them while the bulge in his pants was getting bigger by the second. The girls couldn't stop giggling!'

Turning serious Janice hugged Sandy again, 'I'm so glad we can be close like this! Apart from Harry and the girls, I've not had anyone I could really talk intimate girl stuff with for a very long time!

When I was living with Luke, I had to stop going to visit my old girlfriends because there was always a fresh crop of bruises or breaks that I didn't dare show!'

Sandy nodded her understanding, 'I can work on Harry, now that I know you're happy and relaxed with this...unusual arrangement we've discussed. It's all very strange to me, even talking about it, but I'm willing to see how things work out. Either way, I'll be happy, just knowing that we have this understanding.'

They separated and Janice crawled out of bed and dropped gracefully to the floor, happily conscious of Sandy's gaze on her.

'I might as well get up now,' she said, searching for something to put on. 'Breakfast is calling, and Harry will want us to go clean the boat's bum after that!'

Sandy chuckled, then wriggled off the bed as well, somewhat less gracefully than Janice and dropped to the floor beside her. She kissed Janice lightly and said, 'Are we good with this as well as with Harry?'

Janice nodded with a smile, so Sandy found the empty mugs and headed for the galley, calling for the girls to start breakfast.

CHAPTER 25

Luke's mobile phone buzzed and vibrated itself in a frenzy, leaping all over the bedside table until he managed to push the slumbering body that was partly draped across him onto the other side of the bed.

He had severe difficulty in saying anything intelligent, but after a sip of water from the bottle on his bedside table, he managed a croak when he finally managed to quieten the buzzing monster.

'This better be fucking good Jimmy, or your arse is toast!'

Knowing that his boss' sayings were all too often very literal, Jimmy swallowed before speaking.

'*Yeah, boss. Whatever you say.*'

'Fuck it, Jimmy! Don't suck up to me! Say what you have to say and let me get back to sleep! Stop buggerising around!' Giving what he'd been trying to do most of the night, that struck him as funny and Luke chuckled to himself.

'*Uhh! Sorry, boss. What I wanted to say was that I'm still in Eden; remember, where we found out from the motel people that your wife and daughters had gone to the Gold Coast with some friends with a car?*'

'Yeah, Jimmy. You told me that last time. Now tell me something new!'

'*Yes boss. So, I sent most of the boys up there to look around, but I thought that I'd stay here to ask around a bit more.*'

'Good, Jimmy. Does this go anywhere, or do I have to drag the story out of you with a pair of vice-grips around your nuts?!'

'*Yes, boss, I mean, no, boss, you don't have to do that! What it is, I found some chick in the newsagency who said that a blonde woman with two girls had been asking around if someone with a boat was leaving soon and wanted three crew.'*

'OK. A boat, that's very inventive of my dearest, dumb blonde wife! That's good, Jimmy, then what happened?'

'She didn't know what happened after that. She didn't see the blonde woman or the girls again.'

'Did she know if any boats left around that time? I mean, come on Jimmy, think for yourself, please.'

'Yes boss. She said that she thought that some guy with a cat left town, perhaps heading for the Whitsunday Islands, but she wasn't sure.'

'Ok, Jimmy. That's a good start, but we need just a little bit more information than 'a guy with a cat left town,' heading north. I mean, who give a shit whether he's got a cat, dog or a fuckin' goldfish!'

'Yes, boss. But I did ask the refueller fella about boats leaving and I asked about a bloke with a cat. It was odd. He laughed when I asked that but did say that a boat left to go north. He thought the bloke said he was going to Brisbane, then maybe the Whitsunday's.'

'Did you lean on him a bit to see if his memory improved?'

'Yeah, well, I started to Boss. But a few of the local fishing boat fellas rocked up and sort of chased me off. Anyway, the doctor says I'll be able to use my arm and hand again in about a week, once the cast comes off. Jeez it's difficult wiping your bum left-handed!'

'Oh, spare me! You really are a fucking moron, Jimmy. Don't you know what subtle means? Now that you're got the locals watching out for you, you won't get any more info out of them! Get the hell out of town right now and get up to the Gold Coast or Brisbane. I don't suppose you got this bloke's name; the one with the cat?'

'Yeah, I did, Boss. Just after I bashed this blokes head against the counter in his office, he said his name is Harry!'

'Great! Just fucking terrific! A bloke called Harry with a cat on his boat heading for Brisbane or the Whitsunday's. They should be really easy to find, you idiot!'

Luke took a deep breath or two, something he often had to do when talking with Jimmy.

'Okay, Jimmy. I hope you've got a crew heading up to the Whit-sunday's as well?'

'Yes, Boss. I've got all three places covered, and as well, a waitress in the Fisherman's Club told me that a blonde woman with two girls was in there for a meal one night and she said that they were waiting to be picked up by two friends in a car to go to the Gold Coast.'

'OK, Jimmy. It looks like the Gold Coast might be the place, but still keep checking the other two places, and ask around up there about a bloke called Harry and his fucking moggy on a boat!'

'On it, Boss.'

EAST TELEGRAPH BAY-THREE HUMMOCK ISLAND, SUNDAY MORNING

B reakfast over, Sandy stuck to her word and held another self-defence practice session on the foredeck. From what I could see, they were doing really well, and I'd hate to be faced with the two of them if they were determined to defend themselves.

While that was going on, I set about assembling the stuff necessary to clean *Firebird's* bottom while still in the water. Scrubbing brushes, Scotch-Brite pads, plastic scrapers and the all-important Hookah gear for me to go right under the hulls. The gear I had consisted of an electric motor-driven compressor mounted in the left stern step locker, and two 35m lengths of floating yellow air-hose connected to two full-face masks that gave much better vision and allowed limited speech underwater.

Moving the boat into shallower water was as easy as winching in the anchor chain until the bows were almost over the anchor and with such a light breeze, I wasn't worried that we might drag. When the troops were ready, I told them what to do.

'That looks like fun, can we try that later?' Zoe asked, eyeing the tangle of bright yellow hoses and masks that was the Hookah setup with interest.

'Sure, no problem. Two hoses can be used at the same time, so when we've finished, I'll show you what to do. It's fun.'

All the scrubbers would float, so we just stacked everything on the stern platform and got ready to jump in.

Naturally, the twins just dropped all their clothes and with Jasper in attendance, dived cleanly in on the deep side, grabbed their brushes and set to work, with little screams each time Jasper nuzzled them, a game he has learned to love, not having had girls to play with before. Sometimes I quite envied what he was able to get away with doing to them!

Janice and Sandy wore bikinis, of course, both looking very sexy and when I asked Janice about their secret women's business discussion earlier, both she and Sandy just gave me the Mona Lisa smile thing and said nothing.

I thought I'd work on the opposite hull, this being better for my blood pressure, so reluctantly dragging my attention back to work, I was pleased that the very expensive anti-fouling I'd had applied last haul-out was still working well. There was some slime and a few small patches of weed, but none of the hard barnacles or coral growth that was so hard to remove. Therefore, work went quite quickly as I moved along in a cloud of dislodged slime and fine weed. Looking over to check the ladies occasionally, or maybe a lot more than just occasionally, I noticed that they too, were making good progress and also surrounded by a green-tinted haze of slime and weed. The usual school of tiny fish gathered to suck up the unexpected feast, darting right in under fingers to get the choicest morsels.

It only took two hours for both hulls to be cleaned and everyone was exhausted when we finished. They also had a lot of fun along the way, with the sleek, black form of Jasper always in the mix.

At some stage, Janice and Sandy had separated from their bikinis, and it was the first time I'd seen Sandy naked. She was a delightful sight, and also appeared to be a regular user of Mr Gillette's finest, the same as the twins. We played in the water for a while after the work was finished, just relaxing, although on several occasions I became the focus of Sandy's attention. I didn't mind that at all, and apparently Janice didn't either.

Having long given up on trying to work out the mysterious ways of the female mind, I went with the flow and enjoyed the attention. The girls didn't seem to notice, which I had come to realise is not quite the same thing as actually not noticing.

Finally, around midday, everyone's spring ran down and we

wearily dragged ourselves back aboard, each having a quick shower on the way. I waited until last, washing then putting the Hookah gear away, before rinsing myself off. I sort of hoped that all the naked females would be dressed before I got out, but that hope was doomed from the start.

Angie and Zoe whipped up a late lunch of sandwiches with mugs of hot tea as, despite the warm air, the cool water had sucked the heat from our bodies.

I looked around at my weary crew; even Jasper was quiet, stretched out on the daybed.

'No more work today, crew — just relax and mess about.'

That raised a few tired smiles as the girls went for'rard and promptly went to sleep on the trampoline, leaving Jasper with Janice, Sandy and me. We chatted in a quiet, relaxed manner for a while, before the ladies gave each other what seemed to be a significant look.

Janice stretched, yawned mightily, and then announced she wanted to lie down for a while.

'Do you want me to join you?' I asked, starting to get up, but she waved me down.

'No, I'm good. I'm just a bit tired. You stay and look after Sandy; don't leave her alone.'

So I settled back, getting comfortable again on the cushions and Sandy scooted close beside me as Janice smiled approvingly before heading below.

I looked at Sandy, now tucked in close against me. 'Am I missing something?'

She smiled back, 'I think Janice just wanted us to have some quality time together. She seems very good like that. Don't you think it's a good idea?'

I smiled, 'Sure I do. But only if it doesn't cause a problem; this boat's too small to stir up jealousies or hissy fits!'

'I think that you'll find that as long as we're discrete around the girls, Janice doesn't have a problem. Does that help?'

I looked at her; all smiles and an almost innocent look in her green eyes. 'So, if we just wander off below to your cabin, we can fool around all we want? Is that the go?'

She gave a devilish grin. 'What a great idea! Why didn't I think of that? Let's do it!' And promptly took my hand and dragged me to my feet.

Slightly bemused by the turn of events, I followed and before long and with great enthusiasm, we carried out my apparently great idea. Sandy naked in the water was one thing but rolling around on a bed with her was something else again. She was alternately gentle, playful, and very athletic and the sudden and unexpected nature of our coupling made the eventual outcome truly delightful. I think we kept the noise down sufficiently and didn't mess around too long in case the girls wondered where everyone had gone, but although it was still nearly an hour before we did make it back to the cockpit, they were still asleep on the trampoline, while Janice, when I snuck in to check, was fast asleep on our bed.

I made tea, and as we sipped, I grinned at her, 'That was fantastic, but very unexpected! Was that what you and Janice were discussing?'

She just nodded and smiled almost shyly now we'd started a new phase in what was already a complex set of relationships.

'I've always wanted to get with you, but it just couldn't happen last time, so this seemed a good opportunity, so long as it wasn't going to mess things up with you and Janice.'

'So obviously she didn't mind?'

Sandy smiled. 'No, dopey. She doesn't mind. She loves having a real man to sleep with for once, but she knows she's going to have to move on once this all settles down. She seems to have a very pragmatic view of the world when it comes to sex.'

I grinned, 'Yes. I've certainly noticed that! It's been passed on to the girls.'

'Wait 'till Janice wakes up. You'll find that nothing has changed between you two.'

At that point, the girls came back from up front and sat chatting, although they did give Sandy and me a few funny looks and exchanged a grin or two between themselves.

She was right; when Janice came out, she gave both of us a kiss and chatted on as if nothing had happened.

FIREBIRD...EAST TELEGRAPH BAY
- THREE HUMMOCK ISLAND, MONDAY MIDDAY

Promptly at 12:00, the anchor came up and we severed physical contact with Three Hummock Island again. Zoe was on the wheel, while I yanked the various strings to hoist and set the sails, so that we departed with hardly a sound, ghosting away from the pristine white beach with just a slight chuckle from the tiny bow-waves.

Everyone was well-rested, especially the older crew as we had indulged in several of the now traditional NQ teas after dinner and once again, the ladies ended up quite pissed, to the great amusement of the twins who hadn't seen Mum pissed before. I admit that I too was more than a little bit merry as well.

It didn't seem to matter what we did or said, the girls thought everything was hilarious, which set the mood for the evening. Tiredness finally set in, so we all headed for bed about the same time. I was relieved to find that, as predicted, Janice was her usual self or even more tender and loving than before. Sandy dropped around for another night chat and this time I didn't bother going through the pathetic attempts I'd indulged in before to cover myself, which gave all of us something to laugh at.

With the three of us in a happy mood, it was a funny late-night chat and she'd reluctantly departed for her own bed at a reasonably decent hour.

I asked Zoe to steer a straight course for a spot about one mile off Wynyard's Inglis River mouth. The breeze picked up as we left the lee of the land, blowing out of the North at about 15 to 20 knots, which gave us around 12 to 15 knots boat speed. With about 50 nautical miles to run, we should be anchored by 16:30 and I was looking forward to some more of Mavis's beer and a lovely steak. The swell was higher than our last run, but was rolling in onto our left quarter, so it was a soft and easy ride with some good surfing runs to liven things up.

As expected, we were off the entrance, dropping sails and with the engines fired up by 16:30 and anchored in our previous spot 15 minutes later. After I'd set the anchor with a firm burst of reverse, I looked around to see that the little harbour looked exactly the same, as if time had stood still during out absence.

The crew needed no encouragement to get ready for shore leave and ten minutes later, with a lonely Jasper left on guard-cat duty again, we were puttering quietly shoreward, tying up beside the carpark where we did last time.

'Jimmy! You're back,' cried Mavis from the cool, dim depths of the bar, as I groped my way in with sun-dazzled eyes.

'Yup. We're back. Good to see you again, Mavis. You don't look a day older!'

She almost giggled as she swung into action. 'Two schooners of Cascade and two Lemon Ruskies, wasn't it?' she sang out.

'Yes, it was, but we've still got our ring-in bikie chick with us, so you'd better make that three schooners of Cascade thanks.'

'No problem, Jimmy. Jeeze, she must like boats more than bikes to be still staying with you blokes.'

'Yeah, well. You know how it is. Give 'em a good feed occasionally and make 'em work and they'll stick around.'

'Yus! That's wot I say,' came the same old gravelly voice from the far end of the bar.

My eyes having now adjusted for the dimness, I spotted old Ernie propping up his corner.

'Gidday Ernie. How are you going old fella?' I called, 'Mavis! Better sling Ernie another one when he's ready, if you don't mind. I'd better look after the town's senior citizen.'

Ernie took that beer payment as his due with a slow nod. Mind you, if he moved it any faster, he'd probably get a headache. I decided to wind him up a bit.

'Hey Ernie. I guess that Mavis's beer prices aren't too bad after all, you're still here.'

'Now hang about, you young whappersnipper. That's enough cheek outa you! And here I was just starting to think that you weren't such a bad bloke after all. Even for someone who needs two bloody boats bolted together to get around. Although, if my weary old eyes don't deceive me, you've gone and brought that bikie chicky-babe back for me to perve on! I suppose you can do something right at least! Now I've gotta go out and have a close-up look at her, just to make sure you haven't damaged her. When she's sick of you, she's going to want to come fishing with me, but only if you haven't ruined her for a real man!'

'Turn it up, you silly old fart!' Mavis yelled as he nearly fell off his stool. 'You haven't been a real man for 50 years!'

Giving her the finger, he weaved a wobbly path to the door and stumbled over to our outside table.

'Here I am, darlin'!' he cried, spotting Sandy and her glowing auburn hair, 'I've still got a space on my boat for you when you get tired of that sissy boy in the bar. We've got lotsa fish to catch to support old Ernie in his declining years. You stick with me and I'll look after you.'

Sandy favoured him with a dazzling smile, before jumping up and giving him a big hug that nearly popped his eyeballs out.

'Gidday, Ernie. Good to see you again mate.'

When he'd caught his breath, he swung his rheumy gaze around the table taking in Janice and the girls.

'Well, bless my soul! All the lovely ladies have come back to see old Ernie! Fairly makes my poor old heart go thump-be-de-thump to see the likes of you all again!' He sketched a little bow that would have pitched him into the middle of the table if Sandy hadn't had a firm hold of his arm.

'Oops,' he burped, 'sorry about that. Thought I felt that there deck move under me for a moment.'

Sandy sat as I arrived with the drinks, so Ernie stood back, 'Say, Skipper. If you're staying overnight again, that's still a good spot. No one will bother you there, I'll make sure of it!'

'Thanks Ernie, appreciate that. In fact, we might even stay for tomorrow. We need to get some supplies.'

'No problem with that. There's a Supermarket up the main street, but you'll need a car to cart your stuff, so you'd better use mine. I never use it. It's the old white Holden around the back of the pub. The keys are in it, so help yerself when you're ready.'

I was slightly overcome with his kind offer.

'Gee thanks, Ernie. That's very generous of you and it'll will be a great help!'

'No problem, young fella,' he patted my arm. 'You've repaid me ten times over by bringing these lovely ladies back for me to chat to again. See you tomorrow, I hope.'

With that, he waved and wobbled down the stairs to the street.

'What a lovely old feller, 'said Janice, 'that was really kind.'

'Yes, it was,' I replied, 'because tomorrow after Robert gets in and you've had a chance to chat, I'd like you and the girls to go shopping.'

I looked around, 'Angie, can you please make up a list of stuff we need? And don't forget more OP Rum! Damn stuff seems to evaporate in this climate!'

The ladies giggled and Angie grinned, 'No problem, I've already done most of it.'

'I've got some cash left,' Janice offered.

'No, that's okay thanks. My credit card is healthy and not on anyone's watch list at the moment. I'll give it to you with the PIN in the morning so you can use it.'

She nodded acceptance as we got stuck into the drinks and soaked up the calm of the lovely evening.

After some more drinks and a terrific feed, the crew were ready to head back aboard.

Dusk had draped a soft blanket of friendly gloom over the little harbour, relieved only by small clusters of yellow lights on the wharf, as we puttered quietly across the mirrored surface to *Firebird* and an enthusiastic welcome from Jasper.

As it wasn't late, the girls decided to watch a movie after feeding Jasper, while I made three NQ teas that I served in the cockpit. We'd just settled in when Sandy's pocket buzzed with a summons from one of her burner phones.

'Hello?'

'...Oh, hi, Annette! How're things with you?'

'...Yep. We're all good thanks. Great to hear from you.'

'...It's taken a lot of organising, but we're expecting a visit from Janice's Dad tomorrow so we can bring him up to speed on all the extra stuff we've found.'

'...No. Not at the moment. We've restricted that info for now, as I'm sure you'll understand, but we were talking about how we really need to get the hard evidence to you somehow.'

'...Yes, of course. But we weren't going to do anything like that! Way too dangerous! But we did consider asking Janice's Dad, Robert, if he could make a visit to deliver it and discuss the whole situation with you, once he's briefed.'

'...We thought somewhere away from the city, like Yass or Cooma, that isn't too far away. What do you think?'

'...Great! We'll ask him and if you want to call this time tomorrow, we'll have an answer.'

'...Yes, we thought you'd prefer it that way. But here I've been rabbiting on, what's your news?'

'...Oh! Oh, really! That's...very interesting! No, that's okay. I'll pass it on later. Just so long as your tracks are covered, that's the most important thing.'

'...Yes, I agree. We'll have more for you tomorrow night.'

'...Thanks, Annette. Really appreciate the info. Bye for now.'

I'd been trying to read the play of expression on Sandy's face and didn't like what I saw, but I waited for her report.

She glanced into the saloon to make sure that the girls were still too engrossed in their movie to overhear, then looked at Janice and

I. 'She was just reporting that while she's under the radar with her Human Trafficking investigations, that ACP investigator, Alistair Swinford, is still sniffing around to see if anybody is asking anything more than routine questions about paedophile rings. She's agreeable to meet Robert in person if he can get up there without drawing attention, and Yass would suit just fine as a meeting place.'

I was certain she was holding something back, but Janice seemed to accept what Sandy had reported. She also made things easy by saying that she had to go and pee. Once alone, Sandy quickly and quietly said, 'The real reason for the call was that Annette has finally found evidence to support your auction theory. There was a recent email to Luke that requests information on the availability and current condition of the new and unused white goods that had been advertised for sale! It also made reference to negotiating the price of the goods, with reference to a previous shipment of 'Made in Australia' white goods that arrived in 'damaged or apparently used condition' and were 'not as advertised or as paid for.'

I felt as if I'd been struck in the belly. 'Ah, shit! Sometimes I really hate to be right! Particularly now.'

'Well you *were* right and now you've got to tell Janice! This is the perfect time, seeing as we actually have some hard evidence. Forget about our previous suspicions for now; just pass this on and let her deal with it.'

I nodded miserably, concerned what this news would do to Janice's rather fragile emotional balance, but when she returned, I laid it on her as gently as I could. After checking that the girls were still totally absorbed in watching Hollywood's version of what teenage boys and girls seem to do, her response was far from what I expected.

She said with almost icy calm, 'So you think there's been an online auction where the twins have been offered for sale, and some slime-ball in the Middle East or somewhere like that has made a substantial offer?'

'Yes, we do,' Sandy answered, 'the who and where doesn't matter so much at the moment; that can be traced in due course through Annette's human trafficking investigations, but what *is* important is that this explains why Luke is trying so hard and so expensively to track you down. Or, more specifically, to track the girls!'

Janice just shook her head as if the depths of Luke's depravity and self-interest were beyond expression and understanding. Which they were! 'Okay. That explains a great deal more. It's infinitely worse than just selling naked photos of the girls on their website, but at least I have a handle on what's going on! This is going to shatter Dad! He used to really like Luke and always admired his drive to succeed in business!'

'Maybe he won't be too surprised,' I replied, mightily relieved that we didn't have Janice as a basket case, 'he's had to be wondering why Luke has been chasing you so hard, and I'm sure he's drawn his own conclusions! Tomorrow, we'll share all this information and we'll be able to work on the problem together.'

That seemed to be a good time to pull the pin on the evening, so we cleaned up our mugs and went to bed, leaving the girls to finish watching their epic face-sucking, bed-hopping teen drama, although it wasn't long before we heard the movie finish and all lights were out.

FIREBIRD... WYNYARD HARBOUR, TUESDAY MORNING

Next morning, everybody was up early, with Janice subdued, the girls very excited about seeing Pop again, while Sandy and I were just keen to get the next phase of the drama underway. With Robert's plane due in at 09:55 and a diversionary drive involved, Janice and I took the RIB ashore at 10:40 and waited in the car park. We'd just parked ourselves on a seat in the shade of a tree in the pretty little park, when the sat-phone rang.

...'Yes, Robert, it's me. How're things going?'

...'Ok. That's interesting, how certain are you?'

...'Yes. I understand, but that could be coincidental. Maybe still act as though it is.'

...'Look. Stay there and walk around for another ten minutes as though you needed a break, and then come back here to the Wharf carpark.'

...'There's not usually that much traffic, so you'll soon see if there is.'

...'If you aren't followed back to town, either they are on their way to Strahan because they weren't game to turn around or it was innocent in the first place.'

...'Ok. No problem. I'll see you soon. Bye.'

'What's up?' Janice asked, a worried look on her face.

'Robert thinks he was followed after he picked up his rental car. He turned onto the wrong road once and a light blue Camry followed, but passed him when he stopped and turned around. That would've been coincidence, but just before Yolla Yolla, he thought he saw it behind him again, so he stopped in the village and called.'

'So, what now?'

'He comes here if there's no tail and we carry on as planned. If it *was* the bad guys, they won't be able to find him in Strahan, but they won't expect to anyway, since they'll expect him to be at Salmtas's base and they know they can't just drive in and ask for him because it is security controlled.'

'But what if they look around here in Wynyard for him?'

'We'll park his car behind the pub so it's out of sight, then once we're on the boat, he's out of sight. He flies out in the morning, so we might have to keep him on the boat overnight; I could drop the dining table down and he can sleep there.'

Janice blushed a little, 'I don't know how he'll react to us sleeping together, but that's ok, he's got a lot of other stuff to get used to.'

I thought for a moment, 'Maybe we can ask Mavis to look after him tonight, in fact, that might be better. I can run him ashore later tonight in the dark and it'll certainly be more comfortable for Robert. I'll ask Mavis to keep him off the books!'

She nodded, but her worried frown deepened and her eyes glistened. 'I know we've been chased for weeks, but we didn't see them before, then suddenly, they're maybe right here and on Dad's tail! And on top of that, there's this frightful auction! It's just reminded me that it's all very serious, isn't it?'

I hugged her, surprised to find that she was trembling. 'Of course it's serious. It always has been, we've just been isolated from it for a while. When you're swanning around on a boat, it's easy to lose touch with the real world.'

Fifteen minutes later, a white Kia Rio swung off the street into the car park, and then stopped, the driver looking around, but not spotting us at first under the shade of the trees. I pressed her shoulder to stop Janice from bounding to her feet while we looked back up the main street for anybody or any cars that seemed to be taking an undue interest in the Rio. After a few minutes, I lifted my hand and she bounded across the park and banged on the car's window. Robert jumped violently and obviously had his door locked, but motioned Janice away, before rolling forward to the nearest parking spot.

I left them to have what appeared to be an emotional reunion, before I wandered over to where they were still holding hands and talking flat-out. Janice finally stopped and turned.

'Dad, this is Harry who's been playing nursemaid and driving us around.'

Robert was a tall, lean, good-looking man in his mid-50s, with good tan, a full head of grey hair and a neatly trimmed beard. He was dressed so as not to stand out in this quiet town, in jeans, a neat and stylish polo shirt and joggers on his feet. His bright blue eyes swung onto me and I received the benefit of a beaming smile and a firm handshake.

'Harry. We meet at last,' he said in the rich, smooth voice I'd heard over the phone, 'it appears that I'm rather deeply indebted to you for looking after my little girl and precious grandkids!'

'Hello, Robert. It's very good to see you too. It's actually been a real pleasure to have Janice and the girls aboard, so not much of a chore at all! However, we have so much to discuss and really need your advice.'

'Understand. But please call me Rob. Much less formal!'

He glanced over his shoulder toward the town centre, 'I really don't think I was followed back here, since there wasn't much traffic heading toward Wynyard like you said.'

'I agree. We looked carefully after you pulled in, but couldn't see anybody paying attention, so let's get you aboard.'

'Can I leave the car here?'

'No. I'll stash it over behind the hotel and let the landlady know. We might have you stay there tonight, we're a bit tight for spare beds.'

'Oh, okay. That's a good idea, about the car I mean and I guess about the hotel room as well.'

So he unloaded his fat, soft leather briefcase and left his overnight bag in the boot. I ran it around to the back of the hotel and parked it beside what must have been Ernie's old EH Holden still in very tidy condition; one of GMH's better products. Ducking into the back door of the pub, I found Mavis in the kitchen and let her know what was happening and shamelessly practiced a slight deception with Rob's name.

'John will pay cash if you can keep his stay off the books, please Mavis. It's a bit complicated, but it's all above board and involves looking after damsels in distress and putting down a wife-beating husband!'

She teared up a bit as she patted my arm, 'Don't you worry about that, dear boy. Ernie's already told you that we keep secrets around here, as well as respect other people's business! I know you're a good man and so does Ernie, so that's all that matters!'

'Thanks Mavis. We'll leave the hire car here if you don't mind, but Janice will be in later to use Ernie's to go do some shopping. Oh, and we'll all be in for an evening meal as well!'

She patted me again. 'Good on you, love! It's the most fun we've had around here for years!'

I re-joined Janice and Rob, who were waiting by the dinghy and handed over the hire car keys, before we headed for *Firebird*.

'That's an impressive boat,' he commented with considerable enthusiasm, as we drew closer, 'I've never had a chance to sail on a big cat.'

'I hope you'll get the chance, as soon as this rubbish settles down,' I offered, 'in fact, we'll definitely do so!'

His smile was genuine when he replied, 'Great! I'll hold you to that!'

Getting aboard, he still had to run the triple gauntlet of the twins and Jasper who needed to meet and greet the new arrival.

The girls smothered Robert for a while then I had to introduce him to Jasper. His first reaction was rather funny, since he'd not spotted the big cat at first, with the twins all over him on the stern boarding platform, but when he was finally released from their exuberant and affectionate embraces, he climbed up to the cockpit, to be greeted by Jasper who had planted himself in the walkway and refused to budge until the introductions had been made. Not that

Rob had any intention of forcing the issue; in fact, he retreated a step in the face of Jasper's inscrutable green-eyed stare and daunting size.

Without taking his eyes off Jasper, he exclaimed, 'Holy crap! What the hell's that? I know it looks like a cat, but I've never seen one like that outside a zoo, and that's with heavy bars between us!'

By now, everyone was laughing at his reaction and that, more than anything else, helped settle him down quickly, so I stepped between them.

'Jasper, this is Rob and he'll be staying with us for the day. He belongs to Janice and Angie and Zoe.'

Rob looked at me briefly as if I'd gone troppo, but then he noticed Jasper blink a couple of times and saw his lips turn up in what passes with Jasper for a smile. He then held out his massive right paw to Rob who very carefully took it and gave a gentle squeeze, obviously feeling the steely, sheathed claws.

'Well I'll be damned!' he said in amazement. 'He looked like he understood what you said! And I've never seen a cat shake hands!'

'He actually did understand, Dad,' Janice confirmed, 'he's a pretty smart pussy.'

'I can see that,' Rob said with a rueful chuckle, 'he really had me going there for a few moments.' Jasper sensed his concern and stepped forward to gently nuzzle Rob's hand. Rob tentatively rubbed the smooth, black head and was rewarded with a rumbling purr. A look of delight confirmed that Jasper had once again spread his intangible magic and won over yet another human.

Sandy had hung back while the Jasper stuff was going on but was brought forward and impressed Rob with her beauty, background history and calm professionalism.

With formalities over, we spread around the cockpit table, while the girls bustled about the galley to make an early lunch for everyone. While the twins were still present, we limited the discussion to the beatings and the search by Luke's men, reserving the revelation and inspection of the files for later. Nevertheless, there was still a great deal to discuss, as well as Janice and the girls having a lot to catch up with, so Sandy and I let them talk things out and didn't push things along too fast.

Finally, lunch was served and appreciatively disposed of, so I looked at Janice.

'Would you like to go shopping with the girls? Use Ernie's car; it's the old, white Holden behind the pub and the key's in it.'

She'd been expecting the question, and although Rob raised his eyebrows at the strange request that took his family away at such a time, he fortunately kept quiet.

Janice readily agreed to go, stirring Angie into finding the grocery list. They were all still dressed for shore leave, so it wasn't long before the three were heading for shore, Jasper happy for once that he wasn't left alone. Earlier, I'd told Janice to take her time so we could show Rob the nasty stuff and get those discussions out of the way before they came back.

I looked at him and explained my odd actions, 'The reason Janice has taken the girls ashore is so we can tell you in private what we've discovered concerning what this is all about and why Luke's spending so much money trying to get the girls back.'

So between Sandy and I, we laid out the whole sordid, nasty story, fitting Janice's revelations about the beatings into the supposed reasons why it had all started and included our guesses about the girls' auction, only just now confirmed by Annette.

While he was still in shock that someone he'd respected and who'd married his only daughter could have done all these things, I went inside to fetch out my laptop, Janice's affidavit and the sealed envelope that Janice and I had put together.

I held it out to him, 'Please take this, read the document and check the seals on the envelope.'

With a questioning look, he read the affidavit carefully, and then looked the envelope over.

'OK. As an officer of the Court, I can accept that the recording in this envelope has been secure from the time it was made, and that it is a true copy of the original, which has also been kept secure from the time it was made.'

'Good,' I said, 'please open it.'

He did and found the portable HDD that had the recorded copy of Luke's computer main HDD. I pushed the laptop over to him. 'Please plug it into the USB port and open the main folder.'

He did so. 'OK. What am I looking at?'

'That is most of the contents of Luke's iMac desktop computer, including all the files on the desktop plus all the files in the Documents folder. Several documents on the desktop show details of property purchases by Luke, and they need your scrutiny to help you tie things together like we have. The folders and files in the Documents folder are very large and contain thousands of photos and dozens of videos of the paedophile ring's activities.

Regrettably, in the photo files, there are a lot of photos of your granddaughters, going back many years, although blessedly, they are happy, innocent photos taken of happy, carefree girls enjoying life. They are not pornography by any stretch of the imagination!

Also, in both the photos, which we believe is their main database collection, and the videos, are candid, undisguised shots of adults enjoying the fruits of their depraved lust, and these you may find quite astounding! They will also serve to bear out the dramatic statement I made to you that this could easily be a Government-toppler!

I must add that several faces that even I recognise are in high positions in the ACP and several State Police Forces, which is why we've been treading very softly!'

After that lengthy speech, Sandy and I sat back and let him digest it for a few moments, before he started clicking the mouse and the expression on his face grew darker and darker. He only skimmed the files, as I did initially, but finally, he pushed the laptop away and leant back, as if that was sufficient to make the whole, dreadfully sordid mess go away.

'That's almost unbelievable, and if I hadn't seen that stuff, it would have been! But there it is, and to top it off, my granddaughters are being auctioned to some overseas scumbag by my son-in-law! Just horrific!'

He rubbed his face with his hands, suggesting he was trying to make it all go away.

Sandy leant forward and gently touched his shoulder, 'It's all very real, Rob, but you'll come to grips with it. Janice, Harry and I have and now you absolutely have to! We need your advice and help, and we all need to make a plan that stops this in its tracks, protects the kids currently involved and protects Angie, Zoe and the rest of us from those very powerful and very deranged people!'

He looked up, a strange, haunted look on his face, but it was quickly replaced by one of steely resolve. 'This is the worst personal mess I've faced since my darling wife died, but you're right, we've got to help work this out for everyone's sake.'

We updated him with the plan to have him get a copy of the files to Annette as soon as he could sensibly arrange it; then told him of our thoughts about bringing Hilary Jones into the know.

He thought for a few moments. 'Yes, I will get the files to Annette. That will be the best thing to do and I'll do so as soon as it suits her; probably later this week, I hope. There's not much on my plate for the moment, but this is far more important anyway!'

'Don't forget that you're under surveillance. We don't know how tight it is, but it is there, and you should give every impression of business as usual. That's why I suggested this charade today.'

He nodded, 'You're right. I'm a bit green to this side of the business, but I'll learn quickly. Now, about Miss Jones, it's probably a very good idea. I've met her and she's quite a package. Very much the real deal, forthright and squeaky clean, with very high principles concerning corruption. This'll be just what she'll love to get her teeth into!

Did you want me to contact her too?'

'No, I don't think so. Just having you visit Annette will be enough of a risk that you'll have to very careful of. We think it might be best if we get her down here, perhaps for a few days so she can see the girls and talk to Janice. Then she can see the files if she wants to go on with it!'

Rob gave a feral grin. 'Oh, she'll want to go on with it all right! That's a very good plan of yours, to have her talk to the main players in person will make it much more believable.'

He grinned again, 'Oh, and I believe that she loves cats!'

That comment raised a few laughs that were sorely needed, as I added, 'Not being sure how an investigative journalist works, I wondered if we need to make the point that she cannot release any info to a paper until the whole ring has been identified and all the kids, including Janice and the girls, are safe?'

'No, you don't really have to say that, but you can if you want. Hilary won't be offended.'

He looked thoughtful for a moment or two, before adding, 'What we'll really be achieving with all this planning, is to kick-start independent investigations on three fronts. Annette at ACP, Hilary when she starts digging, and Sandy's boss when she reports back most of what you've found out. I'd mention the existence of the files to Sandy's boss too. Wait for him to decide what he needs to do but warn him of the consequences of acting too soon. As you've already mentioned, the whole lot could disappear underground very quickly.'

Sandy nodded acceptance. 'We've been waiting until you were up to speed before we moved on advising my boss. We weren't sure just how much of this stuff to feed him, but I guess you've answered that question.'

Rob nodded. 'I'd advise him ASAP so he can decide how to proceed. He'll have to work out who he can trust.'

We took a break from planning while Sandy made us mugs of tea and we sat chatting absent-mindedly while thoughts tumbled around in all our heads, so that we were surprised to hear the outboard droning alongside and the happy cries of the girls. Two hours had passed and the shopping party had returned.

Many hands soon had the RIB unloaded of a veritable mountain of cartons of food, booze and other stuff. Janice handed my card back with a smile. 'Thanks anyway, but Dad gave me a great wad of cash, so we used that. The supermarket didn't mind.'

'Ok. That's fine and thanks for chipping in.'

Zoe and Sandy were busy stowing groceries under Angie's direction, so I took the time to update Janice on what we'd discussed with Rob and let him fill in any blanks. She was agreeable to everything, but added, 'I think that Sandy should call her boss immediately, so he's updated and knows that his trust in her suspicions was well and truly justified, so he can start gently stirring from that end. Then I think Dad should make contact with Hilary Jones since he knows her and she'd remember him. Then you can talk to her and make the necessary arrangements. I really think that we'll have better protection if some pressure starts being applied to these animals!'

'But,' I came back with, 'don't forget that the more pressure that's applied, the greater the chance that they'll be driven underground. And it still may not stop the hunt for the girls, since the sale can still go through if they can just get their hands on them! So the pressure builds for us as well, unless you want to try for a place in the National Witness Protection Program?'

Janice looked defiant, 'That's true, but how about all the public faces we've identified? Once the entire collection has been carefully checked, it'll be very difficult for them to argue with a photo! And no, I don't think that the NWPP is a good choice, since it's administered by the ACP and with the number of ACP persons already part of this mess, who are we going to trust? I don't think the State ones will be any safer because they're compromised as well!'

Rob ruefully nodded agreement with his daughter's assessment, 'You're right and that's well put. It's not going to work if they have the fox guarding the chickens! So far, right here on the boat is the safest you'll be until the Queensland Police or the ACP produce some senior persons who aren't involved in this mess!'

By now the girls and Sandy had finished re-stocking the pantry and the cellar, so she re-joined us. The girls showed zero interest in getting involved in our briefing session and decided to go sunbake on the bow trampoline. Fortunately, they also decided to wear bikinis, but given their miniscule size, the nearby golf course soon had a stream of players apparently searching fruitlessly for lost balls, playing out of the rough or just resting in the shade. It thankfully created a chance for us to make some phone calls on one of the burner phones, where Sandy went first, catching Superintendent Casey on the first try.

'...Good afternoon, sir, it's Sandy.

'...Yes, I'm sorry about the delay, but I've discovered a great deal and a lot of new stuff has been happening, so I waited until I could lay it all out for you.'

'...No, I won't wait so long again.'

'...Yes, sir. I've got it! May I make my report, please? Then you might understand why I waited.'

'Yes, sir, sorry, sir. I'll be careful.'

After the apparent tongue-lashing, she proceeded to lay the whole tangled scheme out for him in a remarkably concise and easy-to-follow way. He only interrupted three times to clarify a point and even seemed to accept that she wouldn't reveal where she was, apart from being with the star witnesses.

Finally, she'd wrapped the whole thing up for him, knowing that he had recorded the conversation, but would destroy the tape as soon as he'd checked a few items.

'So that's where we're at right now, sir. Two of us have the witnesses under unofficial protection, her father is a barrister and has also been fully appraised of the situation, the bad guys are on our trail, but not too close at the moment and we're keeping moving to stay off the radar.'

'...Yes, he's an ACP undercover operative.'

I raised my eyebrows at this, but she ignored me and ploughed on.

'We believe that any further investigation you commence should be fairly low-key, since we haven't yet fully identified all the main players and don't want them to go to ground and destroy any evidence.'

'...Yes, I understand that, but until we can work out who to trust, we are all in danger. These people are playing for their reputations and careers and won't give those up without a fight.'

'...I appreciate that, sir. Yes, we will. Bye for now.'

She cancelled the call and handed to phone to Rob.

'As you might have gathered, he wasn't happy that I didn't report in every day, but he's over the moon now that he knows what's going on. I had to promise him a copy of the files, but I'm not sure how to get them to him.'

I looked at Rob. 'Maybe when you deliver a copy to Annette, you can ask her to make a copy and send it on to Superintendent Casey at Southport. That would isolate us a little bit.'

He nodded, 'I can do that alright.'

'How about we try to contact Hilary, do you have a number?'

Rob nodded and dived into his briefcase. It looked worse than a woman's handbag, but he eventually found his organiser. 'Yes, I do,' he held it up in triumph, so I passed him the burner mobile.

CHAPTER 29

The short, slim woman, her long, striking red hair pulled back into a girlish ponytail, sat relaxing in a rocker chair on the wide porch, feet propped on the carved wooden railing and gazing out over the peaceful, rolling countryside. The loudest sound was the chirping, whistling, cackling calls of the various bird types she and her partner had attracted to the house by spreading copious quantities of seed. Her partner, Debbie Thomas, a solicitor, ran a small, very successful and female-only practice in nearby Dandenong, specialising in women's issues, usually concerning abusive husbands.

They both loved the old timber house, with its wide veranda on all sides and the high ceilings. Although it cost a fortune to maintain, the wide hallways passing front to rear and side-to-side, kept the house cool during the long, hot summers. Of course, it was difficult to heat in winter, but they had several fireplaces and wood heaters to beat back the worst of the icy winds that roared down off the nearby high country and brought an occasional flurry of snow.

She sipped appreciatively on a glass of Brown Brothers' Chardonnay, a wine style she'd grown to really like over the last couple of years. Though relaxing her body, her mind was as active as ever, mulling over a very strange phone call that she'd received less than an hour ago. It was from Rob Jameson, a barrister she'd met socially a few times and a man she respected for his forthright attitude and unimpeachable character. She'd looked up his bio previously and had just finished refreshing her memory.

He'd said he had a story to tell her, but before he revealed details, he insisted that she think hard about whether she wanted to or even needed to get involved in something that he described baldly as potentially being a 'government-toppler'! He'd just tossed out a few tantalising hints of what it was about, while continuing to suggest that this was an investigation that was truly worthy of her involvement and talent.

'The man should be a bloody politician the way he spoke heaps and said bugger-all!' she muttered to herself.

On impulse, she dialled Debbie's mobile, pleased when it rang which meant that Debbie was out of the office and probably heading home.

'...Hi, Hon. Just wanted to know how far out you are?'

'...Great. No, nothing's wrong. Something's just been tossed in my lap and I just need to bounce a thought or six off you.'

'...Thanks. See you soon.'

Ten minutes later, Debbie, a tall blonde in her mid-forties, a handsome rather than beautiful face hiding a razor-sharp mind, was sitting on the porch with her, still in business clothes but barefooted, a glass of Chardy in hand.

She gave Hilary an affectionate look, 'Okay. This sounds a bit mysterious, although by the look in your eye, the 'something that's been tossed in your lap' is a big story, maybe huge. Am I right?'

Hilary's distant, thoughtful look softened as she gazed at her friend, confidante and lover.

'Yes. That about sums it up.' She then related Rob's conversation verbatim, her total recall memory being a very useful tool for an investigative journalist.

'So, what do you think?'

'What was the next step he suggested?' Debbie countered.

'If I want to find out more, and there is some danger involved in the next step, on account of the high level of corruption involved, the type of which hasn't been specified yet. I'm to call the same number back as soon as possible and talk to a chap named Harry who'll pass instructions for the meet.'

'Does it have to be face-to-face?'

'Yes. That was a no-argument requirement.'

'Should I come with you?'

'I didn't think of that, but I can ask if they'll accept it. I'd certainly feel happier having you and your brain along.'

'OK. Call him and set it up.' Debbie responded decisively. After just a few moments, she added, 'You've been moping around ever since you wrapped up that money-laundering thing. You probably need something to get your teeth into.'

She giggled girlishly, 'Something else, that is!' Drawing a chuckle from Hilary, she re-filled their glasses then picked up the phone from the floor and handed it to Hilary.

FIREBIRD — WYNYARD HARBOUR

The crew of the *Firebird* had just landed and tied up in our usual spot adjacent to the carpark, when my pocket rang. I looked at Rob, but he just shrugged. 'If that's Hilary, she'll most likely be taking the bait, at least as far as a briefing, so it's all yours. Get her here ASAP and away from curious eyes. I still think everyone's way too exposed here.'

I suggested to Janice, 'How about you take the girls to the pub and get some drinks organised. We won't be too long.'

She gave me thumbs up and the four ladies moved off.

'...Yes, I'm Harry...Oh, good. Hi, Hilary, good of you to call back, but do I detect another person on the line?'

'...Ah, okay. Hi, Debbie.'

'...Am I to take it that you're interested, Hilary?'

'...You do? Good. Yes, all right. I don't see any problem with that. It'll be a bit squeezy, but we'll make it work. Rob is flying out in the morning, so another legal mind working on this would be very useful right now, and if you'll be more comfortable, that suits us.'

'...Yes. There's quite a few of us at the moment; each deeply involved in this thing.'

'...Yeah. Sorry to be dark and mysterious, but this is not for an open line. Face-to-face only. So are you still wanting to hear more?'

'...Excellent! Here's the way it has to work, because there's a bunch of seriously bad guys looking for us and have been for a couple of months. We're under the radar at the moment due to our...let's say, particular circumstances, but we can't afford to take any unnecessary risk of our trail being picked up. I promise that you'll understand why when we talk.'

'...Okay. Firstly, are you both able to travel and be away for three to four days?'

'...Great. How soon can you move? Like, first thing tomorrow morning would be really good. We're in a rather exposed position right now and need to move on.'

'...You can? That's really good! As I said, you'll understand a lot of the 'why's' once you're here.'

'...Oh. Yes, I'd better do that. Do you have a pen? Oh, okay. That must be very handy for a journalist.'

'...Book the morning flight to Burnie through King Airways. Yes, that's the Tasmanian one. There's a flight that leaves Tullamarine at 08:45 and lands at Wynyard at 09:55.'

'...Yes, I know. It's very confusing seeing as Burnie is actually 20 kilometres away. Please pack very lightly in soft bags; you won't be going out. I'll pick you both up at the airport. Do you have all that?'

'...Great. Are there any questions about the travel side of things?'

'...That's good. Save the rest until after the briefing. Oh, one more thing. Would you mind leaving your mobile phone at home? Perhaps just use Debbie's from this time on. Like for the bookings as well.'

'...Okay. Only call if you have to take a later flight but try really hard to get the first one. It'll be a great help.'

'...Thanks Hilary and you too, Debbie. Tensions are building with this and the more we can spread the load the better. We're really looking forward to meeting you tomorrow.'

'...Ok. Bye for now.'

There wasn't much more to talk about, so by unspoken agreement, we stayed off all business and let Rob enjoy the pleasure of being with his family again. It turned out to be a happy, relaxed time, helped by the knowledge that wheels were turning in other places. We had some more fun with Mavis and Ernie, as well as enjoying another of Mavis's wonderful dinners that just got better each time.

The locals appeared to accept us without question as well, although I feared for Ernie's blood pressure in the morning when he saw that Rob had left and two more ladies were joining the crew. He very kindly agreed to allow us to use his car again for two airport runs, although it wasn't far, being only a few kilometres from the centre of town. Almost walking distance!

We wrapped up things at the pub early and were soon back on board. That evening, I called a final council of war, since Rob had to be on the 06:30 flight out, which meant a very early rising to be able to make check-in time. Once again, the girls declined an invite to join us and called up another movie to watch, cuddling up with Jasper in the saloon.

I looked at Rob. 'Your job is to set up a meet with Annette ASAP. When, where and how is up to you, but you both understand the vital need to be near-invisible.'

He nodded his understanding.

'Next, you have to send a certified copy of the files direct to Bob Casey at Southport Police Station. We'll make two more copies of the files tonight. I've got two more drives aboard and I can buy some more tomorrow morning uptown on my way to the airport.'

More nods from both, so I looked at Janice.

'While Rob is still here to certify them, you need to make another two, no, make it three copies of your original affidavit verifying the security of the chain-of-evidence to cover the two new copies we'll make now with one spare.'

I looked back to Rob. 'We'll only communicate via the burner phones, dumping one each week. Buy some more, and when either of us changes, we'll send a text message with the new number. We'll get Hilary and Debbie aboard and I think we'll head out for the islands immediately. For your ears only, we might go a bit further to the northeast side of Hunter Island. There are a couple of bays that look just as good as those on Three Hummock Island, just in case we've been noticed there too often.

We might stay there three days, or whatever time it takes for Hilary to get a proper feel of the situation and get to know Janice and the girls.'

This time I looked at Janice.

'You realise that she's going to have to ask a lot of questions of all three of you?'

'Yes. I expected that, so Sandy and I anticipated Hilary's positive response last night and briefed the girls to expect two more crew and that they'd be questioned, but as they only know about the beatings and none of the rest, their part shouldn't be too heavy.'

I nodded, 'Ok, that's good. But it raises two more questions; firstly, when should the girls be brought up to speed on the paedophile business, and should they be told about the auction?'

Both Sandy and Janice shook their heads, but Sandy replied. 'I think we can leave them out of that for now, but we definitely need to plan to tell them everything before long.'

Janice agreed, and then asked, 'What's the second question?'

'Where are we going to put Hilary and Debbie? I was going to make up a bunk on the dining table, but that's a bit ordinary at best!'

Sandy smiled, 'No problem. I'll move out of my cabin and sleep on the table. There's plenty of room for them and I'll be fine in the saloon.'

Up to now, I don't think that Rob had given any thought as to where we all were sleeping, but I could see that he was mentally counting beds and cabins and coming to conclusions that he prudently chose not to voice. Or maybe he just knew his daughter's temper even better than I did.

At that point, we decided to head for bed and Janice volunteered to run Rob ashore to let him get to his hotel room and to say goodbye because she wouldn't see him in the morning, as we had deemed it too risky for her to be seen driving around town and hanging around the airport.

Rob said his goodbyes to the girls and puttered off quietly with Janice, who returned within 10 minutes or so, subdued but happy with how things were going.

CHAPTER 30

LUKE'S MOBILE, TUESDAY AFTERNOON

'Yeah Jimmy. This better be good, I'm busy!'

'Sorry boss. I wouldn't have disturbed you at this time but I wanted to report like you told me.'

'Terrific. Get on with it and I'll decide if it was worth my time being disturbed.'

'Yes, boss. Well, we may have a lead on the location of the packages. You know young Tony, the one with the funny eye? Well, he and Alfie were detailed to follow your wife's father, regardless of where he went, so they tracked him onto a flight to Burnie.'

'Where's Burnie? I've never heard of it! Where the hell is it?'

'Uh. It's in Tasmania, boss. North coast. Anyway, only Tony managed to get on the plane and he stuck really close to him. When they landed, he followed him to the rental car counter where the father hired a car, so Tony did the same. I mean, he pretended to be just another tourist or worker. He says that there was really a lot of workers on that flight, boss.'

'Bloody hell, Jimmy. Will you get on with it? I don't need a lecture on the demographics of airline passengers into Burnie. Who gives a fuck! Just tell me what happened!'

'I'm trying boss, but you keep interrupting me and I lose my train of thought.'

'Jimmy, if your train of thought was still on the tracks, you'd have been my general manager way back, but I'm afraid that train was derailed a long time ago! Now get on with it.'

'Yes boss. Anyway, Tony manages to spot his car and follows him out onto the highway heading south. That one only goes to Strahan and Queenstown, although you can get to Hobart, but it's the long way around, if you get my drift.'

'Yes, Jimmy. I've got your drift. Now if you could just drift along the lines of the story, rather than playing RACV tour guide of Tasmania, I'll be much happier.'

'Yes, boss. Oh, I forgot to mention that Tony overheard the old bloke telling the hire car chicky babe that he was just going to Strahan on business for the day and would bring it back in the morning.

So Tony follows the old bloke and about 8 kms out, he turns onto a side road that heads back over to Burnie, but then stops and turns around...'

'Hang on a minute, Jimmy. You just lost me! How can a side road head across to Burnie when he's just left Burnie? Come on!'

'Well, actually, boss, they just left Wynyard, not Burnie.'

'Jimmy. Are you taking the piss out of me? 'Cause if you are, I'm gunna rip you a new arsehole when I find you!'

'No, boss, I wouldn't do that. You see, it's like this Burnie airport is right beside this little place called Wynyard. It's not at Burnie at all!'

'Well why the fuck don't they call it Wynyard instead of Burnie? Things are confusing enough without bloody airport names being fucked up!'

'Yes, boss. Well, Tony's pretty smart, so he just drives past and gives a little wave as he does, real friendly like, and waits until he sees in the mirror that the old bloke has turned around and got back on the main road. Then he turns around himself. But this time he hangs way back so he won't get spotted, but then the dude stops again in the middle of a little town, jumps out of his car and uses his mobile. Tony had to just drive past again, but although Tony waited in a hiding place down the road, he didn't see the bloke drive past.'

'OK. So what does Tony think happened?'

'Well. He's not totally sure, 'cause he did have to get out of his car to take a piss, and while he did, some cars went past, but Tony didn't think the old bloke was in any of them.'

'So Tony wasn't really watching the road all the time and some cars did drive past. Did Tony go to Strahan?'

'Yes, he did, boss. But he couldn't see the dude or his car anywhere. What do you think happened, boss?'

'I think this 'pretty smart' Tony is a fuckwit! Obviously the guy has driven past the idiot while he's taking a piss! He went to Strahan like he meant to, on business or pleasure we don't know, now that you clowns lost him! It may be innocent, but then again, it's the best lead we've had since you lost them in Coffs Harbour, so we'd better be sure.'

'Yes, boss. Sorry, boss. Uh. What'd you like us to do?'

'How about finding my runaway packages, you moron! Get some of these clowns to sniff around Strahan, this Burnie place and maybe send that smart Tony to check out this Wynyard joint as well.'

'Ok, boss. I'll get onto it right away and I might go down there myself.'

'Bloody good idea, Jimmy. You're supposed to be directing this clusterfuck! Get in there and sort it out!'

'Yes, boss. I'm on it.'

CHAPTER 31

Janice and I were up at 06:00, even though she really didn't need to be, so we had a quiet cuppa on the foredeck while I hosed the overnight dew and accumulated dust off the decks and lower rigging. It was a glorious morning, the water like polished glass with not a breath of wind stirring in the soft pre-dawn light. Janice would have gone ashore earlier for a last goodbye to Rob, but I'd firmly dissuaded her from doing that as I was still a bit nervous about the car that was maybe following Rob the day before and didn't want to take any more risks than we were. We'd already stayed way too long in a populated place, but as it was the quickest way to make the contacts that would hopefully kick-start the investigations, we had to live with the danger.

With Hilary's and Debbie's flight not due in until 09:55, there was no rush, so we just soaked up the peace, waving to a couple of keen early golfers and to the skipper of a lone fishing boat chugging quietly out for the day's work.

With the boat washed and windows chamois-wiped, the rest of the crew surfaced, Angie needed little persuasion to start breakfast. By the time the twins had their daily hand-to-hand session with Sandy on the tramp mats and the other daily chores were done, including tipping the usual huge mass of Jasper's poop overboard and hosing his grass mat clean, it was time for me to move.

I'd asked Rob what Hilary looked like and all he could remember was that she was quite short and had flaming red hair.

For a bit of exercise, I rowed the RIB ashore, tying up in our usual spot and was ambushed by Mavis wanting a bit of a chat while she was hosing down the front veranda of the hotel. Consequently, by the time I legged it around to the back of the pub, I was almost late. Thirty seconds later, however, I was motoring sedately up the main street as I remembered Mavis's directions: left at the third roundabout, next right, next left, over the railway line, left, then follow the road around to the terminal.

The carpark was surprisingly big and a King Airlines Saab 340 was just taxiing in to the terminal.

Despite the early hour, there were quite a few people waiting to greet the arrivals, so I parked myself at the back and scanned the incoming group.

There was a bunch of obvious workers, some touristy types and toward the rear of the gaggle, an attractive woman with bright red hair, who, even at a distance, seemed to radiate energy. A tall, blonde woman who moved with an almost feline grace accompanied her. They were dressed casually in jeans and shirts and while each had a computer bag slung over their shoulders, to their credit, neither carried the obligatory huge handbag.

I stepped in front of them and held out my hand to the diminutive redhead, 'Hi, Hilary, I'm Harry.'

She looked slightly surprised at being recognised so readily but covered it quickly and shook my hand with a firm grasp. I turned to her companion who was my height and had a gentle smile on her face. She beat me to it and stuck her hand out first, announcing, 'Hello, Harry, I'm Debbie.' Being a solicitor championing the cause for abused women, I'd expected a severe, militant man-hating type, not this charmingly pleasant lady with the direct gaze and blue eyes.

I saw them take in my extra casual dress of boat shorts, T-shirt and thongs, although I had shaved that morning and applied a liberal dose of anti-stink in all the suitable locations.

With a cheeky grin that belied her 50+age, Hilary commented, 'I gather by your outfit that we're not heading for the local Mercure?'

I chuckled, 'No. Afraid not. But although we are heading into an environment that can be totally inhospitable, you will have a comfortable bed and hot and cold running water.' I ignored their raised eyebrows, and chatted the usual crap about weather, the flight and the temperature, until the baggage was unloaded and set out for collection. The ladies collected two smallish, soft overnight bags and waited expectantly for my lead. The old Holden confused them further, until after I'd parked it at the back of the hotel and led the way around the side and over the road, thankfully avoiding having to make explanations to Mavis.

The dingy was a giveaway and their eyes immediately scanned the tiny harbour latching onto *Firebird* as the likely transport.

'It's a good thing we don't get seasick,' Debbie commented dryly to Hilary, who contented herself with a, 'nice boat, Harry.'

They were reassuringly surefooted and we made the short journey without comment or issue, except when Hilary added as we came closer, '*Very* nice boat, Harry!'

Zoe was ready to take the painter and the bags, while the visitors hopped out on their own and made introductions.

'Would you mind hoisting the RIB up and securing for sea, please?' I asked Zoe, 'I'd like to leave immediately'

She nodded, 'Sure thing, Harry, but you'd better do Jasper's introductions first. He's excited about having more visitors and been watching you all the way from the hotel!'

I chuckled and led the way up to the cockpit where my beautiful big cat was waiting in his usual greeting position. The ladies' reaction was predictable and, as always, highly amusing to the initiated, but both were utterly delighted with him from the start and accepted that his sniffs and very intimate nuzzles were his due. As usual, he won them over quickly by rubbing against them and wanting to be scratched.

Meeting Angie, Janice and Sandy was rather more conventional, so I asked Angie to show the ladies their cabin to let them unpack and explain the toilet and water arrangements while Zoe and I got us underway. Angie must have given them the short version of the visitor's briefing, because by the time I had the engines started, the anchor stowed and Zoe had the RIB lashed securely to the underside of the daybed, Angie led the two ladies back out into the cockpit.

'Stunning boat,' Debbie said to me, 'I take it that you live aboard full-time?'

'Yes. Normally just Jasper and myself but we do pickup homeless waifs on the odd occasion.'

Janice poked her tongue out at me and smiled, 'We'll explain everything once we get settled on our way and clear of the harbour, but would you like a late breakfast or some tea or coffee in the meantime?'

They looked at each other and giggled. 'We're not used to such luxuries on a sailing boat, but we'd love a mug of tea and something to eat if it's no trouble. It was a very rushed early start to make check-in on time.'

'No problem,' Angie answered, 'I'll fix that. How about toasted crumpets with honey or jam?'

'That'd be great,' Debbie answered for both, 'can I help?'

'Nah. Not for now. But you can watch to see where stuff goes, 'cause after this, you're on your own. It's no big deal really, Harry's got it set up just like a house on shore so it's easy.'

I turned the wheel over to Zoe to navigate the by-now familiar twisting, shallow channel using the reverse lead process, while I joined the group around the cockpit table, waiting until Debbie and Angie re-joined us bearing food and drinks.

'There's a great deal to cover,' I started, 'and I don't want to bombard you with the whole lot at once, so I'd like to go slowly and let you build up the picture. For now, I might just explain a bit about each of us and how we came to be together on the high seas like this.'

Hilary nodded, 'That's fine by me. Debbie is along, not only as my partner, but also as my legal advisor and confidant. She makes sure that I don't set myself up for a lawsuit!'

'In that case, you've got plenty of work ahead of you on this one,' I smiled at her, 'we're all going to need serious legal representation before this mess is sorted.'

With the girls close by, I let Janice tell her story, up to the time she lobbed on my gangplank, then took over to very briefly outline my background. I saw Debbie take some notes from time to time, but Hilary took none, apparently relying on that brilliant eidetic memory.

We took a break in the narrative once we cleared the channel and were safely off the coast where the breeze started to lift and we could set the sails. As had become usual, Zoe steered while I hoisted, sheeted and trimmed until *Firebird* was scudding along at 15 to 18 knots with the moderate swell just ahead of our starboard beam. The speed and motion proved too attractive for the twins, so they decided to play and sunbake on the trampoline. Maybe in deference to our guests, they didn't strip off completely, but just shed shorts and tops, scampering for'rard clad in just brief panties, already squealing with delight as the cool spray flicked up by the windward bow pelted them.

I noted Hilary and Debbie cast appreciative looks at them, before Debbie said sincerely to Janice, 'Absolutely lovely girls. They're a real credit to you and remarkably well-adjusted despite the recent events.'

Janice nodded her thanks, just grateful that they'd taken her earlier suggestion and removed themselves to allow for more involved discussions between the older people about the stolen files and the old mansion.

I engaged George, the autopilot, before returning to the table.

'We've been a bit circumspect with the girls around, as they're not aware, at this stage, of the actual reason why their father is chasing them so hard, so please respect that when you talk to them or if they're within hearing range. It was a big enough shock to Janice, Sandy and me at first.'

Hilary looked a little bit annoyed. 'Ok. We'll be good little girls and watch what we say. Now, what the hell is it that you've dragged us all this way and gone to this much trouble over?'

I took a deep breath. 'Janice told you that before she left, she had the opportunity to copy Luke's computer Desktop and Documents folders?'

They nodded in synchronisation.

'Well, I think the best way is for you both to have a look at some of the files that were in that folder. They're arranged in annual sub-folders, spanning about 10 years, with mostly JPEG photos but there is some MP4 video. To save time for this preliminary look, and since there are a lot of images, I suggest that you just skim through a few photos from each year, just to get a feel for what we have. In particular, we'd like you to see if you recognise any faces as you go. That point is very important, but we can fill in the gaps later, and you'll have your own copy to look at privately in depth and to take away when you go.'

Hilary and Debbie exchanged silent, meaningful looks as I ducked into the saloon and retrieved my personal laptop from under the nav station. The boat's laptop, that sat available to any-one on top of the nav desk, was the one used for all other business as well as the library of books and movies.

They shifted into the shade and sat close as I woke it from sleep mode and selected the first year's sub-folder. Debbie drove the scan and they moved quite quickly, pausing occasionally to point and nod, before moving on. Debbie stopped disturbingly often to jot down a name, but they scanned on in silence, only their deepening frowns revealing the inner turmoil they were feeling.

While they scanned and jotted, Janice sat and watched the end-lessly entertaining view of the ocean slipping rapidly past with its heaving, ever-changing tableau of waveforms and I reclaimed the driver's seat, pushing Jasper onto the other half, since he'd wisely chosen to remain dry in the cockpit instead of joining the twins jumping around under the continual spray off the bows.

Nearly 40 minutes passed before Hilary muttered, 'Enough!' and Debbie gratefully closed the folders and flipped the lid closed, returning the laptop to its electronic slumber, both of them sitting back with a sigh. Sandy went to the galley and started brewing teas all 'round, while I raised an eyebrow at Hilary.

'So? Is it worthy of your time?'

She shook her head, not in denial, but in dismay at the depths of depravity on display, although there was a hint of excitement in her voice.

'We've seen some nasty stuff over the years, since paedophile stories are unfortunately quite common, but the scope of this, the timespan and the adults we can identify so far, just beggars belief!'

She looked at me, 'When Rob was trying to pique my interest, he used the term 'Government-toppling'. I love that and might borrow it if I may because I believe that it best describes what we are sitting on! I mean, we spotted a former deputy Prime Minister and two current frontbenchers, one from either side of the House! And as you said, that's just a small sample of what's in there. How bloody arrogant can these arseholes be? Didn't they think that someday these photos might leak?'

She'd virtually repeated my words of several days or was it weeks ago?

'It does seem pretty stupid of them,' I replied, 'so, I presume that you did recognise other faces?'

'Oh, my goodness yes. Apart from the three Federal pollies, there are at least 15 persons known nationally, in business and in the Victorian Government, as well as a handful of celebrities who'd pay a fortune to suppress this. You're sitting on the biggest piece of potential blackmail in Australian history. You could be the richest people in Australia if you went down that track!'

'No thanks,' I replied, 'I just want them behind bars and all those kids in a safe, caring place. I'm glad that you've found more than we did, but you may not have recognised a few faces that belong to very senior members of the ACP and the Victorian Police Force up at Assistant or Deputy Commissioner level!'

'Oh shit, oh dear! That does make it more difficult.'

She looked at Debbie, who replied, 'Yeah. It'll certainly make it harder to prosecute those guys. They'll have covered their tracks very well apart from these photos.'

Hilary replied, 'True, but exposing them to public attention when the time is right should get around all that, and that's where I come in.'

We acknowledged the wisdom of that before I looked at Debbie and asked her the same question I'd asked Rob.

'Based on how Janice has described how she acquired these files, do you see any problem with them being admissible in Court?'

She thought a few moments. 'No. Not really. A chain of evidence has been established, thanks to your quick thinking, although Defence would argue that they were personal and private files and can't be admitted into evidence, but I'd counter by saying that as Janice was his legal wife at the time, that as the computer was in their shared home, the room door was open to access by anybody in the house at the time and the computer was up and running, she had the right to look at and copy those files if she so desired. Also, the fact that she hadn't been specifically told not to go in the room or to use that computer adds to her right to view and/or copy stuff on it.'

'Great! It was something that had bothered me, since this is obviously the best proof of what's been going on.'

She nodded. 'Yep! Good call. But so far, I don't see a problem in that regard. What did Rob say? You must have asked him.'

I smiled, 'Essentially the same as you, although we did spend a lot of time talking through where and how to proceed from here. The problem of conducting an investigation without setting off alarm bells has been bothering me a lot.'

'Yes. We understand that, but there are other ways to verify things without asking direct questions that might raise red flags.'

She smiled, 'Relax. This is my field of expertise and I've handled this type of investigation many times before. The trick, as you've said, is not to alert the subjects too soon. They must remain totally unaware that a case is being built against them until it's too late. Then we strike on several fronts.'

I nodded and reminded her, 'But don't forget that there are an unknown number of these arseholes in the Ring and we don't want any getting away if we can help it.'

'True,' Debbie replied, 'but usually we find that once several are in the bag, they'll rat out the others very quickly, hoping for a deal with the Prosecution.'

'OK, that's reasonable, but now you've mentioned striking on several fronts, you also need to know about the parallel investigations that we've already started, one of which has produced possible proof that endangers the girls even more!'

They both raised eyebrows, so I told of Sandy's boss in the Queensland Police and more importantly, the contact with Annette in the ACP, her legitimate investigations, the phone tapping and email interception and what she'd discovered in an email to Luke.

'So, not only does Luke want to salvage some pride in getting his family back under his thumb, he stands to possibly lose a great deal of money if the sale of his virgin daughters can't go through because he can't find them.'

Hilary and Debbie shook their heads in disbelief.

'Well. Think about it! It's the only thing that makes sense of the way Luke has been pouring so much money into this search!'

After thinking further, they finally agreed that my theory and the supporting email connected a few scattered dots and did explain many things.

We also told of Rob's possible encounter with a tail after he arrived in Wynyard.

'So they may be closing in on us,' I concluded, 'which is why we're getting out of Wynyard so quickly. I hope that you weren't seen, although we've visited the port twice now and chatted with the locals, so there's plenty of people who've seen the boat and us. And that's a bit of a worry, but it was the quickest way to get Rob and yourselves up-to-date.'

Hilary agreed, 'Yes. That sounds reasonable. Time does appear to be getting tight, especially if the hunters are getting close. Really, your best option is what you've been doing; stock up and stay in remote areas, moving every few days or so.'

I smiled, 'Yeah. That's what I figured, and we'll get back to that after we drop you off.'

Hilary looked wistful. 'If I didn't need to be in contact with the outside world so much, and co-ordinating the investigation through Debbie's office, I'd like to come with you, but we'll make the most of these few days to get the full story, then I'll go do some digging.'

A devilish grin lit up her face, 'However, to properly answer one of your earlier questions, this has the potential to be the biggest story by far that I've ever been exposed to, so thanks for the opportunity.'

I retrieved the sealed envelope with the copy of the HDD with all the files on it and passed it over to Hilary.

'Don't forget that you'll need to look at all the real estate stuff on the Desktop section as well, on account of that's where the records of the purchase, renovation, income and upkeep of the mansion are. That'll probably be a separate line of investigation for you.'

'I won't forget,' she promised. 'We've got a huge amount of ground to cover and will need some help, but that's where Debbie's staff will be invaluable. We trust them implicitly as they all are dead set against child exploitation of any sort, and this is the worst. Debbie has a real estate section, well, one solicitor and a paralegal, who normally look after divorce settlements, so this will be easy picking for them.'

I got the feeling that having Debbie and her resources on board was almost as good as having Hilary herself, and started to feel a lot more comfortable about how things were unfolding.

The girls came back aft for lunch and had a quick shower off on the stern platform, so we decided to stop discussions at that point, to give Hilary and Debbie time to assimilate what they'd learned and think of questions they needed to ask. They also needed some time to relax and enjoy what was proving to be a new and exciting experience for both.

Debbie showed the most interest in the nuts and bolts of running the boat and I was soon deeply involved in discussion and demonstrations of how stuff worked, much to the amusement of the rest of the crew. A trip up to the bows turned out to be a real thrill for her and it was lovely to see her professional reserve melt away with the showers of spray from the dip and lift of the bows. Before she got her shore-going clothes too wet, I suggested that she change and try coming for'rard again.

She took that suggestion with enthusiasm and even talked Hilary into changing into a fairly staid one-piece swimsuit, although Debbie herself shaped up very nicely in a small blue bikini. The pair of them proceeded to have a ball, screaming with laughter as they alternated bouncing around on the trampoline, with perching on one of the two bow seats and hanging on as they were occasionally dipped into green water, or just pelted with spray.

Having a pod of dolphins suddenly appear was icing on the cake as the beautiful mammals cavorted around the bows, looking up at the humans with their ever-laughing faces. Both ladies were quite exhausted after 20 minutes of this, so when the dolphins gave a final farewell flick of their tails and disappeared as quickly as they'd arrived, they came aft.

I showed our two dripping guests where the stern shower was and how it worked. Angie had already cautioned them on the water-conservation procedure, so they didn't take long, greatly appreciating the hot water supply as the breeze was chilling them down. Zoe had kicked me off the wheel, so Angie was waiting for them with thick towels to dry off and perching in the cockpit out of the wind soon warmed them up.

'Absolutely fantastic!' Hilary enthused.

'Yeah! Amazing,' added Debbie, a grin from ear to ear, 'that's the most fun I've had since I was a kid!'

Hilary grinned and kicked her in the shin.

'Oh, this was fun type fun, sweetness, not the same as our fun!'

It was such a departure from their normal, professional manner that we all cracked up laughing and it really was a pleasure to see two people who seemed to lead such serious lives, where they were dealing with all manner of awfulness every day, being able to let down their professional masks for a while and just be like kids again.

I plotted a course on the Chart plotter for Zoe to follow that would take us to a small bay on the east side of Hunter Island, called Shepherds Bay. On the maps, it was the northernmost sandy beach on the east side of the island, very protected from almost any wind, and appeared to be just like our beautiful bay on Three Hummock Island, only smaller. But was just a bit further west and would take maybe another hour of sailing. Not that I thought that anyone would mind the extra time scampering along as smoothly and quickly as we were.

So, in this manner, the afternoon passed very pleasantly with informative conversation with Hilary and Debbie, and we came to appreciate what sharp minds they had. Inevitably, they started asking questions of all of us, and Debbie's notebook was always at her elbow, but this was the process I'd hoped would naturally evolve, without any real pressure on anybody — just as long as Hilary got the facts.

It was a great sailing run yet again, although I cautioned Zoe that she needed to bend our straight line north a little so we cleared the point off Stanley by a healthy margin, and as we were due to pass the south tip of Three Hummock Island by 15:00, we should be anchored in Shepherds Bay by 15:30, according to the smart-arsed Chart plotter.

Marvellous what modern technology can do!

So, she steered us safely and about on time, as predicted, we could see a gleaming, white strip of sand showing clearly against the dark vegetation of the surrounding coastline. Hunter Island was considerably rockier than Three Hummock Island, so there were only a few protected sandy beaches on this side of the island. The west side was very exposed to the relentless procession of swells and weather systems that marched impassively west to east around the southern part of the globe with virtually no land to impede their progress.

Fifteen minutes later, we rounded up into the northerly breeze, diminished slightly by the landmass. I furled the headsails first, then let the main shiver and flap, which applied a braking force until we stopped, then, as we began to move rearwards, dropped the anchor and let out a safe amount of chain. The flapping main applied enough force to dig the anchor in, so that once we were stopped, I could lower the main into its stowage place in the boom.

Zoe gave me a little clap.

'That was really neat. I've watched you sail off from anchor without using the engines, but that's the first time you've sailed in and anchored without them.'

I smiled at her enthusiasm. 'The trick is to get rid of the headsails early, to slow down, then when you come up into the wind, the flapping main puts the brakes on and the boat will slow quite quickly. The two big mistakes are to drop the main too early and forgetting to steer the boat straight back downwind by using the rudders in reverse.'

She nodded understanding. 'Can I try it sometime, if we have an easy approach?'

'No worries! I'll just talk you through it. You'll do it easy.'

Now that we were secure, I joined the others in looking around our new home. It was a pretty little bay with a curving white sandy beach, only about 600 meters long, with a low, rocky headland curling protectively around to the north. A pair of rocky headlands, separated by a very small beach, marked the other end of the bay.

With the north wind blowing, we were tucked in close to the end of the beach at the north end, just 200 metres from the small headland, over a clean, sandy bottom. The stiff breeze that had brought us here in such fine style was barely enough to ruffle the crystal-clear water and carried a medley of scents from the various bushes making up the scrubby cover. In that respect, it was very similar to our old anchorage, but was a lot more secure in virtually every wind direction.

'Just fabulous,' breathed Hilary, 'to borrow a well-used old saying, 'you can feel the serenity!"

'Amen to that,' added Debbie, 'I didn't know such beautiful places existed, and it's only just across from Melbourne.'

As we were tucked in close to shore, with the first rocks leading to the headland not far away, I decided to drop the stern anchor over and walk it out a way to keep us securely in position. When I told Zoe, she dug out the blow-up plastic float we had used previously, inflated it and passed it down to me to rest the anchor and some chain on. Even though the anchor was alloy, the chain was heavy and piling a bunch of it on the float made the swim out 50 meters much easier. I tipped the chain over first, and then dropped the anchor clear of the links. I signalled to Zoe to haul in some slack and watched to make sure the sharp tip dug in cleanly once she'd tied the anchor line off.

Seeing me paddling around the boat in my jocks, inspecting things from the waterline prompted the rest of the crew to get wet. Hilary and Debbie were still in swimming gear from their earlier play on the foredeck, but Janice and the girls just dropped their shorts and tops and jumped in wearing panties only. Naturally Jasper wasn't about to let a chance go by, so he leapt in off the top of the cockpit roof with a massive splash, much to the delight of our newest visitors.

The girls showed Hilary and Debbie how he'd tow them around by hanging onto his tail and Jasper graciously let the visitors have a turn, adding to their ongoing enchantment with my beautiful, and at times almost mystical cat.

CHAPTER 32

In a small, but neat and tidy villa in one of Canberra's many leafy inner suburbs, a plain-Jane burner phone sitting on the kitchen bench warbled happily.

'Ah, fuck it,' was the weary curse directed toward the sound, until the curser saw the origin of the sound. Then her interest quickened.

'Hello.'

'...Oh, yes Robert. I was told to expect your call. How are things with our friends?'

'...Excellent... You do move quickly!'

'...Well, I suppose I can understand that.'

'...That good? Or bad as the case may be. I suppose that it depends on which side of the line you stand! Ha-ha.'

'...Yeah, sorry. No, I'm not busy tomorrow.'

'...A pleasant drive in the countryside? How romantic!'

'...Oh. No, I suppose not. Maybe, I'll just pretend. I'm getting good at that!'

'...Ok. I'll be serious, I can be sometimes. What you do is drive into Yass from the Canberra side, stay on the main street and on your left at the traffic lights, there's a pub that serves pretty good pub grub and we can talk without being disturbed. If you see my only indulgence, a little, black Mercedes Benz AMG SLK55 parked out front, that'll mean there'll be a dark-haired old tart in the public bar, wearing a red shirt and with a schooner of beer in front of her.

Just another thought, if you think you've been followed, don't acknowledge me or stop in the bar, but walk through to the beer-garden and I'll have one of the staff come out to show you to a private room.'

'…What do you mean, which traffic lights? Get a grip Robert; this is Yass, not poncy bloody Melbourne, there's only one set of lights in the whole fucking main street which is very long and full of roundabouts, so I don't think that even a big shot Melbourne barrister like you could miss it!'

'…Yeah, alright. I'm sorry. It's been a total shit of a week and I've been looking forward to a bit of relaxation and unwinding, but this'll have to do for now. At least I'll get out of town for a while.'

'…Yeah, that'll be good! Black shirt, black pants, Jeeze Louise, you'll look like Johnny- bloody-Cash on an off day.'

'…Sorry, sorry! I'm doing it again. But why not wear a green polo shirt? Even if it does have one of those poofy crocodile-things trying to bite your left tit, you won't stand out quite as much as the all-black ensemble!'

'…No? Well, heaven forbid that I should try to tell a man how to dress. What the hell would I know?'

'…You will! Outstanding! You just scored some brownie points!'

'…Oh, I know you don't care about that. It was a bit of a joke Robert. You sound like you really need to unwind big time! Your sense of humour is non-existent!'

'…Do I? Well, if you must know, I've already had two glasses of red and was about to go for another refill.'

'…Yeah. It's a Merlot, McG something or another. Bloody good drop for a cheapie. I'm doing my favourite job, the bloody ironing and I can't drive the fool thing straight if I'm not half-pissed.'

'…Yes, of course I'll be sober tomorrow! What the hell are you, the booze police? Give it a rest!'

'…No. Of course not, I've only had two glasses so far!'

'…Yes, no problem. I can be there by 12:00 easy. Where are you that's got so much noise?'

'…Oh, really? A bar! How amazing! I thought that you'd shun

such places of debauchery where alcohol is freely available. Well, in that case, I'll see you in Yass. Goodnight, Robert.'

CHAPTER 33

FIREBIRD...SHEPHERD'S BAY, HUNTER ISLAND – WYNYARD, FRIDAY PM – SATURDAY AM

We'd verbally covered a great deal of ground since Hilary and Debbie joined us on Wednesday, and by Friday afternoon Hilary finally indicated that she probably had enough info for the moment. She and Debbie had a determined look and were anxious to get back and start setting things in motion, as well as go through the files again more carefully, looking for identifiable faces.

They'd fitted into the boat lifestyle very well and seemed to really relax in-between talk sessions. There were lots of beach walks for relaxation and although the bay was smaller than our last abode, it was just as beautiful and very sheltered. Jasper loved the extra company and always came with us. The girls kept their bikini pants on, which helped maintain a slight sense of decorum, but otherwise went topless most times.

Sandy graciously slept on the lowered dining table on Wednesday night, although admitted that it wasn't near as comfortable as the double berth back aft.

Thursday night, due to everyone relaxing even more, all the adults got a bit pissy on NQ teas, to the vast amusement of the girls. Hilary and Debbie kept telling lots of very funny stories about their exploits before we all staggered to our respective beds. There were lots of giggles from the left rear cabin and just as many from the right forward one as well, especially when Sandy wandered in to have a chat. She hadn't bothered to dress for the visit, which was fine by me and apparently by Janice as well.

She ended up climbing into bed with us, which was a lot less distracting for me than to have her sitting naked and cross-legged at the foot of the bed as she had on previous occasions. I was interested to see that she chose to climb in beside Janice, so we talked and laughed at silly things for a while, before I decided I was tired, then turned my bed light off and left them to it.

Although a big bed, it was still very cosy with three adults, even though Janice was petite, but I slept well, only coming half-awake a couple of times when I was jostled to realise that Sandy was still present and that the ladies were apparently very pleased with each other's company. They were both asleep when I awoke as usual at 06:00, so I left them undisturbed, dressed and retired to the galley for my morning cuppa, where I was joined by Hilary who needed some reviving with a strong coffee.

She gave me a cheeky grin, 'Thanks to those NQ teas, I guess we all played up a bit last night!'

I grinned back, 'Yep. A bit of an unwind occasionally does a power of good!'

'Here, here! But on a more serious note Harry, you'll have to keep an even lower profile than before, once we start poking around. The usual effect of one of our investigations is that slimy things start crawling out from under rocks and that will turn up the pressure on the search for the girls and Janice.'

I nodded, 'Yeah. You're right. We may have been a little bit slack in that regard at times, but after we drop you off, we'll come back out here and hole up. I think we're good for food and supplies for a while, but if necessary, we'll run down to Strahan or even just across to Stanley to top up the pantry.'

Janice and Sandy wandered up soon after looking bleary-eyed but happy and after the usual round of kisses and hugs, they hit the galley. The girls weren't far behind, so in the bustle of activity around the galley, Janice gave me another kiss and whispered in my ear, 'You were a very good boy last night.'

I pulled back and grinned at her, 'Really? I don't remember doing anything.'

'That's what I mean. You just rolled over and went to sleep.'

She wouldn't elaborate, so I mentally shrugged and let it slide, happy that they were happy and that she was happy with me.

The only flight Hilary and Debbie could get seats on for Saturday was the 10:15 departure, so Debbie booked them using the satellite Internet, as there was no mobile service out on the islands. Rather than sail back to Wynyard that afternoon and risk exposing the ladies to the extra public scrutiny that they would attract, since we were starting to look like a floating harem, being more than a little top-heavy with females, I decided we should make a very early start on Saturday morning as the wind forecast was for strong northerlies, with another cold front bringing a southerly change on Sunday.

The crew didn't seem to mind the prospect of a 03:00 wakeup call, with a 04:00 departure, but Zoe asked about navigation.

'It won't be any different than what we've already done,' I reassured her, 'night sailing isn't a problem when electronic aids like radar and the chart plotter show us the way and reveal any moving obstacles. Plus, this bay has no obstructions on our track, so it's another straight shot to a point off Wynyard, but still stay at least 2 miles off the Nut at Stanley.'

Next morning, things went smoothly as Zoe and I had made most of the preparations the evening before, and to my relief, the wind had started blowing late yesterday afternoon. Everyone was up at 03:00, although I'd told our guests that they could stay in bed until normal get up time if they wanted, but they declined, wanting to be involved in everything.

It was worth their while, as it turned out, as a full moon was shining brightly, turning the choppy sea into an ever-changing, metallic-silver landscape that *Firebird* charged across at the very decent speed of 18 to 20 knots, with the odd higher burst. I had to put a small reef in the screecher and rolled the main down a little, but that just made the boat sit flatter and relieved some pressure on the bows, as the wind was over our port quarter.

The clouds of flying spray tossed up as the bows dug into the smooth backs of the swells, glittered in the moonlight like millions of diamonds cast aloft by the sea gods to light our way, lending an air of ethereal beauty to the scene. The ladies were totally enchanted with the sight and watched in silence for a long time.

Debbie finally turned to me with a smile of utter delight on her face. 'Harry, this sail alone makes everything worthwhile! It's incredible! No wonder you love this life. Will you invite us to come out again, please?'

I smiled back, pleased with her, 'Yeah. It's times like this that makes the uncomfortable times fade away as bad memories, but you're very welcome to come visit whenever you want.'

She nodded thanks and understanding and returned her attention to the endlessly charming, changing vista in front of us.

Dawn at sea with a clear sky is always a magical time, but this morning was special as light slowly pushed the cloak of darkness back behind us into the west, while some low cloud on the east horizon caused faint orange bars of the still-hidden sun to slowly grow more distinct and spread like the fingers of a giant orange hand, stretching for, but never quite reaching the apex of the sky. I'd warned the ladies to look for the green flash that is occasionally seen just as the upper rim of the sun breeches the horizon line, but on this occasion, it didn't happen.

Once daylight had lit our heaving, wet world, and the celestial light show faded for another 24 hours, there was a general call for food and Angie volunteered to make everybody a decent, hot breakfast. Debbie cheerfully assisted, seeming to really enjoy getting involved as part of the crew, while Hilary and I quietly re-hashed a few of the more important points of our discussions of the last few days. I suggested that they buy a selection of pre-paid mobiles for contact with us and change them every week or so. They had both the boat's mobile and sat-phone numbers, plus there was always email via the satellite Internet.

The rest of the run was uneventful, and we dropped the anchor in our usual spot by 09:00. Zoe dropped the RIB into the water while I finished securing the boat, and without delay, goodbyes were said, then I loaded the ladies and their gear. Angie and Zoe asked if they could come as well and stop at the chemist and newsagent to stock up, so after a quick consult with Janice and Sandy, I agreed and we all jammed into the dinghy and motored slowly ashore

Ernie's old Holden was in its usual spot and as we were lucky to avoid tripping across Mavis or any hotel staff who might ask awkward questions, we were soon headed for the Airport, passing up the main street that was slowly coming awake for the Saturday morning rush. I snagged a park quite close to the terminal and asked the girls to stay with the car while I saw our visitors checked in safely. I was a little longer than I'd planned, but after a few more words to Hilary, I hustled back out to the car. There was some sort of confrontation happening out front and I had to work my way around a small crowd who were jeering and booing a scruffy-looking fellow with long greasy hair who was having a very one-sided shouting match with a towie and two security guards over his parked car being hooked up to a tow-truck. Since the two vehicles were stuffing up the access for arriving and departing passengers with their baggage, the idiot scored zero sympathy from anybody. It would have been funny to watch if I hadn't been in a hurry, so I left them to it. Driving past on the way out, I saw that the tangle had been cleared and orderly traffic flow restored.

Back down the main street, the girls said they needed to go to a chemist and then the Newsagency, so when I spotted a chemist just next to the big supermarket, I got lucky and scored a park just in front of it. The girls knew the Newsagent was just a little way further down the street opposite the post office, so I said I'd stay where I was. Janice had given them some cash, so they happily darted over the road to do their stuff.

I noticed a cafe not far back and suddenly fancied a milkshake, so I locked the car and wandered back. The café was very clean, and the owner was a nice old Greek bloke and we had a good old chat for a few minutes while he built the drink with pride, which included a raw egg, a different addition that he said made his 'shakes taste the best in Tasmania.

I was game to try anything once but had to agree that the taste was better than any I'd had before. After I'd been brought up-to-date on the local gossip, but before he got started on the doings of his extensive family, I made my escape, so we parted the best of friends and I strolled back down to the car. Traffic was quite heavy for a small town, even for Saturday morning, so I leaned back against the brick wall surrounding the small park to enjoy my beautiful 'shake and watch the rest of civilisation bustling about while I waited for the girls. It wasn't long before a screech of tyres, a very loud bang and the tinkling of broken glass, just a little way further down the street, announced that at times, civilisation shouldn't bustle quite so much.

Moments later, a growing chorus of angry shouts added to the spectacle, so I wandered down to see what the fuss was all about.

CHAPTER 34

JIMMY, WYNYARD AIRPORT,
SATURDAY MORNING - 10:00

As the port propeller of the Saab 360 whined to a stop, the door with its set of folding steps popped open, the Flight Attendant holding on carefully so she didn't follow them down as the stairs unfolded. The First Officer, who looked too young to have left his Mother, made an appearance, adjusting his new and still very shiny flight-crew cap to what he thought of as a jaunty angle, before trotting down the steps to secure the lower prop blade so it didn't start turning again in the stiff, gusting breeze that had made his attempt at a smooth landing such a cockup. The Captain's total lack of comment was an even worse condemnation of his arrival.

Despite his attempt to look like a highly experienced, fearless professional aviator, the first passenger to emerge, a burly construction worker, shot him down in flames by commenting loudly, 'Better go back to flight school, sonny. That was a real teeth-rattler!'

The First gritted his teeth and gave a twisted grimace that had to pass for a smile, mortified to hear a badly stifled giggle from the pretty flight attendant he had been desperately trying to impress.

The next passenger down the steps was a large, overweight man of medium height, the small amount of hair he had left arranged in a dopey-looking comb-over. His beady little eyes were set too close together and he leaked perspiration from every pore, the smell of which easily overcame the anti-stink he'd slathered on earlier. Suddenly, every fly on the airport zeroed in on the new attraction.

'Better check the landing gear after that one,' he advised the hapless First with a sneer, 'you've broken some-bloody-thing. It's a friggin' wonder people fly at all with drivers like you trying to kill 'em!'

'Yes sir. Have a good day, sir and thanks for flying with King Airways.'

'Bloody well wouldn't if I didn't have to!' the man grumped as he stomped off to the terminal, unaware that his comb-over was standing up like it was trying to take off, his eyes already scanning the Arrivals area for the expected familiar face. As he pushed through the doors, a short, skinny man with tangled, greasy hair hanging over his long narrow face giving him the look of a malnourished ferret, and a left eye with the highly disconcerting habit of peering in any direction other than where the right one was pointing, stepped forward.

'Gidday, Jimmy,' he announced in an irritating, high-pitched, whiny voice, 'good to see ya mate. I've got the car just outside the door, all ready to go. Jeeze, I'm glad you came. I reckon we might be onto something here.'

'Yeah. Gidday Tony. I gotta get my bag first, though. Then you can tell me all about it.'

'Oh. Yeah. I think bag pickup is right over there.'

Ten minutes later, they pushed through the doors to the outside, to see a white Toyota Corolla with a tow-truck backing up to it, under the direction of two large, pissed-off security guys.

'Wadda youse think youse are doin'?' Tony squeaked. 'That's my car!'

'Is it now, mate?' the nearest guard sneered, after giving him a quick once-over. 'In that case, you can have the pleasure of collecting it from the impound area in about two hours' time. It's not far from here. You can probably walk if you want to save your money to pay the fines and charges!'

Jimmy stood impassively; being unusually patient while Tony spluttered, ranted and nearly got his hand crushed trying to stop the tow-truck operator sliding the lift bars under the front of the Corolla.

'Aw, c'mon mate,' he whined to the towie, a man as big as both

Security guards together, and looking three times as tough, 'give us a break! My boss is going to be really pissed with me!'

The towie looked up for a moment, pointed a finger the size of a sausage roll at a sign behind Tony and declared in a calm, deep voice, 'Maybe you should have thought of that before you parked your heap-of-shit in a tow-away area, blocking everybody else from doing the right thing! Mate!'

Tony glanced over his shoulder at the incriminating sign and shrugged, 'Yeah, but, you know!'

'Don't, 'yeah, but' me, sport, 'cause I don't give a shit! Complain to the airport management, they love to hear from arse-holes like you!'

He quickly finished securing the Corolla, then with a practiced hand, filled out a form, tore off the top sheet and handed it to Tony, who stood, narrow shoulders slumped, misery all over his face.

'There you go, sport. Holding depot is in town, address on the bottom of the form. Vehicle will be available after 14:00 today and you can pay the fine and costs there, or you can deal direct with the rental car company. They'll love to see you too! $150 fines plus the $300 towing fee.'

Tony took the sheet of paper, glanced at it and gave the towie the one-finger salute.

The towie and the security guys laughed, saluted him back, then he climbed into his truck and drove off, the rented Corolla trailing obediently behind.

Jimmy looked at him. 'You really know how to fuck things up, don't you? Even when you were tailing that dude, you had to take a piss facing away from the road! Why couldn't you keep your eye on the traffic?'

Tony looked down and scuffed his shoe on the footpath, ''Cause I can't go if people are looking at me, that's why!'

Jimmy took a deep breath, visibly holding himself back.

'Oh, I see. So I suppose that in a public toilet, you can't use the urinals in case somebody sees your almost non-existent dick and cracks up laughing?'

Tony looked up with a pleading expression, 'Yes. That's right. It's a phoebe or something. I looked it up one time. Jeeze, I'm glad you understand Jimmy.'

In a soft voice, Jimmy lowered his face so their noses were almost touching and quietly said, 'I don't give a flying fuck if it's a phoebe or a phobia. You're an idiot and shouldn't be allowed out in public on your own, unless you're on a leash with a minder. Now get inside and get another car. Now! Before I rip your bloody arm off and stuff it up your smelly little arse!'

Jimmy followed a rather frightened and subdued Tony as he scuttled back inside the terminal, to make sure there were no more fuckups. Watching while Tony alternately argued with and was barked at by the hard-faced lady behind the counter, Jimmy finally turned away to check out any good-looking females waiting for the outbound flight and almost bumped into a small group of three people; two women and a man, who were talking intently and not really watching where they were going. Exercising a degree of politeness, he really didn't know he had, he stepped aside, although his attention was immediately caught by the shorter woman's brilliant red hair that flowed in shimmering waves down to her shoulders. Her companion was a tall, almost regal-looking blonde with great tits and tight jeans. The guy with them was still talking softly, but intently and although they meant nothing to him, he automatically took note of the guy's instantly-forgettable face and appearance, which in shorts, T-shirt and thongs rated super casual even by Jimmy's standards.

As they moved away toward the boarding gate, Jimmy watched the ladies' very shapely bums and legs from behind while he continued to wait for Tony to finish getting reamed and bored by the rental car clerk. Then, as the final boarding call was announced, the ladies separated from the guy with kisses and hugs and hustled through the gate. Jimmy took a final wistful look at their rear view, then turned to see Tony extract himself from under a continuing torrent of abuse, clutching a sheaf of papers and a set of keys.

'Are we right to go now?' enquired Jimmy politely.

'Yes, Jimmy. Good to go, but bloody hell, they know how to charge in this place. They wanted me to go and retrieve the car myself, but I said we were in a hurry.

Then that Nazi bitch with the really smart mouth really paid me out and charged an extra $200 for them to retrieve it! And that was on top of the fines, tow charge and the cost of the new car!

So I've had to fork out $650 plus the charges for the new car! Can I claim that back off expenses? What'd you reckon, Jimmy? I mean, my card's nearly empty!'

Jimmy bent down again, once again generously giving Tony the full benefit of his lack of dental hygiene, 'I think that if you don't shut the fuck up, I'll tear you a new arse-hole. You'll need a new one 'cause the old one'll be a bit blocked off by your arm, which I'm about to rip off at the shoulder and stuff up there!

I also think that if you tried to claim money back from the Boss for cocking things up, he might just rip your stupid bloody head off and piss down the hole!'

'Oh! Well, you don't have to carry on about it. I mean, we all make mistakes. Anyway, the car's over this way.'

Five minutes later, they were seated in yet another Toyota Corolla, engine running and air-con on.

'Now, you little turd-burger! What's the big news you've got that dragged me down here?'

'What? Oh, yeah. Well, after I lost the old geezer the other day, I thought I should hang around, so I checked into a Motel and had a bit of a wander about. Later that night, I was down by the harbour having a beer at some old pub, when I thought I saw the bloke we're chasing come through the back door and duck upstairs. I asked the barmaid who they had staying there, but she said that no one was. They had rooms to rent, but no guests at that time.

When I asked again about the bloke I saw, she said maybe I'd seen her brother who lives upstairs. I suppose it could've been some-one else, but it sure looked like the guy in the photo you gave me.'

Jimmy looked at his sidekick with distaste.

'So, when was this?'

'Umm...Four nights ago...Tuesday it must have been. I mean, I only saw him for a couple of seconds as he walked past the doorway and climbed the stairs, but it looked like him to me.'

Jimmy thought for a few moments, the refrigerated air helping to dry up some of the reeking sweat that'd soaked his clothing. 'Ok. Drive around town to let me have a look. Maybe swing past that pub where you reckon you saw him.'

'Ok, Jimmy.'

They cruised slowly down the main street, busy with Saturday morning shoppers, when Tony made a strangled sound, swerved violently left toward a narrow space just past the pedestrian crossing, nearly hitting some old dear in the process, then jammed the brakes on so hard the motor stalled and Jimmy was pitched hard forward against his seat-belt.

'Jesus! What the fuck are you doing now, you bloody goose?' roared Jimmy, rubbing his left shoulder that had thumped hard into the door pillar.

'Look Jimmy!' Tony spluttered. 'There they are!'

'Where what are?'

'The girls! The girls are right there! Just up ahead past the Real Estate place. They just came out of that Newsagent! I'm sure it's them! Come on, we can grab them right now!'

Tony's panic swerve and crash stop caused a young female learner-driver to rear-end the Holden ute that had jammed its brakes on hard to avoid running into the back end of the Corolla that Tony had left sticking out half across the traffic lane. The resultant horrific bang, crash and tinkles from the shower of shattered glass and plastic distracted Jimmy who didn't know where to look. But Tony, with a rare display of focus and determination, took off like a man possessed, out of the car and across the road, oblivious to the chaos he'd caused behind him. Not even the sound of car doors slamming and a series of angry bellows directed in his direction was able to deflect his unerring course toward his two hapless subjects, standing on the footpath outside the newsagency clutching the latest editions of Cleo and Cosmopolitan magazines, while they looked toward the source of the noise and shouting. That distraction also made them overlook the scrawny, scruffy little man striding toward them, his gaze unwavering.

In the meantime, Jimmy had finally extracted himself clear of the octopus-like embrace of his locked-up seat belt and was heading across the road after Tony. He was desperately trying to catch up to stop the stupid little turd from making an even bigger scene, right in the middle of the main street on Saturday morning with a bunch of angry Taswegians, intent on revenge, for the damage done to their cars bearing down on them from behind!

CHAPTER 35

The girls had bought what they needed at the Chemist and wandered down to the newsagent, Zoe swinging a woven hemp carry bag. It was a bit weighty with a large bottle of nice-smelling shampoo and another of conditioner. There was also a large container of body wash that they both liked as well as tampon supplies and more sunscreen. As much as they loved the boat, the sailing and the beautiful islands, there were times they craved the company of others, so the laid-back rush of Wynyard on a Saturday morning was great. They were thoroughly enjoying being back in the normal world for a brief time. At the newsagent, they grabbed a copy of each of the new teen magazines, plus a good selection of newspapers for the oldies. After paying, they walked outside, while Zoe stowed the magazines and papers carefully in the bag. Because her attention was on the bag, the first time she knew that something was wrong was when Angie said, 'What the fuck…?'

She looked up to see a weird little guy, long greasy hair flapping around his face, dodging around horn-blowing cars, charging straight at them, his mouth twisted in a feral snarl and a rant of what sounded like, 'Now we've got you, you rotten little bitches!' spilling from his foam-flecked mouth. There was a much bigger guy lumbering along not far behind the first one, yelling abuse at him, while several other guys were walking swiftly after them, yelling abuse at the two in front.

For Angie, Sandy's training kicked straight in as the little guy ran straight up to Zoe and grabbed her arm. Hardly pausing to consider, she drew back her right leg and delivered a resounding kick straight to the outside of his left knee, which immediately bent much further inwards than nature ever intended. With a howl of agony, he collapsed onto the footpath, his long, ragged fingernails raking down Zoe's arm and drawing several streaks of fresh blood. Seeing the damage done to her sister, Angie drew back again and delivered another very hard kick straight into his stomach that doubled him up in further agony.

Stunned shoppers, already distracted by the noise of the car crash, gave the trio a wide berth, opening the way for the large man to charge in, this time grabbing for Angie, still off-balance from the second kick. He hadn't reckoned on Zoe's reflexes however, as, despite the pain of the gouges down her arm, she spun a 360° circle; her right arm extended like a discus thrower and caught the big man right across the side of his fat, meaty face with the heavy bag. He gave a howl of pain and rage as the collection of bottles inside the bag split his cheek open from his eye to his chin and relocated his jaw, now in several pieces, to the far side of his face, a position that the various tendons and muscles couldn't quite accommodate without tearing painfully.

It wasn't a look that improved his appearance and certainly made speech impossible, although the incoherent gurgling sounds suggested that he had something to say.

Angie tossed a quick grin and a muttered, 'Thanks, sis,' at Zoe, before looking around to see Harry sprinting through the traffic, incongruously carrying a milk-shake container in his hand. 'Come on,' she said, grabbing Zoe's hand, 'here's Harry and I think we'd better nick off quick time.'

They dodged away from the two downed assailants and met Harry in mid-street, just as several irate locals from the damaged cars arrived, ready to inflict their own brand of justice on the two clowns who'd caused the damage.

'Good on youse, girls,' one of the bigger drivers called, 'we'll look after these dickheads now!'

With the situation now sufficiently muddled to render the concept of what had happened to whom and why a complete mystery, the girls quietly turned Harry around and calmly walked back over the street, past an angle-parked Corolla with the L-plater crying her eyes out sitting in the gutter. Clouds of steam spouted from under the bonnet of her Hyundai Excel that had rammed the tail of the Holden Ute, while a stream of bilious-green coolant spread across both lanes. There were plenty of helpful bystanders to comfort the pretty young girl, while her father was over outside the Newsagent, still bellowing with rage and apparently exacting some revenge.

By the time the police arrived, the girls had convinced Harry to turn the car around and make an orderly escape. At the scene, confusion reigned supreme and the best the police could make from the mass of conflicting stories, was that the Corolla driver must have been on drugs, had gone nuts, stopped in the middle of the road, causing the accident between the ute and the L-plater, then tried to attack two girls on the opposite footpath. The locals, who assumed both men were dangerous and were trying to run away from the smash scene, subsequently did their civic duty and made sure they didn't escape again. Their injuries, induced by several extra kicks, including a particularly good one right in Tony's shrivelled little nuts, were put down to the abrupt stop of their car and the chase across the road where they must have tripped over a rubbish bin and fallen badly. The list of serious injuries tallied up by the Ambo's when they arrived ten minutes later was enough to make them shake their heads and tell the police that they had to be transported to Burnie Hospital immediately and requested a high-speed police escort.

CHAPTER 36

Once he was settled in his business class seat, Robert mentally reviewed the weird and somewhat unsettling conversation he'd had with Annette the previous night.

At first, he'd thought that her ball-busting attitude was because she was drunk, but she'd really paid him out big time on just two glasses of red! He was prepared to forgive her though, as her job obviously created a lot of stress, but he really hoped that she was easier to get on with in the flesh. She certainly sounded interesting, with a deep, husky voice that sent a shiver down his spine. Admittedly, he should have given her more notice of the meeting, but he was very keen to show her the files and pass over her copy, as well as hopefully stay a step ahead of the crew that was chasing them.

Nevertheless, he wore jeans and a green polo shirt, sans crocodile, just to placate her dress code sensitivity.

From a prosecution point of view, he was pinning a lot of hope on Annette and her small team to do most, if not all of the identification of the adults in the pictures and video. Apparently, the ACP had some of the best equipment in Australia to get that nasty task done quickly and with a high degree of accuracy.

After landing in Canberra, he drifted around the terminal for a while, checking for any watchers, but couldn't see anybody acting oddly, like hiding behind an upside-down newspaper, so he wandered over to the rental car area and booked a white Kia Rio for four days. His idea was that if someone did get that far along his trail, they might think he was getting a head start on the business week and wouldn't expect him to disappear into the countryside.

Finally, fairly sure that he was tail-free, he located the car and consulted the GPS unit as to the best way out of town to the north. Of two options offered on the device, he chose to go through the suburbs as an extra precaution against surveillance and set off cautiously, unfamiliar with Canberra's curving street layout and seemingly endless road works. He also took the additional precaution of ducking down the odd side street to further confuse any tail, relying on the GPS to put him back on the path to Yass, which it did, although with an annoying series of 'Recalculating' or 'Make a U-turn' commands when he went a different way to the one insisted on by the machine.

Despite the crowded Saturday morning roads, he was soon on the Barton Highway headed north, pleased that he'd managed to avoid the attention of the ever-present speed cameras, cunningly tucked behind trees and bushes. The little car hummed along very nicely, and he felt his mood lifting as the kilometres rolled past. Despite his obsession with being punctual, Rob didn't hit the outskirts of Yass until 10 minutes past midday and was surprised that he didn't really care!

He soon saw what Annette had meant about the main street of Yass; it was very long and there were a whole lot of little roundabouts to dodge around until he spotted a set of traffic lights in the distance with a number of cars parked against the kerb outside a grand old wooden building, one of which just happened to be a pretty little black Mercedes AMG SLK55 with the solid hardtop neatly folded away in the small boot.

He'd long admired the little Benz, particularly this very potent AMG 5.5 litre V8 version, and guessed that it must have raised a few eyebrows at the ACP, but maybe she had something rather more ordinary as an everyday drive.

It was a bit crowded out front, so he parked around the corner and wandered into the front bar. It was rather dim inside and he didn't see her at first, but as advised, there was a tall, slim woman perched on a stool at the bar, wearing a red shirt, with a schooner of beer in front of her. He took a moment to size up this woman who was so handy with a scathing word or six, and had to admit that from behind, she looked good with broad shoulders, a slim waist and hips encased in tight blue jeans.

Her long, shining dark hair hung loose down to the middle of her back, and he had just noted that her beer was at half-mast, when she stood and turned to him. He belatedly realised that she'd been checking him out in the mirror behind the bar from the moment he walked in. However, her front view was even more pleasant, as she was very pretty, looked to be a very well preserved early 50-something and filled the front of her shirt very nicely.

With a quirky smile on her lips, she held out her hand as he approached and gave him a firm shake, her skin warm and dry.

'Do I pass inspection?' she asked in that sexy, husky voice he'd heard last night, but which was so much better in the flesh!

He had the grace to blush slightly, before replying, 'Most definitely so! I'm guilty of attaching visual stereotypes to phone voices, and I'm delighted to say that I was a long way off the mark!'

She chuckled warmly, 'What a back-handed compliment and a charming recovery.' The truth was that despite the shots she'd taken at him last night, she was more than impressed with the look of the tall, lean, well-spoken barrister, having a soft spot for handsome men with chiselled features and a good tan. 'Grab yourself a drink and come over to one of these tables at the back. We can talk more privately there.'

With a beer in hand, Rob followed her over to a table set at the back of the lounge. As he dug his laptop and the portable HDD out of his quirky hippy-style shoulder bag, he said,

'I'm sorry to give you so little notice about this meeting, but I was very keen that you should see the files for yourself as quickly as possible. And please call me Rob.'

'No problem, Rob. I'm equally keen to see them and get stuck into the ID process. But you must tell me more about our runaways; like, where are they and how are they all getting along?'

Rob could see no reason to keep the secret of the boat from Annette, so told a short version of the story, including the not-so-secret fact that his daughter, Janice, had decided to hop into bed with her rescuer and protector and the various antics of the surreal boat-cat, Jasper.

As an icebreaker, it couldn't have been better, causing Annette, after her laughter had settled, to say, 'I wonder if I could talk Harry into taking on another temporary crewmember after all this is over?'

Rob chuckled, 'Looking like you do, I think he'd be delighted! In fact, I wouldn't mind a few weeks on board either.'

Annette grinned at the compliment, 'Dear Rob. What a lovely thing to say!'

'Well. It's true! Anyway...' Rob's phone rang softly, interrupting him.

With a quick apology, he dug it out of his pocket, only to realise that it was the burner phone in his shoulder bag that was making the summoning sounds.

'Uh, oh!' he said to Annette. 'Speak of the devil, this is Harry now on the sat-phone.'

'Hi Harry. How are things? Oh, sorry honey. I just assumed it was the big fella.'

'...Oh, shit! Are they Okay?'

'...Great, but what happened?'

He listened for some time without saying much more, although he belatedly remembered to tilt the phone away from his ear so Annette could listen as well, slightly distracted when she rested her head against his, giving him a strong whiff of a very heady perfume.

'OK, got all that and Annette caught some as well, she's here with me.'

'...Yes, dear, we're out of Canberra, but just remind me, when you put a hole in the egg, do you suck or blow?'

'...Yeah, I know. I'm getting good at it; I've been taking lessons from an expert. So, you think that Luke's guys are out of things for the moment?'

'...That long? Outstanding! Good one for the girls and public sympathy! But I'm not sure that'll be the end of the hunt!'

'…I'm glad you agree. Oh! Annette wants to have a quick word, hang on.'

He passed the phone over.

'Hi Janice, glad the girls are ok, but I just wanted to let you guys know that there's been some more emails to/from Luke discussing the 'condition of the white goods. Nothing more specific, I'm afraid, but we keep listening and reading.'

'…You're welcome. I'll let you know immediately if we get more. I've got some of my team at work today, sifting through emails and voice recordings, so stuff could turn up at any time. Anyway, I'll let you go hide out wherever you can hide in a 60ft cat, while I try to persuade your grumpy old man to buy me a bottle of red wine. I think we're going to be in for a long, nasty afternoon!'

'…Yeah, I'm learning that. Take care and bye for now.'

She passed the phone back to Rob who said his goodbyes and terminated the call.

'What's this 'grumpy old man crap?' Rob demanded with a cheeky grin.

Annette pushed his shoulder, 'Just go get a bottle of Merlot and two glasses. As I just said, it's going to be a long afternoon!'

'But we've got to drive!' Rob protested in horror.

'Oh, fuck it, Rob! Take a chance and live a little! We're not going to be looking at happy holiday snaps, are we?'

'No.'

'Well, I at least and probably you too, need to be suitably fortified in that case. You do drink red wine, I hope?'

'Sure. I even like Merlot.'

'Thank Christ for that! Well then, get your arse over to the bar and ask Matthew nicely if he'd open one of the best ones. We'll work out the driving bit later.'

Slightly bemused by this bewitching woman and her quirky moods, Rob dutifully trotted over to the bar, watched by the barman with a smile on his face.

'I'm guessing she wants the best Merlot,' he said, reaching under the bar to produce a really dusty bottle that had no label.

Rob blinked at the price, but flashed his plastic, collected two glasses and as he was turning away, Matthew quietly commented, 'She must like you. She doesn't share the good stuff with anybody else!'

Rob raised his eyebrows at that piece of country pub wisdom. 'Ah...thanks Matthew, I think.'

Matthew chuckled, 'Enjoy!'

The bar was only sparsely populated, and the table Annette had chosen was tucked around a corner from the obligatory sports section where a row of monitors showed all manner of horse racing and betting odds in vivid colour and stereo sound. Several locals nursed their beers, cheered winners, groaned at losers and blew the grocery money on 'sure things.' Rob noted that there was a power point handy to their table in case his laptop needed a recharge. He had a feeling it would!

After he'd poured two glasses, tried a sip and thoroughly approved of her choice, he said. 'Firstly, and from a legal standpoint, I'm comfortable with the way Janice and Harry have created and preserved a chain of evidence, as well as the fact that Janice didn't steal the files. At that time she made the copy, they were not locked or hidden in any way, were openly available and not password protected. So, my considered opinion is that she simply accessed files that were on a computer in her house and one that could be considered the joint property of her husband and herself.'

A suddenly professional Annette nodded thoughtfully, 'That sounds good, but could it be argued that because Luke normally kept his office locked, he didn't really intend to allow anybody else free access, and the one time that Janice was able to gain access was an unintended consequence of the unexpected visitor?'

Rob smiled, 'Damn! That's a good defence argument! But I guess that a judge would have to think long and hard about whether intention to prevent an action occurring takes precedence over that action occurring by happenstance and that if someone took advantage of that piece of happenstance, the advantage gained should be allowed!'

It was Annette's turn to smile. 'Good comeback, Counsellor, and it may be correct, but it's not cut and dried, so that if a ruling went against us on the issue of how the files were obtained, we would be in the position of having them ruled as inadmissible.'

Rob looked rueful, 'Yeah. I've been running that one around in my head for weeks and still can't find a definite answer. Short of consulting with a judge, who might be compromised, we won't know until it comes to trial.'

'Ok. We won't worry about that for the moment, but we need to plan for a backup set of evidence, like what might be found in that mansion in Melbourne. I believe that it will be a major key to the whole thing. A raid on that place, without warning, using that runaway girl as probable cause for a warrant, could yield everything we need. Especially if we find a duplicate set of jpeg and video files on computers there.'

'Yes, you're right. That would be the best back-up, but I presume that no action is planned against that house so far on account of the Thai girl?' Rob asked.

'No, not yet thank goodness! Although that's strange, because she told the coppers she'd been illegally transported from Thailand and held in the house against her will.'

'So does that mean the ACP told the Victorian coppers to lay off, or are they just dragging their feet?'

'I don't know the answer to that one, Rob, maybe a bit of both. Anyway, it's safe for me to keep probing 'cause it's right in my territory!'

While they'd been talking, Matthew brought out some plates of hot finger food, like little spicy dumplings, mini spring rolls with real pork and veal mince, and some peppery Kransky chipolatas, all with an array of dipping sauces.

'Thanks, Matty,' Annette said as the first round was delivered.

Matthew just smiled and returned to the bar.

'You must be a regular,' Rob commented, 'he knows all your tastes.'

Annette gave him a look, 'So the little bugger should! He's my younger brother and I've got a half-share in the place.'

'Bugger me!' was Rob's totally inadequate reply, 'you *are* full of surprises! And I must say, the food's excellent.'

'Yeah. We got lucky by finding a young fella who was just out of prison but had trained as a cook while he was in there. It's hard to find work being a convicted felon, but we gave him a chance and we've found that he's a good worker and a bloody good cook. So far it's worked out really well, and he's paired up with the girl who helps with the bar and the kitchen, so everybody's happy. Trade is building quite nicely, so we'll probably have to take on another kitchen hand and maybe a casual bar person as well.'

'I'm really impressed,' Rob commented, looking around more carefully than he did earlier, 'it looks like you've made some renovations as well.'

'Yep. We closed for a week, got some tradies in, fed 'em lunch and dinner each day, as well as some free beers after 5, and they put in 14-hour days. We did three weeks work in one! Matthew and I have a fancy suite each upstairs, and there's another ten really nice ensuite rooms for rent.'

'That sounds like a neat package.'

'Yes. It's working out quite well. Turnover is up 50% already from when we bought it from an old bloke who didn't bother to modernise the place or serve decent meals. That's where the money is; serve good food at reasonable prices to keep the patrons around and they'll keep drinking! Free bowls of nuts and the occasional serving of hot, salty finger foods keeps the beer thirst going as well!' She added with a sly grin.

Rob fired up his laptop as his answering smile slowly faded. 'That sounds great, and I'd like to see more later, but we'd better get to work.'

YASS, ROBERT JAMESON, SATURDAY

With the folder list on-screen, Rob suggested, 'Why don't you do a fairly quick skim through each folder of photos, starting with the oldest going back ten years. There's no real indication of how long these scum have been operating; that's just as far back as this collection goes. There are an awful lot of photos!'

The professional Annette took over again as she wordlessly slipped on a pair of reading glasses, took hold of the mouse and with Rob sitting close beside her, started skimming through the files. She had a notebook beside her and occasionally jotted a brief note, referenced to a date, photo and folder number.

After 30-odd minutes, she stopped and started at the ceiling for a few moments, her eyes closed and a pained look on her pretty face.

'Bloody hell, Rob! These are seriously bad people!' she finally growled, 'I've identified ten well-known faces already! They don't seem to care that they can be identified! Are they so confident that they're so well-protected, they can afford to be so open?'

Rob nodded, 'Yes. We asked the exact same question, and I think that you're right, they are confident that they can't be touched.'

'Well,' she said briskly, taking a solid swig of wine, 'be a dear and fetch another bottle please. My shout.'

Rob looked at his glass, getting a shock that already they'd knocked over a bottle between them, but dutifully rose and went to the bar.

'I guess it's the same again,' he said cheerfully.

'Yep thanks Matthew, Annette's shout. That stuff slides down way too easily! I don't know how we're going to drive back to Canberra.'

Matthew laughed, 'There's no way you were driving anywhere tonight! Sis had me organise a room for you upstairs. She stays here every weekend anyway, so there'll be plenty of time to sort out your business in peace.'

'Oh. Well, that sounds pretty good then. I can relax.'

'Yep, you sure can. We'll look after everything, in fact, if you let me have your car keys, I'll have Josie take it 'round the back where it'll be safe and out of the way.'

Rob handed them over as he took the fresh bottle of liquid smoothness and headed back to Annette who was still scrolling and scribbling alternately.

After re-filling their glasses, he asked, 'How's it going?'

She didn't look up, but merely said, 'Stunning! Just stunning! I had no idea Janice had grabbed so much stuff, and these are just the still photos! I see there are a whole bunch of videos as well, but I may only watch one of two of those.

Oh. And I think I found some of your granddaughters! They stood out because they were the only ones where the girls looked happy and relaxed!'

Rob grimaced. 'Yeah. That's how they are! Bloody Luke has been taking naked shots of them for years. Apparently, the girls are quite happy being naked anywhere, anytime and certainly didn't mind dear, darling Daddy taking their pics!'

He gave chuckle, 'Mind you, according to Janice, they wouldn't mind who took their photo, so long as the environment was happy and relaxed. That's the way she raised them and I'm proud of what she's done. They're great kids!'

'Yes, they certainly seem to be, although they're not really kids any longer.'

'Yeah. I suppose you're right. It's a Grandfather's habit to see them as kids for life!'

Glass suitably replenished, Annette turned back to her review of just some of the vast amount of material stored on the portable drive, while Rob alternately sipped his wine, studied Annette and looked around the pub. She and Matthew had done a great job of renovating the interior and he was interested to see what the upstairs accommodation was like, so he wandered over and asked Matthew if he could see his room and maybe have a quick wash.

'Sure thing,' Matthew said with a grin, handing over a key attached to a brass tag with a neat #1 stamped on it. 'It's the second door on the left at the top of the stairs. Sis has the first on the left and I've got the one opposite. I hope you'll find it comfortable.'

'I'm sure I will,' Rob assured him, before collecting his overnight bag from the table, where Annette, oblivious to his movements, was deeply engrossed in the display on the computer screen.

The wide, grand staircase that ascended from the back of the comfortable, inviting lounge area, had beautifully carved and polished dark wood balustrades and turned through 180°, ending at a long high-ceilinged hallway that stretched through to the front of the building. It was carpeted in a thick and tasteful design and lit with dim antique-style wall-mounted lamps. As advised, Rob's key opened the second door on the left to reveal a very spacious and comfortable room with the same high ceiling as the hallway and was well lit by ornate French doors opening out onto the wide, fully-roofed veranda that circled three sides of the upper floor.

A queen-size bed was set against the wall to the right, while a door to the left presumably led to the en-suite. A quick look confirmed that, so Rob had a quick pee and washed his face to freshen up a bit, as the unaccustomed consumption of so much wine in the afternoon made him feel like crawling into bed.

Somewhat refreshed, he left his bag on the bed and went back down to re-join Annette, first stopping at the bar to tell Matthew how great the room looked.

'Thanks Rob. We worked pretty hard on the makeover. We wanted to keep the old feel of the place, but with modern, reliable fittings and facilities. Sis chose all the fabrics and colours, I'm hopeless at that!'

'Well it certainly worked out well. I hope it pays off in the long run.'

'It's starting to,' he replied, 'we've done deals with several touring coach companies who do winery tours, so we're getting a few tourists from them and there's a number of regular travellers who like the extra comfort and convenience of having food and drink in the one place. We also keep things quiet at night by closing by 11 or 12 o'clock at the latest and not playing the jukebox after 10pm.'

'That's a good incentive for guests, but don't the locals want a bit more entertainment at night?'

'You're right, they do. But we fixed that by inviting local talent to play live music Friday night, then Saturday afternoon and night, but they must be acoustic only, no amplifiers or drums. Sis and I vet them first to make sure they sound all right, so it's a quieter sort of pub music, but it's been attracting a growing crowd who seem to appreciate not having their eardrums bashed into submission by low-talent, greasy-haired twits who scream three words as lyrics and only know four chords. We find it really suits the overnight guests.'

Rob chuckled, 'That sounds like my sort of live pub music. So, who's on tonight?'

'Oh, you'll like them! It's a young girl singer and her brother with guitar. She's got a beautiful voice and he harmonises with her really well. If she was older and not still at school, we reckon she'd be snapped up by a talent scout as a support act for one of the major touring groups.'

'Must be good,' Rob commented.

'Yeah, she really is! But for now, we're very happy to have her play as often as she wants, and so are the locals. They're very supportive, as you'll see in a few hours time.'

Rob glanced at the old station clock above the bar and was surprised to see that it was going on 5.30. 'Wow! Where's the day gone? It seems like I just got here!'

Matthew chuckled, 'Yeah I know what you mean, but hopefully

Sis will take a break soon and you can have a feed. The tucker's pretty good!'

'If that finger food you brought out earlier was anything to go by, I'm sure dinner will be just great,' Rob assured him, before heading back to Annette who was standing beside her chair, arching her back to relieve the muscles, and stretching her arms above her head which did most attractive things to her shirt front and jeans. Rob was slightly surprised to feel an unfamiliar stirring in his loins as he idly wondered what she'd look like naked, then was rather embarrassed when she put her arms down and looked at him with her very direct gaze, seeming to catch his thoughts. Her cheeky grin confirmed his fears but did nothing to stop the tingling sensation in his crutch.

'I don't have to ask what you were thinking,' she said, still grinning, 'you depraved beast! It was written all over your face!'

Rob sat down quickly, face red, while mentally composing a smooth, suave reply, but when he realised, he was staring straight at the front of her very tight jeans, he stammered out an apology, 'Oh bugger. I'm sorry. You must think I'm terrible. I'd better blame an excess of that lovely wine for my dreadful manners!'

Annette laughed before stepping up to him and briefly hugging his head against her flat, hard belly.

'There's nothing to be sorry about, dear man. You just paid me a lovely compliment, but perhaps we should have dinner first? It would be awfully unseemly to rush off to bed while the sun's still up!'

Rob wasn't sure he'd heard right but smiled back and nodded agreement. 'Dinner sounds good, but I might go up and shower first. All this wine has slowed me down a bit.'

She looked appraisingly at him, 'Good idea. How about we meet back here in 30 minutes? You might as well take your laptop with you, I've seen all I need to for now, so we'll talk it over tomorrow. It's been a long day and I need to unwind a bit so a good feed and some quiet music will be a good start!'

When Rob came back down, suitably refreshed, Annette was propped back at what must have been her usual place at the bar chatting with Matthew, her hair showing signs that she'd just washed it.

'Feel better now?' she asked, as Mathew moved away to serve a thirsty customer.

'Much,' he replied, 'I needed to freshen up, but I may not be staying up late tonight.'

Annette smiled, 'Good idea. We've got a lot to discuss tomorrow and I'm too tired to do anymore work tonight. As well, I need to let my mind work over what I've seen today and come up with a plan of action.'

They sat down to a beautiful, three-course meal, and had just finished the main course of a superb Beef Wellington, when the young girl singer and her brother appeared and without ceremony, set up on the tiny stage nearby and started singing.

Matthew was right, she had a beautiful voice and her brother complimented her at every stage, harmonising perfectly and never trying to overpower her voice. They sang a range of material from ballads to folk and country rock numbers, but whatever it was, the very enthusiastic crowd of locals clapped and cheered loud and long at the end of each song.

Their final song, which must have been their signature closing, was a glorious rendition of 'The Last Goodbye' from the movie, 'The Hobbit-Battle of the Five Armies.'

The applause shook dust from the ceiling and caused more than a few tears to stain cheeks, both male and female.

By the time a generous serving of Grandfather Port had been disposed of in the nicest possible way, Rob was ready to retire and Annette looked ready to do so as well. So, without messing about they made their slightly wobbly way upstairs, where Annette simply unlocked her door and pulled Rob in after her. Switching on a dim bed light provided enough illumination as she removed her clothes and waited while Rob made a slow visual inspection of her body, before taking off his own gear.

Apparently, she was sufficiently impressed with his body's

response to her nakedness to flick the bedclothes back and lie back across the bed. Rob didn't need a written invitation and soon found a position that gave maximum pleasure to both. Annette was not content to simply have him inside her, she wanted some action as well and for the next hour, she tested Rob's stamina.

The end result, however, was most satisfying for both of them and they lay for quite a time without moving as their bodies cooled.

They slept a few hours before Annette demanded a repeat bout, during which Rob was pleasantly surprised to discover that he was more than able to meet her demands. She woke him the next morning wearing a dressing gown and carrying a tray laden with a hot breakfast that would feed a troupe of truckies. Rob initially shuddered at the thought of all that food, but suddenly his stomach discovered that it needed filling and he scoffed down his share along with a fair portion of Annette's, much to her amusement.

'Do you always finish off your lady friend's food?' she asked, with a girlish giggle.

'Nah. Not usually, just yours,' was his reply which earned him a swipe at his head. That in turn, lead to a wrestling bout where Annette quickly lost her dressing gown and the two behaved somewhat badly for a while. By the time Rob looked at a clock, it was going on 09:30.

'Bloody hell! Look at the time!'

Annette smiled. 'And where were you rushing off to at 09:30, that's so important?'

'Ah...well, I don't know! I mean, shouldn't we be doing something?'

'I think that we have been, dopey,' she teased, 'several times in fact, and very nice they were too!'

Rob blushed, 'Yeah. I've got to admit the whole weekend so far has been terrific.'

'But you need to get moving doing something other than rolling around in bed with me, is that right?'

He blushed again, 'Well no. I mean, I... Oh bugger it woman!

I don't know what I mean. I'm just not used to being able to relax with delightful company, without having to rush off somewhere.'

She grinned, 'Well saved, Sir Knight. For that, I'll let you share my shower.'

They actually made it downstairs by 10:00, just as Matthew was opening up the front doors.

'Morning, Sis, morning, Rob,' he called cheerfully, 'I trust you had a restful night?'

'Terrific,' Rob replied, with a reasonably straight face, the whole effect being ruined by Annette breaking up into giggles as she headed for the kitchen and some more tea.

'It's okay, Rob,' Matthew grinned, 'it's great to see Sis relaxing for once. She works terribly hard and has enormous pressures on her at work, so this is her refuge from all that. This is the happiest I've seen her for a long time.'

That statement eased Rob's fears that he was just another in a long line of Annette's partners, brought out to her country love nest for a weekend frolic, then booted out the door on Monday, never to darken her life again.

'Yeah. She's a special lady all right,' Rob said, 'I've gathered a bit about her job and the pressures involved. It must be hard breaking into what's predominately a man's world.'

'That's the problem. The better she is, the more resentment builds up against her from her male colleagues, but if she makes mistakes, she's dumped on from a great height! So how can she win?'

'Like in most things, I guess. Do the very best you can and hope the right people up top notice.'

'Well said, Rob. That about sums it up. By the way, what'd you think of our singers last night?'

'Fantastic! You were right that she could hold her own anywhere. I know a couple of decent music promoters in Melbourne who'd jump at the chance to take her on when she's ready to turn professional. Neither of the two I'd recommend would do the wrong thing by her, and I'd be happy to look after the legal side of things.'

Matthew looked thoughtful. 'Thanks Rob. That's a decent offer. I'll mention it to her, but she really wants to finish school first.'

'No problem. The world can wait.'

As we drove sedately away from the increasingly congested main street, I was more than a little angry over the attempted kidnapping and kicked myself for letting my security lapse to such an extent that the girls were nearly grabbed. For the fourth or fifth time, I apologised to them, only to be told yet again with exaggerated patience that I was forgiven and that they must take some blame since it was their idea to visit the shops.

They were in a remarkably upbeat mood, probably still on an adrenaline high, feeling very proud of their self-defence prowess.

'Do you think Sandy will be proud of us?' Zoe asked for the third time.

'I know she will,' I responded, 'I certainly am! You both absolutely flattened those guys.'

'Are you really?' Angie asked, pleased with the praise.

'Hell, yes!'

She leaned over and kissed me on the cheek, but then she looked thoughtful for a moment. 'But in hindsight, that was pretty dangerous, wasn't it? I mean; that little guy who grabbed Zoe was almost frothing at the mouth and his big mate looked worse. I think we just got lucky because they didn't expect us to fight back so quickly.'

'And,' Zoe chipped in, 'how dumb was it to try to grab us in the middle of a crowd; with their car on the other side of the road, traffic jammed up, and a bunch of angry Taswegians chasing them? How stupid were they?'

I smiled at her as I drove around yet another corner at random, just in case there were more of Luke's men on our tail. 'Well put,

Zoe. They were definitely the 'B' team, but I'm certain we won't be so lucky next time. Your Dad's shown that he's still very determined to scoop you up and I think that next time he'll try a lot harder with a much better crew.'

Angie thought some more, and then asked the question I'd been dreading.

'But why is he trying so hard, Harry? I mean, I can understand that maybe he'd want us to get back together, although after what he's done to Mum, I know that'll never happen — but to have guys all over the country looking for us seems rather extreme! We can't make any sense out it!'

I pulled over on a quiet street and stopped in the shade of a tree, turning sideways to face both of them.

'As you've come to realise, there's a lot more to this than you've been told so far. Your Mum, Sandy and I wanted to protect you from the whole story, simply because it's very nasty and your Mum didn't want you to have all that on your mind as well, but I think that the time has come for you to learn the full facts.'

I smiled, 'Unfortunately, mums often think that their little girls are always 10, regardless of their real age or level of maturity. You guys have certainly shown me that at 18, you're mature enough to handle anything life can and will toss at you. However, I'll wait until we're back aboard and we've told your Mum and Sandy what's happened already.'

They looked puzzled and a little apprehensive.

'But what could be so bad that none of you want to tell us?' Angie almost wailed, nearly melting my resolve.

'Look. This will really have to wait 'till we're back aboard before you bombard me with too many questions. I want to have a quick look at the crime scene before we leave.'

The quick switch of topic disconcerted them for a moment, but Angie rallied quickly.

'Why go back there, Harry? Won't that be a big risk?'

'No one's looking for me and if you two keep your heads down, I might find out if those two arseholes were acting alone, or if we have others close behind them. That's vital knowledge we really need.'

They nodded their understanding, so I worked out where we were and headed back to the main street. We'd only been away for about 15 minutes and there was no pursuit of any sort, but I told the girls to slide right down below window level anyway.

I approached by way of a side street and one glimpse of the log-jammed main street ahead made me park at the back of a pub just down from the Newsagent. After telling the girls to keep the windows up, lock the doors and not to talk to anyone, I trotted up the street, confident that they were safe while I found out what was going on.

As the street was blocked solid with stalled traffic, it would have been impossible to do a drive-by. Two Ambulances and three Police cars were the cork in the bottle, and they weren't moving for anybody.

As it was too narrow to turn around, the bulk of the traffic had nowhere to go, so their occupants happily added their numbers to the seething mass of humanity surrounding the scene. Looking back down toward the harbour, I saw a police car starting to get drivers to turn their cars around and go elsewhere, but it was a slow process. Two Constables outside the Newsagency were trying in vain to hold onlookers back, so I eased my way into the press of shoppers and asked an old dear what was happening.

'Oh, it's all very confusing, dearie. There are two men that are badly hurt on the ground there and that's who the Ambo's are working on. Somebody said they thought that they were the ones who ran away from a car accident just over there in front of the Post Office, attacked two girls just here for some reason, then were bashed up by the drivers of the cars that were involved in the accident!'

'Oh dear,' I appeared shocked, 'so how are they?'

'Oh. I'm not sure, but they're still in there being treated by the Ambo's,' she laughed, 'although someone else said that the girls walloped them before the drivers got to them, but I'm not too sure about that. I mean, I don't think that two young girls could have done much against two grown men!'

I laughed with her, 'No. That doesn't sound right at all. So how bad are the men?'

'Well, like I said, I'm not really sure, but my friend Gladys was at the front for a while until the crowd started pushing too much for her, and she said that they're in pretty bad shape!'

'Oh dear. So they won't be walking away from this, then?'

'No way!' she stated emphatically. 'Gladys said that she heard one Ambo say to her mate that they could be crippled for life!'

'Goodness me! That's terrible. So, what are the Police doing about it? Have you heard?'

'Ha! That lot couldn't find their backsides in broad daylight,' she cackled, 'The drivers all went back to their cars as soon as the wallopers arrived and looked innocent. The men who attacked the girls weren't going anywhere, that's for sure! So the coppers have to try to get something that makes sense out of two busted up bad guys.'

'But what about the girls? I asked. 'How are they?'

'Now that's a funny thing,' she said thoughtfully, 'they must be all right, because someone said that straight afterwards, they ran off over the road and disappeared. Someone else said they had dark skins and might have been African or Aboriginal, so probably that's the last we'll hear from them. Nobody recognised them, anyway, so they're not from around here. We get some indigenous people from other areas coming through here at times. The girls are probably frightened to death by the whole thing, the poor things, I know I would be!'

I prowled around the crowd a bit longer and was listening for any fresh scraps of info when I managed to overhear a woman telling the Police Sergeant heading the response team, that she saw the small man attacking the girls and it looked like he was trying to grab them.

'He was almost foaming at the mouth!' she said indignantly, 'the filthy little germ! I saw him grab one girl by the arm, but she pulled away. He must have had something sharp in his hand, though, like a knife, 'cause her arm was badly slashed and bleeding afterwards.'

'So, you think it was a weapon of some sort?' the Sergeant asked, scribbling in his notebook.

'Well, it must have been. I mean, she was cut up and bleeding quite a lot from where he grabbed at her, but I must admit that I didn't really see the weapon, so it must have been small,' the old dear responded. 'But I'm afraid I didn't see much after that. It was all so very violent! All those young men fighting! But I know I did see the girl's arm slashed and bleeding badly! Why would someone attack a young girl like that? We never have violence in this town!'

After that fascinating exchange that had just escalated the crime to assault with a weapon occasioning actual bodily harm and attempted forcible abduction, nothing new was added, apart from the Ambo's reporting to the Sergeant that their patients' condition was deteriorating rapidly and they needed very urgent hospital treatment, available only in Burnie, 15 minutes away. The Sergeant started barking orders into his radio arranging for an Officer to ride in the ambulance, with a Highway Patrol car to lead the way to Burnie hospital. He also asked for a 24-hour guard to be put on both men.

With that happy news, I eased back out of the crowd and made my way to the car. The girls were happy to see me, the shakes setting in a little by now, but reported that no one had taken any notice of them. In short order, I drove to a service station where I filled Ernie's fuel tank, and soon we were parked out back of Mavis's pub. We managed to make it to the RIB without meeting anybody we knew and quietly headed home.

If Janice was initially puzzled by the unsettled demeanour of the girls when they came aboard, as well as the deep scratches on Zoe's arm that had almost stopped bleeding, then she was utterly horrified when they told her and Sandy the whole story. I calmed things down slightly by pointing out that, to the best of my knowledge, the episode was closed as far as we were concerned.

From what I'd pieced together, the Police wanted to talk to two girls of African or Aboriginal origins, one of whom had been attacked with a sharp weapon of some description. Their two assailants were in hospital with a number of very serious injuries, incurred under mysterious circumstances and were under 24-hour Police guard. They were no doubt facing a long list of charges that should see them locked up for a long time, particularly with their previous records. Oddly, there had been no mention of blonde hair, only dark skin colour, due to the tanning they'd built up over the last couple of weeks, so between normal public misperception, bad reporting, lousy memory, lack of the primary victims and two attackers who were already convicted felons, it was all a delightfully muddled mess!

While she cleaned and competently dressed Zoe's arm, Sandy did say how proud she was of their reactions, which cheered the twins up considerably.

CHAPTER 39

Following an early lunch, I collected everybody for a round-table conference, where I outlined what I thought of our position, which basically was that Luke had lost our trail for the time being, although having a positive sighting as a fresh starting point, we could probably expect that a crew of far more competent searchers would descend on the town asking more pointed and aggressive questions about us and our movements.

We had little option but to scoot back into hiding again and strike Wynyard off the list of safe havens for now.

'Before we go too much further, I need to clue Mavis in as to what to expect,' I said to the crew. 'At least she and Ernie can be on their guard and might be able to apply a little misdirection. Some of that 'know nothing, say nothing' routine that Ernie was banging on about would be a great help!'

I looked at the girls, 'While I'm gone, hold off those questions until I get back, then you'll be told everything, I promise.'

That earned me a questioning look from Janice, but I held up a hand to stall her for a moment, 'Angie, will you and Zoe go through our food and supplies to check our stocks? We can get supplies from Stanley, but we might have to make the run down to Strahan after all, just to avoid being seen in one area too often.'

The girls nodded and jumped up, keen to do something, so I looked at Janice and Sandy.

'Ashore, the girls asked me why Luke is chasing them so hard and I've promised that we would tell them the whole truth about what we know. After this, they need to know, and it may help stop them being grabbed again.'

'But it's going to be devastating for them to hear all that stuff about their father.'

I took both her hands and squeezed them, looking into her eyes that were starting to glisten, 'It'll be a whole lot worse if we don't. They're already puzzled as to why Luke is trying so hard to catch them, so concealing the story any longer will just do more harm than good. They'll handle it, trust me. I'm the Skipper!' I added the last as a weak joke, but it seemed to have the desired effect, or maybe my impassioned plea was more effective than I thought.

I looked at Sandy, 'You might like to give Bob Casey a call and bring him up to date on all the goings-on and after that, would you mind calling Annette as well?'

'Good idea. I keep forgetting about him. I'll do that right away then call Annette.'

I said to Janice, 'We also need to call Robert with the same update. You might like to do that while I'm ashore. You know what to say but also let him know that we're pulling our heads in for a while, so that comms will be via email or the sat-phone only. I'll call Hilary and Debbie as soon as I get back.'

She nodded, so before there were any more doubts or discussion, I hopped back in the dinghy and motored ashore, finding Mavis in the bar with a lively and rowdy lunch crowd building.

'Going to have a schooner, Jimmy?' she called out.

'Not today, thanks Mavis,' I replied, beckoning her closer. She left her bar wiping for a moment and wandered over to the clear space where I leant.

'Wot's up, love?' she asked, shrewd eyes scanning my face for a clue.

'We're shoving off,' I said, 'and may not be back for a while. There was a bit of a fuss up the main street this morning, you may have heard?'

'Oh goodness, yes. The whole town's talking about it. Never had so much drama in sleepy little Wynyard!'

'Well, for your ears only, remember that wife-bashing situation

I first told you about as to why we were here and keeping a low profile?'

She nodded, 'Yup. Sure do. I told you then and I'll repeat it now, we keep our own secrets and look after good people's as well.'

I smiled, 'I'm glad to hear that again, Mavis, because the husband in question sent some thugs to try to grab the two girls. That fuss this morning was an abduction attempt that went horribly wrong for the bad guys, but the husband is still trying very, very hard to grab the girls. He doesn't want his wife, just the girls, if you get my meaning?'

Her eyes went wide and the genial, smiling hostess façade slipped away, to be replaced by something a great deal harder and more competent.

'Well bugger me!' she exclaimed rather eloquently, 'that explains a lot! I'm glad you told me.'

She then gave me a careful look, 'I'm guessing that means we might be getting a visit in the near future from some other gentlemen looking for a couple of blonde girls, will we?'

'Yep! That's exactly what's likely to happen!'

'And I guess that it would be much healthier for them if there was no talk of girls on a boat?'

'That would be fantastic! But be careful. When they do turn up asking questions, they're likely to be a lot tougher than the last pair of clowns, so please don't take any risks.'

She gave a deep belly laugh, 'Now don't you worry about that. We can look after ourselves with strangers and we know how to handle those nosy dicks that try to find out our secrets. You might say that we're quite expert at it!

What I'll do is have a word to Ernie and a couple of the others and we'll fix it up. We won't deny that we'd seen the girls and their Mum around town, but we can say that they got the shits with being chased and harassed all the time and jumped in their car and drove back to the mainland. I can always drop a hint that I heard them talking about going to…?'

'The Whitsunday Islands are nice this time of year,' I supplied with a grin.

'That's the place,' she beamed, 'Whitsunday Islands. Always wanted to go there meself, but never did find the time. Still, one day, you never know, some good-looking bloke with a flash sailing boat might come by and whizz me away to those very islands!'

I laughed with her, appreciating her strong will and ready support for travellers in trouble.

'You never know, Mavis, someday a bloke just might fancy picking up a good-looking sort and sailing off to do just that!'

She had a sudden glisten in her eye as she ducked under the access flap across the bar top and gave me an eye-popping hug that raised a chorus of whistles and ribald remarks from the far end of the bar.

'Look after the ladies Jimmy,' she said softly, 'Ernie said you were a good'un and he's never been wrong. Don't worry about this end; we'll take care of things for you. Just come back to see us when all this rubbish has shaken down. Promise?'

I had a bit of a catch in my throat as I kissed her and left the bar, waving to the regulars up the back as I went.

Back aboard and with the dinghy secured for sea, I made immediate preparations for sailing. Sandy reported that Bob Casey was both delighted with her progress and appalled by the near-miss grab for the girls.

Janice also reported her success with speaking to Rob who had nothing new, but who became surprisingly frantic when told that Luke's minions had got so close to success. She was surprised that he was meeting with Annette so quickly and passed on that she had little extra news apart from some more email traffic with Luke referring to the condition and location of the 'white goods' previously referred to.

Angie gave me a questioning look when she handed over the list of supplies she'd arranged into a spreadsheet, so I said, 'I want to roll ASAP, so we can talk while we sail. How are the food stocks?'

'Pretty good, but we're down on fresh fruit and veges again and we really should have bought more bread-making supplies.'

'Ok. Let's call in at Stanley. It's about a two-and-a-half-hour sail, so there'll be time to do a really good stock-up and still get to Shepherd's Bay by dark. The supermarket is an easy walk from the boat ramp, and we can get a taxi back with all the stuff.'

'OK, Harry. That sounds good.'

I gave her an affectionate pat on the bum that made her giggle and got on with getting us moving. With Zoe on the wheel and the engines rumbling contentedly, I left her to once again take us safely out to sea, while I called Hilary. They were in their car, heading home and were shocked to hear what had happened so soon after their departure, but acknowledged that for them, it didn't change things too much, apart from increasing the urgency of chasing leads and information. They thanked me again for a wonderful trip and promised to call on the sat-phone number when they had some news.

By then, Zoe had us safely clear of the bar and the shallow approaches and with the breeze already established we set sail for Stanley.

Once the sails were trimmed properly, I called the round table conference again, after putting George to work looking after the steering and the radar on alarm watch. I deferred to Janice to start proceedings, which she did in a very hesitant manner, but soon got into stride. Each time she seemed to be avoiding an issue, I chipped in with an elaboration of the point.

'But what was Dad doing with our photos?' asked Zoe, 'I mean, we don't care who sees us, as you all know, so what's the big deal?'

'The big deal,' I explained, to give Janice a breather, 'is that your father was trading your photos to other men, and also some women, all over the world!'

'Oh!' Zoe replied faintly, 'but what was he trading them for?'

'More photos of other young kids. That's how these groups work. To get a supply of photos from others, you have to come up with some of your own.'

'Okay,' said Angie, 'that's a bit tacky, but still no real biggie for us! I would have thought that we were getting a bit too old for the 'young girls' thing! Anyway, there's got to be more than that!'

I looked at Janice and Sandy and shrugged helplessly. 'Have you heard of paedophiles and what they do?'

'Sure we have,' Angie said, 'They prey on young kids for sex and all sorts of awful stuff....'

Her eyes widened and a stricken look slid into place on her face.

'Aww no! Dad can't be mixed up in something like that!'

I waited a few moments for both to think it through, and then gently said, 'I'm afraid to say that not only is he mixed up in a world-wide ring, but he owns and runs a big house in Melbourne that caters for just that. Sort of like a brothel, but just for paedophiles and their filthy habits.'

The girls looked horror-stricken and shook their heads in denial as Janice and Sandy scooted in quickly and tried to comfort them.

'Your Mum had the opportunity to copy a lot of files off his computer before you all left, and as most of them are photos and videos, they prove all that we've said and much more! There are also a lot of very well-known people who can be identified from the photos, which is why your Pop and Hilary and Debbie have been involved. We can't just blow the whistle on a few; we need to catch all these people before they go undercover and do it all over again somewhere else.'

The girls looked at each other for a few moments, silently communing in that uncanny way twins so often do, before Angie spoke with determination in her voice.

'Ok. We accept what you say about Dad, the paedophiles and the photo files. But there must be something else you still haven't told us! Because as bad as all that stuff is, it still doesn't explain why Dad is trying so hard to find us!'

Sandy and Janice looked at me in mute appeal, so I drew a deep breath and said,

'You're right, there is more and it's the main reason why we've kept quiet about all the paedophile stuff. Being blunt, I believe that you are both virgins?'

They both nodded, but weren't particularly put out by my question, 'OK. There is a small but very lucrative market amongst the very wealthiest of the paedophile set, for young, virgin, Caucasian females. The price goes up dramatically if there are identical twins and more for being genuine blonde, even though at 18, you're almost past the most sought-after 'young girl' stage.

Therefore, we believe that there is active bidding underway between members of that small group for the pair of you. And that, my dear girls, is why half the Australian underworld is out looking for you. They don't want your Mum, and don't even know or care about Sandy or me, just you two!'

That rocked the girls more than anything else and Janice and Sandy re-doubled their efforts to comfort them, but Angie's reaction was not what I expected. She got a furious look on her face, before saying, 'So that rotten, stinking piece of foulness who calls himself our father has not only bashed our Mum repeatedly, but has set us up to be sold as sex slaves? Is that the situation?'

I nodded. 'I'm afraid so, that puts it very simply, but effectively. Now you know why we've been going to such lengths with your Pop, Hilary and Debbie and several other people we haven't met yet, to get names to go with the pictures and wrap this whole filthy mess up. But while that's happening, we have to keep you out of their clutches.'

They were quiet again, until Angie said, a little more calmly, 'How sure are you of the auction thing? I mean, is there some proof, or is it just an educated guess?'

'It started out as a wild idea I had, prompted by the same reasoning you've just applied; why is he trying so hard to get you? But a contact Sandy developed in the ACP in Canberra has got proof of the auction process through telephone and Internet taps that have been placed on all your father's phone lines and connections.'

Angie looked at Zoe who was huddled silently in Janice's arms and they did the silent communication thing again. 'We'd like to hear all of what's going on to nail these arseholes, if you don't mind.'

So I stepped through the whole investigation to date, including the fact that a few senior ACP officers were part of the problem and explaining why the investigation had to proceed quietly, but at least it caused Angie to slowly lose her bleak expression in exchange for one of extreme interest.

'All these people getting involved, it's amazing! So, is there anything else we can do to help?'

'No. We just have to keep you two from being grabbed again while we wait for the right people to put together the case against your father and all the others in the Ring, so they can all be grabbed at the same time.'

She nodded understanding, but then added with the voice of maturity, 'Ok. But there is one thing that occurs to me.'

We three adults looked and waited. 'If someone was going to pay a squillion for us, how is he going to be guaranteed that we're still virgins?'

I coughed and promptly handballed that one to Janice or Sandy, but before either one could come up with a reply, Angie added, 'What you need to understand is, there's no longer any physical evidence. That went many years ago for one reason or another that we don't need to go into here, so how can our status be proved one way or the other? I presume that the price on our heads would drop dramatically if we were used goods, so to speak!'

Janice and Sandy looked a bit disconcerted, but I started laughing, as both the logic and associated absurdity of the situation appealed greatly to my warped sense of humour. The huge cost of the search, all the time Janice had wasted dragging herself and the girls around the countryside, when it could have been stopped at the beginning if Luke had bothered to ask a female the right questions!

It also would have helped if he had an understanding of Middle Eastern cultures that were not used to females having freedom to do as they wished, so to them it was only natural that if a female wasn't a prostitute or married, she had to be a virgin, particularly if she was young and in almost all cases, would have the physical evidence to prove it.

Without physical proof, there were no virgins and that made the whole auction thing a farce! Presenting for sale a matched pair of pretty, young blonde girls would probably attract a good price as sex slaves, but it would be a mere fraction of what Luke was hoping for.

When I explained my thoughts, everyone saw the funny side, which helped a little to lift the pall of gloom that had settled over the girls' normally sunny demeanour. The temptation to have Janice call Luke right then and explain his terribly stupid mistake and try to get the search called off was very strong, but fortunately common sense prevailed as that news would have alerted him that we were privy to his phone calls and emails and probably his files as well.

We did agree that the info could possibly be used later as a last resort plan to nullify the need to recover the girls. Maybe.

FIREBIRD... WYNYARD - SHEPHERDS BAY, SATURDAY

We dropped anchor just off the boat ramp in Stanley Harbour at 14:30. It was a pretty little place, totally dominated by the dark and rather brooding presence of the 'Nut' as the huge, oval-shaped mass of rock shielding the town from the northeast was called. As Janice, Sandy and I motored ashore in the RIB, we saw there wasn't much activity on the commercial slipway, but several tinnies were either being launched or retrieved at the two public boat ramps, the left one rather hemmed-in by a curving rock wall.

An attention-getter was a beefy guy with a loud voice giving a confusing set of directions to his wife/girlfriend who was trying to back a very nice-looking 20-foot half-cabin tinnie with a humungous 200hp outboard hung off its stern, down the left ramp. He seemed incapable of translating the movement he wanted the trailer to make, as to how the steering wheel should be turned, so time and again, the trailer, seemingly with a mind of its own, came within centimetres of the rock walls either side of the ramp.

Finally, a very shapely young lady leapt out of the cab and stormed up past the front of the Ford F-350 to the head of the ramp, crossed her arms under her generous boobs and glared down at the red-faced goose.

'For fuck's sake! Either say what you want or do it your bloody self! It's not as though I haven't done this before! You don't know your left hand from your useless tiny right nut, you fat wombat!'

'How dare you call me that!' was the spluttering answer. 'Get back down here immediately!'

'Get fucked!' was her screamed reply, accompanied by a glare of renewed intensity and an obvious refusal to move, so the guy stomped back up to the ute and proceeded to share the glistening paint from the stern and sides of his new boat with both rock walls before managing to thread the eye of the 5 metre wide needle that was the end of the boat ramp, before triumphantly running the trailer at speed into the water, making a giant splash that nearly swamped the pair of old dears just loading up their little tinnie in the next ramp.

He didn't seem at all fazed by the fact that the back half of his gleaming red F-350 ended up submerged, right up to the crew-cab. He did, however, become a little more agitated when his boat, no longer secured to the trailer and without the benefit of a bow line to hang on to, floated serenely away before clunking to a stop against the far end of the rock wall. He started to wade into the water after it, then stopped to throw his bulging wallet and mobile phone back at the truck where they missed the cab window, bounced off the oversize side mirror which promptly shattered, then fell into the water anyway.

Briefly, peace descended on the ramp as the red-faced goose was stricken speechless, although just as he was winding up to yell at somebody, he had another attack of speechlessness when his boat lurched sideways away from the rough embrace of the rocks with a loud clunk, the stern settling lower and lower in the water.

'Forget the drain bungs as well as the bow rope, did we, SKIP-PER?' the girl's voice echoed down the ramp and over half the harbour. 'You fuckin' great goose! You couldn't launch a wet fart properly, let alone a boat!'

Although nearly helpless with laughter, it was probably just as well that we were not far away, as I pointed the bow of the RIB toward the sinking big tinnie. With our soft bow jammed between the half-submerged stern and the tilted outboard, I pushed the wallowing mass of sinking metal toward the ramp, yelling at red-face who was dancing around with broken bits of mirror glass stuck in his bare feet, while retrieving his soggy wallet and busted mobile from the water, 'Drive forward enough to bring the trailer up. Quickly, before this thing sinks completely!'

Fortunately, the girl sized up the situation, trotted back down the ramp, pushed the tub of lard aside so he slipped on the weed-covered ramp, landing on his arse, and jumped in the cab. She eased the truck forward enough so that as the trailer partly emerged, I managed to roughly push the thing onto the guide rollers.

'Now hook the winch cable on the bow eye,' I called, revving my outboard up to full power to hold the still-settling mass from slipping backwards, 'and try to crank it in before it slips back off the rollers.'

She quickly and competently followed my instructions, her partner having parked himself on the rock wall to extract more shards of glass from his feet, and finally the soggy beast slowly emerged from the water, two large jets of water spouting from the open bungs in the transom. She waved and bowed her thanks, her boobs almost falling out of her bikini top, causing the old geezer in the next ramp to cop a smack across the ear from his wife just for looking. The girl kicked her useless partner in the shins, before carefully driving the rig back up the ramp to let it finish draining.

Still chuckling, we motored around to the other side of the commercial slipway where there was a convenient little loading dock. We shared a laugh and a cheery wave with the old couple as they drove out of the parking lot, before strolling off toward town.

We'd left the girls aboard, comfortable with the thought that with Jasper to mind them, they were very well protected. Oddly enough, they weren't keen to explore the delights of Stanley, as quaint and pretty as it was. It was only a few hundred metres along the waterfront road to the supermarket and didn't take us long to find the supplies we needed. Plus, some treats for the girls and Jasper.

One of the very obliging staff kindly offered to drive us back to the dinghy with all our stuff and that saved even more time, although it still needed two trips in the dinghy to get the shopping and ourselves back aboard.

'Bloody hell!' exclaimed Angie, in mock indignation, as she surveyed the mass of bags and parcels. 'That's the last time you guys go shopping by yourselves! Where am I going to put all this stuff?'

Naturally, she was laughed at before Sandy and Janice helped her find space while Zoe helped me get under way. Fifteen minutes later, we were beating into a strong, hot northerly, spray whipping across the foredeck. It was my least favourite point of sail, but in this case, there was no choice since a vigorous cold front was expected in the morning, so we needed to be in a sheltered anchorage tonight.

Although as uncomfortable as expected, we still made reasonable time and had carefully dropped and bedded-in both bow anchors in Shepherd's Bay just before nightfall.

The cold front squall line struck during the night this time, and although not as vicious as last time, it still was enough to shake Sandy's normally calm demeanour and get her worried. Yet, once again, we rode out the screeching gusts and torrential rain without a problem, apart from losing a heap of sleep. I managed to chase all the ladies back to bed, Sandy sticking with Janice, while I maintained watch. Once I was certain that the wind was dropping and that we were secure, I retired to bed with the ladies for a couple of hours of sleep.

I didn't wake until late morning, the ladies considerately leaving me to indulge in a rare, luxurious lie-in, although it was a lousy day with cold, gusty winds driving sheets of rain across the anchorage and moaning around the mast. The girls had the boat buttoned up and all was warm and dry, the familiar shipboard routine kicking back in with board games played, movies watched and lots of sweet snacks and hot tea consumed.

Zoe was happy to dry Jasper off after he had to go outside for his toilet, but he loved being involved in human activities and having the choice of so many bodies to drape himself over.

The day passed happily, as we kept a close eye on the girls, but they seemed to have largely shrugged off their shock of discovering dear old Dad's unhealthy obsession with young kids and trying to sell them. That depression seemed to have been replaced with a new level of maturity and a firm resolve to bring all these rock spiders to justice, dear Dad included.

BURNIE HOSPITAL & LUKE AT HOME, MONDAY MORNING

Hospital routine also carried on as before, except for the highly unusual presence of two large, uniformed and very imposing young policemen, one seated outside a double room on the second floor, while the other was permanently inside. The outside guard checked all staff coming close, while the inside one hovered closely over each nurse who came to do the hourly Obs of the latest two semi-comatose patients.

Not having any Health Insurance, they were both at the mercy of the Public system, which although of high quality, meant lengthy and painful delays waiting for surgery, given that their wounds were considered non-life threatening. Consequently, Luke received a very perplexing and frustrating phone call from Jimmy's phone the following Monday morning.

'Hello, Jimmy. I hope you've got some good news for me this time.'

'I am hoping that is so,' announced an unfamiliar foreign voice, 'Is that Mr Emery?'

'Yeah. Who are you and how did you get this phone?'

'My name is Doctor Rajid Singh, and I am calling you from the North West Regional Hospital in Burnie.'

'Another bloody wog. What's going on? Why are you using this phone? It's not yours! Are you trying to flog me something?'

'Such interesting manners of speech you have in this country, Mr Emery. In my country, if some person were being flogged, it would mean a grievously painful beating for a serious offence. However, I am a Doctor, I am not trying to sell you something and I know that this is not my telephone. I am trying very hard to explain the situation, if you

would give me the opportunity to do so. Also, I must record my most strenuous objection to being called a 'wog'. It is a very derogatory term to use when addressing a fully qualified doctor in the medical profession and in particular, one that is trying to help two stricken colleagues of yours. It is my belief that they are your colleagues because one has your telephone number on his telephone, and it is this telephone that I am presently using to have discourse with you.'

'Yeah righto! I don't need your life history, just get on with it and tell me what the fuck's going on.'

'What is going on, Mr Emery is beyond my understanding? I can only tell you the very small portion that has been brought to my attention. This telephone was found in the possession of a man who was brought here by ambulance from Wynyard on Saturday morning in a very damaged condition. Another man, who appears to be his friend or colleague, and who is also very grievously injured, accompanied him.

The Policemen who came with them in the ambulance vehicle have them under 24-hour guard and they are remaining most closely to them and this is very disrupting of the smooth functioning of this Hospital. The other patients are not happy to see so many guns and other implements of restraint and destruction, although some of the younger nurses seem to be very enjoyable with this situation. I do not know why this is so...'

'Jesus Christ! Is this a reading from War & Peace? Will you get the fuck on with it?'

'You should not be taking the Lord's name in vain, Mr Emery, this is not a good thing to do. Also, I do not think that you are a very nice person and if it wasn't my duty to assist my patients, I would not continue to talk to you!'

'Oh, spare me from a sensitive wog! OK. I'm sorry for being rude and I won't do it again. Is that better? Can we proceed with your report now?'

'Ahh! That is an improvement, Mr Emery, and it proves to me that you do know how to be polite. Yes, we most certainly can proceed with my report. Now, to answer your previous question; your first colleague is

not able to talk and has a concussion, so I have been using the telephone that was in his possession to make telephone calls to the persons that were listed as having been 'recently called'. I happened to take notice that your number was one of the most frequently called numbers, except for one very curiously named number, listed as the 'Daily Asteroid' but I thought I would try your very frequently called number first.'

'Yeah, terrific. You're a real Samaritan! Will you please get on with it?'

'Yes, Mr Emery. Now that you are conversing politely with me, I shall proceed. The name of this man is James Fitzroy and his companion has the name of Anthony Jacobs. Do you have the intimate knowledge of these gentlemen?'

'Bloody hell! What do you think I am, a bloody woolly jumper? Of course, I don't have intimate knowledge of them, but I do know them, if that's what you mean, in fact, they work for me. What did you say the problem was with them?'

'Well. Despite my not understanding your relationship to an item of warm clothing, that is a most interesting and useful piece of information about the two gentlemen and very good to know, because we have no other knowledge of them, but now that we do have the knowledge, that will be most helpful for the police men.'

'I don't give a shit about what is or isn't useful. Why do I always have these sorts of conversations with people? First that bloody wombat, Jimmy and now some wog Doctor in Tasmania! What's wrong with you people? Just tell me! Please?'

'Oh dear. Mr Emery, you are doing it again and I am compelled to be delivering you the warning that you are calling me a wog once more. I must ask that you desist from this insulting practice, or I shall be forced to conclude our discourse!'

'Yeah, okay. I apologise for calling you a wog, but I'm buggered if I know why you're so upset about it. The old bloke down at the shops calls himself that!'

'Ah, yes, Mr Emery. But I am not the old bloke down at the shops. Now perhaps we can proceed with my lengthy report, as I have a great

amount of work to do today and your gentlemen are taking up most of my time. Now we have had the big mystery with these gentlemen. They are both of them very badly damaged. Mr Fitzroy's jaw is broken in three places and he has lost several teeth. He is not able to talk, nor will he be partaking of the solid food for several months. He has also sustained a very grievous injury to his testicles that is causing him a great deal of distress, both physical and mental. I regret that it will be a long time before he can be taking the pleasure with the ladies again.

His colleague, Mr Jacobs, has sustained a very bad injury to his left knee to the extent that the entire joint will have to be replaced with an artificial one. He has also sustained an injury to his testicles, and one has had to be removed. He too, will have to be refraining from any form of sexual arousal or activity for a long time. Additionally, he has three broken ribs, a punctured lung and severe contusions to the face, but he will recover from those in the fullness of time.'

'Yeah, yeah! Do I really need all these details? I mean, that's your job, isn't it? Just fix 'em up and send them on their way.'

'If you will allow me to continue, Mr Emery, there is a very good reason for my lengthy report. That reason is that Mr Fitzroy wishes for me to communicate his thoughts to you from a note that he managed to type on the Head Nurse's laptop computer. The note reads and I am making this quotation directly from the computer — **'Hello, boss. I'm sorry we are in hospital and I hope you can help us with money and a lawyer 'cause we need both very urgently. The cops have grabbed us, but I don't know all the charges yet, although there has been talk of attempted abduction, assault with a deadly weapon and public affray, but I promise, we didn't take any of our clothes off, really boss! I don't know where that one came from. But anyway, there're quite a lot of charges apparently! We got in this trouble 'cause we found the girls for you in Wynyard and almost had our hands on them, but they somehow managed to clobber us and get away. I don't know where they've gone, but at least they were there on Saturday morning, by themselves. We didn't see your wife, although your father-in-law was there as well but it was a few days earlier that**

Tony spotted him in a pub on the waterfront. Please help us out, boss. We're going to be laid up for a long time and that's before the wallopers get stuck in for their pound of flesh.'

That is the ending of the message, Mr Emery. Do you have a reply for Mr Fitzroy?'

'Yeah. I've got a reply,' Luke snarled, 'tell them that they're incompetent idiots, deserve what they've got and can get fucked! They're sacked!'

'Oh dear. That is not very compassionate behaviour by you. I'm afraid that will not please Mr Fitzroy very much. He is most distressed by this whole affair!'

'Listen you Indian...person. I don't care what you think or how distressed that fuckin' busted-arse wombat might be, but those two clowns have cost me a great deal of money and have maybe blown a deal worth millions.'

'Very well, Mr Emery, I will pass that message on to your employee, Mr Fitzroy. Please do not try to make the telephone call to either gentleman, however. They are not in any condition to answer, but I shall let you have my telephone number if you do have a change of heart and wish to communicate with or to help them. They really do appear to be in a very bad situation and will need help.'

After he hung up the phone, Luke held his head in his hands in despair. The Middle East deal was hanging by a thread, with the potential buyers wanting better proof than just his repeated assurances that the girls were safe, which meant unmarked, undamaged and intact, and now his tame goons had cocked things up again. Worse, they'd drawn a large amount of Police attention to him as their employer. There'd been no word that Janice had made a formal complaint against Jimmy and Tony for attempted abduction, but perhaps that was still to come. And what was that bit about not taking their clothes off? The man's gone loopy. It must be the concussion.

Maybe it was time to pull his head in and go low profile for a while, but he really didn't want to pass on the chance to make such a big score with the sale of the girls. But there again, what guarantee did he have that they were still virgins? He really didn't know a great deal about the medical side of that condition; maybe he should have consulted somebody before getting into this mess? And if he'd been able to keep them close to hand, almost in a lock-down situation, he might have been able to be more certain of that, but now with them running around loose over three states, who knows what grubby little appendages might have been actively reducing the value of his prize assets.

That he felt not a shred of compassion for them, nor even the fact that they *were* his own daughters, didn't bother him in the slightest, even fleetingly, as he steadfastly remained focused on making the most of what he desperately hoped was their still un-molested value. Having spent so much money on the search already, he decided to take a last shot at retrieving them by hiring a small team of professional investigators he'd heard good things about, then get rid of all the other incompetent fools still combing the Eastern states at vast expense.

CHAPTER 42

A smooth, husky female voice quietly purred, 'Steel Associates, how may I help you?'

Ignoring the quiver down his backbone, Luke replied, 'I'd like to speak to Mr Xavier, please?'

'Certainly sir. May I have your name?'

'Luke Emery.'

'Just a moment Mr Emery. Mr Xavier will be right with you.'

There were several clicks on the line and then a cultured British accent quietly announced, 'Xavier.'

'This is Luke Emery, Mr Xavier.'

'So my secretary said,' he replied, 'and I am aware of you, Mr Emery, or at least your very unsavoury reputation. But hopefully this call is only about business, so what can I do for you?'

'I need three people found, and as quickly as possible.'

'Broadly speaking, who are these people, Mr Emery?'

'One adult female and two 18-year-old females. They're my wife and two daughters.'

'Ah yes. I know of your efforts to locate them, but are you aware that many other persons are also on their trail?'

'...'

'May I take that silence for a negative? I thought so. Very sad, the state of this mercenary world! I also believe that your efforts to date have been somewhat embarrassing.'

'What! What do you mean by that?' Luke spluttered.

'Just look at the results to date my dear fellow. Two employees with severe injuries in hospital under police guard, some of which were *apparently inflicted by the two young ladies you seek! Were your men fools or simply grossly incompetent? Only you know that.'*

'But I...'

'No Mr Emery. You're the Captain of your ship and all responsibility starts and stops with you. Which tars you with the same brush, so to speak.

But, to return to business — are your family to be just located, or are they to be removed from wherever they are found and delivered to a nominated address, with or without their consent?'

Finally, Luke got a chance to speak, the extent of Mr Xavier's very detailed knowledge having rendered him temporarily lost for words. And what was that bit about other guys looking?

'Well, I'd like them found and delivered to me at my home address, if that's possible?'

'My dear fellow, of course we can do that. Anything's possible if one is prepared to pay for it!'

'Ah...yes. That was my next question. What are your fees?'

'Quite modest, my dear man, quite modest, considering that we work on a no live delivery, no pay basis!'

'Yes, yes! That's terrific! But how much?'

'This job, taking into consideration that we actually have to locate the subjects and transport them against their wishes, will be $25,000 per day or part thereof.'

Luke actually spluttered for a moment while his tongue tried to catch up with his racing thoughts.

'But...but, that's ridiculous! I can't afford that!'

'Oh, what a shame. In that case, we might have to find them ourselves and place them on the open market. I believe that there are some very handsome offers floating around at the moment for a matched pair of, shall we say, young and unmarked, white goods!'

'You can't do that. That's unprincipled. It's unethical! You're the service supplier, not a competitor!'

'My dear Mr Emery, we can be whatever we like! There are no rules in this game, as you apparently need to learn. The market decides

what is reasonable, and if the goods are as described, then the return is obviously very lucrative. Why should we pass up this opportunity for a fast earn, as the saying goes. By the way, Mr Emery, the goods are as described, aren't they?'

'Well, to the best of my knowledge they are. I mean, I don't have a medical certificate guaranteeing the condition and I'm certainly not in a position to verify it myself!'

'Oh, dear. That is a serious problem, Mr Emery, because a medical certificate is exactly what you should have, at the very least, and to have the items running around loose, subject to the vagaries of nature, so to speak, is very, very careless of you.'

'Yeah, yeah! Whatever! But I'll bet that they are still as described. Their mother will be looking after them.'

'You may well be betting very heavily on that belief, Mr Emery. The people you are negotiating with are well known to be, dare I say, unscrupulous in the extreme if they believe that they are being made a fool of or misled in any way. They have a very distinctive way of rectifying that type of situation. In fact, so distinctive that it's been a very long time since anybody made that mistake!'

Luke swallowed to try to unstick a suddenly dry throat, and he lost a lot of his previous bluster.

'Ok, but I'd still like to come to an arrangement with you, if you will do the right thing and not mess me around.'

'Very well, Mr Emery, based on the very uncertain current condition of the items you seek, we will confine our interest to the locating and seizure of the persons discussed and their delivery to your home address as requested.

Additionally, I will need a recent, good-quality colour photograph of each of them, the girls with their clothes on, if you please. One of my associates will call at your house within 20 minutes of me receiving verification from my bank that four days-worth of fees have been lodged in advance.'

'FOUR days-worth! Oh, shit! Very well.'

'Excellent! Our terms are as follows: You are to make a single day's

payment at 10:00 each and every day of the operation, so as to remain four day's in credit. Any variation or delay in this payment system will cause immediate and permanent termination of the operation and total forfeiture of the remaining fees in credit.

If you follow these instructions to my satisfaction, all remaining credit will be transferred back to your account at the successful conclusion of the operation.

In the very unlikely event that we are not successful, for reasons beyond our control, all credit will be transferred back to you after I verify that the targets are not available. Are you agreeable to these conditions?'

'Well, I suppose that I am, but why is that bloody daily rate so high?'

'Because we are the best Mr Emery, and we take all the risk. We are, after all, talking about committing forcible abduction or kidnapping, unlawful restraint and assault, among several other minor crimes, some of which would cause my associates to be incarcerated for a very long time were they to be caught.

The fact that you have called us suggests that you aren't willing to personally take that risk, Mr Emery, nor do you have the training or expertise to direct such an operation. The results of your lack of competence in this area are currently languishing in Burnie Hospital. Need I say more?'

'No, bugger you!' Luke snarled in frustration, 'I'll do what you ask, but you'd better produce results!'

'Really, Mr Emery. Such petty insults and threats should be beneath you, but I suppose that is too much to hope for. You really should give up such an unhealthy lifestyle. I mean; living in the shadows and messing about with children the way you do is particularly dangerous to your health and not conducive to a long life. Or a free one in the longer term, if I may be so bold as to offer a small piece of gratuitous advice!

As for results, I've said all I need to on that subject, but we will need what current information you have as to the whereabouts of the targets. A brief summary should be presented to my associate when the photographs are collected. I think that now concludes our discussion for the moment. Either myself or my secretary, Miss Julie, will be in touch when we have information or need a question answered that might assist our operation.'

There was a sharp click and Luke was left staring at a dead handset, his mind whirling as he contemplated the cost of $25K per day, with $100K up front. Numbly, he replaced the handset and set about transferring the required money to Mr Xavier's account, the details of which had been texted to his mobile, as well as writing a report listing all the info he'd gathered from the search over the last disastrous week. Along with the positive sighting in Wynyard, he included the various references to the Whitsunday's and a boat with a cat.

As promised, about 20 minutes later, a knock at the door proved to be an attractive young lady who declined to come inside, waiting patiently until he'd finished the report and rounded up some photos of the three. One of them included him, so he took scissors to that, before running it through the copier. Everything went in an envelope that he handed to Xavier's associate who departed with a quick smile that could have meant anything but said nothing.

CHAPTER 43

FIREBIRD...SHEPHERD'S BAY, HUNTER ISLAND... SUNDAY

We'd had a wet and bouncy beat back to Shepherd's Bay on Saturday, after clearing Stanley Harbour without any further incidents with moronic boaties. The strong, gusty northerly hammered us most of the way until we gained some respite in the lee of Three Hummock Island, not long before dusk.

I think we were all relieved to be tucked up safely again in the beautiful little bay, with two anchors well dug-in in preparation for the southerly blow due to hit that night or next morning.

The girls didn't seem to have any lingering after-effects from their encounter, and the deep scratches on Zoe's arm didn't get infected, thanks to Sandy's quick and effective first-aid. Jasper knew there had been trouble, making a concerned mewling in the front of his throat while he sniffed the girls over very carefully in a motherly sort of way, paying particular attention to Zoe's scratches. He licked all around the dressing with his rough, but antibacterial tongue.

Sunday was spent lazing about, the ladies looking very enticing as they stayed in pyjamas all day, with the much cooler south wind howling through the rigging with a high-pitched scream, while a deep, droning counter-tone was generated by the hollow carbon mast acting like an 80-foot bass organ pipe. Still, the heavy insulation I'd had built into the cabin top and sides for temperature stability also did sterling service as sound insulation, so it wasn't too noisy inside.

As with previous fronts, there was nothing gentle about the arrival of this one, which came belting in from the Southern Ocean like a brawling bully, the gusty winds hammering every-thing in their path and pushing roiling sheets of low cloud that raced over the low-set island, seeming to just clear our masthead. It also dumped regular, sharp-hitting rainsqualls that rattled on the decks like little hammers and churned the usually placid, transparent water into seething patches of foaming white. There was no danger to the boat and I was just happy that it was getting a free freshwater wash.

Mid-morning, the sat-phone rang and it was Annette, our ACP contact lady.

'*Hi Harry. It's good to speak to you. Is everybody well?*'

'Yes thanks Annette. All well, although it was a close call on Saturday.'

'*Ah yes. Rob let me listen in on the phone call from Janice. I've also skimmed the files and am stunned with the file content! That is such great evidence, but getting back to your near miss, you were lucky the bad guys were clumsy and/or incompetent. It could have been nasty.*'

'Exactly. We're just about to have a round-table about that and to make a plan for the future. By the way, how did you and Rob get on?'

'*Well, let's say that it was a rather rocky start, but everything worked out rather well. Anyway, I won't keep you from your round-table, but I called to pass on a piece of info that you need to fit into your planning. Yesterday afternoon, Luke made contact with a gentleman who calls himself Mr Xavier and who runs an organisation called Steel Associates. His real name is Terry Johnson, a bent Pommy ex-copper and current well-spoken thug who left the UK in a hurry 15 years ago, just ahead of some very heavy local Mob interest after he did the dirty on the wrong people.*

He set up a Security and Investigation service out here using UK immigrants like himself; some ex-military and other bent ex-coppers. They specialise in muscle-for-hire, celebrity protection and snatch-and-deliver, all for exorbitant fees. The business has proved extraordinarily successful, as they are quite good at what they do, but the short version of all this is that Luke has engaged their services at $25K per day, to take over the search and deliver operation for Janice and the girls, the cost of which even Luke is apparently finding it hard to cope with.

Oh, and he's said that it's really only the girls he wants. Getting Janice back would be just for revenge, so she might like to try really hard to avoid that!'

'I presume that Luke's updated them with all the latest info on the aborted search?' I asked.

'Yep. 'Fraid so. The first instalment of money's been paid, so the contract is active now and you can expect a crew to arrive in Wynyard very soon asking very pointed questions. I do hope that you're not still there?'

I chuckled, slightly bitterly, 'No. We've learned that lesson, even if it's a bit late. We're back in isolation again, but we may move again shortly, after hearing that. How serious do you think these guys will apply themselves?'

'Very seriously, I'm afraid. Please don't underestimate them! In their line of business, they've got a reputation to maintain, so excellent service is paramount. They even have a 'no gain, no pay' clause in their contracts, although customers have to pay up front to kick things off. But if Steel Associates can't deliver for whatever reason, all the funds are refunded to the customer without argument.'

'That shows an impressive level of confidence,' I observed dryly, 'but makes it a lot harder for us.'

'Yes. But hang tough, Harry. We're making progress already with identifying the faces and thanks to computer-aided facial recognition, we can put names to about 60% of them, so the initial plan is that once we have as many as we can, we, that is Rob and my small group, plan to hand all the info over to the various State Police Forces to make the arrests. We need to time things carefully, however, as we'd like the Victorian Police to raid that house in Melbourne at the same time as the arrests start, as it seems to be some sort of Ring headquarters, apart from being their kiddies play centre. If we can wrap that place up at the same time as individual arrests are being made around the country, we stand a good chance of grabbing a lot more evidence, including some of the kids involved, like that Thai girl who escaped. These bastards are very slippery and they'll lawyer-up in an instant.'

'Well, that's a good bit of news. We didn't know how you were going to proceed, given that the ACP is so compromised.'

'Yeah. It bothered us for a while as well. But going through the various State Police Forces seems the best approach as it will be a saturation approach, where one small group, or even a whole State Force can't do anything to suppress the info or stop the arrests.'

'Yeah, I can see how that would work, and we'd better copy Hilary in on that as well. It might affect her investigation. Can I ask you to let her know when you're about to start the arrest ball rolling? Perhaps her story will help nail the whole thing down tight.'

'Actually, I'd forgotten about that! Yes, it will help make sure that no official can try to sweep anything under the carpet. I'll talk to her.'

'Great, thanks for that. So those files were really good?'

'Oh, they're brilliant! By themselves, they're admissible in Court, but if we can add more data from the house, particularly if we can rescue some kids and score some fresh photos, that should wrap the whole case up nearly watertight!'

'That's great, thanks Annette! We'll have a chat about all that here, but basically, I think our best bet is to go into deeper cover and wait to hear of developments.'

'Good idea! Bye, Harry. Take care and keep your head down.'

The others looked at me expectantly, so I brought them up to date on Annette's info, before we had our council of war to review our mistakes and devise a plan for the future, in light of the bad guys closing in and the new data. I looked around the table at the crew.

'Unfortunately, I've been a bit careless about security,' holding up a hand to stall any protests, 'and we've all become a bit complacent. However, the extra exposure we incurred in Wynyard was still justified by the necessity of the face-to-face contacts with Rob, Hilary and Debbie, and I still believe that the wider we spread this information, the safer we'll be and the less chance these rock-spiders have of getting away with it.'

That drew nods of agreement, as Janice asked, 'But what's our best move now? Do we stay here, or will we be safer on the move?'

I waited to see if anyone else had the same idea as me and was pleased when Angie spoke up, 'What's wrong with doing both? We should stay on the move, but we'll get tired of sailing back and forth constantly, or even around Australia, for that matter. If we stayed in one place for just three or four days, then moved on to someplace else, wouldn't that make it much harder for the new bad guys to get a line on us?'

I smiled my appreciation at her, 'That's my choice as well, so it means that we need to plan some comfortable harbours to stop at, while staying within reasonable range of Melbourne for now, and also some places where we can re-supply without attracting too much attention.'

Zoe flashed a rueful grin at her sister, 'Bugger! I'll bet that means even less chance of us meeting some boys.'

Janice gave her a motherly look, 'Probably for the best for now. You'll have your chance in good time.'

'However,' I added, as a comforting thought for them to hang onto, 'you never know whom you might trip across while boating. Aren't school holidays coming up?'

'Oh, yes. They are,' Zoe noted, 'do you get many families on boats during holidays?'

'Oh, sure. We may not see too many in the more remote places, but when we go closer to civilisation to re-supply, there'll be lots!'

That brightened them up, as I remembered the fun they'd had ashore in Wynyard, despite the near-abduction.

'Ok. So, the plan is, when the weather lets up a bit, we might head back east to what I think should be a very sheltered little bay on an island called Erith Island, about half-way across Bass Strait. It's north-west from the bay we first stayed in on our way down from Eden.'

'That sounds good,' Janice offered, 'so you think that would have the desired effect of dropping from sight for a while?'

'Yep! We've been here twice now, for days at a time and even though we haven't seen anybody, a passing boat might have seen us and since there are a few people on the other side of the island, some of them might have walked across and spotted us. Therefore, we need to disappear again.'

Sandy added, 'Yeah. This place might be a bit too well-used for now!'

'Exactly. I thought that, on account of the weather, we might spend another two days and nights here then head for Erith Island first thing Wednesday morning. The southerly will still be blowing so we'll have a fast and reasonably dry run to the northeast that'll take most of the day. After we've had a few days there, we might look at a couple of remote, but sheltered bays around Wilson's Promontory that look suitably isolated from land access. Then, if supplies are getting down a bit, we can run east to Lakes Entrance for a bit of civilisation.'

The girls looked pleased with that prospect, as Janice said, 'We've been there on holiday. There's a huge lake system there. Maybe we could hide out there for a while?'

'We could, but there will be lots of boating activity. Although, just thinking about it, maybe that won't be such a bad thing, sort of like hiding in plain view, but we'll need to make sure we don't stand out too much.'

Sandy gave a derisive snort, 'Oh, yeah. Sure! Get a grip, Harry. You don't really believe that sailing around the Lakes in a 60-foot cat with a very attractive female crew isn't going to stand out too much!'

That raised a general giggle at my naiveté, so I grinned sheepishly, 'Yeah, righto. I guess that we've been sailing back and forth so much already, I've forgotten what we look like to outsiders.'

Sandy replied, 'That's the big thing. We do stand out, particularly as Janice and the girls are very blonde. How about at least a hair colour change for the girls? Or even a wig since their hair is short?'

The girls looked unhappy with that suggestion, but Janice looked thoughtful. 'That's a pretty good suggestion, but I doubt that we'll find wigs anywhere we're likely to go.'

'You're right there,' I came back with, 'but, what about a haircut and a colour change?'

'We're already fairly short, so no way am I going to get a butch haircut!' both girls exclaimed in unison. 'However, going pink or green might be fun.'

'Sorry. I think that if you have a colour change it will have to be black or brown. Pink or green is going to draw even more attention!'

I looked to Janice for a ruling on that, so she said, 'Ok. If we can find the right colour and type of dye, I don't want either of you coloured for life!'

They immediately started an argument as to who was going to be a goth and who would be a brunette. Half-listening, it crossed my mind that the goth look might be a most effective camouflage.

The rest of Sunday
The female crew stayed in their pyjamas, or what passed for those in the case of the girls and kept me distracted all day. Outside, the wind still howled, and rainsqualls still hammered across the scrubby island, churning the water into froth as they blasted at us, but the anchors held securely, and the diesel heaters did their usual efficient job. Reading, board games and video movies were the order of activity, interspersed with curses directed at Jasper when he went to pee or poop and came back wet and dripping, insisting on drying off by rubbing against every set of legs he was allowed near.

At one point when he was dry and sprawled contentedly across the laps of both girls, he let go a huge and silent fart that immediately filled the saloon with a noxious miasma. With the five humans choking and gagging, he raised his head, sniffed, then cast a puzzled look at his rear end, as if to say, 'did I do that?'

'What the hell caused that,' Angie spluttered, opening a forward window a fraction to let some fresh air in.

'It was that bloody can of PAL that you guys bought to try on him,' said Zoe in disgust, 'they cause the worst farts! I'm going to use the rest for fish bait.'

Order was slowly restored as the air cleared, while Jasper stared around, apparently puzzled at the antics of his humans.

Despite being confined to quarters, everyone was in high spirits on account of having an action plan and the prospect of going to see some new places. After a simple evening meal of Angie's tasty toasted sandwiches, the girls found a comedy movie that we all could enjoy, while I made us older folk some NQ teas. The girls asked to try a sip, which I was happy to do, but they weren't too enthused, so I just made three. The movie was a hoot and with us all scrunched together on the lounge, another round of NQ tea went down as easily as the first. 'Jeeze, Harry' Sandy slurred, getting stuck into hers, 'are you trying to get me pissed so you can have your wicked way with me?'

'Maybe,' I replied airily, a comment that provoked derisive howls from everyone.

'Oh, all right then. Yes! How's that?'

'That's better,' Sandy purred, a smug smile on her face, 'honesty is always best.'

'I dunno about that,' I grumped, 'it always seems to get me into more trouble!'

The third round of NQ tea was finished just before the end of the movie and by then, frequent yawns were in evidence, so there was a general rush to pee, brush teeth and head for bed. It was no surprise that Sandy joined Janice and I in our preparations of bed, then joined us in it. What was a surprise was that Sandy took the centre position between Janice and I, instead of outside on Janice's side where I couldn't reach her, but she and Janice seemed to like the arrangement just great!

On this occasion, with the wind howling outside, it was my turn to enjoy a rare treat with Sandy's lovely body beside mine, so we made the most of it.

CHAPTER 44

A chime sounded softly in the multi-line 'phone set on the ornately carved desk.

'Yes?'

'Mr Peter on line 4, Mr Xavier.'

'Thank you, Miss Julie.'

'Xavier. You have a progress report for me?'

'Yes Mr Xavier. We concentrated our resources on the last point of sighting in Wynyard, Tasmania, and have finally developed a lead. Numerous locals we questioned, particularly the patrons of the Hotel near the harbour, have positively identified the subjects and their mother from photos we showed them, but all claim that they left town, either by car or by air, and in company with an older man who could be the mother's father. However, some thought that he left several days before them.

We cannot find any trace of the ladies on the airline records, including from Melbourne onwards, nor did they seem to have hired a car locally.'

'Continue.'

'The only dissenting piece of information was gained under some duress from a young girl who worked at a Hotel near the harbour. She admitted that the subjects might have spent time in the company of some people off a yacht that was moored in the harbour. Although we have a rough description of the yacht, we are unable to corroborate the girl's story, although we believe that she was telling the truth.'

'I urge caution, Mr Peter; you know I don't like hurting civilians in the course of an investigation. Just what form did this 'duress' take?'

'She was intercepted on her way home from work by two of our men, blindfolded, and taken to a local football ground where she was pegged out

on the grass. All her clothes were removed, and she was questioned for some time, but she was not molested or hurt in any other way. After questioning, she was untied, allowed to dress and allowed to make her way home. Unfortunately, her level of anxiety at the time was gauged to be extreme, although she managed to depart the scene without outside assistance'

'Hmmm. I consider that to be excessive and unnecessary force, Mr Peter. That will draw additional attention from the Police who, as you are fully aware, are already quite agitated about the happenings in the middle of their town on Saturday morning. Connections will be made that will hinder the investigation.

I require that you immediately discipline the two operatives who made this interrogation. As their supervisor, I will deal with you when this matter is resolved. A successful resolution would go a long way to mitigating your treatment somewhat. Kindly do not fail me again.'

'Yes, Mr Xavier, that will be done, and may I offer my apologies for their precipitous action?'

'You may, Mr Peter. Apology accepted. Now, what is your plan for taking best advantage of this scrap of information?'

'With your approval, Mr Xavier, I will commence a search for this yacht using a chartered seaplane. We believe that the yacht made several visits to the town, so therefore, it is logical that it is hiding in an unpopulated area that isn't too far away. There are a number of ports and off-shore islands to the north west of the town that are within a reasonable distance, and it is my intention to focus our search there.'

'Very well. That action and associated expenditure is approved but do try very hard to minimise any further civilian casualties! We want a clean pickup of the subjects without drawing any further attention from the Authorities!'

'Yes, Mr Xavier. It shall be as you say.'

CHAPTER 45

FIREBIRD... SHEPHERD'S BAY
– HUNTER ISLAND, MONDAY

Next morning was late in arriving for the whole crew, it would seem; even Jasper was slow in calling for his breakfast, so we three stayed put and I indulged in a glorious repeat romp with Sandy, despite Janice giving a very bad imitation of still being asleep. In fact, by that stage of our joint relationship, none of us cared who did what to whom, as it was all happy and with no tensions.

Finally, we roused sufficiently to take turns to use the bathroom, not bothering to dress, which amused the girls as we passed back and forth below the companionway, where they sat having breakfast at the table.

I pulled on pants and a sweater and ventured out on deck where I noted that the weather had improved a little, but low cloud still streamed across the island and the wind blew hard from the southwest. A quick check around the wet decks in the very chilly wind revealed that all was well, so I shook the contents of Jasper's toilet mat overboard and left it for the next shower to rinse clean, while I dived back into the warmth down below.

Inside I found that the girls were watching another movie and the ladies had returned to the warm bed, so I made a command-level decision and joined them!

Where, not surprisingly, one thing led to another and I surprised myself and delighted Sandy by rising to the occasion yet again and gave a thoroughly successful performance that left me quite drained and temporarily weak.

The girls bravely ventured down with mugs of tea after a while, so I roused myself sufficiently to sit up and be revived by the hot, sweet liquid.

'We put extra sugar in, Harry, figuring that you might need it,' Zoe remarked cheekily.

I poked a face at her, 'Ha ha ha! Very droll!'

A great deal more of the day was spent in the warmth of that bed, dozing, chatting and laughing about little things that had happened, so it wasn't until late afternoon that we rolled out, showered and dressed to find the rain gone and a rather wan sun just on the point of slipping below the roiling cloud banks to the west.

In a burst of enthusiasm that failed to communicate to anybody else, I managed to stir everybody into action and after launching the dinghy, we made it ashore for some badly needed exercise. Jasper went a bit nuts after several days cooped up, so we played with him while we trotted up and down the wet, sandy beach, keeping moving to ward off the chill. Finally, the ladies cried enough, and we returned aboard where I stowed the dinghy under the daybed platform in case of a night shower.

Tuesday

Morning dawned much brighter, although the wind still blew strongly from the southwest and was bloody cold. I hauled the second anchor up as we were laying very comfortably to one, even in the strong breeze. We were sitting down to a feed of fresh, hot pancakes for morning tea, when the sound of a low-flying aircraft stifled conversation.

I ducked out clear of the cockpit overhead in time to see a single-engine floatplane, a Cessna 206 by the quick glimpse I had of it, roar low overhead in a steep bank. There was only one passenger and the pilot, but the passenger had a camera to his face.

The winds and low-level turbulence were kicking the aircraft around quite badly and I took time to admire the pilot's skill as he made a curving approach to the small bay and lined up for a crosswind touchdown on the smooth water close in to the beach.

With a curse on my lips, I turned back to the cockpit, pancakes forgotten.

'Bugger it! This is trouble! Janice, take the girls and get below! Go right for'rard into our dressing room, get on the floor, but crack the hatch first and keep listening for what happens.'

They went, Angie having the presence of mind to grab three plates, mugs and cutlery as she left, dumping them in the sink on the way past.

I looked at Sandy. 'You'd better grab your Glock and some extra mags. I don't think these guys will be messing around with too much small talk.'

She hustled below as I tripped the concealed latches on the fittings that hid two pump-action shotguns stowed in the back of the steering station seat, grabbed two boxes of rounds from under the chart table, and retrieved my very special handgun, a LAR Grizzly Mk IV .44 Magnum semi-auto pistol with an 6.5' barrel, from another concealed locker behind the circuit-breaker panel. One shotgun was a Remington 870 Express that took a sabot rifled slug for hard-hitting, long-range action, while the other was another Remington 870, but this was the TAC 14 short-barrel model loaded with 3' Nitro Magnum shells.

I dumped the opened boxes beside the guns on the helm seat and had all three weapons loaded and ready by the time Sandy came back up, her Glock loaded, a spare magazine stuffed into each pocket.

I turned to Jasper who, alerted by my tone, was lurking like a black shadow in the doorway to the saloon and pointed to a spot on the cockpit floor, just beside the port boarding stairs, 'Bad guys, Jasper, stay low!'

He looked at me, flattened his ears out sideways, which with his dilated pupils gave him an evil, devil-cat appearance, and gave a soft growl before slinking across the cockpit floor to crouch like a sphinx in the shadow of the stern seat. Sandy took a quick look at both of us, shook her head in wonder and then focused back on the Cessna.

Unfortunately, the floatplane made a good touchdown on the upwind float and taxied toward us, the pilot using his water rudders hard to counter the weathercocking effect caused by the strong wind gusts.

Sandy tucked her Glock into the back of her shorts, which worked for her, while I did the same with my LAR Grizzly, except that at close to 2 kg and around 320mm long, I wasn't going to be doing much leaping about. Not if I wanted to keep my pants in place or avoid shooting my bum off!

The pilot was finally able to swing around so he was approaching us from downwind, which meant straight at our stern. However, because we were swinging around somewhat now that we had just one anchor set, his task was more difficult. Still, he had already shown that he was an excellent pilot. His passenger climbed out on the starboard float holding a mooring line, although his partly un-zipped padded jacket was bulging suspiciously on the left side.

'Watch him, Sandy,' I called over the clatter of the idling six-cylinder IO-520 Continental and the muted buzz of the three-blade prop, 'that dude's armed!'

'On him!' she called back, without shifting her eyes from the passenger who had clipped one end of the mooring line to a ringbolt on the underside of the Cessna's wing. The rest of the coil of line he held in his free hand.

Sandy had propped herself casually against the starboard stern seat, one foot up on the seat, back leg braced, her right hand on her hip, very close to the Glock in her waistband. I hoped that her prominent, bikini-clad breasts would provide some level of distraction for our unwanted visitors, but I was prepared for them to be immune to such things.

I remained glad that I wasn't!

I was standing casually beside the helm seat, the three weapons out of sight beside me, while I held onto the overhead grab rail with my left hand and pasted a sappy smile on my face.

'Smile for the nice gentlemen, dear,' I called, as the pilot cut the engine, swinging the 'plane left at the last second, to place the right float beside our port stern. This allowed the passenger to step lightly across to our boarding platform and take a round turn on a cleat with his mooring rope in one smooth movement. Sandy had to duck slightly as the Cessna's right wing swung dangerously close over our stern seats and very close to our cockpit overhead where I could have reached out to grab the wingtip quite easily. But didn't.

With a big, false smile, our un-welcome visitor spoke. 'Morning Missus, good morning, Sir. Please excuse our slightly dramatic arrival like this, but we'd like to discuss a matter of mutual interest with you.'

I didn't move as I replied in a calm, level tone, 'Consider yourself excused, so long as you take your wing-tip out of my face and your aeroplane away from my boat. Preferably in the next 30 seconds! Permission to board is refused and will be noted in the ship's log! Under maritime law, your continued presence constitutes an act of piracy, the penalties for which are rather severe!'

The pilot hadn't moved, and I could still see both his hands gripping the instrument panel coaming, his eyes temporarily glued on Sandy's chest. The passenger was only put off stride for a moment, before shaking his head and replying, 'That's not very hospitable, sir, seeing as we've flown out here on this very unpleasant morning, at great expense and in great discomfort, I might add, just to talk to you.'

'Not interested,' I replied, 'my previous statement stands.'

'But please, at least allow me to introduce ourselves. I'm Mr Peter and my very capable associate over there is Mr Jordan. We are from the investigative firm of Steel Associates and have been hired to locate and return three female persons to their rightful father and husband, Luke Emery.'

'What makes you think the persons in question are here?' I asked in my most relaxed manner, draping my right hand casually across the back of the helm seat beside me.

'Oh, it's amazing what people talk about under enough duress, and unfortunately, the ladies in question weren't quick enough to vacate the cockpit when we flew over.'

He smiled, but the expression didn't reach his eyes, 'The wonders of digital photography, you see. I made a quick review of the photos I took during our flypast and I'm afraid that I've identified all three before they departed the cockpit.

Now, with their presence established, I do hope we can avoid any unpleasantness. If you'd just ask the ladies to present themselves, we can comply with your request that we be excused. We'll even let them take a small bag with them, but as you can see, we do not have a great deal of spare space, so luggage must be limited.'

'Gee,' I replied, 'what a wonderful offer. They'll have to consider that one very carefully. Like for the next 30-odd years perhaps!'

'Oh, no, sir. Very droll! But we don't have that sort of time to spare, so I really must insist that you call the ladies up here.'

'That sounds like an 'or else' is attached. Care to elaborate?' I challenged.

'Or my associate and I will have to take rather more drastic measures to ensure compliance with our request. Either way, sir, the ladies will be leaving with us in the next 10 minutes. That is a certainty!' He smiled at his cleverness then made the huge mistake of advancing up the stern steps, stopping just at the top step, failing to glance down to see the motionless black head and partly open jaws almost beside his right foot.

I love ultimatums and hate bullies, so I turned my head and raised my voice. 'Janice! Would you come up here please? Alone.'

There was a faint answering call and after a few moments, she spoke from the doorway, 'I'm here.'

'Ok. Stay right there and answer this question. Do you and the girls wish to go with these gentlemen and be re-united with your supposedly loving husband?'

'No and most emphatically no!' was her instant reply.

'Thanks, Janice. Please return to your previous position.'

I shrugged and smiled at Mr Peter. 'Well, there you have it. You've heard from her directly. The lady says no, so I'm afraid I'll have to ask you yet again to remove yourself and your aeroplane from my boat.'

Mr Peter slowly shook his head in mock dismay, his close-set eyes showing no such emotion, 'Oh, dear. I was so very afraid that it would come to this. I do hate to inflict pain, but you've left me no choice.'

He made the mistake of turning to call to his colleague in the pilot's seat, while reaching into the left side of his jacket, his hand coming out with a black pistol clutched in it.

'Mr Jordan, would you mind coming up here? We may have to do some additional persuading of... Ahhhhhhhhh!'

His rising-pitch scream was caused by a combination of fright, terror and incredible pain as a huge black shape launched up from seemingly nowhere and clamped a set of razor-sharp fangs around his right arm. He stumbled backwards as the 25-odd kilogram weight of Jasper, sounding off with his own ear-piercing, unearthly yowl of rage, thumped into his chest, causing him to miss the step behind and perform a backslide down to the boarding platform, his head bashing painfully on each riser. Jasper stayed clamped to him, his jaw continuing to wrench back and forth at his forearm, claws raking every other part of his body within reach, sending clothing, then blood and chunks of torn-off flesh spraying in all directions. Vainly, he tried to dislodge the maddened beast that was slowly succeeding in ripping his lower right arm off, his screams sounding undiminished.

Mr Jordan, meanwhile, showed that while he had no intention of getting out of the aircraft's cabin, he wasn't averse to doing his bit for his colleague by groping under his seat and coming up with what looked like a mini-Uzi machine pistol. What he was doing didn't deter Jasper literally ripping the shit out of Mr Peter, so Sandy snatched her Glock from her waistband and opened up on the pilot.

That finally gave me my chance and I grabbed up the compact TAC 14 and aimed for the cockpit as well.

I saw Sandy get some hits, which certainly slowed the pilot from bringing the mini-Uzi to bear on us, although he did squeeze off a short burst that seemed to go straight up through the wing over his head. While airframe bits deflected some of Sandy's 9mm rounds, at least she had plenty of them, a very nice feature of the Glock. But the TAC 14's 00 pellets hardly spread at that range and acted like one solid mass of steel shot that just blew through everything in its path and kept on going. The first seemed to hit the rear of the engine, which didn't do it much good, but the next sort-of removed most of Mr Jordan's head, which ended the whole argument right there!

I lowered the TAC 14 and after checking that Sandy was safe and had ceased fire, stepped forward to see how Jasper was doing with Mr Peter. It was not a pretty sight with blood, guts and bits of flesh all down the steps and over the boarding platform. Jasper was having a great time pulling out a length of large intestine, but I decided to call him off, which he did very reluctantly, spitting out the tasty morsel and giving me a reproachful look as he slunk past, blood dripping from his muzzle, as if to say, 'You spoilt my fun!'

I patted him and offered a 'Good boy. Well done!' but that didn't seem to be well received, as he sat at the top step and sulked, not even bothering to have a wash.

Mr Peter was a just a little bit worse for wear after Jasper's attention, appearing to be barely alive, his right arm hanging by a thread of tendon and with blood spurting in great gouts into the water. Jasper's claws had neatly disembowelled him, and the contents of his abdomen, spread courtesy of Jasper, added to the horrific scene. Not to mention the stink!

'I don't think he'll be any further problem,' I commented dryly to Sandy as I carefully emptied the TAC 14 of the remaining shells before laying it down.

Sandy was doing the same with her Glock, by removing the magazine and clearing the chamber, 'Love your perceptive nature, Harry,' she quipped, trying the lighten the tension.

'Ok. Let's see if these clowns have anything interesting on board that might help us, then we can see about some garbage disposal!'

Mr Peter had somehow made a few feeble movements toward the Cessna's float, bobbing just beside his head, but he clearly had only seconds to live. I approached him carefully, but caution wasn't necessary, so I hauled his remains half across the float, stepped over him and pulled the door open.

Mr Jordan was definitely having a bad-head day and had made a rather disgusting mess over his side of the cockpit. There was also a very strong smell of fuel, so I hurriedly grabbed a laptop and camera from the middle seat, along with a briefcase and passed them back to Sandy. As an afterthought, I grabbed the Mini-Uzi and a gym bag under the pilot's seat that seemed to hold a bunch of spare magazines, boxes of ammunition and another pistol.

A quick look around showed nothing else useful or of importance, so I left the door open and stepped back to *Firebird*.

'What do you want us to do with that lot?' Sandy asked.

'There's fuel pissing everywhere in there. I think that short burst he got off went straight through one of the wing tanks, so we might just untie the thing and let the wind carry it off a way before we fire a flare into it. The water deepens quickly about 100 metres out, so that should hide the evidence. Sharks will take care of the bodies.'

CHAPTER 46

So that's what we did. It would be a sad end for a very nice aeroplane, but with bullet holes and blood and guts everywhere, there'd be no easy explanation for its condition, even without the bodies. We didn't even need to push it away after untying it, the gusting wind doing that job in very short order. In fact, I had to move quickly to dig out the flare pistol from the locker under the helm seat before it had drifted too far.

The wind turned its nose toward us as it drifted and we saw a stream of fluid pouring from the inboard end of the left wing, soaking the side of the machine and splashing into the water. I waited until the wind had blown the fuel slick away from our stern, before firing a flare into the shimmering pool of fuel gathered most densely around the left float. There was a soft whoosh as the Avgas ignited, a cloud of black, greasy smoke unfortunately going up with it, but within seconds, the once-proud Cessna was a seething mass of flames.

'Feel like some target practice?' I asked Sandy with a grin.

'Sure,' she answered, 'but why waste rounds on it. Most will burn anyway.'

'True, but it's over pretty deep water already and the quicker it sinks, the less attention it can attract.'

'Oh, right,' she caught on, 'the floats.'

'Yep. Try your hand with the LAR Grizzly.'

I handed her the gun and she grunted as she felt the weight of it.

'Bloody hell, Harry! What possessed you to get a cannon like this?'

'I've always wanted to be able to say, 'Make my day', haven't you?' I grinned.

'Oh no. Got it. Dirty Harry! You idiot.' She thumped my arm, adrenaline fuelling her muscles so that I stumbled, before adding, 'I wanted a handgun with massive stopping power in case of boarding incidents just like this one. I didn't need to conceal it, so being large doesn't matter. Therefore, I could go as big as I wanted, but .44 Magnums are big enough and ammo isn't too hard to find. Still, I keep a good stock just in case.'

I handed over a full magazine and watched as she checked the rounds for freedom of movement and correct seating, then expertly slipped it into the butt, clicking it home precisely without the dramatic slamming tactic of an amateur that could damage or jam a cartridge.

The high spring tension on the slide also made her grunt for a second, but then she braced herself, settled her grip and squeezed off the first round. There is nothing subtle about a .44 Magnum, both in recoil or in sound, but Sandy was pleasantly surprised that the recoil was so manageable. Despite the range, her first shot was on target and I had to remind myself that she was rated Expert Instructor in the Police Force.

A great chunk of aluminium tore off and spun away from the left float, the whole aircraft becoming difficult to see through the smoke and flames.

After that sighting shot, she squeezed off the remaining six rounds and really tore up the float closest to us, causing the Cessna to settle very quickly on that side. A quick magazine change and she stitched a line of holes up the wing, while I joined in with the 870 Express, pumping two loads of rifled slugs into the wing tanks as well. That did the trick, and as the aircraft settled wings-level in the water, gouts of escaping air and fuel showed that the job was complete. Minutes later, the fire consumed the remaining escaped fuel and the remains slid quietly underwater.

The strong wind did an excellent job of dispersing the smoke and the waves spread the small oil slick. Hopefully, within a few hours, that would be gone as well, as the wind was set to continue all night and the next day.

I grinned at Sandy as I cleared both shotguns and she did the same with the Grizzly.

'Great job, partner, but we'd better clean up Jasper and the mess on the boat before we get Janice and the girls up.'

She grinned back, her chest still heaving from the adrenaline pumping through our systems, hard tips showing through the bikini top. Being in a gunfight tends to do stuff like that and it doesn't matter how experienced one might be. It takes a while for the system to burn the adrenaline off, so the bit of necessary target practice was part of the wind-down process.

'I'll take Jasper, if you like, while you wash off the boat.' Sandy offered.

'Done.' So, she coerced the reluctant Jasper over to the starboard stern shower, while I unrolled the saltwater wash hose from the left stern locker and quickly hosed off the blood and muck. With the high pressure delivered by that hose, it all came off cleanly and it wasn't long before I'd finished and rolled the hose up again. I then helped Sandy with Jasper, who at least had stopped sulking now that he was the centre of attention again.

With everything clean again, I called inside for the others to join us, which they did in very short order, all looking quite fearful and worried. Sandy and I got hugged and kissed before Janice looked around and asked the big question, 'Where are they? We heard all the shooting and didn't know what was happening. We were waiting for them to come busting down below to drag us out, but all we heard were gunshots. We didn't even hear them fly away!'

She looked around the cockpit and saw the pile of guns on the helm seat. 'Bloody hell, Harry. Where did they all come from? And why is Jasper soaking wet? What happened up here?'

The relief of coming out on top of the encounter started Sandy giggling at her barrage of questions and I had a few chuckles myself, but before Janice became upset, I held up my hand.

'Okay. Hold it. We'll tell you everything, but let's have a cup of tea and sit down so we can tell the story properly. Sandy and I are just a little bit wired at the moment.'

Janice peered closely at me, 'Are you alright? Are both of you OK?'

I gave her a little hug, 'Yep. We're both fine. Now, how about that cuppa?'

The twins had been watching and listening with wide eyes, not saying anything, but my question broke the spell and Angie spoke as Zoe disappeared back inside to the galley, 'Oh. Yeah. Sorry Harry. Won't be a moment. You just sit and relax.'

So we did and in short order, the girls produced tea and sandwiches. I waited until we'd all had a bite and some tea before starting.

'To start at the end, I can say that those guys won't be a problem again and it may be some time before the others pick up our trail again.'

With that reassurance, Sandy and I proceeded to tell the whole story. We didn't gloss over anything, particularly Jasper's part in proceedings, causing the three of them to look at the great devil-eyed, killer-cat, laying on the settee with his still-damp head on Zoe's lap, accepting her scratching and patting as his due and purring like a small motor.

'So, Jasper killed one of them?' Angie asked, interrupting our story.

I looked carefully at her before answering. 'Yes, he did. And it was to protect those he loves, because bad guys were threatening us. He could have been shot since they were both armed, although Jasper didn't quite give the ex-Mr Peter a chance to complete his draw and just as well! We'd prefer not to go into details, but he's wet because Sandy had to hose him off.'

Both girls were silent for a moment, before Zoe gave Jasper a hug and said, 'Cool!'

Janice had her own questions after looking over the pile of guns on the helm seat.

'Are these all yours, Harry?'

'Not quite,' I replied with a grin, 'I told you once before that I had a few guns tucked away, but the Glock is Sandy's service pistol and the machine pistol is a Mini-Uzi we took from the bad guys, as well as another pistol that was in the bag full of magazines.'

Sandy coughed. 'I also happened to hang onto the pistol that Mr Peter was trying to draw. The two pistols, Glock 19s and the Uzi are in 9mm, and although my service Glock is .40 S & W, we have plenty of ammo for all of them and can easily get more.'

I smiled at her, 'Good work. I hate throwing guns away. They can be very useful at times.'

That generated a general laugh, until Janice prompted me to finish the story, mainly about getting rid of the bodies and the aircraft, which I did without embellishment.

'Was that the best thing to do?' she asked, 'I mean. Wiping out all trace of them?'

'Yeah. We reckon it was. If they and the aircraft totally disappear, there's no evidence that they ever found us, so we've temporarily cut that line of investigation. They'll have to know about the boat from reports, but there'll be no reports from this morning onwards, so we're confident that our trail is broken for the moment.

However, I think that we should get out of here within the next hour and head for Erith Island. It's a 10 to 12-hour sail, which means arriving sometime tonight, but that shouldn't be a problem with the nav gear we've got. That way, if they do send a crew out this way looking for their mates, they won't trip over us.'

Those thoughts were met with approval, including from Sandy, our new Chief of Security.

While the girls cleaned up the morning tea things and stowed the galley for sea, I checked on deck that all was secure. The dinghy was still secured and we only had one anchor out, so there was only the main to get ready for hoisting. I fired up the generator to do some battery charging and power the winches, although the two wind generators had been working well since we arrived, and the batteries weren't down much. The wind was still strong out of the southwest, so it was going to be a fast, wet ride. I sent Janice around to close all hatches and portholes, and dog them down well.

Sandy gathered up our augmented weapons collection and took them into the saloon for inspection and cleaning.

I was rather pleased that I'd saved the mini-Uzi. They have a well-deserved reputation for reliability, although at 1,000 rounds/minute, they chew through the 25 or 32 round magazine very quickly. Like in less than 2 seconds!

I'd not been able to get one before, even with my ACP contacts, although by using the common 9mm Parabellum round, they were easy to feed, so it was a very welcome addition to my arsenal. It even looked to be in good condition, but Sandy would let me know after she'd stripped and examined it more closely. The other gun she'd plucked from Mr Peter's near-lifeless hand, as well as the gun in the pilot's bag was the smaller-framed Model 19 that was more easily concealed as a carry weapon. Sandy's Glock was the full-size service version Model 22.

As a bonus, the pilot's bag also contained several hundred rounds of 9mm ammunition in addition to five extra magazines for the Mini-Uzi, also fully loaded, so we were well-stocked with ammo for now.

I was careful getting underway as the winds were still strong and gusting wildly. It wasn't my normal choice of conditions for a sail across the top of Tasmania and half of Bass Strait, but at least we would be running or on a very broad reach that would be more pleasant. We had to go regardless, so it would be interesting to see how *Firebird* handled the conditions.

It was nearly 12:00 by the time the anchor was stowed for sea and with the 50% reefed main already hoisted and flapping madly, I unfurled the inner staysail and let it haul our bows around. As we came around beam-on to the wind, *Firebird* really started to accelerate, momentarily overpowered, but with the pressure quickly easing as we turned onto a broad reach to pass clear of the bottom of Three Hummock Island. I took the wheel until Zoe was ready and delighted in the way *Firebird* really picked up her heels and scooted.

Even with greatly reduced sail, our speed soon climbed into the high teens, going over 20 knots in the gusts of which there were plenty. The wind was averaging over 30 knots, so I expected that once clear of the influence of the two main islands, the wind would increase further. And so it proved as we rounded the southern tip of Three Hummocks Island and bore away on track for Erith Island, the mean wind speed climbed to over 35 knots and the seas started to build.

We covered the 5.5 nautical miles to the rounding point in just 15 minutes, giving an average speed of just over 20 knots. With the higher wind speed, and since the track to Erith Island was now almost straight downwind, I deliberately steered a little to the south of that direct course so that there was no danger of the sails being caught by a slight change of wind direction and being ripped over to the other side. Called a gybe, it was generally a mast-breaking experience if it happened in gale conditions! For additional security I fitted a simple sheet brake to the main to prevent such a disastrous event.

We slowed slightly with the more downwind heading, but it was safer and more comfortable as there was less chance of being overpowered. I made some small adjustments to the mainsail reefing percentages to balance the steering, but it was still exacting work keeping the boat running straight, especially as the waves built further once we were away from the land shielding and we started some serious surfing.

It was an exhilarating ride without doubt, and I was totally enjoying myself, especially after the gross unpleasantness of the morning. I turned George the autopilot on to see if he could cope with the sea conditions, and to my surprise, it coped very well, keeping us straight while surfing at speeds up to 25 knots and correcting in time to prevent broaching. However, I could hear the steering motors working very hard to achieve that sort of performance.

Zoe was hanging around, keen to take the wheel, but a bit concerned whether she could handle it, so I let her have a go and after a while she was doing well, learning how to anticipate a yaw before it developed into something worse.

She did admit that while great fun, it was also very hard work and needed total concentration. So when she tired of wrestling with the wheel, she turned the task over to George who did the job without tiring, apart from the high drain on the batteries.

And so we fled on into the afternoon and an uncertain future, riding the remains of the tempest, leaving any regrets or concerns over our actions of the morning further and further behind in our boiling wake, along with two dead bad guys and a wrecked aeroplane. There was, of course, the minor matter of when they would be missed and what sort of a search would be triggered, but for now, as far as we were concerned, out of sight was definitely out of mind. By mentally looking ahead, not behind, the carnage behind us became of lesser consequence as the miles streamed past.

The ride was remarkably good, given the conditions, and none of the crew seemed bothered. In fact, everyone went about normal on-board routine as though we were still at anchor. After our evening meal, which was tasty toasted sandwiches and hot tea. I asked the crew sitting around the table, 'Does anybody have any regrets or problems over our actions this morning?'

There was only a brief moment of thought, before they all shook their heads.

'Excellent. In that case, I'd like to leave that one as far behind us as possible, literally and metaphorically. Sandy and I can live with the doing and seeing part, but I'd like the rest of you not to dwell on what happened, but you do need to voice any concerns you might have.'

Only Angie spoke straight off, 'From my point of view, and I think Zoe agrees, those guys were going to take us no matter what, and they had loaded guns to enforce that, so I reckon they got what they deserved! I've got no regrets.'

Zoe nodded agreement.

'Okay, that's great.'

I looked at Janice, my eyebrows raised questioningly, but she smiled gently and shook her head, 'I think Angie said it just right. They wanted to harm us, but thanks to you, Sandy and Jasper, we kicked their arses instead. Good riddance and no regrets!'

'Excellent! Needless to say, this morning's events should never be mentioned to anybody outside our close circle, no matter what the provocation or how much you trust them. I'd prefer not to have to argue the finer points of self-defence and piracy in Court!'

Janice answered for the three of them. 'We understand and I'm sure we can keep that secret!'

We left it at that and I moved on to talk about our arrival at Erith Island.

'It's 18:00 now, and according to the chart plotter, we should make Erith at about 9 or 10 this evening. We'll have to be careful as we get closer, but there aren't any major obstacles on our direct track for now so there shouldn't be any problem. We've got the radar and the forward-looking sonar running continuously and know exactly where we are.'

That seemed to reassure everyone, so I continued to keep an eye on radar and the chart plotter, but apart from a few freighters and some large fishing boats, the Strait was very quiet tonight. The wind didn't ease as dusk fell, but as we made the course change at Norfolk Point to thread the 800 metre-wide channel called Murray Pass, between Dover and Deal Islands, I reefed the mainsail a bit more. That dropped our speed a little, then about 500 metres out from the anchorage at Erith Island, I dropped both sails altogether and fired up the engines.

With them at 50% power, we slid sedately into increasingly sheltered waters, the wind easing a little, but the waves dropping away to nearly nothing as we approached our parking spot close in to the beach at the southern end of West Cove.

As reported in the Pilot books, the anchorage was good sand

with a few weed patches, but we dropped the pick close in to the beach on clean sand. I shone our very powerful High Intensity Discharge spotlight around the bay to check for company, but we were quite alone.

As Erith Island has quite high hills, the average wind strength had dropped considerably, but perversely, the hills produced some very powerful bullets or strong gusts, that howled down the hill slopes at ridiculous velocity, before roaring out across the water, shaking the mast and the whole boat like a dog with a bone. It was a little un-nerving to the crew at first when these hit from near-calm conditions with no warning, but after we'd snugged everything down securely, everyone was too tired to be bothered by them, so we slept well.

FIREBIRD...ERITH ISLAND, WEDNESDAY MORNING

Next morning, I was up early and a quick check revealed that no changes had occurred to our anchored position during the night. I'd made my usual couple of brief inspections during the night, by standing up in bed and sticking my head through the big access hatch, unless I needed to go aft for a pee. The clouds had lifted considerably and patches of blue sky grew steadily larger which brightened the view of our surroundings, now shown to be a very pretty little bay only about 500 metres across, open to the East, with scrub-covered hills around the other three sides. One kilometre away to the East, Deal Island provided shelter from all but the very worst easterly gales, although they were quite rare. The small anchorage was still deserted and I knew that the island was uninhabited, so with a bit of luck it would stay that way for a while, although as a stepping-stone from the Mainland to Tasmania, we could expect other small boats at some stage.

After checking *Firebird* for any signs of wear or damage from our fast and rough flight across the top of Tasmania, I treated the deck and fittings to a fresh-water wash off. Then it was time for a mug of tea, as the crew, apart from Jasper, were still fast asleep. The surrounding hills gave the little bay a different aspect to our last anchorage at Shepherd's Bay and to my mind, made it a much more interesting vista than the low scrub covering of our last two hideouts.

I looked forward to some bush walks, having little concern about meeting other people.

The water covering the sandy bottom was absolutely gin-clear and an amazing variety of small aquatic life could be seen busily going about their business, occasionally chased by a larger predator.

I also remembered that these islands were the last stronghold of the Australian Fur seal and hoped we might see some.

That inspired a mental note to get our resident fishing experts, the girls, on the job as soon as they were up, as we needed to supplement our pantry. Jasper, who sat happily by my feet as I perched in my favourite seat up in the port bow, showed no sign of his terminal encounter with Mr Peter yesterday and was his usual affectionate and playful self.

I hadn't long finished my tea, when there were signs of life from the galley and soon Zoe showed up balancing a large plate of hot, buttered toast and two mugs of tea. She parked herself on the trampoline nearby, Jasper in close attendance to scrounge some toast.

'Angie and I wanted to thank you and Sandy for what you did yesterday,' she said between mouthfuls of toast. 'We didn't get around to it in all the rush of getting away, but we appreciate what you did and understand how difficult it must have been to kill both those men.'

I smiled at her, 'You're welcome. Actually, killing bad guys who're trying to kill you isn't too hard, when it's done in the heat of the moment. It's the cold-blooded stuff that few of us like. But I'm just glad that we were able to come out on top without any of us getting hurt.'

'Amen!' she replied, 'Now we just have to keep one jump ahead of them.'

'Yes, and that's the difficult part, since this lot are obviously much more capable and we don't know how long we have to keep ducking and dodging. I just wish that the various Authorities would hurry up and co-ordinate their raids so this whole mess can be put to bed and everyone can get on with their lives!'

She looked wistful. 'You know, despite all the bad things that have been happening, it's going to be very hard to give up this lifestyle and go back to Uni and a new onshore life. We can see why you love boating and being on this beautiful boat!'

I smiled gently, 'It's going to be hard for me too, princess. I've become very fond of you two and your Mum. But you do need to finish your education and plan a career, if that's what you want.'

She looked down at the deck and said in a soft, sad voice, 'What we'd like most of all, Harry, is for all of us to stay here with you, Sandy and Jasper. But I guess that's not going to happen.'

'No, princess. Unfortunately, that's not going to happen. But what can happen, if your Mum agrees, is that you can come join Jasper and me and hopefully Sandy as well, when you have semester breaks. We won't always be close by, but that's what aeroplanes are for. You get to come to us.'

She looked up at me, her eyes brimming, 'Oh, could we? That'd be absolutely fantastic!'

I smiled and nodded. 'Yep. Why not? Once this nonsense is over, we can get back to a normal life. I'm sure many of your girlfriends travel for their holidays.'

She looked around as if seeing the boat and the setting around us in a new light, 'Well, yes they do. But nothing like this. And no one has adventures like we've had!'

'No one would want to have adventures like you've had!' I countered with a grin, 'But once all the bad guys are locked up, you can talk about it all you want. Or not, as you wish. Your call.'

She gave me a shrewd glance, 'You're very understanding, aren't you? I mean, you've only set rules when we've needed to be protected, but you cut us a lot of slack most of the time. We expected you to act like a father figure, but you're like an older brother who's looking out for us, and that feels really good. You've treated us like adults and even though we're 18, that doesn't happen very often.'

It was my turn to find a piece of rigging to inspect carefully so I could avoid an answer.

Zoe giggled, 'Sorry Harry. No reply necessary, but I've got to go tell Angie that we can come and stay with you in our holidays.'

'Only if your Mum is happy with that,' I called out to her disappearing figure.

'Yeah, yeah, whatever!' was the frivolous reply.

A happy shriek from the large hatch over the girl's cabin suggested that Angie thought my offer was a pretty neat idea, but I wasn't prepared for the delightfully naked body that erupted as the hatch was flung wide open and Angie sprang through it before wrapping herself around me.

'Oh thank you Harry. We were so frightened that we'd never see you, Jasper or this lovely boat again. It would be absolutely wonderful to spend our holidays on board. We're sure Mum will be happy with that as well.'

I tried hard to confine my hands to just stroking her velvet-smooth back, but it was difficult! Finally, she backed off and I tried to regulate my breathing again.

'You're very welcome, especially if you keep greeting me like that every morning. I could get very accustomed to that!'

She gave a cheeky grin as she went back below via the cabin hatch, creating a disturbingly erotic sight as she did.

'I'll happily do that for you, Harry. Anytime, anywhere.'

I waited a while to allow my heart rate and other things to subside, and I'd just picked up my empty mug to go below, when there was a soft 'Whoosh' under the bow behind me. Turning, I saw to my utter delight, a grinning, heavily whiskered face with huge brown, expressive eyes poking up from the water. Moments later, with another soft 'Whoosh', a second, much larger seal reared up beside the first, flippers gently moving as they kept perfect position.

Turning my head slightly, I called quietly back to the cabin,

'Girls! Quickly, come up here, but don't make too much noise!'

I heard noises behind me, then two bodies, one still naked and one clothed, pressed in beside me and hung over the pulpit rail.

'Oh, wow!' was the joint response, as the seals, far from being frightened by the extra audience, seemed delighted to see the girls and deliberately splashed water up at us with their flippers. Zoe darted back to call Sandy and Janice up as well, and moments later, they joined us in marvelling at the playful, happy creatures. Our visitors weren't put off either by Jasper sticking his sleek, black head over the side to peer down at them, even when he mewled softly, almost like asking the question, '*Who are you guys?*' Although he showed signs of wanting to jump into the water with them, I told him 'No' until we saw how the seals behaved around humans in the water. I'd read that the males could grow to well over 300 kgs, which was a lot of seal to wrestle with if push came to shove.

Still, it was hard to imagine the happy pair below us having any aggressive habits against humans.

'Can we feed them?' asked Zoe. 'We've still got some decent-sized bait fish un-frozen.'

'We shouldn't,' I said, 'but bugger it! Go get some and see what they do.'

She darted away and quickly returned with a handful of decided smelly mullet we'd been saving for fish bait. Leaning over the bow rail, she dropped one to the biggest seal and laughed when he reared up almost to her fingers and caught it neatly with his gleaming mouthful of massive teeth.

'Far out!' She laughed. 'That's awesome!' She threw one to the smaller seal we thought was probably the female of the pair and she caught it just as easily, gulping it down in two quick bites and a toss of her head. She was a pale brown on the top of her head, with a creamy throat. Her much larger mate, was darker in colour, and had a distinct ruff of fur around his neck. They both seemed happy to be close to us and after accepting more fish, dived and splashed around the anchor chain as if putting on a show for their feed. After we ran out of baitfish, we continued watching until they splashed their flippers at us a few last times as if saying goodbye, before flashing away.

'Magic!' seemed to be the common reaction to the encounter as we sat down to breakfast in a mood of wonder that some wild animals could interact so easily with humans and we all hoped that the seals would return soon.

After breakfast, we went ashore to walk the beach for a while, until I suggested that we should return to make contact with the various persons who needed to know about yesterday's attack and its gruesome outcome. It took until lunchtime to get the word out to everybody and they were unanimous in their approval for our actions.

Bob Casey, Sandy's boss was really chuffed to hear how the fight went, but the only news he had to offer was that Greg James, Sandy's old partner, was out of hospital, with the wounds received from the bashing now healing quickly, and that he would make a complete recovery. He would also be returning to his former position and duties at Southport and was delighted at Sandy's promotion to Sergeant and independent undercover operative. He was also dead keen to join us but knew that wasn't going to happen.

Annette didn't have much to say, except that her side of the investigation was proceeding well, with virtually all the adult faces in the photos and videos now identified, and the list of public figures had grown disturbingly long.

'We may not be too far off being able to ask for a bunch of search and arrest warrants,' she advised, *'but it might be a week or so before we can make the co-ordinated raids we believe will have the best chance of netting all these persons at once. As you realise, it's no good picking up just one or two, the rest will bug out immediately. They plan for this, so we have to be careful.'*

'Thanks, Annette,' I replied on the sat-phone, 'we know why the delay has to be, so we'll continue to do our best to keep a low-profile, but we'll need to head for civilisation within a week to restock the larder.'

'Understood, Harry. Just keep hanging on and we'll move as fast as we can. If anything changes, I'll call you immediately.'

'Thanks, and make sure you don't turn over the wrong rock,' I said.

She chuckled in her warm throaty manner, *'Will do. Bye for now guys.'*

Rob was suitably cryptic as to how the visit to Canberra/Yass had gone. He said so little, in fact, that Janice immediately suggested that he'd got on extremely well with Annette and that his long bout of celibacy was over.

Hilary and Debbie were appalled to hear of the attack and wanted all the grisly details for the eventual story. When told we were soon heading for the mainland, we had to promise to let them know when and where before we could terminate the call.

After lunch, the clouds had blown away completely although the wind was still fresh and so was the temperature, so we went ashore again and ventured into the bush. There were walking tracks everywhere, both human and animal, although we knew that there wasn't anything large on two or four feet left on the island. There were supposed to be white-lipped snakes about, but we didn't see any. Maybe it was too cold.

Anyway, the bushwalk was fun and different and Jasper had a wonderful time chasing anything and everything that moved. We covered a lot of ground and our legs really felt it by the time we were back aboard, so we all slept like the dead that night.

We had three more lovely, relaxing days at Erith Island before the shit hit the fan again.

CHAPTER 48

'Good Afternoon, Steel Associates. How may I help you?'
'Good Afternoon, Miss Julie, this is Mr Raymond. Is Mr Xavier available?'

'Certainly Mr Raymond. Good to hear from you. Please hold and I'll transfer you.'

'This is Xavier.'

'Good Afternoon, Mr Xavier, this is Mr Raymond with a report.'

'Please go ahead, Mr Raymond, recording starting.'

'I'm stationed at Wynyard at the moment, and as discussed, Mr Peter and Mr Jordan chartered an amphibious seaplane from Hobart to continue the search along the coast to the west of Wynyard, including the islands to the north-west.

They took-off yesterday morning from Wynyard airport at 09:00, but they haven't reported in or been sighted since. My assistant, Mr Steven had been driving west along the coast and reported a seaplane flying past Stanley at 09:24, heading at low-level along the coastline to the northwest, but that was the last sighting or report I have received.'

'Was their plan to return to Wynyard at some time during the day?'

'Yes Mr Xavier. They were to do that after they had looked at all the ports along the coast to the west, and then make a sweep over the islands just offshore. Apparently, there aren't many private yachts in that area, so the subjects should have stood out. The weather has been quite bad in this area with low cloud, strong winds and rain showers, so visibility would be very poor from the air. An alternate plan was for them to visit the islands first in case the conditions were better off shore, but I don't know which plan they followed. They would have needed to refuel at some point regardless. The aircraft has a total endurance of about 5 hours.'

'How long will it be before the Company that owns the seaplane gets worried and wants it back?'

'Ahh…That's where there's a bit of a problem, Mr Xavier. The Charter Company wouldn't hire out the aircraft to our own pilot, insisting that they supplied their own pilot but as you know, we didn't want a civilian aboard during the operation. Therefore, Mr Peter offered the pilot a sum of money to spend the day in a motel, but he was reluctant to do that, saying that he could lose his job if anything went wrong. Therefore, Mr Peter made the decision to heavily sedate him to help him sleep the day through without making a fuss.

If Mr Peter had returned as planned, the pilot could have returned to Hobart this morning, with no further problems.'

'I can see that there are already some problems with that arrangement, Mr Raymond! Would you care to share the rest of them with me?'

'Yes sir. The problems are that because the seaplane hasn't returned, and it was due back in Hobart this morning, the pilot has protested most vigorously about being drugged against his will and the Motel owners have called the Police in to investigate, since it occurred on their premises. The Charter Company also has naturally become involved as well and wants to know why their pilot was forcibly grounded and where their aeroplane is. They're making noises about hi-jacking charges amongst various other charges related to the unlawful detention of their pilot.'

'Are you telling me, Mr Raymond, that you didn't have this pilot under your direct control at all times? That you allowed him to lie in a motel room without supervision or restraint? And am I to understand that the Police and the Civil Aviation Safety Authority are now investigating a kidnapping, drugging and aircraft hi-jacking situation? In addition to which, they're also looking for a missing aircraft?'

'I'm afraid that is the situation, Mr Xavier. I must offer my most sincere apologies for my lack of foresight in allowing Mr Peter's plan to proceed without sufficient supervision.'

'I have to say, Mr Raymond, that I am extremely disappointed with the performance of all three of you. I could go so far as to say that I am stunned that you and Mr Peter have allowed this situation to degenerate to such a degree! Have you, at least, been able to avoid the attention of the Police?'

'Yes, Mr Xavier, I left the area immediately the pilot woke up at the motel and started making a fuss. I'm currently down the coast at Burnie but avoiding all contact with the public.'

'Very well. Kindly avoid attracting any attention from any Authorities. I need you to gather as much information as possible about the situation as it develops. It may require you to move back to the Wynyard area to achieve that objective but keep a very low profile.'

'Yes sir. I can do that and will report as soon as I learn anything new.'

'All right Mr Raymond. If you can complete these requests effectively, I will consider a slightly lighter punishment for your extremely incompetent handling of this situation! Report regularly and get results!'

Yes, Mr Xavier. Thank you for the opportunity to redeem myself. I'll not let you down again.'

'One more thing before you go, Mr Raymond. It has come to my attention that our client has taken additional steps to retrieve the packages, by putting out a general contract. It was only a rumour previously but is now confirmed. Naturally I am very unhappy that the field may become cluttered with amateurs trying to achieve the same result as ourselves so I would be obliged if you would also look out for any evidence that 'bounty hunters' are in your area and report immediately if you learn of any.'

'Certainly Mr Xavier. I'll do that, but so far, I've not seen nor heard about anybody like that.'

'Good! Keep looking and listening and report regularly.'....

Mr Xavier then treated himself to a very rare outburst of cursing, followed by an even rarer triple shot of Speyside's finest 50-year single-malt Scotch Whiskey.

CHAPTER 49

FIREBIRD...THURSDAY

On Thursday, the seals were back for a feed, but this time they brought their baby with them to show him off. Although it probably wasn't quite right to call a 50 kg seal a baby, since he ate a fair share of the fish we tossed down. They played around the boat like the previous day, diving under the hulls time and again and circling the whole boat several times at high speed. After that, we bushwalked again, covering the island more easily as our land legs built up strength.

Jasper loved the walks. He always liked the beaches, but the bush was such a different environment where he had so many different smells and things to chase after that he was exhausted when we returned to the boat.

FIREBIRD...FRIDAY

Friday was a lot warmer, so we all ventured into the water for a welcome swim and found it bracing, but not too cold. Having a warm northerly blowing really helped! We hadn't been in long when the girls let out a shriek that would have raised the dead, had there been any handy to try it out on. The cause was a large, grinning, be-whiskered face that popped up in the middle of our little group, followed by two more, one a lot smaller than the other two. Our seal family had come visiting and seemed delighted to have their new human friends in the water with them.

I was very wary now we were in their environment, especially with the seal pup present, but when the girls just started playing with the pup and the adults equally, they responded in kind. Although fast, strong and agile, they seemed to sense that humans were fragile and played gently, not minding if the girls cuddled the pup. Jasper joined in as well, and the seals treated him as just another playmate, diving under him and lifting him gently up on their backs almost clear of the water.

Jasper took it all in good spirit and splashed them when he could, or batted them with a soft paw, no claws. They didn't demand their daily feed while we were playing, but Zoe decided to feed them anyway, so we stayed still in case they got a bit carried away and chomped on a hand instead of a fish, but my fears were groundless as the seals ate in a most genteel fashion. They didn't snap at or near any of us but made sure that the pup got a decent share. Once the feeding was over, they played around us for a little while longer before making several leaps right out of the water as they took their farewell and disappeared as three brown flashes toward the channel.

We dragged ourselves wearily out onto the stern, rinsed off then lay around in the sun to dry off, enjoying the warmth after days of cloud and cold winds. The big sunbed hung out over the stern was the most popular spot with all four females sprawled out over the white, padded mattress, heads pillowed on each other.

'What an extraordinary experience!' said Sandy into the languorous silence. 'Those seals were almost as switched on to human emotion as Jasper is. For totally wild creatures, they were so gentle with us.'

A collective '*ummmm!*' was the only reply she was going to get from the sleepy group, so she slipped back to drowsing.

FIREBIRD – EAST COVE, ERITH ISLAND
– BASS STRAIT, SATURDAY

Saturday was a repeat of the previous day weather-wise and a return visit by the seals just made it special. They were as frisky as before and just as careful not to harm us, even during the feeding. We were all feeling the effects of being in another beautiful, peaceful place and losing all the tension of the last encounter with our followers. Just after lunch, however, as we had settled down to various low-key interests, our peace was disturbed by a powerboat that quietly eased into the bay from the north side of the main channel and anchored at the very furthest, northern end of the bay, about 500 metres from us.

It looked to be about 44 ft long, with lovely sweeping lines that would be very sea-kindly. It had a slightly raked centre wheelhouse with a trunk aft cabin and looked a lot more business-like than most of the top-heavy, plastic gin palaces that are flogged off as boats these days. Nevertheless, being a good sea boat didn't ease my sense of foreboding, even though I tried to tell myself that I was just being paranoid.

The tension however, racked up a few notches when Sandy eased up beside me and said quietly, 'Nice boat, but they might need watching!'

I was standing in the saloon, the binoculars to my eyes, watching the visitor though our tinted windows, 'Yes, my thoughts too. There's not been any movement on deck as they dropped the anchor remotely which is a bit unusual in good weather, but maybe it's an older couple. Still, it's a very pretty boat and I'd be annoyed if it did turn out to be crewed by bad guys. Pretty boats are supposed to belong to good people and that's my piece of philosophy for the day!'

Sandy laughed, but then followed me over to the chart table, intrigued when I started flipping switches on the main panel. 'Okay. What are you up to now?'

'A magic new toy I had installed a few months ago, just before I came south, but I've not had a chance to use it properly,' I explained, 'it's a mast-head camera system, with full-colour Electro-Optical and passive Infra-Red cameras, both with 100X zoom and powerful image stabilisation. It can take 4K stills and video, record internally or onto a separate SSD and/or be viewed in real-time on a monitor. It's in a streamlined, waterproof housing that blends in with the masthead so it can't be seen normally and is not obvious even when it's opened up and operating. It also does facial-recognition and Automatic Target Tracking.'

I flicked another switch to display the image on the chart table monitor and was rewarded with a razor-sharp picture of the shoreline to the south of us.

'Wow,' exclaimed Sandy, 'how clear and sharp is that!'

She was even more impressed when I worked the little joystick and zoomed in on a bush, where an unsuspecting sparrow was having a tug-of-war with a large worm. Every detail of the little bird was sharp and distinct, right down to the individual barbs of each feather.

She laughed delightedly, 'Ok. Now you're showing off, but what if that bird is in a bush just on the edge of the beach?'

By way of answer, I slowly rolled the zoom back, letting the shrinking picture tell the story. Luckily there were cross hairs to mark the target, because the little bird and his prospective meal had disappeared from normal view, but were, according to the laser range finder, 573 metres inland. I couldn't even pick out the bush under which the epic struggle for survival was taking place.

'That wasn't the limit of the zoom, either,' I quietly informed her, 'and we can get a similar performance at night under either a low-light setup or go to full processor-enhanced Infra-Red for very hi-res under total blackout conditions.'

She smiled, 'I'm impressed. It should be terrific on any covert surveillance job.'

'Yeah. And so it should be for about $350K installed.'

'Holy crap, Harry! I hope you didn't have to pay for all of that?'

I grinned, 'No way. I had quite a bit of help from Auntie.'

Sandy grinned back, knowing that the ACP, who I did some work for at times, would have been happy to fund the whole thing. After all, where else were they going to get the best and most effective water-borne covert surveillance platform in the country, crewed by an operator trained at vast expense and conditioned in war.

I panned the camera around to the north, pulling the zoom back to wide-angle until our mysterious new neighbour appeared in picture. A click on one of the joystick buttons locked the cross hairs onto the centre-mass of the hull and I slowly zoomed in. Oddly for such a beautiful day, various blinds and curtains covered nearly all the windows and portholes, so there was very little to see. We could, however, clearly see the name of the boat, *Orion* printed on a circular life-ring hung on the side of the wheelhouse.

I thought that I saw a hint of movement deep in the shadows of the wheelhouse that had no curtains, but it was hard to be sure. Time for the hi-tech!

I moved a switch on the dedicated camera control panel and the picture changed to a monochrome, pale greenish blur that flared and faded a few times as the sensors and filters sorted light intensities out. Abruptly, after a few more moments of fuzzy crap that made me think I should go get my money back, the picture cleared to a sharp green-grey scale image. It took us a few moments to interpret what we were seeing, but suddenly realised that we could see a very sharp outline of the boat and a slightly less sharp view of what was inside it! Virtual X-ray vision, courtesy of the computer-enhanced, Hi-Definition Infrared!

There were two persons in the aft saloon, one male and one

female. The vision wasn't clear enough to get an idea of age, but they weren't kids at least. The man seemed big and quite well built, while the woman was — well, female, with the required curves and bumps that are normally necessary to qualify for that sex. As we watched, the man came aft from the wheelhouse and sat down with her, drinking something hot, to judge by the flare of light from each mug, while a bright area nearby must have been the cooktop in the galley. Of greater interest were what looked like two handguns they seemed to be cleaning?

After a while, the man got up and moved up into the wheelhouse again, where he stood still for a long minute looking at us through binoculars, before returning to the aft saloon and resuming his seat.

'Periodic check on us, I guess,' I said to Sandy, who nodded agreement.

'I don't like the look of those handguns they're cleaning,' she commented, 'whatever they are, they're trouble! I'm guessing that they're not here to fish or to fool around with each other!'

'Yeah. We'd better tell the others and have a round table.'

'Do we need to keep a constant watch on these characters?' she asked.

'Not for now,' I replied, 'although we can keep the camera on and start recording. The IR is the latest passive type with no cooling gas required, so it can be operated indefinitely. We might, however, flick back to E.O. mode to keep watch. I don't think they'll start anything during daylight.'

Yeah,' Sandy agreed, 'probably come for us late at night.'

I looked at her, 'Just thinking ahead, maybe we shouldn't advertise who's on board. They'll expect Janice, the girls and me, but perhaps you might stay out of sight as best you can, either in the saloon where the tinted glass will block vision, or down below. I might get Jasper to do the same, although he's easier to hide since his boobs are smaller!'

She poked her tongue out at me, but agreed, so we called the others inside from where they were still lying around in the sun or reading in the cockpit, to gather around the dining table and discuss the latest threat. They wanted to have a look at the picture generated by my whiz-bang camera, so I flicked back to I.R. to show them the benefits of X-ray vision. Suitably impressed, we sat around to discuss our responses.

'So, are these two more of the same bunch of goons who've been chasing us all along?' Janice asked.

'No, I don't think so. I'm going to call Annette in a moment to see if there have been any calls from Luke to involve anybody else in the search apart from Steel Associates. I wouldn't expect a Steel snatch and run crew to comprise a man and a woman on a fairly slow boat. I mean, the guys who hired a seaplane to find us and came armed with a sub-machine gun, wouldn't turn up as a couple out for a 3-day cruise.'

'But maybe they haven't found out about the last crew we whopped?' Angie said, with considerable insight. 'In which case, they mightn't know that they need more bodies and weapons to attack us!'

I smiled at her enthusiasm and belief in our invincibility. 'Good points, except they'll certainly know that their crew is missing, but maybe not where or how and may never do so. And you're right that they don't know how well we can fight back, especially now that we have extra weapons.

As for finding the evidence, there are a lot of bays and harbours to search and the winds should disperse any fuel or oil slick very quickly. The Authorities will be searching for the aircraft once the owners report it missing, but hopefully, they'll never find the wreckage. But even if they do, it should be put down as a drug deal gone wrong, given all the bullet holes in the thing.'

'Ok,' Sandy agreed, 'that all sounds plausible, but where have these dudes come from?'

'My guess is that Luke hedged his bets and put out a general contract, so that any low-life who fancied his chances could have a shot at the reward.'

Sandy chuckled, 'Yeah, that'd be right, but I bet the Steel mob aren't happy about it, if they know.'

'If they're half as professional as they've shown so far, they'll know! Now I'll just call Annette and see if she can to confirm the theory.'

At that, I took a breather and placed the call, using the sat-phone. I still hadn't established if Annette was able to take encrypted calls yet without raising suspicion, but I got lucky and caught her at her desk with all her files at her fingertips.

'*Hi, Harry. What's new?*'

'We're still in the same location as for our last call, but we have visitors, a male and a female in a 44 ft displacement cruiser called *Orion.* Their behaviour is a bit suspicious since they've been keeping us under covert surveillance since they arrived. We've got some rather hi-tech camera gear on-board that has allowed us to see inside the hull to an extent, and at present, they're cleaning a pair of handguns between visual check-ups on us.'

She whistled. 'That must be some camera you've got if it lets you play Superman! I'd like to see that sometime.'

I chuckled, 'When this is over, I'll be happy to show you the whole thing, but in the meantime, a couple of quick questions.'

'*No such thing from you,*' she fired back, '*but go ahead.*'

'Firstly, could you look up the boat name and check the registered owner?'

'*No problem. Next?*'

'From the transcripts of Luke's phone and email intercepts, has there been any reference to him issuing a public or open reward for finding Janice and the girls?'

She was quiet for a minute and I heard her keyboard clicking as she searched. 'Ah, yes, here we are. I thought I'd read something about it. He issued a reward notice quite some time ago, and I can't see any reference to it being withdrawn. In fact, now you mention it, I think I read recently that he might have increased the amount to something like 40 or $50K.'

My heart sank with confirmation that the couple in the Orion were probably private bad guys. 'Terrific! That sort of confirms our suspicions that they might be bounty hunters.'

'*Gee, Harry. That's just what you need to liven up your day. I mean, really, you've had several days slacking around, so what do you expect?*'

'Ha, ha. Very droll! But thanks for the confirmation. We'll get back to you when we've got more information.'

'*Ok guys, I'll chase up the boat registration and let you know. Meantime, hang in there and please be careful.*'

We disconnected and I relayed the guts of what Annette had said.

'So, they probably are after us,' summed up Janice, 'but they're not the professional guys like last time, just some private dudes out to make a dollar or two out of the girls.'

I nodded. 'Yep. That sums it up. But don't forget that they're carrying guns, so they obviously don't mean to mess around. That also suggests they don't mind if people get hurt, unless they think that just flashing guns will make us hand you over.'

'OK, so how are we going to handle it?' Zoe asked, looking at me. 'I presume that you've got a plan. You usually seem to.'

I grinned, 'As a matter of fact, smart-arse, I do. It's not very complicated, since the bad guys don't have a lot of options. Basically, they have to come to us, and Sandy and I agree that they won't do anything in daylight, and almost certainly won't come over until they think we've been asleep for a while. Therefore, it's important that we give the impression that we don't suspect a thing while we make preparations to greet our visitors in a manner befitting their low-life status!'

'Good plan, Dirty Harry,' Zoe grinned, 'so, what do you want us to do?'

'Sandy will stay out of sight so they won't know our full numbers, and Jasper will too, once I've spoken to him.'

The beast in question was lying on the saloon floor, carefully watching and listening, his ears pricked forward.

'Janice, you and the girls might like to go and lie around on the foredeck for a while, sunbaking and reading like you normally would. I want this pair to get a good look at you and the girls so they can confirm that you are whom they think you are. I'll move around the boat doing normal maintenance chores.

Oh, and Janice, if you'd like to wear a big floppy hat and baggy clothes, then if necessary, you and Sandy can make separate appearances on deck by just exchanging clothes.'

'And what do we wear?' Angie asked with a cheeky grin.

I laughed, 'Probably what you usually don't, I suppose. It won't hurt to give our hidden watchers a dose of high blood pressure! The male one anyway.'

That drew a general laugh, until Janice got back to practicalities. 'But what's going to happen tonight? I mean are we just going to let these guys come to us? Can't we go to them? What if....'

I held up my hand to stem the tide of questions, 'Whoa! We can't approach them with any aggressive intentions in case they really are just a couple with odd habits having a boating holiday. So, we have to let them show their intentions first, but with our spy camera, we should have plenty of warning of their movements, intentions and firepower. It's a case of hope for the best but prepare for the worst!'

She nodded, 'But I'm worried that we have to let them come aboard before we can react!'

I smiled, 'That's not a big problem when the unwary are involved. Apart from our considerable firepower and better planning, there are a few other little surprises I have in store that will help us keep the upper hand, so don't worry too much for now.'

She subsided, only slightly mollified by my words, so we broke up the conference and let Janice put more clothes on, while the girls did the reverse. With towels in hand, they wandered up on deck, chattering brightly while Sandy and I monitored our watchers.

The guy was up in the wheelhouse again, binoculars raised and stayed there for quite some time, eventually being joined by the woman, their attention apparently focussed on the two naked young ladies on our foredeck.

I clued Jasper into what was going on, much to Sandy's amusement, as I spoke in plain English and he actually seemed to understand. When I finished, he happily assumed the Sphinx-pose on the saloon mat. In case he needed it, I moved his grassy toilet mat to the stern boarding platform, since the breeze caused us to lie with our sterns mostly hidden from sight of the *Orion*.

'So, what is the plan of action for tonight?' Sandy asked, now we were alone.

'After lights out, you and I keep watch,' I replied, 'while Janice and the girls keep out of sight. They won't want to go to bed at all, or at least not to sleep, but we have to make things look normal, although we can have an early night. They won't come over straight away.'

'Maybe we could play board games for a while. That would look normal.'

'Yeah, it would. But don't forget that with our internal lights on, they can see inside quite easily, even with our tinted windows.'

The penny dropped. 'Ah yes. So, once it's dark, I'd better stay below, or at least out of sight until lights out.'

"Fraid so,' I grinned, 'It's a pity I can't join you. I know of a terrific way to pass a few hours.'

She giggled and looked forward to where the girls were stretched out in the sun with Janice propped up against the bow rails, reading.

'Nothing much going on for now, by the look of things. Feel like a bit of messing around? We can resume the planning bit later.'

My arm didn't need much twisting, so in short order we were naked on Sandy's bed doing lots of lovely messing around, before getting down to some serious business. It all went so well, that it was a good hour before we emerged, relaxed and somewhat sleepy, to find that nothing had changed, either with our crew or the watchers, so we did resume our planning session.

CHAPTER 51

FIREBIRD...EAST COVE – ERITH ISLAND,
BASS STRAIT, SATURDAY

That evening, we went about our routine as usual, except that Sandy and Jasper stayed down below, out of sight. Sandy stayed involved in the conversation by perching on the companionway steps. We cooked, or at least Angie did, ate, washed up and played games — Scrabble being the best one so that Sandy could still join in.

Jasper found it all very interesting and possibly a bit puzzling, as he alternately sat with Zoe or Sandy. We deliberately made an early night of it, and everybody headed off to bed with a great show of yawns and stretches. I made my usual lap around the upper decks, making sure that everything was in its place, including the placement of two artificial grass mats that I folded double-thickness and laid on the upper step of each of the stern boarding steps. Under the cover of the cloaking darkness, I carefully poured a bucket of seawater over each mat, soaking it thoroughly, before securing the twin stainless wire safety lines tightly across the top of each entrance.

Several items that normally lived in the cockpit were removed to the saloon and the shorter of the two boat hooks, with a razor edge ground into both sides of the curved, bronze hook was propped up in the forward corner of the cockpit. After making sure that Jasper had his final pee, I returned inside, leaving the door unlatched. Making sure the masthead anchor light was switched on, I turned on a couple more switches on the auxiliary panel and set the digital radar to short-cycle auto switching with close guard zone, before turning out the saloon lights. Janice and the girls already had their cabin lights on, and all had decided that it would be more comfortable to sit up in bed reading, rather than sit in the darkened saloon, so I joined Janice and Sandy.

For once everyone was fully dressed and stayed that way.

We read and chatted quietly, the hatch over our heads wide open. After a while I called for lights out and made sure the girls had complied. Then the wait started!

There was no fooling around with either lady tonight as they were both too uptight and edgy, Janice repeatedly asking about this and that, until I had to tell her to be quiet so that we could hear what might be happening outside.

With all the early-warning systems in place, including the most sensitive of all, Jasper, it probably wouldn't have mattered if we'd had a party raging! I think we all dozed a bit despite the tension, until about 02:00 when there was a soft, repeating two-tone chime from the speaker above the bed, suggesting that the radar had detected a moving target within the guard zone I'd set earlier. Sandy and I were moving even before Jasper padded in to give a soft growl and Janice slipped out of bed to her shelter spot in the forward dressing room.

We were already dressed in snug-fitting black gear, Sandy looking particularly erotic in a pair of Angie's black tights that were *really* tight on all Sandy's more generous-curved bits, plus a dark blue tank top that was equally too tight. She also looked very menacing with her Glock 22 strapped around her waist and a black bandanna around her head. I had the compact mini-Uzi strapped across my chest in a makeshift quick-reaction rig, with extra magazines in pouches at my waist.

We each had a Gerber Mk II knife strapped to a calf to complete the strap-on arsenal, being as much for show as anything, but still very effective and frightening at close quarters. As we gained the saloon, I grabbed the Remington TAC-14 pump-action shotgun I'd positioned earlier, while the girls scurried past in a crouch, heading for Janice as part of our plan.

At the nav desk, the radar was still beeping softly, so I killed the alarm and looked at the heavily dimmed display. It showed a sharp target heading slowly for us, about 200 metres away.

Flipping the radar off, it's job now done, I selected the low-light camera and dimmed the green-toned, high-resolution picture of a dinghy with a male and a female aboard and powered by a small outboard, starting to take a curving track that would keep them well seaward of us until they could make their approach from a downwind position. This showed good planning on their part to start with.

As they got closer, the camera clearly showed that it was the same man and woman as before and that they were wearing holsters for their handguns. At about 100 metres distance, the man shut down and tilted the outboard, then they picked up a paddle each and stroked firmly in unison toward our stern. A few minutes later, they reached the starboard boarding platform and silently tied up. 'Showtime,' I muttered quietly, trying to damp down the adrenalin pumping through my veins. They were out of sight for a few moments before we saw the man's head poke above the upper step, the woman close behind him.

'Close one eye,' I warned Sandy as the man reached out to unlatch the safety lines across the top of the steps.

I'd just closed one myself, when there was a series of very bright blue flashes and a choking scream from the man who seemed to be doing a new and very active version of a jive dance on the top step, apparently hanging onto the safety lines for balance. The woman grabbed him to help and promptly screamed as well, before falling backwards down the boarding steps.

'What the fuck...' Sandy said softly beside me as the man finally collapsed in a heap on the steps, a dying shower of blue sparks showing curling wisps of smoke rising from him in several places.

'It's a boosted amperage version of an electric cattle fence,' I muttered back to Sandy, '80,000 volts at 200 to 300mAh — the high voltage breaks down the skin resistance and the current level hits the heart rather hard so it's probably lethal with that length of exposure. But we'll see. Watch his mate though, she only got a very brief hit and could still be dangerous.'

'Good one, Harry,' Sandy muttered back, reaching out to slide the cockpit doors open in the next stage of the plan, 'I'm glad you didn't warn me! I might have been worried or something!'

I gave her a quick pat on her thinly clad rump, before reaching over to the control panel and flicking two switches. One turned off the electrified safety line system, the other turned on a pair of 320mm LED spotlights that I'd rigged to shine down on the boarding steps. There was one on the other side in case they'd used that one instead, so the effect was to light up the whole stern like daylight and totally blind the woman who was stumbling around on the lower step, while Sandy and I had our sunglasses on and could see perfectly.

I unhooked the safety lines and bent down to inspect the crumpled mass of the man but pulled back at the sharp odour of burnt meat and the stink of voided bowels. Instead, I poked him with my boot, but didn't get any sort of response, so I pushed harder and the odorous remains sort of flopped and squelched back down the steps to the disoriented woman's feet.

The jolt of electricity that had fried her partner had still had a considerable effect on her, even though she'd only copped a brief hit. Apparently, it was still sufficient to scramble her balance and co-ordination, as she was making awkward attempts to draw her gun. The trouble was, the gun was on her hip and she was groping roughly in the vicinity of her crutch. Or maybe it was just a bad time to have an itch.

However, she must have been recovering quickly, since she finally did manage to find, draw and fire the thing; three, flat sharp cracks echoing across the water, causing me to drop and Sandy to draw and fire her Glock in one fluid motion, hitting the woman's right shoulder and making her drop her gun.

By the time I lifted my head, Sandy had stepped down, carefully avoiding the messy, smelly lump of the former partner, and retrieved the woman's pistol from beside his remains. She dug his pistol out from underneath his carcase while she was there and pushed the shocked woman back up the steps. I looked her over carefully as she came closer, but she seemed to have no other weapon visible on or under the skin-tight jumpsuit. Sandy roughly shoved her down into a seat, before expertly clipping handcuffs on her wrists, thoughtfully threading the chain through the hole in the seat back to prevent her bailing out over the side.

I turned the big lights off, switched the normal cockpit lights on and called Janice and the girls up. I did ask them, however, to bring the first-aid kit, but to stay back in the saloon, just in case things turned nasty. We then turned our attention to our captive.

She was a good-looking woman in her mid-thirties, I guess, her long, dark hair tied up in a ponytail. As we'd seen on the IR camera view earlier, she was nicely proportioned and would have been very pleasant to look at under normal circumstances, especially in her jump suit. Unfortunately, large, melted patches of fabric, with painful-looking, blistered skin showing through, marred her appearance. Despite the burns, the bullet graze line across the outside of her shoulder was probably the most dominant pain source. Sandy quickly flushed the wound with saline solution, dusted it with antibiotic powder and bound a pad tightly over the injury.

The woman's eyes were part closed with pain, and by the smell hanging over her, she seemed to have lost bladder control at some point, but at least she smelled better than her partner.

Sandy was on a roll, so I let her carry on with the bad cop routine by smacking the woman hard across the face to focus her attention.

'Ok, blossom. Let's hear your story! And don't think about making up a load of bullshit! Anything I don't like the sound of, I'll smack you around some more. Let's start with your names.'

'I'm Teri Adams and the fella you electrocuted was my cousin Gerry Adams. I suppose he's carked it?'

'Yes, he has,' Sandy replied, with a distinct lack of emotion, but drawing a little gasp from the listening girls in the saloon. 'I guess he learned the hard way that it's not polite to board someone else's boat without asking permission.'

Teri gave a mirthless laugh and shook her head in dismay. 'Oh fuck! What have we done? I mean, look at you guys; you look like commandos with shotguns, big knives and that dinky little sub-machine gun. Gerry said that it'd be a pushover. Just come over here in the middle of the night, wave our guns around, and then demand the girls be handed over.'

I stepped forward and spoke quietly, 'And who were you supposed to hand the girls over to when you got hold of them?'

'The dude who posted the reward. I don't know his name, but he's in Melbourne, I think. Anyway, I've got his number back on the boat. The deal was that as soon as he got the girls back, he'd hand over $50K in cash, no questions asked! And now Gerry's dead and I may as well be. It's not even our boat — I just borrowed it for a few weeks!'

Sandy gave her a hard kick on the side of her thigh. 'Oh, cut the crap! We're not interested in that shit! You two came here to kidnap two girls at gunpoint and you expect sympathy? Give me a break! Do you know the penalty for kidnapping?'

Teri looked at the floor and shook her head slowly, so Sandy enlightened her.

'Try 25 years just for the kidnapping bit, then toss in the assault with a deadly weapon, unlicensed firearms and unlawful trespass and you might see the light of day when you turn 70!'

As tears flooded down her cheeks, I thought it was my turn to play semi-good cop, so I asked, 'Who else is involved in this little kidnap scheme?'

She looked up at me, 'No one. I swear. My uncle owns the boat and he lets me use it when I want, so there was no problem to bor-row it for a while, but he didn't know about this caper.'

'OK. But how did you know that we were here?'

She shrugged. 'We didn't. The dude who let the contract said that the latest news on your whereabouts was that you were on a boat with a cat and running around the Bass Strait ports and islands. This just happened to be the second island we looked at 'cause it's closest to Melbourne where we started. We checked Deal Island just over the channel yesterday, and if you weren't here at Erith, we were going to cover the rest of the Flinders group, then move west. You could say that we just got lucky or very unlucky as it's turned out.'

That long-winded speech seemed to drain her meagre resources as she slumped further in her chair and closed her eyes, fresh floods of tears running down her cheeks.

Sandy looked at me and jerked her head toward the saloon. We stepped inside and closed the heavy sliding door, still keeping an eye on our prisoner.

'What the fuck are we going to do with her now?' Sandy demanded angrily. 'This is such a total cockup! These people are absolute morons to think they could just waltz up to us in the middle of the night and demand that we meekly hand the girls over, then watch them sail away!

Oh, yes, don't forget these,' she added as she handed me the two pistols taken from Teri and Gerry.

I was surprised how light they were, for what seemed like a full-size pistol.

'Ok. I'll bite. What are they?'

'An amateur's idea of a good close-range pistol. They're Kel-Tec PMR 30s, loading a .22 Magnum cartridge. It's actually a very good gun, light, accurate, reliable and with a nearly flat trajectory out 20 metres or so and a 30-round magazine. Not a lot of stopping power at a distance, but very good up close if you're accurate.'

'Ok. They'll make a good addition to the armoury. I guess that we can get more ammo when we get more 9mm stuff?'

'Oh sure. Ammo's no problem for them. And they are good things in the right hands.'

'Fine. Now, about our captive; I think you should flash your badge and formally arrest her for actual assault with a deadly weapon, attempted kidnapping and trespass. She'll have to somehow get turned over to the Victorian Police, since we can't keep guard on her for too long.'

Sandy thought a moment, 'There'll be a problem with that. Any official involvement will mean a full investigation and we can't really afford to get bogged down with that at this time!'

'True,' I replied, 'but perhaps when you report to Bob Casey, he might be able to suggest a way around that.'

'Yeah, ok. I'll sound him out. I'll have to report this latest incident anyway.'

'Well, we'll have to report this new confrontation to everybody on the reporting list, so let's do that once we've tidied things up and buggered off. But first, I thought we'd search their boat for any more information or stuff that'll be useful, before heading for the nearest civilisation with both boats as soon as it's daylight.'

'What about the man, Gerry?' Janice asked, a tremble in her voice.

'I'm afraid we'll just have to push him overboard. We don't want to be explaining his condition to anyone official, so the story will be that he fell overboard in the initial scuffle, drowned and drifted away in the dark. I don't think that Teri will be challenging that story and there won't be much in the way of remains left after a few hours with seals and white pointers as clean-up crew.'

The girls nodded agreement, looking far more resolute and accepting of the horrific situation than Janice.

CHAPTER 52

The remaining hours of darkness were busy with clean-up duties. Teri, our captive, was fed some painkillers from the first aid kit, and allowed to use the toilet under very close supervision, before being laid out on the cockpit settee. She was handcuffed to a strong metal upright and had her ankles strapped with tape for good measure.

Sandy shocked the hell out of her by flashing her Police badge with the usual I.D. notifications, before formally arresting her on a list of charges that could see her incarcerated for the next 40 years! The fact that Sandy was a Queensland copper on roving duties was glossed over for the moment until she could contact her boss, Bob Casey, to clarify the situation.

Her cousin's stinking remains were unceremoniously pushed overboard, the normal sweep of tide through the little bay ensuring that the body would soon be swept out into the channel.

I cleaned the stern steps and cockpit of all traces of various body fluids with powerful detergent and bleach. I did find one bullet hole in the cockpit overhang from Teri's three wild shots and that was quickly patched with white epoxy putty. It made me glad I'd ducked when I did!

Janice was given a severe talking to by Sandy and emerged from that experience looking shaken but not overly stirred. The girls helped with the cleaning, treating the whole affair as another part of the wild adventure and wanted to feed our captive some Vegemite toast, although I noticed that they were becoming increasing angry toward Teri. Their main complaint was that a range of bad guys was constantly targeting them, and as she was the only live body they had the chance to vent at, she was going to cop it!

Their level of maturity under the threats to their freedom continued to amaze me! They checked with me before they gave Teri the toast and wanted to know if they could wind her up a bit. I waved my hand carelessly, 'Sure, go for it! Wind her up all you want. She's the one who was going to kidnap you!'

They traded evil grins and when the toast was ready, I heard them say to Teri,

'We thought you might like something to eat, even though you were going to kidnap us and take us back to our paedophile father.'

'What? What are you talking about?' Teri answered. 'Are you saying that the dude who let the contract is your father?'

'Yep,' was the joint answer, 'not only is he a paedophile, but he offered you so much money for our return because he was going to sell us as sex-slaves to some jerk-off in the Middle East!'

'Bullshit! No father would do that!'

'You're half-right. No normal father would do that, but ours isn't normal in any way, and that's exactly what he is still going to do if he gets his grubby little paws on us.'

She looked thoughtful for a moment. 'Do you have any way to prove that?'

Angie thought a moment; 'I might talk to the others about whether there's any value in trying to convince you, but then, why bother. If it was up to Zoe and me, we'll just dump you.'

'What? You mean just let me go?'

Angie laughed, suddenly not play-acting any more, as this stupid, evil woman started to really get to her. 'No, no, no! We can't afford to just let you go! Don't be stupid! I mean that we want to get rid of you permanently!

Can't you understand? You and your idiot cousin tried to grab us, against our will, for money. Just so that our filthy, rotten father could sell us for a lot more money!'

Teri blinked at the change in tone of Angie's voice.

'Do you really think that we care about your fucking miserable future? I mean, we disposed of your cousin's stinking remains overboard without blinking an eye, so getting rid of you won't be a problem. Just look around at where you are! We dump you overboard out in the channels' tide flow, after making a few knife cuts in the right places, then the sharks pull you apart before you've got time to think about swimming to land, and the crabs will pick the left-over bones clean. Bingo! Problem solved.'

Teri's eyes reflected pure horror along with her total conviction that these lovely young girls had the stone-cold hearts of killers.

'But you can't just kill me like that?' she protested weakly.

'Really? Why on earth not? You didn't care what happened to my sister and me when you decided to come and snatch us for money.'

'But we didn't think there was much harm in that! We thought it was just a family dispute.'

'What! A family dispute where the father pays $50K to retrieve the wife and daughters who voluntarily walked out? And you didn't think that was a bit excessive? Get real, you stupid bitch!'

'We thought that was the going rate. We've not done anything like this before.'

'So that's supposed to convince us that you didn't know what you were doing? Wake up bitch! You're the ones who came to us in the night with guns in your hands. You knew what you were doing; the pair of you just got a severe attack of the greedies! More fool you!'

Teri blinked away a fresh flood of tears, 'But there must be something I can do to be useful to you?'

'Buggered if I know what you could do. You're not that good-looking so I don't think anyone fancies you, so that's out. I do the cooking and the Skipper and Zoe run the boat, so that eliminates that. Maybe if you've got a shitload of money you could try buying your way out, although we're all pretty well cashed up, so that probably won't work either.'

She shook her head, a rueful expression on her face, 'Nope. Sorry. Can't think of anything useful.

'But...'

'No! No buts. Like, at the moment, we've got to watch you to make sure you don't get up to mischief — then we have to haul you down to the toilet occasionally, although I'd prefer to just tie you to the stern platform and let you piss and crap yourself whenever you wanted. Much easier for us to hose you and the stern off, and then you won't stink up our toilet! Oh, I forgot that we also have to feed your stinking, rotten body. And as I'm the chief cook, that really pisses me off — having to waste good tucker on you! Have I left anything out? No? Well, there you have it. You represent zero value to us and are a huge drain on our resources and time.'

'Please can I talk to the Skipper? Maybe he'll have a different view of the situation.'

'Hmm, I doubt it. Even though he's a man, waggling your tits and pussy at him won't help you much. You might have noticed that the rest of the crew are female — we get to outvote him. A big cock only goes so far when it comes to voting rights around here!'

Teri saw her last chance blowing away with the breeze, 'But there must be something I'm good for!' she wailed, tears streaming down her cheeks, 'I don't want to die!'

Angie lowered her face so their noses were almost touching, and in a quiet, but hard tone said, 'And Zoe and I don't want to be sold to a pox-ridden, goat-fucking paedophile on the other side of the world either! Think about that, bitch! Now eat your toast before I shove it up your poxy fanny!'

Angie stood up; her face flushed with real anger at the stupidity of this piece of thoughtless trash, while Teri turned her face away and broke out into a fresh flood of wailing, convinced that her demise was imminent. This may not have been too far from the truth, since Angie may have started out joking but she ended up meaning every word.

The girls came back inside to me and saw that we had all heard the entire exchange. I beckoned them, including Janice and Sandy, down to our cabin for a private talk.

'So, what can we do with her?' Angie asked, perched on the end of the bed, 'Is there anything to gain by trying to convince her about our story, or should we just ignore her? Although we do think that she was genuinely shocked about Dad, we don't think she can really help us in any way, so perhaps we'd be better off getting rid of her. That'd wrap things up neatly, at least. No loose mouths to flap when they shouldn't.'

I dreaded to hear her drastic solution to the problem, but pretended to think a moment, 'Perhaps you're right. But bear in mind that cold-blood killing is nothing like being in a straight fight where it's kill or be killed. Something like that leaves a heavy burden on your conscience and your soul, for that matter. It's not easy to live with afterwards.'

'But you and Sandy have just killed three men in the last five or six days. It doesn't seem to bother you!'

I smiled gently at her. 'My dear girl. Despite the fact that we've had serious training to cope with the aftermath of killing, that was survival! They were trying to kill us so they could grab you two. I just said that there's a big difference in shooting someone who's shooting back at you, and deliberately shooting someone in a vital spot when they can't defend themselves. One is called self-defence and is a very normal and healthy response, the other is called execution and is a totally different situation. There are times when it's called for and may even be justified, but it is by far the hardest thing to do.'

'Yes. But look at what she and that other swinging dick were trying to do to us!' Angie wailed.

I drew a deep breath and avoided looking at Janice and Sandy. 'Ok let's try this. I respect your feelings and I'm sure that Sandy and your Mum feel the same, so I'm not even going to consult them privately. We'll let you two decide how to deal with her. Totally your choice! No interference from us. Whatever you do, we'll support you fully and go along with it. We just ask that you think of the consequences that you've got to live with the rest of your life, after you enact whatever choice you make. Is that fair?'

They both nodded, suddenly looking serious as the weight of another human's life was placed in their hands.

I got up and went up to the saloon, where Sandy had been cleaning and checking our haul of weapons. I selected one of the Kel-Tec 30s, found a magazine that was at least half-full and stepped into the cockpit. I didn't look at Teri, stretched out on the seats and sobbing quietly. I just inserted the magazine in the butt of the pistol, worked the slide to jack a round into the chamber, flicked the safety off and aiming out over the water, squeezed the trigger. I was rewarded with a sharp crack, mild recoil and a splash about where I'd aimed, 50 metres off the beam. Ignoring Teri's whimpering and with the safety catch back on, I returned to our cabin.

In front of the girls, I removed the magazine and worked the action, catching the round from the chamber and re-loading it into the magazine, before handing the pistol, butt first to Angie who looked at me with questioning eyes.

'All okay. I just wanted to make sure that the fool thing would work. No point in you going to shoot someone unless you're sure the gun will work.'

She blinked uneasily at me as she gingerly took the gun.

'It's empty, so you can test fire it safely. Pull the slide back fully to cock the action, point the gun at your target, and just pull the trigger. I suggest you aim at her head as it's the quickest way to kill, and with a small calibre like this, it's the least messy. You'd better hold it close to be sure you don't miss, maybe close to her ear, and fire several shots to be certain, as there's nothing worse than a head-shot target who's only wounded; they just flop around, moaning and groaning and that does spray blood everywhere. Very messy!'

That bit of gruesome advice didn't seem to faze Angie too much, although Zoe and Janice turned a faint shade of green as Angie took the gun, nodded grimly and with it pointed it down at the floor, worked the slide then squeezed the trigger. There was a smooth click as it fired. She worked the slide again, with firm determination and fired again.

'When you fire it with a round in the chamber, it will make a loud noise, kick a little bit in recoil, and the gun will reload itself automatically. You just squeeze the trigger a second time to fire again.'

She nodded, her face set in a very serious expression and I feared for the loss of both her and Zoe's innocence if she went through with her plan.

I took the gun off her and explained, 'OK. I'm going to insert the magazine like this, then work the slide to cock the gun. It's now loaded and ready to fire, except that I'm going to put on the safety catch. It's this little lever on both sides of the gun at the rear, just below the slide. When you move it down so the red line shows above, the safety is off and pulling the trigger will fire the gun. That's all you have to do.'

'Ok. Got that Harry. Thanks for your support.'

She and Zoe took the gun and marched determinedly back up to the cockpit. Janice and Sandy both gave me worried looks as we trailed forlornly behind.

I whispered to them, 'Go along with this. They need to make their own decisions about this, and it will be the hardest decision of all. But whatever happens, we must support them to the utmost! Is that understood?'

The last was said in the sternest tone I could muster, and they both nodded.

We stopped inside the saloon, watching as Angie approached Teri, who looked at her, and then at the black, menacing form of the gun held steadily in her hand.

'Oh no, no! Please don't do this. I'll do anything you want, but please don't do this to me!'

'Pity you didn't think of that when you and your moronic cousin hatched this stupid plan that would enslave my sister and me!'

'But we didn't know about that,' she wailed, 'I told you!'

'No, you didn't know about it. But did you really believe that someone was going to hand over $50K, just to get his family back in the spirit of sweetness and light?'

'Well, no. I suppose not. But like I said, we just thought it was a family squabble; nothing like what you said!'

'Too bad, bitch! But now it's time to pay the price for your greed and stupidity!'

Angie raised the gun, flicked the safety off, placed the muzzle close to Teri's temple and started to squeeze the trigger. Teri shut her eyes and howled, although the loud crack of the high-velocity shot silenced her protest.

Angie lowered the gun without taking a repeat shot, a look of immense satisfaction on her face despite the stink of voided bowels and bladder that filled the cockpit. I waved Janice and Sandy back, as I stepped out of the saloon and without speaking, held my hand out to Angie, as she calmly flicked the safety back on and handed the pistol to me, butt first in approved fashion.

'Sorry about shooting your boat, Harry,' she said, 'but it shouldn't have gone too far in.'

'Nah,' I replied, taking a quick look, 'don't worry about it. It won't have gone far. No harm done and it'll be a great talking point later on.'

Beside us, the recumbent form of Teri Adams lay unmoving along the settee, until after a while, her head slowly turned and she stared up at us with a look of abject terror frozen on her face, her eyes wide like a rabbit caught in a car's headlights. Her mouth tried to work, but with little success, her hearing obviously not functioning at all after the concussion of even such a small round fired right beside her ear.

'Nice shooting, by the way,' I commented casually, as I ejected the magazine and worked the action to clear the next round, which I reloaded into the magazine.

'Thanks Harry. But really, if you're going to let us play with real guns, you'd better teach us to shoot them properly as soon as you can. That was fun!'

'Yeah. It is fun, but generally not so much when some bad guy's shooting back. Still, for your first time, you did well. But I'll get Sandy to teach you, she's the professional instructor.'

'Oh, yeah. Forgot about that!' She reached up and gave me a hug and a kiss. 'Thanks for everything!'

Zoe did the same and I knew what she meant and didn't need to reply, except smile and pat them both on the rump.

Teri was virtually comatose with shock and looked like staying that way for some time, so we left her there in her own mess and stink, glad we'd had the foresight to remove the thickly-padded vinyl cushions that normally lined the fibreglass mouldings of the cockpit seats, before we tied her up. It would make her mess easier to clean up later.

Back in the saloon, Janice was almost distraught with concern, flapping her hands and turning left and right like a chook with its head cut off.

'Oh shit, Harry. What's happened? What's going on?'

Angie stepped forward, her hand on my arm to forestall my automatic response.

'It's nothing to do with Harry, Mum,' she stated, eyes firmly fixed on Janice, 'All he did was point out the choices we must make when faced with serious decisions like these. Zoe and I made all the decisions and no one else is responsible. For the record, I never was going to shoot the rotten bitch, but we did want to put the biggest scare into her that we possibly could.'

She gave a wry grin, 'I think we achieved that objective, don't you?'

Janice broke down completely and with tears cascading down her cheeks, enfolded both girls in a mother/daughter hug type thing. When that sob-fest finally broke up, Angie announced, 'This stuff isn't completely over yet! We're still going to stay with Harry's offer, that as we were the ones most at risk by the actions of these fuck-wits, we get to handle the payback; so we'll handle her treatment from here on. She's not getting away without paying as severe a penalty as we can devise, short of kicking the bitch over the side like I threatened.' She delivered a stern look at her Mother, who finally nodded, while Sandy and I happily agreed.

'Ok,' Angie stated, 'we're going to look after this next bit, so could we have the handcuff key please Sandy?'

Sandy handed it over without comment, as Zoe grabbed some cleaning gear from under the galley sink and they headed back up to the cockpit. Janice looked at us and rather ruefully uttered the understatement of the year, 'I think my little babies have grown up, big-time!'

Sandy and I refrained from saying, '*We told you that they have been for a long time!*' but Janice got the message anyway.

Fifteen minutes later, we heard a half-choked cry from the stern area, followed by a loud splash, so we ventured out into the cockpit, with Jasper asked to remain in the saloon, since he was the back-up guard and enforcer. The seats were now clear of bodies, live or otherwise and were squeaky clean, as was the cockpit floor. A pleasant lemon scent replaced the foul odours from before, although a small hole in the rear portion of one seat suggested that either termites had suddenly gained an appetite for fibreglass, or that was Angie's shot hole. A razor-sharp filleting knife lay on the table.

We spied the girls standing down on one stern boarding platform, both giggling — Angie held one end of a mooring rope, Zoe the end of another one.

Stepping closer, we saw that Teri had been stripped naked, her tattered, stained and bloodied jumpsuit nowhere to be seen, while the rope that Angie was holding had been tied tightly around her neck. She'd been shoved over the stern into the water, presumably to clean her off.

Zoe had the handcuffs dangling loosely from one hand, and it seemed that the other end of her rope was tied tightly to Teri's ankle.

In case she decided to get a bit feisty, or object to her treatment, all Zoe had to do was pull up on her rope and Teri was neatly upended. They gave us a demonstration of how well the system worked, even though Teri hadn't become feisty. It must have worked, as all was peaceful, except for Teri's spluttering, choking and gasps for breath. They enjoyed the demonstration so much, they did it again with similar results. It appeared that the only person who didn't appreciate the demonstrations was Teri, but she'd forfeited voting rights several hours earlier.

'Better make sure she's clean, sis. She made a fearsome mess of herself,' Angie suggested to Zoe, slackening her rope off while Zoe moved up a couple of steps before hauling enthusiastically up on hers. Teri promptly went arse over tit yet again and as her leg popped up, her shapely bum followed, all associated bits looking quite clean to us. With difficulty I restrained myself from making a comment.

'How does that look?' Angie asked, looking over her shoulder at us. 'Clean enough to let this piece of garbage back aboard?'

I couldn't help myself and called out, 'Yeah. Looks pretty good to me. Her bum's clean as well!'

That earned me a poke in the ribs from both ladies and a genuine giggle from the girls that was very welcome to hear, as they reversed the load on the ropes and Teri's head emerged, hair plastered all over her face that had turned a bluish tinge, coughing and retching seawater.

'Good work girls!' I called. 'Shall I put the kettle on?'

'Yes, please, Harry. We won't be too much longer. We just want make sure that at least all the surface filth has been washed away.'

'Good oh. I'll call when it's ready.'

They waved and turned back to their unhappy subject, who apparently wasn't going to be invited to the early morning tea party.

When Janice and I brought the tea out, we saw that the girls had handcuffed a naked, shivering and totally dispirited Teri to the handrail beside the boarding steps and for good measure, tied one ankle to a cleat well out of her reach. They were in high spirits and more like their old selves, which was a welcome relief.

'Did we do well?' Angie asked, a little anxiously now the hard part was over.

'You did beautifully,' I responded, 'I'm proud of you, and I'm sure your Mum and Sandy are too.'

They nodded enthusiastically, and the girls beamed, tension flooding out of them as they sipped the hot, sweet tea, to which I'd sneakily added a heavy measure of dark rum. They were too wired to notice and shortly after we had a pair of slightly intoxicated girls loudly replaying the funniest parts of their new involvement with the latest kidnapping attempt.

We had breakfast ourselves shortly after the sun struggled above the horizon, to reveal what promised to be a beautiful day — the wind still from the North and quite warm. Normally I'd recommend that we stay put and enjoy the idyllic setting, but a live captive, Uncle's boat and yet another dead body meant that more planning was needed quickly.

So we sat down inside to yet another round table conference, but with Teri well out of hearing range down on the stern platform.

I opened with, 'Ok. My plan is to go search their boat and retrieve any documents, ammunition and weapons they might have left there. We then check their boat out to make sure there's enough fuel and supplies to be able to reach the mainland.'

'Where are we going to head for?' Janice asked, 'Do we still want to turn Teri over to the Police?'

'I checked the charts and was thinking of Port Welshpool. It's only a small town, but hopefully there'll be a Police Station somewhere close by, but we'll have to come up with a cover story for what's happened. And yes, I really think we should hand her over. We can't keep her and we definitely can't just let her go.'

'Ok. What's your suggestion?'

I looked at Sandy, who, by way of answer, got up and retrieved the sat-phone from the chart-table charger, and dialled a number from memory, putting it on speaker so we could hear.

'Good morning, sir, this is Senior Thomson with a report on my activities.'

'Ah...and a very good morning to you too, Sergeant.'

'Ah...sir. It's Senior Constable Thomson calling, not Sergeant.'

'Oh dear, my fault for not telling you. I have the pleasure to inform you that you've been promoted to Sergeant as of two weeks ago. Congratulations, Sergeant Thomson.'

'I'm overwhelmed, sir and thank you very much, but I urgently need to report of some further happenings.'

'*Of course Sandy. I'm just having a bit of fun with you. Delighted that my request to the Commissioner was approved immediately. But please, go ahead, I'm recording.*'

She then proceeded to bring him up-to-date on the latest attack and our problem with a captive on hand. Once again, he was delighted with the outcome of the attack, but appalled that it had happened again so soon after the last one.

'We have a problem with what do with our captive, sir. We'd prefer not to have to shoot her to keep the news of this mess quiet and we'd have housekeeping problems with keeping her aboard under constant guard!'

'*Oh, I don't think there's any need for further bloodshed, Sergeant. Of course, if the prisoner decides to make a run for it, that's a different matter. However, I just happen to have been to a seminar on Interstate Service Co-operation, where I met the Inspector in charge of the Foster Police Station, just to the west of Port Welshpool. We had some good times and for reasons I won't go into he owes me a few favours, so I reckon I can twist his arm enough to take your prisoner off your hands.*'

'That would be terrific, sir,' Sandy replied, 'Harry tells me that Foster isn't far from Port Welshpool, which is where we plan to head for within the next couple of hours. We could be there early evening or tomorrow morning. Can you let me know as soon as you can if your Inspector friend is able to help?'

'*No problem, Sandy. In fact, I was only speaking to him last week to arrange a fishing trip down that way when I take some overdue leave. I'll get back to you shortly, but in the meantime, congratulations on your promotion, and to all of you for dealing with yet another attempt to grab the girls.*'

'Thank you, sir, on both counts. I'll standby for your call.'

The phone clicked off and Sandy looked at me. 'How about that? What a coincidence that old Bob knows an Inspector down here. Let's hope he comes good with a plan.'

'Yeah. That would make things much easier. I wasn't looking forward to making up a story that would convince a Victorian copper, without coming on too heavy with my warrant.'

Sandy looked at me thoughtfully, 'You'd do that?'

'Very reluctantly,' I replied, 'Breaking cover is never a good idea since people always leak info, no matter how much you threaten them with Divine Retribution or even worse, the National Security Act.'

I let Janice call Rob with the latest but asked her to keep it short. She did, while also asking Rob to let Annette know.

I then called Hilary and passed the short version, even though she demanded full details. I said that it would have to wait for later when there was more time to talk, but I did say that we might be in Victorian waters soon and she was naturally keen to meet up with us as soon as we could.

It was another 15 minutes before Bob Casey called back to say that his mate, Inspector Jack Pearson from Foster, would meet us at the Port Welshpool Public wharf at 09:30 tomorrow morning, if that was suitable. He gave us a number for Jack in case we were delayed but suggested that we might like to call him anyway. With that detail taken care of for the moment, we continued with the plan to check out *Orion*.

Ignoring Teri still shivering on the stern platform, I decided that we'd take their boat's dinghy rather than re-launch ours, so we left Jasper in charge, but out of sight while we all went to look at our prize.

It was an impressive boat, well designed and built, and if I were in the market for a powerboat, it would be my choice of ride. All was ship-shape aboard, so it was probably Teri who was the real boatie. There were two cabins forward of the wheelhouse and both were reasonably tidy. We went through everything and found hundreds of rounds of .22 Magnum ammunition for the PMR 30s, as well as various knives. Gerry had a large amount of cash stuffed in his bag that we grabbed as well as his wallet with Driver's Licence and any other I.D. we could find relating to him.

Angie selected some basic underwear and clothes for Teri, although I got the impression that they wouldn't be handed over straightaway. We left the rest of her belongings, thinking that we could let her pack up in the morning.

I checked the *Orion's* systems as best I could, and it seemed that there was plenty of fuel for the run back to the mainland. It was only 55 nm, and if the *Orion* could make 8 to 10 knots and we left before 12:00, we should comfortably be able to anchor for the night on the west side of Snake Island which sat blocking the direct approach to Port Welshpool. I planned to keep *Firebird* away from the port and hopefully any direct association with the *Orion*, since we'd be leaving it behind for its rightful owner, Teri's uncle, to eventually collect.

I made a note-to-self to ask her for his phone number when she was in a fit state to be spoken to, but in the meantime, I took Zoe on the rounds of inspection, while Angie looked through the stock of supplies for anything we could use.

'How would you like to drive this thing to Port Welshpool?' I asked her.

'What, by myself?'

'Not quite,' I smiled, 'Sandy would be with you to help with lookout duties and pee breaks, and I'd have *Firebird* in close company with the radar going. Plus, we have marine VHF radio to chat on.'

She grinned, 'That sounds like fun. Sure, I'd love to. But are we going into port tonight?'

'No. I'll show you on the chart where we'll anchor around the corner from Port Welshpool overnight. Then tomorrow, Sandy, Teri and I will take the *Orion* up to the Port and meet the Police Inspector.'

She grinned again, 'That sounds great, Harry. Good fun.'

The boat was quite well equipped for day trips, but lacked radar and an autopilot, but with two to handle steering duties, they'd be fine. We tested the engine, a very nice six-cylinder Yanmar diesel that seemed to be overly powerful for the boat size and displacement, but it fired up instantly and idled smoothly.

Perhaps Teri's uncle just liked extra power! I let it run for a while so Zoe could see how all the systems worked, including testing the winch and the gearshift, but the boat had been well maintained and once we saw that everything worked as it should, I shut the engine down.

We found a chart and I drew our course, but as that direct track went through a couple of little islands, I commented that we might have to deviate around those to avoid scratching the paint. That earned me a hard poke in the ribs but was a good sign that she was getting her sense of humour back to normal.

In the aft cabin, Angie, Janice and Sandy had piled up a lot of food we could use, leaving just enough for the crew to nibble on during the trip. I was pleased to see several bottles of rum as well as a pile of tinned stuff, and as Angie was pleased with the haul, so was I.

Loading all our booty into bags, we filled the dinghy and returned to *Firebird*, where Jasper gave us a warm welcome and we received a very frosty one from our captive who seemed to have recovered from her water treatment very quickly.

'When do I get released from here?' she demanded.

I looked at Angie, making an over-to-you gesture. She picked up the ball smoothly.

'When Zoe and I decide, bitch-face,' she snarled, 'and, any more demands like that will make it longer.'

That seemed to be an effective argument stopper, so we ignored her whining protests and got on with lugging all our booty inside. I noticed that the items of clothing for Teri were taken below without comment. When all was stowed to Angie's and my satisfaction, I called a brief conference.

'Zoe and Sandy are going to drive the *Orion* to Port Welshpool. We'll leave shortly and travel in close convoy, but we won't go into port until tomorrow morning.'

I looked at Sandy, 'Take your Glock and extra magazines, just in case, but that's all you should need. There's plenty of basic food and water aboard to keep you going, and we should be anchored in the approaches well before dark. We should...'

My words were interrupted by a shriek of terror from the stern, and after we'd rushed out to see what was happening, we cracked up with laughter. Our naked captive had forced herself up the steps as far as the handcuff's chain and the rope around one ankle would allow. The source of her terror was our newest best friend, the male fur seal, having heaved most of his considerable bulk up onto the stern platform to see if this human had any fish to bribe him with. Not finding any fish, he seemed content to nuzzle her in places she apparently didn't want to be nuzzled, but that wasn't going to deter the seal from giving her a good, friendly going over with his whiskery face and cold, wet nose.

Unfortunately, she didn't seem to appreciate his sociable manner and continued to sound off as though she was about to be eaten alive. We let him have his way with her for a few more minutes, but when the female and her pup popped their grinning heads up to see what all the fuss was about, Zoe went down the steps on the other stern and lured all three away with smelly fish handouts.

I felt *Firebird* lurch as the big male slid back off the stern platform and Teri's shrieks abruptly shut off.

'You fucking mongrels!' she screamed, in response to our continued laughter. 'You knew that he'd come up after fish! You might have told me. Arseholes!'

'What? And miss seeing you piss yourself again!' Angie retorted, as we noticed the pool of yellow she was lying in.

Several more very uncomplimentary remarks were directed up at us, until Angie called out to Zoe who was scratching the little pup's chin, his mother benignly looking on, 'Hey, Zoe! The little princess over here needs to be washed off again.'

'No. No I don't! I'm just fine like this,' was the quick reply to the threat, 'I just got dry and warm!'

'Oh, no dear,' said Zoe, shaking her head in mock dismay, 'that's not allowed. We can't be having our guests getting comfortable.'

She tipped the rest of the fish from the bucket into three gaping mouths, scooped up a load of seawater and marched across to the other steps and tossed it accurately down onto the cursing woman.

'Here we are. Lovely fresh seawater strongly flavoured with rotten fish. Can't be too bad, the seals like it!'

Wisely, Teri shut her mouth as the water washed her urine away and soaked her again as we went to prepare for sea, leaving her there.

CHAPTER 54

ERITH ISLAND – SNAKE ISLAND
– PORT WELSHPOOL – VICTORIA, SUNDAY

Preparations didn't take long and once I saw *Orion* hauling anchor, I did the same so that we got under way at the same time. Zoe was to lead and I'd stay off her starboard quarter. We had tested the radio and found a channel that was fairly free of the endless fishing boat and drill-rig tender chatter. I passed Zoe the course to steer and trimmed sails to stay roughly in position — a comfortable 9 to 10 knots into a short, choppy sea. *Orion* looked to be travelling all right, although bouncing around a fair bit with a lot of spray being tossed over her bow. We were bobbing along much more easily under reduced sail and were very comfortable.

I had Zoe check in by radio every 30 minutes to report boat and ride conditions, but they had no complaints and sounded like they were having fun.

We'd left at 11:15 and the chart plotter suggested in its annoyingly precise way, that we would arrive at our designated anchoring point at 17:42.

And so it was, that after successfully dodging contact with Hogan Island and a cluster of un-named little rocky islets not far off the coast, we entered the wide, sandy channel leading to Corner Inlet, between Snake Island and the chunk of Mainland that was Wilson's Promontory. The water smoothed in the shelter of the land and a couple of miles up the channel, we tucked ourselves in a small gutter against the Snake Island shore, well clear of the channel and dropped anchor at 17:42.

I'd deliberately left the care or otherwise of our prisoner to Angie, although she didn't do much on the trip, except to wander out every hour or so to see if she'd fallen overboard. I had Zoe anchor first, then did the same, but very close so that we could raft up with lots of fenders between the hulls for the night. Two boats tied together tend to disguise the lines of both, so I was happy with this small subterfuge. I made sure that there were the necessary anchor lights burning, but naturally, we all stayed on *Firebird*.

'How's your prisoner?' Sandy asked Angie with a grin.

She laughed, 'Very unhappy that I left her on the boarding platform the whole way over. I think she got seasick since there's a bit of mess around her. I'd have thought her stomach would be empty by now, but I did wash her off with fresh water.'

'That's a bit generous,' Sandy grinned, 'but what's your plan for the night?'

'Ah! For the last part of our diabolical plan, we need the co-operation of Jasper,' she said, looking at me.

I shrugged, 'Let's hear it. If I can make him understand, I'm sure he'll be happy to oblige.'

'Oh, it's not too difficult. We thought that we would put her on the toilet on *Orion*, handcuffed to some pipework, with Jasper on guard outside the door. That way, we don't have to sit up watching her all night. She can have a towel to drape over her, but we should take all her clothes from her cabin and the key to the boat, but I can't see her getting out of there past Jasper.'

We all had a good chuckle over that one and I thought that Jasper would be happy to do the guard-cat bit. It took some organising, but we managed to set it up as Angie had suggested. Angie fed Teri a sandwich and a bottle of water after we'd eaten, then the girls carefully untied her and led her up to the cockpit. Most of the defiance had left her, but both Sandy and I had too much experience with supposedly docile prisoners to take chances. Still, she stayed quiet and didn't curse anybody.

That was until she met Jasper!

The girls had her in the cockpit, both hands cuffed and with

Zoe hanging onto the ankle rope. The cockpit lights were off and she didn't see Jasper's black form in the dimness.

Teri bravely asked, 'What are you going to do with me now?'

We let Angie run the show again. 'We're all tired so we're going to bed. But you're going to spend the night 'cuffed to the toilet on board *Orion*, so you really don't want to play games like trying to sink the boat, since you'll go down with it. You'll have a bottle of water, and the best part is that you'll have your very own, personal guard all night.'

Teri sneered, 'At least one of you gets to stay awake watching. That's something.'

Angie shook her head. 'Sorry. We're all going to be asleep, but you haven't met our other crewmember, Jasper. He's the guard.'

Teri looked around, 'Where is he? I didn't know there was another one of you.'

'Right here.' I said, taking over this bit, 'Jasper. Here boy. Come and sniff the bad person.'

My beautiful big cat rose and silently padded forward out of the shadows, his huge gleaming amber eyes fixed on Teri, who jumped with fright as he seemed to appear from nowhere,

'Holy crap! What the fuck's that thing?'

'This is Jasper and he's looking after you tonight. But be careful how you talk about him. He's a bit sensitive to abuse and you really don't want Jasper feeling sensitive toward you! Anyway, he's going to check you out first, so I'd advise you to stand very still unless you want to be mauled.'

I squatted down beside Jasper's head. 'This is a very bad lady. She tried to hurt the girls, so she's very bad, just like the last bad man you ate,' I emphasised, and Jasper obliged by emitting a soft, deep, rumbling growl. 'She's not to leave the room where we put her, unless I am there. Understand?'

Once again to everyone's disbelief, my big cat turned his head and looked at me and huffed a meaty breath in my face, as if to say, 'Of course I understand. You humans must think I'm stupid!'

Despite her obvious uneasiness, Teri still managed to bluster, 'This is bullshit! I don't know what that thing is, but I know animals and he can't understand you speaking to him like that. You might fool others, but not me.'

I smiled, 'Ok. As you wish. But I still wouldn't try to do anything to get away. Once Jasper starts on you, he won't stop.'

Jasper stepped closer and briefly sniffed her over with obvious distaste, stepped back, and let loose with his loudest and most spine-chilling yowl. Teri would have jumped overboard in fright if Zoe didn't have such a tight hold on her ankle rope; all her bluster was gone in a flash.

With those niceties dispensed with, Angie, Jasper and I escorted our newly subdued and still naked prisoner to the toilet on board *Orion*, sat her down 'cuffed securely to a thick water pipe with her hands behind her back, draped a towel over her head and shoulders and left her, closing the door after turning out the light.

'You can do what you want,' Angie called out, 'but don't forget that Jasper will be lying on your mattress on the floor right outside the door all night. If he hears anything he doesn't like, he's quite capable of breaking the door down, and if he does that, you won't survive. Sweet dreams!'

A string of filthy curses followed us out, until we heard Jasper give one long, savage growl, then abruptly, quiet was restored.

I was up several times during the night to check the boats' position and each time crept silently down near the toilet cubicle to listen, but she stayed quiet. Each time, of course, Jasper was sitting up waiting to be patted, emitting a soft, rumbling purr.

Next morning, we retrieved our prisoner from her improvised cell, which fortunately was still clean, and marched her, stiff, sore, cold and naked over to *Firebird* where she was treated to a hot shower on the stern platform. She remained under close scrutiny, mine included, since I really don't mind looking at any shapely, naked female, especially one taking a shower. We took her restraints off, since Jasper sat just one step up from her, emitting his trademark rumbling growl every few seconds to remind her that even thinking about jumping overboard was futile. We took the precaution of mentioning that Jasper loved swimming and that Snake Island was named for the countless deadly Tiger snakes that thrived there.

The last bit wasn't true, since the Island had few if any snakes, but it all helped keep our prisoner docile.

Right on 09:00 saw Teri, now dressed in her own clothes, with Sandy and me on board *Orion* ready to head for Port Welshpool. At the last moment, I relented and allowed Angie to come as well, leaving Janice and Zoe to mind *Firebird* with Jasper as watch-cat. We hauled *Orion's* dinghy up on the stern davits, so we could more easily tow our own RIB to make the run back down the channel after our delivery. Zoe helped untie us and waved forlornly as we rumbled away up the channel.

There was a steady stream of traffic, private and commercial fishing boats as well as rig tenders moving up and down the channel, so we were just one more in the crowd.

By 09:20, we were nosing into a space on the wharf jutting out between the public boat ramp and the commercial slipway, and Sandy decided to handcuff her prisoner to a handrail out of sight, now that civilisation was close at hand.

We tied up and waited for Inspector Jack Pearson to arrive, although what we weren't prepared for was a Highway Patrol car, complete with multi-coloured stripes and light bar, nose into the dirt parking lot, attracting a lot of attention as it parked. A uniformed female Sergeant and a tall, slim man in neat, casual clothing climbed out and wandered down toward us.

Sandy and I stepped out to greet them, leaving Angie inside out of public view, keeping an eye on Teri.

Inspector Pearson introduced himself as Jack and his Sergeant as Jill Tracy, a solidly- built, amiable woman with a laid-back manner who, nevertheless, looked highly competent.

'Don't say it!' Jack said with a grin. 'We cop that shit all the time.'

They addressed Sandy as Sergeant, showing that Bob Casey had pre-warned them and they accepted her status, but weren't so sure about me. As we swapped brief CVs, I smiled to ease the tension that seems to build when Police Officers meet officially with those they regard as from the 'Dark Side', and said, 'Let's just say that, under the strictest confidence, I'm associated fairly closely with the Commonwealth mob.'

That raised a pair of eyebrows.

'Ah...So is this an official Commonwealth operation?' Jack asked.

'It is and it isn't,' I said evasively, 'there's nothing that you'd discover with a phone call to the front desk. However, such a call could open a very large can of worms at this stage of the operation, but if you really need to have reassurance that this is all legitimate, I can reluctantly show you a document, but you'd both have to sign the National Security Act first.'

Jack waved his hand dismissively, although with a look on his face that suggested that he had just bitten into a particularly sour lemon. 'No need. Bob vouched for Sandy and yourself, so I'll accept that, but I'm sure you understand that we country coppers hate it when something's going down in our area and we know fuck-all about it!'

I glanced at Sandy who nodded, before asking Jack, 'How much did Bob tell you?'

Jack grimaced, 'He's a great bloke with an excellent reputation, but he didn't say much either.' He gave me a hard look then bluntly stated, 'Despite me saying I'll do him a favour, I really need to know a bit more about why we're here to collect a female prisoner under what I regard as very peculiar circumstances. By that, I mean a Queensland Police Sergeant working undercover with an ACP deep undercover operative, turning up with an arrested Victorian citizen accused of attempted kidnapping, attempted murder and assault with a deadly weapon!'

I looked at Sandy again and, bunging it on a bit, signed theatrically, 'OK. I can understand your concern and I don't want to put you or Bob in a difficult spot, so we'd better sit a spell and we'll give you the short, edited version of the situation.'

That at least earned me a reluctant smile as Jack said, 'Any version, so long as it's not the bullshit one, will be very welcome at this stage!'

I nodded then asked, 'We have Sandy's prisoner on board, and she can't be allowed to hear any of what I have to say, even though she's managed to get involved in part of it. There's also a young lady with us who is one of the reasons for the whole thing.'

That really raised his and Jill's eyebrows, so Jack looked around and noted, 'It's a nice day. If you've got any folding chairs aboard that thing, we could sit out on the stern deck. We need to hear this straight. No crap!'

So, we found some chairs, asked Angie to join us and handcuffed Teri back in the forward toilet again where she'd be well out of hearing and couldn't open the door with her hands behind her back. The gaffer tape over her mouth also restricted her ability to yell out.

It was really very pleasant on the rear deck, especially when Angie whipped up some tea and coffee as well as finding some choccy-chip, shortbread biscuits that they'd stashed away.

When we were all seated, I launched into a much-abbreviated story of what had been happening so far. To avoid any official unpleasantness or the need for any premature investigation, I left out the second attack at Hunter Island, but described the first since it was already a matter of Police record and of course the most recent one, but glossed over the demise of Gerry Adams by saying that he'd fallen overboard early in the fight and must have drowned, as his body wasn't sighted again. The news of his death deepened the pall of gloom hanging like a small thunder-cloud over our visitor's heads, especially when I handed over all his identification as well as Teri's to Sergeant Tracy.

Sandy eased the potential drama over the death by adding, 'If you regard his demise as happening in Tasmanian waters, then it isn't your problem. At least for now.'

Jack gave a wry smile. 'Good try Sandy, but I could apply that reasoning just as easily to the happenings involving Miss Adams.

The only difference is that you lot have lobbed on my doorstep with her and this boat!'

It was just as well that Sandy and Angie were there to corroborate my story, Commonwealth copper association or not, since in Jack's view, we were talking about some serious shit going down. I told Jack that the guns they used had been lost overboard and made no mention of either the two bullet holes in *Firebird* or the electrified defence system. Neither he nor Jill were dills however, and both knew that there was a lot more to the story than the heavily sanitised version they just been fed. They were, however, polite enough to at least consider if what they heard could be massaged into a plausible report for the files and to justify the holding of a female on the charges listed.

'So, let's make sure we're perfectly clear on what you're asking,' Jack stated, leaning forward in his chair to emphasise the point. 'You want us to hold this person for a week or two until the various State Police Forces get their collective arses into gear and move together on this paedophile ring?'

I nodded, 'That's about the size of it, Jack. Even though she and her dopey cousin were working independently, if she's released beforehand, she might flap her gums to Angie's father trying to scam some money for the information and that'd blow the whole thing. But if you can think of another way to keep her incommunicado until then, we'll go with it.'

'I know how difficult this must be for you,' Sandy chipped in, 'it's not exactly a clear-cut arrest on straight-forward charges that can be prosecuted and defended.'

'You're damn right there,' he said ruefully, 'in fact, I'm not sure what to do. I mean, based on your report, I can certainly arrest her on a whole heap of charges, that's no problem. But how do I keep her locked up long enough?'

Sergeant Jill leaned over and spoke quietly into his ear at length. I only caught a few words like 'paperwork' and 'lost ... system'.

Jack sat back and thought a few moments. 'Sergeant Tracy has made some helpful suggestions that would be improper for me to share with you at this time, but might be useful, so what we'll do is this. We'll arrest this Teri Adams on charges of attempted robbery and piracy, provided that you and Sandy are prepared to provide written statements at your earliest convenience. An email will do for starters, but sworn, witnessed testimony will have to follow before long.'

Sandy and I nodded agreement.

'We'll leave all mention of attempted kidnapping out of it for now and can hold her, pending further evidence, for another two or three weeks, by means that don't concern you. But I must be informed as soon as the real deal breaks open, or my arse will be well and truly in a sling! I trust that'll be acceptable?'

Sandy and I smiled with relief. 'That'll be terrific and it will be as you say,' I responded, 'now I guess that Sergeant Thomson had better retrieve the prisoner and do the appropriate hand-over duties.'

'No need for that, 'Jill smiled, 'I can base the arrest on your complaint, and we were fortunate enough to be able to arrest the individual concerned before she escaped. That way there's no Interstate politics involved.'

'That'll work for me,' Sandy said admiringly, 'I'll just retrieve my handcuffs.'

'Excellent,' Jill grinned, 'but I'm really busting to hear the full story behind all this. It beats the hell out of arresting drunken sailors and chasing abalone poachers!'

I looked at both of them, 'I'm not exaggerating when I say that if you inadvertently let word of this get out, it won't just be an official reprimand that comes down from on high. Please remember that some of these rock-spiders are very high up in both the ACP and Victorian Police Force and they won't go down quietly. You can't talk about this to anybody in case they're involved. We were shocked to discover who was involved!'

Jack nodded seriously. 'Don't worry. We've got a tight crew at Foster and will keep a lid on this.'

With that, we wrapped up the briefing session. Sandy went to retrieve her handcuffs, Jill accompanying her to make the formal arrest on the modified charges. I passed the contact details for Teri's uncle to Jack, so that the boat would be taken care of, while Jack promised to clear things with the commercial slipways guys who owned the jetty, so we could leave the boat safely there until it was collected.

It was a greatly subdued Teri who emerged from the wheelhouse, 'cuffed and firmly in the grip of Sergeant Jill, to be marched away to the Police car, not even bothering to look back at us.

I'd given Jack our contact details; sat-phone, mobile and email address and promised to have an email report based on the slightly modified charges to him within 24 hours. That concluded our work here and hopefully with all those loose ends tied up neatly, we cleaned up the morning tea things, closed the boat as securely as we could then boarded our dinghy for the 15-minute, high-speed trip back to *Firebird*.

Another 10 minutes after getting back on board saw the dinghy stowed, the anchor raised and *Firebird* under sail, heading down-channel to the open waters of Bass Strait. I kept the wheel, while the ladies checked that things below decks were ready for sea.

CHAPTER 55

FIREBIRD...SNAKE ISLAND TO
LAKES ENTRANCE – VICTORIA, SUNDAY

Fortunately, the next cold front was at least a couple of days away, so the warm nor 'westerly was still blowing quite strongly, giving us a delightful beam reach along the amazing Ninety Mile Beach, that stretches from near Port Albert, just east of our departure point, in an unbroken, gently sweeping curve north east to Lakes Entrance.

As there were no offshore reefs or other hard stuff to create trip hazards, we stayed close inshore for a change of scenery and fairly flew along in nearly calm water, with only the slightest swell to remind us that we weren't in a sheltered bay. Little towns like Woodside Beach, the delightfully named Seaspray and The Honeysuckles, were followed by several more villages that were interesting landmarks to plot our passage, since we mostly stayed just a hundred metres offshore. The ladies were delighted with the change compared to our usual sea-only views when passage-making, and spent most of the day up on deck, where even Jasper found it interesting to see the land slip past so close and so quickly.

The only drawback to being this close inshore was that manual steering was essential in case of unexpected shallows or a rogue swell that might break to seaward of us, but the exhilaration more than made up for the extra work, especially with Zoe to relieve me. The occasional larger swell did hump up, but we were easily able to angle out and over it with no risk. Twice, when we came across people swimming in front of a village, we cheekily veered even closer, staying just clear of the shore break and passing within calling distance of the swimmers, delighting them to see such a large sailing boat travelling so fast and so close inshore.

It was one of those rare, magic sailing days where the warm breeze and cloudless sky added to the thrill of near-silent speed in calm water close to land. It also made the miles fly past and helped us once again to mentally and physically leave the latest round of nastiness behind. It was all so therapeutic that I could see the mood of the ladies lifting hour by hour and felt my own mood of depression being dissipated by the peals of laughter floated back from the foredeck when a pod of dolphins found us and decided to play under our bows for a while.

The calm water and strong breeze kept our speed up, so that thankfully we were approaching the Lakes Entrance bar with a comfortable hour of daylight to spare. The offshore breeze that had made our run so smooth was just as effective at flattening the bar approaches and we were able to cross this potentially very dangerous bar without drama. Once through the narrow entrance to what is probably Australia's most beautiful and extensive lake system, we turned hard left into a shallow channel arm, opposite the one that led to the town itself, but we only went about 400 metres, before anchoring in clear, shallow water over a sandy bottom. There was little boating activity up this arm, so in the morning, I planned to take the dinghy to town for supplies, before finding a cluster of boats we could hide amongst, in line with our latest cunning plan.

Everyone was in a very upbeat mood after the exhilarating sail along Ninety Mile Beach, with the girls particularly excited at the prospect of maybe meeting some kids their own age.

'We can't let you loose in Lakes Entrance,' I warned, 'just remember what happened in sleepy little Wynyard. This place is fairly jumping during school holidays.'

'Yeah, yeah,' Zoe grumped, 'we know, but jeeze, Harry. We really need to talk to somebody our own age for once! Not that you guys aren't fantastic. I didn't mean that! But we'd just like a change.'

I smiled, 'I do understand and no offence taken. But in the morning, your Mum and I will take a run up to town to do some shopping. After that, we'll go looking for a bunch of boats we can try to blend in with. There should be some kids among the boaties there.'

Zoe nodded, 'Ok. I guess we'll have to settle for that.'

Despite the girls getting toey for some teenage company, we had a happy evening with the lights of the town only a few kilometres away. Next morning, the cold front still hadn't fronted, so the warm northerly made a swim before breakfast a pleasant interlude with all the ladies choosing to keep their bikinis dry. After breakfast, Janice and I loaded the dinghy with shopping bags under a plastic spray cover. Clutching a list supplied by the Catering Manager, and with her last-minute admonition, 'Don't you two dare buy anything that's not on the list!' ringing in our ears, we set off for town.

It was a fast and fun run down to the entrance channel, across it and up Cunningham's Arm to the town. I'd worked out where we could safely tie up to minimise the walk with a heavy load and brought along a collapsible trolley to make the task of carting groceries easier, something I'd realised I badly needed shortly after I'd taken to the boating lifestyle.

Supermarkets are rarely located for the convenience of boaties!

The closest spot was beside a semi-circular spit of sand adjacent to the centre of town, so we motored in and pulled up close to the trawler jetty. The sand-spit was already covered in tourists, doing most of the things generally associated with the sun, beach and water.

We hadn't even left the beach when the standout amusement of the day occurred.

The sound of car horns blowing and some raised voices heralded the appearance of an extended family of Orthodox Jews, beautifully dressed in their best finery, emerging in a long line from a bike and boat hire store just across the Esplanade from where we had parked the dinghy. Two plastic, two-person kayaks followed them, each carried by a store employee at one end with a young male family member at the other. For some reason, they formed a long single-file line that halted traffic for several minutes while they all straggled across the road and manoeuvred carefully between the glittering ranks of parked cars.

With the family so immaculately dressed in traditional clothing and looking so totally out of place among the near-naked, tanned bodies of the rest of the tourists crammed onto the small sand-spit, it was an immediate attention-getter! As the kayaks were placed on the sand near the water, I nudged Janice.

'Let's sit a moment, this could be interesting.'

She grinned back and we perched on the low concrete wall beside the footpath overlooking the small beach. The family attracted even more attention when they gave no sign that they intended to do anything sensible, like take off some of their fancy clothes and wear something more suitable for paddling a kayak.

Giggles started when big Poppa, his distinctive hat jammed firmly in place, donned a yellow life jacket, which clashed horribly with the rest of his clothes. Demonstrating commendable leadership, he walked awkwardly down to the first kayak, sand filling his shiny, black dress shoes, and plonked himself down firmly in the stern seat.

Unfortunately, the kayak was still high and dry on the sand, and it took the combined efforts of four of his boys to slide Poppa's 120kg bulk, together with that of the youngest daughter, complete with skirt, leggings, headscarf and life jacket, into the water. It was then very obvious that neither Poppa nor daughter had the slightest idea of what to do with the double-ended paddles. Their problems were compounded when one of the boys, bravely getting his best shoes and pants wet, enthusiastically pushed the kayak away from shore. With cries of encouragement from the tribe ashore, all of them by now looking like yellow-breasted penguins in their life jackets, the two hapless wannabe boaties flailed at the water with their paddles as though they were trying to beat it into submission but doing little to propel them forward.

'30 seconds!' I muttered to Janice.

'In your dreams!' she snorted, '15 at best.'

'Loser buys the first two rounds?'

'Done!'

I lost, as Poppa and child gracefully toppled sideways at the 12 second mark, Poppa's hat remaining in place until splashdown, as the four husky sons in their Sunday best ploughed into the water like a Baywatch Rescue Squad to save them both from the terrors of the deep.

Anticlimactically, Poppa came to rest on his side, paddle still clenched firmly in hand, in about a metre of water, provoking a round of applause and laughter from the assembled multitude. There was more hilarity when he extracted himself from the kayak, stood upright, re-seated his sodden hat and as dignified as dripping clothes allowed, strode back to shore after making sure that youngest daughter was safe. The boys were left to retrieve the kayak.

We detoured via the pub where Janice demanded and enjoyed her liquid reward several times over, before we wandered off to find the supermarket. Angie's short list was quickly filled, although there was enough of each item to fill the trolley. Despite her warning, we added a few treats for everybody, including Jasper who was very tolerant of his diet, so long as there was enough of it.

Back at the dinghy, we noted with surprise that the Jewish family had commendably persevered to the extent that both kayaks were being slowly and carefully paddled around the shallows. We quickly loaded up, then steered a wide course around the adventurous family, before speeding up away from shore.

'There's more boats anchored near the town than I thought,' I commented to Janice.

'Yeah, there are. But no good for us, since the girls would just want to go ashore.'

'True,' I agreed, 'We'll look elsewhere.'

Steel Associates' Office, Monday morning
'Good Morning, Steel Associates. May I help you?'

'Good Morning, Miss Julie, this is Mr James. Is Mr Xavier available?'

'Yes, he is, Mr James. Just one moment and I'll transfer you.'

'This is Xavier. Go ahead Mr James.'

'I have a sighting report for you, Mr Xavier. As you know, I'm currently in Lakes Entrance and I have a positive sighting on the Mother, Mrs Janice.'

'Please continue, Mr James.'

'I sighted the woman in a supermarket, and she appeared to be with an unidentified adult male. They were buying a lot of groceries and I managed to follow them to the closest bay beach where they loaded a small dinghy, then motored away.'

'Excellent, Mr James. Did you see what boat they went to?'

'No Mr Xavier. I couldn't see them go to any particular boat as there are a lot of boats anchored here at the moment and my car wasn't close by.'

'That's very unfortunate, Mr James. So, their boat is either there or nearby. You will have to be much more diligent now that we know that they are in the area.'

Yes, Mr Xavier. But unless they come ashore more frequently, it will be difficult to track them down without a boat.'

'Very well, then hire one immediately.'

'I've investigated that, Mr Xavier, but the only hire boats available here are very small and slow and can only be used in a restricted area of the back arm behind the town. There are larger ones available from places further up the lake system, but they need to be booked many months in advance for school holiday time.'

'I'm not pleased by that news, Mr James. We need to track these people immediately before they disappear again. This contract has cost us way too much already in personnel, money and Police attention and I am very concerned about what might have happened to Mr Peter and Mr Jordan.'

'If I may say, Mr Xavier, I've been advised by some locals that the only way to safely and effectively get around this area is with a substantial boat. Bad weather with strong winds causes many boating accidents and the Lakes' area is huge. What about the Company boat at Blairgowrie? As this is so urgent, could we use that?'

'That's *not* the Company boat, Mr James; it's my very private and personal boat! But I suppose that in this situation, you may be right; I'll contact Mr David to get it ready to depart as soon as possible and have Miss Corrine accompany him. She will be useful in handling the female targets. Do you think that the three of you will be sufficient to find and restrain the targets?'

'*Oh, yes, Mr Xavier. There's only a woman and two girls, with one man who appears to own the boat they're on. I have the appropriate weapons and restraint devices with me and don't anticipate any problem once we locate them.*'

'Hmmm. I seem to remember Mr Peter saying something very similar before he set out in that seaplane! Be careful, Mr James. Things may not be what they seem.'

'*Yes, Mr Xavier. May I presume that Mr David will contact me on his arrival in Lakes Entrance?*'

'You may presume that, Mr James. I'll have them moving within the hour and anticipate that they will be with you later this afternoon or evening. Please keep watching that area for any trace of the targets until your backups arrive.'

'*Yes, Mr Xavier. Thank you, sir, for this opportunity to complete the contract.*'

'Don't make rash assumptions, Mr James. Keep in touch.'..........

Patrons in the Sports bar at the pub were slightly surprised at the outburst of cursing from the chubby, fair-haired man perched on a stool in the corner, apparently directed at the mobile phone still clutched in his hand. Those nearest him heard him mutter, 'Bloody David. That useless, self-opiniated surfie prick! Just because he runs Xavier's boat for him, he gets sent out here. He's not a field operative; he's just a boat bum! And that slack tart Corrine has probably fucked her way through the whole Company by now, but does she even look at me? Oh no. Reckons she's too good for me! Bitch!'

Steel Associates' Office, Monday morning

'Miss Julie, would you mind getting Mr David on the phone, please?'

'Certainly, Mr Xavier. Won't be long.'

...

'This is David.'

'Good Morning, Mr David, this is Miss Julie. Please hold for Mr Xavier.'...

'Mr David. What's your location?'

'Good Morning Mr Xavier. On-board the Seeker sir; just doing a routine check of all the systems as per the maintenance schedule.'

'Very good. So, is it ready to go?'

'Yes, sir. Fully fuelled, watered and provisioned as you have instructed, although the stock of fresh food needs topping up.'

'Good, good. I have an urgent job for you. Load whatever additional supplies you need and take the *Seeker* to Lakes Entrance ASAP. This is a job to locate, pick-up and deliver three females, one adult and two teenagers, back here. If you can't obtain the additional supplies quickly, proceed without them since it's essential that you be there by this evening. Is that achievable?'

'Yes Mr Xavier. No problem with any of that. I can have the food stocks topped up within the hour and the offshore wind will let me make a high-speed run. That will leave plenty of time to get there by late this afternoon.'

'Excellent! You've always been very dependable Mr David and I appreciate that. I'm also getting Miss Corrine to join you, and you will meet up with Mr James at Lakes Entrance. You have his number in the Company notebook, so call him when you get in. Mr James will be in charge of the operation as he has all the details of the targets. Any questions?'

'Do we need any more weapons? There's a handgun and a shotgun aboard.'

'Good question, but no, I don't think so, Mr David. That should be enough. Mr James has some additional items I believe, but the targets are considered soft and shouldn't need anything more than frightening to comply with your directions.'

'Very good, sir. I'll attend to the re-stocking immediately, but when

should I expect Miss Corrine to arrive. I mean, do I wait for her, or leave on schedule?'

'What is you estimated travel time to Lakes Entrance?'

'Around about 5 hours sir. It's 11:00 now, so if I leave by 12:00, I can comfortably be there around 17:00. Do I wait beyond that departure time?'

'No. If she's not there by 12:00, go without her and she can travel by road.'

'Thank you, sir. It will be as you say.'

'A final word, Mr David. Please be careful. We currently have two operatives missing in action under strange circumstances. Something odd has happened and so far, I don't know what it is. That makes me uneasy, so watch your back!'

'Yes sir. I will.'

CHAPTER 56

Whistling happily to himself, David trundled the last load of fresh food down the walkway of the finger wharf to the boarding ladder beside the cockpit of the AB 68 sports cruiser and started transferring it aboard. He'd guessed at numbers for catering, allowing for up to 6 persons for 3 weeks. There was always plenty of canned and frozen food stowed below, but nothing beat fresh stuff. He loved cooking and had even attended classes at the local TAFE to improve his skills. Taking care to avoid scratching the gleaming finish of the upper works, he moved the various cartons through to the galley.

At 68 feet long, the sleek, low-slung boat with its Rosso-red hull, looked like a speedboat on steroids and was a showpiece of Italian marine art, or so David and many others believed. The pair of MAN 19:00 horse-power V12 diesels driving Rolls-Royce water jets, could push the monster to a top speed of over 60 knots or nearly 117 km/h in fairly calm water, or let it cruise all day at 45 knots. The deep-Vee hull design allowed it to maintain a high speed even in choppy conditions, but as with any boat, in really rough seas it was reduced to a crawl, although it was a very seaworthy design and could safely survive the roughest weather.

Below decks, were three cabins, the Owner's luxurious one in the bow, and a twin and a double located under the saloon, all with ensuites. A separate crew quarters in the bow with twin bunks and ensuite was accessed via a deck hatch. The fully equipped galley was amidships with a spacious white leather lounge and dining table opposite that doubled as an office/workstation. There was an upper saloon with the jet-fighter style driving position, a wet bar and another sumptuous lounge area. The driving position had a full suite of navigational and electrified equipment to take care of the running of the boat and the whole thing was fully reverse-cycle air-conditioned.

The walk-through, white-painted engine room was David's special pride and he kept it and the twin V12 MAN diesels immaculate. Being paid to look after, live aboard and occasionally drive the beast for Mr Xavier were dreams come true for the ex-professional surfer, ex-lifesaver, so he took the job seriously, didn't screw around and did look after the beautiful boat very well.

Scoring the job with Steel Associates was a case of being in the right place at the right time, and to this day, he didn't really know exactly what his strange employer did.

That is, apart from talking oddly and surrounding himself with a bunch of very hard, tough men who presumably investigated things using some very dodgy methods. He'd heard that weapons were frequently carried and used by the operatives, but he tried to stay away from that side of things. The run out to Lakes Entrance should be a hoot, especially since the sea would be flat and he could really open the engines out properly, something he rarely got the chance to do as Mr Xavier actually didn't like being out on the water. As great as his job was, it was frequently boring, so any opportunity to leave the dock and cover some serious distance was very welcome.

He'd heard that Mr Xavier had acquired the boat through a very shady deal but being allowed to play with a boat worth around $2 million he didn't care where it came from. He didn't know this 'Miss Corrine' chick either, except that she was listed as an 'operative'. He had about 15 minutes to stow the fresh food, before he was due to cast off, so Miss Corrine had better turn up soon or she'd be hitting the road by herself.

Being a normal male with the appropriate ravenous appetite for females, he hoped she'd be attractive, but guessed that messing around between the hired help was frowned on by the boss, so he mentally tucked his dick back where it belonged and got on with the job. He divided the last of the thick-cut rib-eye fillet steaks and prime lamb chops between the fridge and the freezer and had just started the two diesels to let them warm-up, when there was a yell from the wharf.

"Hey! It this thing the *Seeker?*'

Stepping out into the spacious cockpit, he saw a diminutive female standing on the finger wharf, a large duffle bag slung over her shoulder. At first glance, she looked to be not much more than a child, but closer up, he saw that she was just of small stature, but definitely had all the appropriate female bits in all the right places. Even her features were very acceptable, with long red hair tied in a ponytail flowing down her back and constantly being blown about in the stiff northerly breeze.

'Well, is it or isn't it?' she called back impatiently. 'If you don't know, say so and I'll bugger off and find some other swinging dick who does know where the bloody thing is.'

'Ah... yeah! This is the *Seeker* and I'm David. I presume that you're Miss Corrine.'

'Thank Christ I found the bloody thing! But it's just Corrine thanks. None of that Miss Corrine bullshit! We're in Australia and most of us don't talk like there's a bowl of plums stuffed up our arse! Leave that for our esteemed boss.'

David smiled at her candour and surprisingly she smiled back. 'Sorry, excuse my bad manners and please come aboard and call me Dave in that case. I was just about to cast off. Mr...I mean, Xavier told me that if you didn't make the 12:00 deadline you'd have to drive.'

'Fuck that for a joke! Why drive when I can be carried there in luxury,' she retorted, swinging her duffle effortlessly over the railing, letting it drop to the deck with a metallic clank, before following it herself with a swing of delightfully tight jean-clad legs. Standing before him, she barely came up to his chest, but something in her manner warned that there was a lot more to her than initial looks suggested.

Grinning, she stuck a hand out and said, 'Pleased to meet you, Skipper.'

Dave blinked as she had the grip of a Russian wharfie, and he quickly revised his initial impression even further upscale while he shoved his dick a bit further out of reach.

'Likewise,' he responded weakly, 'grab your gear and I'll show you your cabin.'

'Great! It's been a rush since I got Xavier's phone call, 'cause I really didn't want to drive!' She looked around as he led her through the sumptuous saloon and down the curving stairs to the lower deck.

'Hey. This is really something. I've not been on a boat like this before. It's more like a palace! Are these handrails real gold?'

'No. But they are 18ct gold-plated,' he replied with a grin, as he showed her the double cabin, opening off to the left after a 180° turn to the left off the companionway, 'It was built for an Italian billionaire, but he decided that it was way too small for him, so he dumped it straight back on the market and ordered the biggest one they make, a 145 foot monster that's twice as long as this. Somehow, Xavier got wind of this and did some sort of shady deal to snag it. And here it is! $2 mill or so of Italian design genius and we get to play around with it!'

She caught some of his infectious enthusiasm for the boat and grinned back at him.

'It's really great! I love it. But if it's Italian, it must be fast. Is it?'

Dave smiled, 'Oh, shit, yes. Wait and see. It was ordered with the biggest motors that would fit, so we have about 900-horsepower more than standard. It really does get up and boogie for a big boat. We've got a long run ahead of us and the sea is calm, so I think you'll be impressed! Anyway, stow your gear and I'll get us out of here.'

'Can I help you?' she asked, following him back up to the saloon after casually tossing her heavy duffle on the double bed.

He pointed as they reached the upper deck where the sound of the idling twin V12 diesels was a subdued bass rumble, 'Sure. If you can untie those mooring lines from the boat end and pile them on the dock, we'll leave them here for our return.'

'Ok,' she said and nimbly hopped back over the railing, while Dave took a few moments to admire her tight jeans again. The way the front of her shirt was being jiggled around also caught his interest, just as she looked back and caught him looking.

'See anything you like?' she asked with a cheeky grin.

'Ah...yes, lots as a matter of fact, if you will excuse me saying so. You're very attractive.'

'Thanks,' she said simply, 'you're not bad yourself, so consider yourself excused.'

That wasn't the reply he'd expected and couldn't think of a suitable answer, so he concentrated his thoughts to easing *Seeker* out of the berth without transferring any paint. Two engines and water-jet drive, with a joy-stick manoeuvring control made tight quarters docking easy, even with the gusty wind, so as they backed up, Corrine was easily able to jump back aboard, leaving all the mooring ropes neatly bundled on the finger wharf.

'Thanks for that,' he said, expertly spinning the wheel as he engaged forward drive. The note of the diesels didn't change as the reverse buckets lifted and the sleek boat quietly gathered speed. Two or three people waved cheerily to them as they growled slowly along the bobbing lines of boats tied up in the rows of berths, staying well under the speed limit.

Once clear of the marina complex, he increased power slightly, letting the boat rise gently onto the plane. There were channel markers to follow, as well as other boats going both ways, so he needed to be careful and held the sped at a comfortable 15 knots. The flooding tide was swirling through the heads against the strong northerly wind, creating a choppy sea, so he prudently kept the speed down until they were around the point of Fort Nepean and had turned southeast into calmer water. Noting that the size of the swells rolling in from Bass Strait wouldn't worry a bathtub, he slowly opened the throttles, after warning Corrine.

She promptly tucked herself in beside him at the helm station, holding on to the handrail set below an instrument panel that looked as though it'd been transplanted complete from a jet fighter. As the growl from the engines steadily rose to a mighty bellow, the boat shot forward, a boiling white wake blasting out behind it. In moments, they were doing 40 knots with the throttles only half open and Corrine was bouncing up and down in her seat, yelling with excitement and delight. Dave noted that the boat was riding easily and needed no trimming but kept the speed steady as they soon rounded Cape Schanck; then the mass of Phillip Island slid past as they closed on Cape Patterson and Wilson's Promontory. It wasn't until they made the turn to the northeast past the Promontory, that he decided to stretch the big boat's legs properly.

With Snake Island slipping astern, he could safely angle in toward shore and as they passed the start of Ninety Mile Beach, he opened the engines up to 95% power.

The big V12's exhaust note rose to a spine-tingling howl and the *Seeker* seemed to launch herself into another realm of speed, noise and white-spray fury, with the speedo sitting firmly on 63 knots. Corrine had a manic grin on her face and losing herself in the moment, clutched Dave's arm in excitement.

'Fuck! This is almost better than sex!' she spoke up over the howl of the engines, her head swivelling back and forth as she tried to see everything.

He grinned back at her, 'I'll have to take your word for that. It's been a long time between drinks for me.'

She gave him a quirky look, before resuming her ceaseless scan of everything happening around them.

After a while, he throttled the engines back a little, the speed dropping to a mere 40 knots again. 'Do you want to drive a while?' he asked.

'Fuck, yeah!' she said enthusiastically, so he changed places with her.

'It'll feel quite light and sensitive at this speed, so be very gentle with the wheel movements,' he cautioned, 'think smooth and try a few wide turns to get the feel of it, but don't go any closer to the beach than this.'

Corrine nodded, fiercely concentrating on following his instructions, and he was relieved that she obeyed them perfectly, feeding in a small amount of wheel left and right, to smoothly carve a boiling white arc on the glittering green water. After a few minutes of carving smooth S-turns, he suggested that she tighten the turns a bit more, pleased with her delighted shriek as the big boat just seemed to suck down onto the water and haul around without the slipping and sliding that a propeller-driven boat would carry on with. For its size, the thing turned like a small speedboat, and the grip in the turns was so much that quite strong G-forces were generated, and both had to brace themselves to avoid being flung across the saloon. Finally, Corrine straightened out the course, aligned it parallel to the beach and handed control back to Dave.

To his great surprise, she gave him a quick kiss as they changed placed on the helm seat again.

'Thank you,' she said simply, 'that was one of the most fun things I've ever done!'

He looked at her, 'Really?'

She nodded, 'Yep! Try being a girl in a man's Company with testosterone floating around like a fog! Even to just maintain my lowly status, everything I do has to be better than the men can do. It's very rare to be offered a chance to do something fun and interesting without some swinging dick making a competition out of it!'

Dave saw an opening and casually asked, 'So just what is your job with Steel Associates?'

'Oh, apart from being an escort for female targets, I do the really dirty work when needed. I kill people.'

He was instantly sorry he'd asked the question, but bravely followed up with, 'So who are you supposed to kill this time?'

She laughed at his expression, 'Nobody, silly. On this job, I'm just the token female escort in case the targets need a female around to settle them down, but if things really go tits up, well…'

'Oh, sorry I asked.'

'Don't be. It's just a job like any other, and if it didn't pay so incredibly well, I'd do something else more boring, but much safer.'

'But where did you learn that particular speciality. I mean, it's not something that's offered at your neighbourhood TAFE campus!'

She giggled, 'You're funny. I'm ex-Army and was in Special Forces for five years, where they found that I had a talent for silent killing as well as sniping, but I took a bullet through my side in Afghanistan. They gave me a medal, an honourable discharge with a piss-ant pension and the left-overs of some very lethal training that had quite limited use in the civilian world, so I ended up with this lot. But as you might know, it's hard to leave a Company like this. I know too much!'

'Well, I don't know really. I'm just the hired boat driver and maintainer for Xavier. I don't go on jobs unless it's to act as a nautical wheelman. But I can understand that if you know a lot of bad things about the Company, they may not like you just resigning and disappearing back into the world at large.'

She patted his arm, 'Well put. It's actually really nice to meet and work with a normal person who only lusts after my body, rather than someone who is trying to deprive me of it at the first opportunity.'

She suddenly gave Dave a mock glare, 'You aren't going to try to kill me, are you?' Then laughed at his startled expression. 'Only jerking your chain, lovely man. I know you aren't.'

He grinned weakly, appalled at the turn the conversation had taken, 'Oh, well in that case, put me down as just lusting after your body. But I rather like your mind as well.'

That bit of flattery earned him another, rather longer kiss that was very pleasant for a man with a severe shortage of attentive females in his life at the moment.

SEEKER – DAVID & CORRINE, LAKES ENTRANCE, MONDAY

Just after 17:00, the long, low boat eased into the main anchorage in Cunningham's Arm, Lakes Entrance after an exhilarating, but uneventful run. Even the bar was as flat as a pancake and while Dave would have liked to fill the capacious fuel tanks immediately, the refueller had apparently gone home for the day, so that little job would have to wait until the morning. Seeker looked like a predatory red shark gliding amongst a swarm of baitfish as she growled quietly between the gin palaces and sundry other private boats.

Finally, he selected a clear area that would ensure he remained clear of the generally incompetent holiday crowd, dropped anchor and secured the engines. A large bank of batteries and a very well silenced generator would ensure that all electrical requirements would be met instantly with the minimum of fuss.

'We'd better call James,' he said to Corrine, 'that what Xavier said.'

'He's a fuckwit!' she warned, 'But he's probably in charge because he's already on the job. The trouble is, he couldn't organise a root in a brothel, but I suppose we'll have to work with the goose!'

'I've not had the pleasure,' Dave said, dialling the number listed in the company handbook.

'Haven't missed much!'

'Err...Yeah. Hello? This is James.'

'Good afternoon, Mr James, this is Mr David. As instructed by Mr Xavier, I am reporting that Miss Corrine and myself have arrived in Lakes Entrance with Mr Xavier's boat. I understand that we are to place ourselves at your disposal.'

'*Yeah, righto. About fucking time you got here. Shit! What've you been doing all bloody day? I've been sitting around like a stale bottle of piss waiting for you slack arses! Anyway, I need to get aboard immediately, so come and pick me up.*'

'Certainly, Mr James. Would you care to tell me where you actually are at this moment? We are anchored in the bay opposite the main hotel in the main street.'

'*Where? Are you at the hotel? I'm at the hotel! I can't see you. Where the fuck are you?*'

Dave rolled his eyes, guessing from the confusion that Mr James had apparently spent the day at the hotel and hadn't been sipping lemon squashes! 'No, Mr James. I said that we have anchored the boat in the bay opposite the hotel. I'm afraid we can't actually get any closer.'

'*Well, you need to pick me up then. I'm in the sports bar.*'.....

The phone went dead, and he looked in bewilderment at Corrine who'd come down with a sudden fit of the giggles. 'He's hung up!'

'Yeah, I told you he's a fuckwit, and the stupid prick's pissed as well from the sound of that. Xavier will tear him apart when he finds out. But I suppose we'd better go get him; he couldn't find his arse with both hands in broad daylight, let alone make his way out to a jetty.'

So they launched the dinghy and motored ashore. Local cruise boats used the closest jetty to the hotel, but there was plenty of room for a dinghy to tie up.

They wandered through the hotel; taste buds tantalised by the delicious smells wafting out from the dining area and indeed did find James propped up in the Sportsman's bar. He had two large duffels at his feet, a schooner of beer tilted at a precarious angle in one hand and was waving the other wildly in the air while bullshitting to a couple of pretty girls perched on stools nearby. Corrine stopped short, straining to hear what the Wally was saying

'...So as soon as my crew comes and picks us up, we're going on a cruise around the lakes.'

He leant drunkenly toward the nearest girl, a pretty brunette, slopping beer onto the carpet at her feet, 'You girls will love this trip. We're only messing around since we're supposed to be working for the boss, but this will be a creamy side job on a flash boat, and we'll make some decent...' He belatedly recognised Corrine stalking toward him, a furious look on her face, and swayed back upright.

He plastered a patently false smile on his ugly mug and made a grand, sweeping gesture of welcome, but unfortunately, it was with the hand holding the beer, most of which sheeted in a broad spray over the bare, tanned legs of the girls, with the remainder going over three guys at the next table. Although the girls shrieked in surprise and the guys erupted in anger, James was so far gone he didn't notice and blithely waffled on,

'Here they are. See, here's the lovely Corrine and this other fella, what-is-name! I told you my crew were coming to get us. Come on girls; we'll go and look at the boat, then you can get your gear from the motel and we'll all go for a Lakes' cruise.'

Dave supposed it would have been a real giggle; this drunken, balding, tubby little man desperately trying to impress the two nicely-dressed, attractive girls, but spraying them with beer instead, as well as pissing off three other guys. Nevertheless, Corrine took charge in a very decisive manner, placating the guys at the table by saying that they were taking the drunken idiot home immediately and sending Dave to the bar to get them another round.

She ignored James, who had forgotten Corrine and Dave and was peering myopically into his glass, wondering aloud where all his beer went, instead she spoke to the girls who were trying to wipe up some the beer still dripping off their legs.

'We're sorry about that, girls. He's a fuckwit at the best of times, and worse when he drinks. We actually have come to pick him up, but can we get you some more drinks to make up for all this?'

The brunette chuckled, 'Oh that's all right, no harm done. He seemed fairly harmless at first, but the barman has already told him no more and to get out. Still, he had a nice pickup line with the boat and the Lakes' cruise.'

Corinne gave her a look. 'Oh, that bit wasn't bullshit! We do have a boat. Dave and I just arrived and parked it just across from the pub, but it's not his, we're not his crew and we are supposed to be working. He's going to be toast as soon as the boss finds out.'

They flashed a quick meaningful glance at each other, before the blonde laughed and waved her hand dismissively as they slid off their stools, their short skirts dragging up, showing a lot of bare, tanned thigh that attracted Dave's approving glance. He picked up James's bags and as Corinne helped their very unsteady owner off his stool, the brunette said, 'We were just going in to have a meal. You're welcome to join us if you can park that pissed possum somewhere. We like people with boats.'

Dave looked at Corinne. 'We do need to eat, and I don't feel like cooking tonight, so I suppose we could dump numbnuts in a bunk and come back.'

She shrugged and smiled at the girls, 'Sounds good to me. Let's do it.' She turned to the girls, 'We'll be back in ten, ladies. Have a drink on me while you're waiting.'

'We just might do that,' the blonde said in a delightfully husky voice, 'but we'll have a wash down first, then grab a table in the dining room and wait there. Don't be long though, we're starving!'

Corrine waved as they staggered away with their burdens. The girls chuckled and watched with amusement as the tall, handsome guy with the broad shoulders, and the pretty, diminutive girl who acted a lot tougher than she looked, helped the semi-comatose fool across the road and out along the jetty opposite.

'It looks like they really have a boat, if they're going somewhere in that,' the blonde murmured to her friend, as they watched the dinghy curve away from the jetty and head for the biggest, sleekest and most expensive boat in the little bay.

'Yes. So, if the boat is real, what about the deal shit-for-brains was talking about? Will that be off now?'

'Maybe, but let's sound these two out over dinner and see what we can find out. But will you look at that! They really are going to that beautiful big boat! How good is that?'

Dave and Corrine had a fearsome struggle to wrestle James up to the cockpit, but possibly Corrine's double-handed grip around his neck as they hauled him up may have helped zonk him out even more.

'Where are we going to put him so he won't cause any mischief?' Corrine asked, as they let his limp body thump down onto a cockpit seat. "Cause we'll have to tell Xavier about this immediately. It's practically a terminal offence for an operative to be drunk on duty, but to be this far out of control is much worse.'

David gave her a worried look, 'He won't ask you to kill him, will he?'

Corrine laughed and patted his cheek tenderly, 'No. I don't think it'll be that drastic, but he's finished as far as Steel Associates are concerned and he'll probably be confined somewhere until this operation is over. By what I heard when we walked in there, he'd arranged some private deal with those girls, so we need to find out what it was.'

'Yeah. It's a bit strange the way they're so interested in the boat. However, for now I have the perfect place for this wombat,' David said with a broad grin, 'the crew berths are in a small cabin right up in the bow, with their own toilet and shower, so he won't suffer too much. We can lock him in since the only way out is via the deck hatch! Drag him up this way.'

So, they dragged him for'rard, dumped him carelessly down the steep stairs and jammed him in the tiny shower cubicle, tossing his bags on a bunk.

'That's for when he wakes up and has a chunder or three,' Dave said, 'no way I want him to mess up the cabin!'

'We might check these bags before we go,' Corrine said, 'in case he's got something useful in there.'

It was just as well they did, as a thorough search of both bags produced a gym bag holding two compact, small-bore pistols, thirty boxes of ammunition for them, several pair of handcuffs and three wicked-looking knives with dull black, razor-edged blades, as well as a manila folder full of papers.

'Wow!' said Dave. 'He's well equipped. What are the pistols?'

Corrine picked one, expertly ejecting the magazine and working the slide.

'They're Kel-Tec PMR-30s, firing a .22 Magnum round. A good, reliable little pistol, but limited stopping power unless you're fairly close, in which case they do a bloody good job, especially with hollow-points. Having 30 rounds in the magazine also helps with the stopping duties,' she added with a grin.

'Can you show me how to use one, some day?' he asked, surprised that his interest was aroused in wanting to learn about a gun. Or maybe it was the Instructor who'd spiked that interest.

'Sure, no problem. There's plenty of ammo for them.'

Before they left with the hardware, Corrine checked the fat manila folder.

'This looks like the entire task briefing info. He won't be needing it again after Xavier gets through with him,' she said, 'but I meant to ask earlier, if this is the crew quarters, where do you camp when you're aboard?'

Dave jerked his thumb over his shoulder at the solid bulkhead behind them, 'I live aboard full-time and I usually kip in the master stateroom unless Xavier is here, showing off to mates or clients. But all he ever wants to do is short day trips and never sleeps here, so he doesn't care where I sleep. If visitors are due, I always clean everything up so it looks like nobody lives here. It's surprising what people get up to when they're on a boat, even for a short time. I'm always washing sheets after a day trip!'

She laughed at that, but asked, 'I didn't know that you lived aboard, so how does that work out?'

He grinned, 'Perfect for me and the same for Xavier. I love the boat and it's just like living in a luxurious apartment onshore. I'd be here doing minor maintenance most days anyway, so this way Xavier gets his boat maintenance, 24-hour security and driver all in one package.'

She smiled admiringly, 'Good setup, dude. Beats paying a fortune for some dump onshore. Anyway, let's go have a feed.'

'Yeah, let's. But what's the go with those girls do you think? That bit you overheard dickhead saying to them did sound like some sort of private deal. Surely he wouldn't be stupid enough to try to claim the reward for himself? That might explain why he wanted the girls to help.'

She shook her head; 'I don't know, except that he is stupid enough to try something like that, so we need to find out how much they about the operation. But let's have a meal with them, listen carefully to try to learn some more, but we'll buy our own drinks and decide what to do with them after that.'

'Yeah, ok.'

Corrine was struck by a thought, 'How about this. If we don't learn anything over dinner, I'll give you a nod and you invite them out to the boat for coffee. I've got a few things in my bag that might get us some answers.'

Dave immediately looked worried, 'This won't become messy, will it?'

'No, dear! I actually try *not* to kill people! But despite having nice tits and long legs, they can still be up to no good, okay?'

David smiled, 'OK boss.' Then ducked away from the friendly punch she threw his way.

On the way back ashore, Corrine called Xavier.

'Good evening, Mr Xavier, this is Miss Corrine with an interim report.'

'Good evening to you, Miss Corrine. I must say I was expecting to hear from Mr James.'

'I'm afraid that won't be possible, sir. Unfortunately, Mr James became excessively intoxicated this afternoon while waiting for our arrival and may have been discussing aspects of the current operation with two female civilians. With the assistance of Mr David, I have taken the step of confining Mr James while he recovers and we determine the extent of the security breech he's created.'

There were a few moments of silence. *'That is very grave news, Miss Corrine. I commend you and Mr David on your actions, but I am very disturbed by the lack of control displayed by Mr James. Despite the delay this will cause to your search, I shall dispatch Mr Robert to your location to retrieve Mr James and return him to head office, so I must ask you to remain at that location until he can get there, which may not be until later tomorrow.*

In your opinion, what is the extent of the leak of information to these civilians?'

'Unknown at this time, sir. I overheard some words relating to the operation as we approached Mr James and the civilians in the hotel, but the conversation was interrupted by our arrival and Mr James's advanced level of intoxication. Mr James has also attracted the attention of the Hotel staff who were about to evict him from the premises for being drunk and disorderly. However, Mr David and I are currently proceeding to socialise further with the two civilians to determine what information may have been passed.'

'Excellent, Miss Corrine. Even if the delay causes us to temporarily lose track of the targets, I'd be very appreciative if you and Mr David would proceed with the mission as soon as Mr James has been collected. May I presume that you have taken possession of the briefing files that were in Mr James' care?'

'Yes, sir, I have the files, although we haven't gone through them yet, as we wanted to inform you first and get your instructions as to how to proceed.'

'I appreciate your tact, Miss Corrine; you are proving very capable and I won't forget that. Mr David is also proving most resourceful. Please read the files at your earliest opportunity and if you need further information, contact me directly at any time. So, are the two of you willing to proceed without additional resources?'

'Yes, sir. We can handle things and I'll report every two or three days or as we gain more information.'

'That will be excellent, Miss Corrine. I wish you well.'....

She'd had the phone on speaker, but as they were still slowly motoring ashore, Dave heard the full story.

'He sounds pleased with us, but James is in deep shit!'

'Yep. His arse is grass. He'll be lucky not to end up going swimming with cement boots. Xavier takes a security breach very seriously.'

Dave grinned, 'Yeah. I sort of gathered that. We'd better play things straight.'

'Damn right!'

CHAPTER 58

Back in the hotel, they found the two girls waiting at a table, beer residue from their legs apparently removed. By the cheery glow they both had, it looked like they'd had at least a couple of rounds of drinks while they waited.

'Sorry we were so long,' Corrine said as we joined them, 'taking care of James was a bit more involved than we'd hoped, but all's well now.'

'He'll have a sore head in the morning,' the blonde suggested, 'and I'm Allie and this is Jackie, by the way.'

Corrine made their introductions and suggested that Dave fetch another round of drinks and then they consulted the menu.

'The lamb shanks bourguignon is terrific,' Jackie said, 'we had them last night.'

'That sounds good to me,' Dave said, 'I cook them myself, but I'm always keen to try a professional's version.'

That was a good conversation opener and gave Corrine a chance to watch and listen as Dave, Jackie and Allie bounced recipes and cooking tips back and forth, although by the end of dinner, she still hadn't picked up on anything that sounded out of place.

The girls owned and operated a hairdressing salon in Melbourne and came to Lakes two or three times a year to unwind and see if they could meet interesting people, mainly attractive guys. They were staying at the Motel attached to the pub, as it was handy and reasonably priced.

'So, have you met anyone interesting so far this trip?' Corrine asked cheekily.

'Only you two,' Allie answered candidly, 'they're a pretty staid lot this time, and there's a lot of overseas tourists.'

'How about James, did you know him before this?' Corrine asked innocently.

Allie shook her head, setting her blonde curls bouncing about, 'Nope. Never saw him before. What about you guys? Do you normally work with him?'

'Nah,' said Corrine, 'only once — he was a bloody wombat then and no better now!'

Talk bounced back and forth a bit longer, until Corrine gave Dave the nod and he suggested, 'Would you ladies like to join us aboard for some coffee? I can run you back afterwards'

That livened the girls up as they both nodded enthusiastically, 'Oh yes please. We'd love to see the boat,' said Jackie.

In short order, the girls had been to the toilet and were ready to roll. They boarded the dinghy reasonably gracefully, which meant nobody actually fell in the water, and were soon boarding the *Seeker*.

As Xavier's hired greeter, David was used to putting on the dog and pony show that visitors to the *Seeker* seemed to expect. To the usual chorus of 'Ohhhs', 'Ahhhs' and 'Wows', he led them around the highlights of the boat, finishing back in the saloon where he selected low, indirect mood lighting, including turning on the underwater LEDs around the stern that always attracted fish. Being a temperate evening, he seated them in the cockpit while he went to make Irish coffee.

'Please excuse me a moment,' Corrine said, 'I need to pee.'

She went straight to her cabin, pulled her shower kit from her bag and found a small bottle and a book-sized leather pouch. Leaving the pouch handy, she shook two white tablets from the bottle and ducked out into the galley.

'Which are the girls' mugs?' she asked Dave.

'The two green ones,' he indicated.

She dropped a pill in each mug, waited until he had filled them with brewed coffee and a healthy dollop of Jameson's, then carried them up top, Dave following with theirs.

'Here we are,' she said, 'sorry to run out on you, but when you've gotta go...'

More chitchat was exchanged as they all settled and sipped the heady, steaming brew.

'Nice brew, Dave,' Jackie said, smiling appreciatively, 'you seem to be a very fortunate man having an incredible boat like this at your disposal.'

Dave shrugged, 'Yeah, it's a great thing alright, but I could never afford to run it, let alone own it outright. That's the boss' privilege. He's a very wealthy man.'

They both nodded. 'What's this job you're both here to do?' Allie asked casually.

Corrine picked up on that one by replying, 'Oh, some guys did the dirty on the boss over a business deal, and he wanted us to visit them and suggest that they pay him back what they owe. They're supposed to be on a boat somewhere around here.'

Allie's eyebrows rose, 'No offence, but I would have thought that more people would be required if you're going to play debt collectors on a Corporate scale.'

Corrine smiled gently, 'We can hold our own, but James is being taken back to Melbourne tomorrow afternoon. Then we can get on with looking for these guys.'

'Oh, okay. I hope things all go well.'

Corrine smiled, 'I'm sure they will.'

After that little fishing attempt failed to produce anything useful, talk returned to more general topics as the girls took in the lovely scenery with the lights of the town reflecting off the smooth water, and the endless murmur of the surf just over the sand dunes to the south as an appropriate audio backdrop.

The first sign that Corrine's pills were working were when Jackie gave a mighty yawn apologised profusely, then her eyes slowly closed and she slumped down in her seat. Allie might have been concerned if she hadn't also been affected the same way and just as quickly. Within seconds, both girls were breathing deeply.

'Shit! That was quick,' Dave noted, 'what the hell are those pills?'

Corrine shrugged, 'I don't know, but we use them quite a lot when we need to knock a subject out for a while. Afterwards, they generally have no knowledge of what happened, which is a very useful effect.'

'Sounds like a super Rohypnol or something similar.'

'Yeah, sort of. But there's something else we use as well. Watch them a moment, I'll be right back.'

She went below again, returning with a small leather pouch. From that, she withdrew a small bottle of liquid with a sealed rubber top and a small hypodermic syringe and a sterile packet of fine needles. A sealed packet of sterile wipes completed the kit and Dave watched as she expertly filled the syringe, swabbed the inside of Allie's elbow, then gently slid the needle into a vein. Only a small amount was injected, and the very fine needle seemed to leave no mark.

Jackie received similar treatment, before Corrine packed up the kit, dropped the used needles overboard and carefully rinsed the syringe.

'What happens now?' Dave asked, as neither girl had even twitched throughout the procedure.

'We wait about ten minutes, then they should partially wake up, but be drowsy and very compliant. We need to find out what they talked to James about and this is the quickest way to get the truth.'

'So the pills are like Rohypnol in that respect?' he asked.

'Yes, that part is the same, but it's the stuff I inject that's important as it blocks their ability to be evasive and lie. The pill is just the knockout so I can inject them with the good stuff. If they were conscious, I can't see them holding still while we inject them with anything!'

Dave nodded, 'True.'

Corrine continued to monitor the girls' pulse and respiration rate until after about 5 minutes, first Allie, and then Jackie stirred and mumbled sleepily. Over the next few minutes, they woke up more fully, not seeming to be aware that they'd been knocked out, but also not as aware of their surroundings as before either.

Corrine then asked Jackie a series of simple questions that were verified by just looking at her driver's licence, which they found in her purse on the table.

Dave noticed that her answers were a bit mechanical, even though she spoke clearly but slowly.

Then Corrine cut to the chase. 'What was the plan you discussed with James this afternoon?'

'He told us about the three people you're trying to find and asked us to help him find and grab them instead because there's been a reward of $50,000 offered by the girls' father. If we could do it, he'll split the money with us which he said is a lot better than what he gets paid by your boss.'

Corrine looked at Dave, 'Oh the stupid prick! He really thought he could get away with that.'

She addressed Jackie again, 'So how was the plan supposed to work?'

'He was going to feed us all the information about the where-abouts of the targets and then delay you so that we would get to them first. It seemed like it should work and we know we could use the money.'

'So simple, yet so stupid!' mused Dave. 'Having us do all the work and he'd reap the reward.'

'That's about it,' Corrine replied as Jackie slowly turned her head and smiled at Dave.

'You're nice,' she said, 'I want to go to bed with you. Can we do that now?'

Allie seemed to rouse herself slightly, 'Don't be greedy, Jackie. I want him as well.'

'Well then, we can take him to bed together,' Jackie came up with, giggling, before directing a beaming smile at Dave who was looking a bit uncomfortable.

Both girls then slid back into what appeared to be a light sleep.

Corrine grinned at Dave's expression. 'I should have warned you that they'd have absolutely zero inhibitions while under this drug. The effects will slowly taper off, but they'll still say and do funny things for a couple of days, so we'll have to be careful. It wouldn't do to have a pair of uninhibited nymphomaniacs running loose around town!'

Dave finally saw the funny side of that, but a nagging thought popped up. 'What you just said made me think. What are we going to do with them? As you said, we can't just turn them loose. Even if they can't remember that we knocked them out, they'll still have the memories of what that dickhead James told them and that dopey plan he came up with.'

Corrine thought a moment. 'You're right. I haven't had to think of that side of it before, 'cause there was always someone else to take care of the subject, after I did my thing. But maybe we'll hang onto them for now, since I have to report to Xavier with what we've learned. He might want to send them back with Robert.'

'That wouldn't be a good thing,' Dave put in, 'they'll be treated very badly in Robert's hands. From what I've heard, he's a real arse-hole with females. I mean, apart from being greedy, the girls are innocent and shouldn't be punished for meeting the wrong guy.'

'Yeah. I suppose you're right. I'll try to think of something clever to say to Xavier.'

Leaving the girls snoozing and hopefully slowly recovering in the cockpit, they took Corrine's phone and went for'rard to the bow, confident that James, although just under their feet, was too far out of it to hear anything short of a nuclear explosion and they could watch the girls at the same time.

'*Xavier.*'

'This is Miss Corrine, Mr Xavier, with a further report.'

'*Excellent, Miss Corrine. Please go ahead.*'

'The social discussion we had with the two female civilians was fruitless, so I felt it necessary to use my medical kit.'

'*There was no other way, I presume?*'

'Correct, Mr Xavier. No information was forthcoming in normal conversation and I didn't feel that force was a prudent way to achieve the results we needed.'

'*I concur, Miss Corrine. Go ahead.*'

'The civilians responded very well to the treatment and readily revealed the information needed. It appears that Mr James heard about the open reward posted by our client and decided to set up a freelance operation, using the two civilians as his operatives. He intended to feed them the latest intelligence on the progress of the search as we gathered it, and then divert us sufficiently so his crew could acquire the targets before we could.'

'*That is very distressing news, Miss Corrine and I commend you and Mr David most highly for the way you have handled this situation. Mr James has behaved extremely badly, and I shall deal with him in an appropriate manner. What are your recommendations for further progress?*'

Corrine took a deep breath, unused to having her opinion asked for by the boss. 'Mr Robert should proceed as planned to collect Mr James tomorrow, ASAP. Once that has happened, Mr David and I will depart the town area to continue the search of the Lakes' system. We believe that this is where the targets are currently hiding as it is a vast area of waterways and anchorages with thousands of hiding places.'

'*Is it possible that they have returned to the islands in the Bass Strait?*'

'We think that unlikely, sir. They have apparently been to several of those islands already, and it is logical for them to seek a different hiding place. As it is school holiday time, there are a great number of both private and hire boats using the Lakes' area for the next couple of weeks, so it will be easier for them to hide in plain sight.'

'*Very well. Your reasoning is sound. Proceed.*'

Thank you, sir. We further recommend that the two civilians should accompany us, as they will still remember the deal they had with Mr James and cannot be allowed to roam freely where we have no control over their actions. Given the level of their contact with Mr James, and the attention this search has already gained from the police, we don't believe that a terminal sanction would be wise. They are basically greedy innocents and we think that they can be disabused of that greed without the use of undue force.

In our opinion, they will accompany us without further coercion, so we don't need to restrain them in any way.'

'That would seem to be a risky move, Miss Corrine.'

'With respect, sir, we believe that the risk is quite low. It was revealed under chemical analysis, that both civilians have formed a mental attachment of a sexual nature to Mr David, so this is the basis for our opinion that they will be happy, willing passengers.'

'I see. I must confess, Miss Corrine, that my understanding of this is very limited and I shall bow to your superior judgement at this time, but I do urge extreme caution. It is not company policy to involve civilians in the middle of an active investigation; particularly one that may well be entering its end phase.'

'Thank you for your confidence, Mr Xavier. We will ensure that it is not misplaced and be assured that I am quite prepared to enact a termination solution should our judgement prove incorrect. Our location on the Lakes' system will make that job very easy should it become necessary.'

'Excellent, Miss Corrine. You are indeed the correct person for the job. You are now the lead operative in this matter and I will have Mr Robert deliver additional information about the contract to you tomorrow. Please proceed using your best judgment and keep me informed as to progress.'...

'Congratulations on your promotion,' Dave offered.

Corrine snorted, 'Yeah, thanks. But that just means that as long as we make the right calls, all is well, but just one fuck-up and we're toast. I told you things were tough climbing the rank structure. You should have stayed being the boat driver, it's much safer!'

'Thanks for the tip,' Dave grinned, 'so, what do we do now, boss?'

She kicked him gently in the shin. 'OK. First, check James to see that he's okay and not choking on vomit. Second, we need to park the girls somewhere safe for the night where they won't get into trouble. Third, we need to get some rest ourselves.'

'I'll take care of checking James,' Dave offered, 'but if the girls are still strongly affected by the drugs, can't you just tell them to go to bed and stay put?'

'That's probably true. I've never tried before, but do we want them aboard or ashore?'

'Much safer aboard,' Dave suggested, 'they can have the twin cabin, and if you tell them they have to stay aboard, I can get their gear tonight or tomorrow, whatever works.'

Corrine scowled at herself, 'You're right. I should be thinking more clearly. We can't leave them alone, especially right now. How about I get their room key from Jackie's purse and you go get their stuff. If you're quiet, there should not be any problem packing their gear, then leave the key in the room. The housekeeper will find it in the morning.'

Dave nodded, 'Yeah, righto. Can you get them down to the cabin, or do you need help?'

'Nah! I'll do it shortly. I'll wake them up and suggest that staying aboard is how they'll get to go for a cruise. It's all they're been talking about all night anyway.'

So Dave took the room key from Jackie's purse and went ashore again. Being holiday time, there were still lots of people around, so he didn't stand out at all when he went to the girls' room. He was glad they were a tidy pair and he didn't have to sort out a heap of gear. Still, his packing left a lot to be desired and by the time he'd stuffed their suitcases, he'd probably mixed some stuff up. He also found their car keys and decided to move it out to a safe area in a back street to avoid any questions being asked by the Motel staff. After he carried their bags down to the car, he wiped all things he might have touched in the room and left the key on the table.

Before parking the car, a nice FG Falcon XR6, he dropped their bags in the dinghy, and then found what looked like a safe spot to leave it for a while. Less than 30 minutes after leaving, he was back on board, humping the suitcases up into the saloon.

'Any problems?' Corrine asked.

'Nah. Sweet as. I found their car keys and moved it out of the Motel carpark, though. We don't want the staff wondering why their car is still there when they've checked out early. I found their mobile phones in the room, turned them off and left them in their car. That'll keep them out of contact and they can find them when this is over.'

She gave him an admiring look, 'Bloody good thinking, dude. If you keep this up, I'll have to promote you.'

'No way!' he laughed. 'I'm just the boat driver, backing up the pretty lady. But how are our guests settling in?'

'Pretty good, considering. They wanted to know when their bed mate was coming back, so I had to tell a slight porky by saying that as I was already your bed mate, you didn't have either the time or energy for more, at least for now, so they should just sleep on it tonight and we'd see what tomorrow brings. I'm not sure how that went over, so you may have to fend off some amorous advances for a few days, but otherwise, they're happy to be aboard and going for their 'cruise'.'

'Bed mate, huh! Good thinking! I didn't know how I was going to get out of that one. Two uninhibited females at once might have been a bit too much of a drought-breaker for this little black duck!'

Corrine gave him a look. 'So that bit earlier today about being a long time between drinks was for real?'

'Yep! Living on the flashiest boat on the marina doesn't always guarantee a bedmate. And of the few offers I do get, most aren't worth even looking at. But anyway, you just scored the job of carting their suitcases into their cabin. I'm not going near them for at least a week!'

Corrine laughed at the big, tough ex-surfer, ex-lifesaver, being so scared of two females that he wouldn't even go to their cabin.

'So where are they now?' Dave asked.

'In their beds, of course and pretty much asleep by now. So you'd be safe going in there, but don't worry; I'll play porter and drag all their baggage around. Don't worry about me! I'll be alright.'

After poking out his tongue to her, Dave checked on James in his comfortable little cell, but he was still curled up in the tiny shower recess, semi-comatose. After stowing the dinghy and locking the outside doors, he figured Corrine must have gone to bed. so he showered in his palatial en-suite and went to bed in the comfort of the massive king-size bed, where he slept the totally restful sleep of a truly innocent spirit.

CHAPTER 59

SEEKER...DAVID & CORRINE, LAKES ENTRANCE, TUESDAY

David woke early as was his habit and after basic ablutions like peeing and washing his face, wandered out to the galley to make a cuppa. He'd only just boiled the kettle, when Allie wandered out of their cabin, half-asleep, but looking very alluring in just a T-shirt that must have shrunk in the last wash. It did absolutely wonderful things for her chest and the lower edge of it remained decent by at least a centimetre. That was, of course, provided she didn't stretch up to touch the deck head, which she immediately did as part of a big stretch.

As a typical male, Dave catalogued the information automatically: didn't shave, didn't need to shave, hair colour matches.

She un-stretched and caught the direction of his look, or maybe she just felt the intensity of it, and giggled, 'Hello, Dave. Good to see you too. Can I have a cup of coffee, please?'

'No problem. I'll just brew up a pot. Does Jackie take coffee as well?'

'Oh, my goodness yes. Kick-starter, and all that.'

While he messed around, setting up the expensive Italian coffee machine to do its hissing, bubbling, gurgling thing, she stepped close and said in her disturbingly husky voice, 'Thanks for getting our gear from the Motel last night. Corrine told us about it and I'm really sorry that we got so pissed that we passed out. We must have been really tired. It was good of you to let us stay aboard and to come cruising.'

When he turned around, she was so close he dragged his upper belly across her firm, thinly-clad boobs, her tousled blonde head coming up to about his chin level.

'No problem But I've moved your car into the side street beside the Hotel, almost outside the bottle shop. I hope you paid for your room in advance?'

'Hell yeah!' she replied. 'This time of year we had to book six months in advance, but the chance to go cruising the lakes in this beautiful boat is worth the lost room time. We had about a week to go, so the motel won't be looking for us.'

'That's good,' Dave replied, trying desperately to keep his eyes up on hers. 'Anyway, you're both here now and we'll see how things work out.'

'I'm sure we will,' Allie purred, eyeing him off as she took her large mug of steaming coffee. 'Wow! That smells fantastic! So, do you really live aboard and cook for yourself? I mean all those recipes we talked about last night at the pub. I can see how you had the right conditions to make some of those dishes. This is a terrific kitchen.'

'Galley,' Dave corrected her automatically.

'What's that?'

'I said it's called a galley on board a boat. Kitchen on land, galley on a boat.'

'Oh. So there's a lot to learn about boats.'

'Yep. If you want to, that is. Most visitors couldn't be bothered. They come for five minutes, ponce around playing the big shot and they go again.'

'You take this boating thing all very seriously, don't you?' she observed, backing off a bit and leaning back against the dining table opposite the galley, looking highly desirable.

'Yes, I do. It's a way of life that's clean and rewarding, and totally unforgiving of fools and errors at the same time. On land, the various Governments have set up so many safety nets to protect fools from themselves that people don't realise that they aren't in control of their lives any longer. But on the water, messing around in boats, it's just you and nature. Nature isn't a thinking being; while it can be either benign or devastating, it's just what it is, uncaring, but intolerant of fools and their stupidity.'

He paused for a sip of tea. 'And that's the lure of boating, you have to cope with what is dished up at the time. It's about you being prepared for something that can wipe you out in the blink of an eye if you don't pay attention to every detail, or stun you with the raw beauty of a moment. It's also called living on the edge and nothing compares to that!'

Dave looked down for a long pause, 'Sorry. I climbed on my soapbox for a moment there. My bad!'

Allie stepped forward and touched him lightly on the arm. 'Don't be sorry for feeling strongly about something. That's an emotion many of us seem to have lost in recent times. And it's very sad that most of us will never regain that ability.'

Dave looked up to her eyes and a flash of understanding passed between them.

'Thanks for understanding, Allie. I appreciate that. Most people don't get it.'

She laughed. 'It must have been the booze last night, although I didn't think we had that much. I don't normally do philosophy very well.'

Dave grinned back at her, 'Well. You've done alright in my book.'

Jackie chose that moment to wander out dressed in much the same way as Allie and disturbingly, did the stretching thing the same as Allie. It had the same effect on the hem of her T-shirt as it did with Allie, and he was forced to make a similar evaluation of her nether regions that matched Allie's.

Without being asked, Dave presented her with a steaming mug, white and two.

She grinned with delight.

'Thanks, Dave. I see my business partner has been telling tales.'

'Only minor good ones,' Dave smiled.

Jackie took a sip of her coffee and said, 'Look. I know that James was a drunken fool and was shooting off his mouth yesterday, trying to get into our collective panties, but you really didn't have to honour his offer and take us with you. Not that we're complaining, mind. It's just that I feel a bit guilty by intruding.'

Dave shook his head, 'No, that's okay. If Corrine and I weren't happy with the plan, we'd have dropped you back at the motel last night with no hard feelings.

Still, we'll get you to do whatever jobs you can to help, and it won't hurt our image to have two more attractive ladies running around in skimpy bikinis making us look just like the rest of the holiday boating crowd.'

Jackie gave a cheeky grin, 'How do you know that they're skimpy?'

He grinned back, 'Who do you think packed your gear last night?'

They both laughed, then Allie asked, 'What's the plan for today?'

'Well, as we told you last night, we're actually on a job, looking for some guys. We had a tip-off that they were spending a few weeks on a boat in the Lakes' system, but there's an awful lot of area to cover, so we'll just have to keep cruising around, hoping we trip over them. We do have what we think is the name of the boat, however, so that should help.'

'What's the name?' Jackie asked, 'we can help you look for it, at least. It's not confidential, is it?'

Dave thought a moment, 'No. That should be ok seeing as you're here with us. The name we've been given is the *Firebrand* or something like that. The information source was a bit vague apparently. Our first job today is to get rid of James, so the boss is sending a colleague to collect him. He won't be here until around midday, which means we have to stay put, although we might run down to the trawler base and refuel while we wait. We did a fast run from Melbourne yesterday and this thing's a bit thirsty.'

'OK. That sounds good. We can help with cooking and cleaning or any other boat stuff that you care to teach us.'

'Doing the cooking and cleaning sounds good; that'll free up Corrine and myself to run the boat and look around for our guys. But outside of that, you two are free to lounge around. Provided you wear the skimpy bikinis,' he added with a chuckle.

'And speaking of cooking, I'd better take Corrine in a coffee. It's time she was up.'

The girls headed back to their cabin with their coffees, Allie cheekily flipping the back of her T-shirt up to show off her nicely rounded bare bum.

'Careful you don't catch cold down there doing that,' Dave said after her.

She flashed a grin over her shoulder, 'Never happen. It's way too hot!'

Corrine appreciated her coffee and promised to be up and dressed in five minutes.

After breakfast, they up-anchored and rumbled sedately down to the Fisherman's Co-op, where the capacious fuel tanks took just under 3600 litres to fill them up again.

'Going to be around long?' the refueller asked, "Cause I'll give you a discount if you have a few more fills like that.'

'We'll be drifting around the Lakes for a week or so, but if you make it worth my while I'll definitely come back here.' Although only 5%, it was a reasonable discount and Dave was pleased as he handed over Xavier's Platinum Visa card.

Robert called Corrine on her mobile at 11:45 to say he'd arrived, by which time they had tied up at the ferry wharf in a short-term parking spot to make things easier, now that Jackie and Allie were aboard voluntarily. Robert was a large, brutal-looking man with knife scars crossing his face, little piggy eyes set too close together and an abrasive manner. He was rude to Corrine, ignored Dave, but nearly tripped over his dick when he saw the girls. Dave made sure that he didn't have time to question Corrine about their presence, but insisted that he handed over the additional briefing notes before he dragged a very sick and sorry James out from the crew cabin. No one was listening to his plaintive bleating as Robert grabbed him roughly by the scruff of his shirt and marched him back down the wharf without saying any goodbyes.

'I'll leave the fore hatch open to air for a while, before you go down to clean it out,' he told Jackie, who'd volunteered to do the duty, while Corrine was reporting to Xavier that Robert had collected James and passed over the additional briefing notes.

'But in the meantime,' he told Allie, 'let's shove off before something else goes wrong.'

'Have you worked out where to start looking for the guys you're chasing?' she asked.

Dave looked thoughtful, 'Although still a bit hit and miss, we might as well work our way around the system methodically, so we can go clockwise or anticlockwise. Let's flip a coin.'

He found a 20c piece in his pocket and flipped it, letting it drop to the carpeted floor. Allie bent down to look.

'Heads! That's clockwise'

FIREBIRD...BUNGA ARM, GIPPSLAND LAKES, A REMOTE
ANCHORAGE EAST OF OCEAN GRANGE VILLAGE, SUNDAY

Maybe because of the school holidays, the various secluded anchorages in the Bunga Arm, not far to the east of the diverse collection of eco-houses and fishing shacks known as Ocean Grange, were surprisingly crowded with boats. The first anchorage seemed to have the biggest collection that was mostly hired bare-boat cruisers, but there were a fair number of private ones as well. The seclusion, very good weather protection and being just a 200m walk to the ocean beaches was probably much of the attraction. Since the progressive and bustling town of Paynesville was only ten minutes away in a fast dinghy, it seemed an ideal place to park for a while.

We cheekily sailed in on the dying breath of the northerly breeze, dropping the pick well clear of the main concentration of boats. There were a few small sailing monohulls, what looked like an Antares 44 catamaran, a bunch of hire cruisers, all tucked in amongst several privately owned, top-heavy gin palaces. Their cockpits and flying bridges were fully wrapped in clear plastic, like they hadn't been used yet, but apparently to ensure that not the slightest trace of nasty fresh sea air could sneak inside to taint the owner's martinis.

Most boats were anchored in clusters off a small, curving sandy beach where a lot of tents had sprung up ashore, apparently to reduce congestion aboard, so we anchored a bit further along, near the end of that first stretch of beach, just off the mouth of a small creek. Beyond that to the East there were a few boats anchored here and there off any little sandy spots on the surf side of the arm that offered easy landing, and due to the lateness of the season, the mozzies were hardly noticeable.

As the evening gently settled its soft, grey mantle over the anchorage, boat lights came on like scattered fireflies, accompanied by the sounds of happy boaties indulging in the traditional nautical ritual of getting pissed at sundown. It was a remarkably similar ritual to the one they'd indulged in at lunchtime but needed repeating as six hours had passed since then.

Despite Bunga Arm being over 12 km long, there wasn't much tide flow, although the water level still did its usual up and down thing, so swinging around on the anchor wasn't a problem. Being a minimal-draft cat, we were parked in shallow water, less than a tinnie throw off the tip of the little peninsula formed by the creek, and were close enough to talk to various people who wandered past on their evening walk, offering a cheery wave as we hoisted our own drinks to them, doing our bit to maintain the time-honoured tradition.

We were all tired after the exhilarating, but long sail from Snake Island and the earlier negotiations with Jack Pearson and his Sergeant. During that fast sail, Angie had managed to slow-cook a roast on the Weber gas BBQ hung outside in the cockpit, and proudly produced a beautiful leg of lamb complete with roast veges and greens. As chief cook she was in her element!

Even though Janice and I had gone shopping in Lakes Entrance, I hoped that we had stayed anonymous by keeping *Firebird* well out of sight. Next time we needed supplies, I intended to visit Paynesville, as it should be far less likely to have a surveillance team in place. I also believed that another layer of protection had been created by the rather terminal solution we had applied to our last encounter with Steel Associates' operatives, as they were now down two associates along with all the knowledge of what boat we were on and where we might be. They were also thankfully ignorant of our ability to effectively defend ourselves.

Spending a few days or so hiding in plain sight amongst a bunch of half-cut holiday boaties seemed a good idea and I thought that we might have a chance of staying under their annoyingly vigilant radar.

The twins were also happy that there were so many boats around as they had seized on the idea to go prowling for boys and some peer-company immediately, but we had to stop them roaring off in the RIB by suggesting that they stood a far better chance of spotting teenagers in daylight!

FIREBIRD, MONDAY

I was up at dawn next morning after a great sleep. Even Sandy had stayed in her own bed for once, making lots of room to stretch out. I treated the decks and fittings to a fresh-water hose-down to get rid of salt accumulation and was joined by Jasper who made his usual noises about going ashore for a romp, even though he'd had plenty of shore leave on Erith Island. So I dutifully lowered the RIB and rowed him the short distance ashore where he had a lovely time chasing seagulls and leaving a few carefully buried treasures well above the tide line. He only managed to frighten one older couple, but then charmed them just as quickly with his corny, *'I'm really just an overgrown kitten'* routine by rolling over on his back, paws curled cutely. Nevertheless, they took some convincing that he wasn't a juvenile black panther. By the time he'd worn himself out and I'd had a run and a workout on the sand as well, I could see movement in the galley.

'Can we take the dinghy and have a look around?' Angie asked, when brekkie was finished and washed up. 'We won't be very long.'

I'd already discussed the security risk with Sandy and Janice, so I nodded. 'Yep. That's okay. But still be careful and do keep an eye on the time. We'd like to walk over to the ocean beach later in the morning so I can try out my surf rod. The fresh fish stocks are getting low.'

They beamed in unison. 'No worries. We'll watch it. But if we meet some nice teens can we invite them back here? I mean, if we get invited on board their boat, we should repay them.'

I shrugged, 'I don't see any problem with that. However, it might be best if you didn't openly invite the parents if you can avoid it without being rude. The less we have to explain the better; however, our general story is that your mother, Sandy and I are old friends and I invited you all on an extended cruise as your Mum has just gone through a divorce and she needed a break. You're getting your Uni assignments by Internet to keep up with lectures and work-load. That's close enough to the truth that you don't have to try to remember a complex set of porky pies.'

They nodded solemnly. 'Good story. Got that.'

A quick toilet visit, and they were off, wearing their most effec-tive boy-attracting gear of tight, slashed shorts and brief bikini tops, while ponytails and ball caps completed the setup. With their sun-bleached almost white hair and dark tans, they did look a lot different to when they joined me in Eden. Still, as a matched pair they were still very distinctive as they purred off in the RIB, Zoe driving as usual.

Janice went to wash her hair, paint nails and other female stuff, while Sandy changed down to one of her bikinis and sat around in the sun, chatting and looking quite delectable, while I replaced the washers in the outdoor shower and cleaned the head. She was such a distraction that I was on the verge of taking her below for a round or three of hide-the-sausage, but I restrained myself, not knowing how long the girls would be cruising for boys.

My relationship with both ladies had changed considerably since the time Sandy and Janice had a D & M discussion. Although I wasn't given much say in the bedtime arrangements, I certainly wasn't complaining. Janice and I still shared the forward cabin, while Sandy joined us most nights, unless we were all very tired. We had discussed the longer-term situation and had come to the very practical and amicable decision that while Janice and the girls would have to return to a more normal life ashore sooner rather than later, we could enjoy the relationship we'd started for now, but Sandy and I perhaps had a more long-lasting relationship in mind. I didn't go into how they resolved things, just happy that there was harmony.

After about an hour, the girls returned, chattering excitedly as they tied up the RIB and came up to tell all.

'What did you discover?' Janice asked.

'Well,' Zoe started, 'there are lots of teens among the various boats and even camping ashore, but most are a lot younger. Some of the older ones didn't seem very sociable, so that cut the choices.'

'There is a sister and her brother who sound really neat,' Angie chipped in, 'They're French, and sailed over from New Caledonia for an extended holiday. They're on that white cat with the blue trim and the black mast on the far side of the anchorage. Their parents are very nice, speak good English and invited us to visit anytime. The brother is very yummy! I really fancy him!'

I chuckled and Janice gave me a motherly glare before she held up her hand. 'Whoa. Settle down you two. You're acting like sex-starved sailors just into port!'

Zoe wailed, 'Mum! But that's exactly what we are! You guys get to have all the nooky you want, wherever you want, while we're stuck with some toys! We're old enough to join the real world!'

Sandy burst into semi-stifled giggles, I laughed outright, and Janice didn't know whether to laugh or cry, but luckily chose laughter.

'Ok. Ok. I suppose we deserved that. Maybe it does seem a bit unfair from your perspective, but you can't just go up to the first good-looking boy you find and drag him off to bed!'

Angie poked a face at her. 'Why not? That's the way all our friends seem to do it! Maybe things were different when you were our age, but times change and perhaps you need to change the way you think about us!'

She sat back after delivering that little speech, while Zoe gave a little 'Yay!' of agreement.

Janice smiled, 'Ok. Of course you're capable of deciding whom you want to go to bed with, but you've got to be a bit selective about it. Particularly the safe sex issue!'

'Mum! C'mon. We're aware of all that! But it's not as though we've got a great deal of choice of partners, now is there? But the French guy, Dominic, really is cute and very nice as well. So is his sister, Helene. She seems to have a really good sense of humour and their parents seem to be very friendly, and liberal-minded, but they do seem a bit odd, in a nice sort of way!' She stopped to giggle then added, 'They even serve them wine with lunch and tea each day! I'm sure you'd all like them, so maybe you should invite them over. I mean, they've got the only other cat here and are from New Caledonia, so I'm sure you'd have lots to talk about.'

Janice held up her hands in surrender. 'Ok. You can ask them over if they want to come. Just give us some warning first. But surely those two weren't the only two teens you saw?'

'Oh, no. There are two brothers we think are about our age or maybe a bit older and are very good looking. They seemed interested in us too, but they said they've been taking a girl from another boat out most days going fishing or swimming or something just up from here, so we may see them go past.'

'OK. That sounds like at least you'll have some others to talk to who aren't involved in trying to kidnap you!' Janice said with a grin to defuse her words.

'Yeah. We'll be fine, Mum. We'll work out who we can invite back here without creating an International incident or having to call the Police.'

Janice wisely left that one alone as we split up to do various jobs or just lie about in the sun like Sandy had gone back to doing. I still felt like whizzing her off down below, but decorum prevailed, so with the plumbing repair attended to, I adjourned to the chart-table to download the latest chart updates I'd been putting off. I was doing so when I noticed the twins had gone for'rard to sunbake topless on the trampoline, while Janice was out back chatting quietly with Sandy.

After a while, my work was interrupted by the sound of a small outboard close-by, followed by a hail. I looked for'rard to see the girls standing by the starboard rail, happy grins on their faces, waving and chattering to the occupants of the dinghy idling close beside us. I stepped forward to the part-open tinted windows to listen and saw that there were two good-looking guys in the dinghy, with a pretty, dark-haired girl in a bikini sitting on the middle seat. It was obvious that the guys were very keenly checking out the twins, although the girl didn't seem to be too put out by having some competition for their attention. I wasn't too sure about the guys, though. They both had plenty of trashy tats and looked to be a lot older than the twins.

'Where are you guys going?' I heard Angie ask, puffing her chest out a little in a vain attempt to match the girl in the dinghy who had a very substantial and well-shaped chest.

'Just up the arm a way,' replied the guy in the bow, fending off from our topsides, 'we found a small beach that others don't seem to go to and it's great for swimming and just messing around. Fishing's good as well, if you're into that.'

'Sounds great,' Zoe chipped in, 'we might buzz up there tomorrow.'

'Yeah. That'd be cool,' replied the bowman with a chuckle, 'you look like you're dressed for a bit of fun in the water.'

Zoe blushed a bit. 'Oh, we always get around like this. It's much more comfortable than wearing clothes all the time.'

'Love your thoughts,' the guy at the outboard spoke for the first time, 'maybe we'll see you up there tomorrow. It's the first little beach beyond this next scrubby stretch.'

'Ok,' said Angie, looking a little put out that he didn't insist they go with them now, 'we might see you then.'

With another long, appraising look at the girls, the two guys and their girlfriend roared off to up the Arm, leaving the twins looking longingly after them. As the dinghy receded in the distance, Zoe came back to the saloon and asked for the binoculars. I handed them over, and then she returned to the trampoline, joining Angie in muttering excuses to each other for not handling the situation well enough.

'That would've been fun,' I heard Zoe exclaim, 'two lovely guys and three girls. She's a lucky bitch having them to herself. I'll bet they do a lot more messing around than swimming or fishing!'

Angie grimaced, 'Yeah. I reckon you're right. She'll be wearing one of them within five minutes of them getting up there, lucky bitch! Did you see the bulges in their shorts?'

Zoe giggled, 'Yeah. They nearly fell out of the dinghy trying to get a better look at us though, even though that bitch has got bigger tits. Let's hope she's a dud fuck, anyway.'

'Maybe. But at least she gets to practice pretty often!'

'Yeah, bugger it!'

As they subsided, still muttering at lost opportunities and swapping the binoculars as they peered after the dinghy, I returned to the chart table, but something about the two guys still didn't sit right with me.

Janice wandered in to see what I was up to and saw the girls still peering up the beach with the binoculars. 'What are they looking at?'

'Those sleazy guys and their girlfriend fooling around from what I can gather. They seem jealous that she's getting the attention of both guys!'

Janice laughed, 'They would! But I must say that I didn't much like the look of them. Too many tats and I reckon it's been years since they were 18!'

'Just what I was thinking,' I chuckled, just as Zoe came back with the binoculars and replaced them carefully in their case.

'Checking on the boy supply?' Janice asked.

'Yeah, we were! But after talking it over, we reckon that those two guys are sleazebags and that girl's a slack tart, so we won't bother seeing them again!'

'Well I'm glad to hear that,' she smiled, putting the kettle on for morning tea.

'But we might run over and visit Dominic and Helene. Or can we bring them back here if they want?'

Janice glanced at me, so I nodded. 'Yeah, sure. Whatever you want to do is fine. Just take care.'

'We will, Mum. Thanks.' And they went below to change, although the result wasn't a lot different.

Things must have been quiet on the French cat, as the twins were back on board within 15 minutes, with Dominic and Helene in tow. Dominic was a good-looking lad of medium height, with dark hair and a strong, stocky build. Helene in contrast, was tall, slim and pretty, very much like the twins, but with long, dark hair. They spoke perfect English with just a slight accent as both attended University in Melbourne, although a different one to that the twins were attending. They were dressed more conservatively than the twins, Dominic in neat shorts and a polo shirt, while Helene wore baggy shorts and a floppy shirt that revealed very little.

We went through the usual introductions to Jasper, with Helene breaking into giggles when he nuzzled her crutch. 'That tickles,' she said.

'Yeah. That gets us too,' Zoe said, 'and, when he gets to know you better, the furry deviate will nuzzle you there all the time! He does with us.'

They politely thanked us for inviting them aboard, as Angie and Zoe bustled around making tea and coffee as required and some basic information was traded. The youngsters were bright, very intelligent and well educated, and held a conversation very easily. It came out that Dominic was 18 and Helene 19, and I couldn't help notice that Dominic enjoyed looking at all the ladies, both older and younger, but he seemed to particularly admire the twins, so there wasn't much wrong with his basic inclinations. As they chatted about their home life, it seemed that they had picked up a typically laid-back continental attitude to sex and nudity from their parents, much like the way the twins viewed things. Then, after tea and coffee was served and the twins sat down with us, Janice asked. 'Did your parents mind you coming over to visit?'

Helene traded an amused look with Dominic, then giggled, 'Oh, no. They're happy to have any quiet time alone they can.'

Dominic explained with rather startling candour, 'Dad's a psychiatrist specialising in sex therapy and has just started experimenting with a new-type of synthetic testosterone that a biochemist friend in France invented. The tests were going well, until Dad decided to see what would happen if he doubled the dose, but it's had some weird side effects!'

Janice raised her eyebrows, as much at the very personal revelation about people we hadn't met, as wanting to know what the weird effects could be.

'Why would he want to try doubling the dose?' she asked.

Helene giggled at the look on her face, 'Most of his male patients have issues with sexual performance and some those who he prescribed testosterone for overdosed with some weird effects. So, Dad wanted to try this new version to see if he could eliminate the side effects of overdosing.

He had to use this time away from his normal work schedule, since it's turned him into a male nympho! He's got an erection most of the time and needs sex four times a day, every day! Mum loved it for a while, and she says she still does, but we can see she's getting tired and a bit sore. But Dad needs the trial to run its full course so he can see if there are any other side effects, which means we have to put up with another ten days of them having sex every time he needs to, which is often in odd places at odd times.'

It was such a bizarre story that we all had a good laugh at their parent's expense.

Dominic finished the tale with a chuckle, 'And a 44 ft cat is a bit small for us to dodge them every time, so although it's been an interesting learning experience, we get off the boat as often as we can to save tripping over our parents! Anyway, Mum and Dad can still laugh about it, since we all got over the embarrassment bit after the first couple of days.'

I couldn't help chuckling, 'It sounds to me like a great thing, but I guess some things can be overdone!'

Both Janice and Sandy leant over and smacked me on the arm, grinning as they did. 'Bloody chauvinist pig,' Sandy said.

But then to our embarrassment, Angie candidly explained, 'Harry sleeps with both Mum and Sandy most nights.'

Both our visitors looked impressed with that. 'Really?' Dominic said with renewed interest, eyeing Sandy and Janice off afresh, 'that's cool!'

I quickly stalled that line of questioning by asking about their boat and the trip over from New Caledonia.

'Pretty easy,' Helene replied, 'it's an Antares 44 and Dad says that it's really well designed, so we have plenty of room and it sails quite well. We mostly had light winds and slight seas, so it was much the same as sailing around the islands back home. There was a bit of a blow north of New Zealand, but it didn't last very long and the boat stayed dry and warm. Coming in through the bar here was probably the most exciting thing, since the wind was against the tide and that made the waves stand up, then just flop over. We took a few on board, but it wasn't a problem. And as you know, cats run straight on waves, so it was all rather fun.'

I agreed and said, 'Well, after all that, you're welcome to come and go here as you please, whenever you want.'

The girls agreed enthusiastically, while Dominic and Helene smiled and thanked us before they all went for'rard to the trampoline to chat about young adult stuff. I went back to updating charts, and checked on them occasionally, but they seemed to get on extremely well. The girls obviously had the hots for Dominic, or just Dom as he preferred to be called, and Helene seemed happy to sit back, obviously used to the effect her good-looking brother had on other girls.

It was pleasantly warm outside in the sun and wasn't long before the girls stripped down a bit, conservatively for them, just to basic bikinis. Helene happily followed suit, removing the baggy shorts and shirt to reveal a beautiful, tanned body in a tiny bikini, the top of which struggled gamely to hold her bigger breasts. Dom removed his shirt to reveal a good tan and an impressive set of muscles that the twins openly admired and promptly poked at and felt. He didn't seem to mind in the slightest.

Getting tired of playing with charts, I was happy to be interrupted by the buzz of an outboard approaching at high-speed. It slowed as it got close and I saw the twins sit up with a marked lack of enthusiasm and wave without bothering to get up. I couldn't hear what was said, but the girls weren't encouraging, so the motor revved up again and they were gone.

The four teens huddled together and there was much laughter and arm waving. Soon, Angie came aft and said, 'They wanted to know if we were going to go with them tomorrow, but when they saw Dom and Helene, they changed their minds and pissed off.'

'Excellent. Good riddance.'

'Yeah. After what we saw this morning through the binoculars, we're not missing much.' She went back up for'rard and chatter resumed.

Our visitors stayed the morning, the four teens talking and laying on the trampoline in the sun, and it wasn't long before the three girls had shed their tops and Dom was down to small, tight-fitting bikini thing that attracted a lot of openly hungry glances from both girls. When they got too hot, they went swimming off the stern, with Jasper enthusiastically joining in the splashing and wrestling. When they got out, we chuckled at the antics of the twins who were taking turns to hose Dom, although I didn't bother telling them to save the water, since Jasper was getting washed down as well. They finally finished playing with the shower, and traipsed for'rard, not bothering to dry off, all three girls flushed and excited and Dom apparently very happy to be the centre of female attention.

Late in the morning, Angie came aft to ask if Dom and Helene could stay for lunch and we all sat around the cockpit enjoying Angie's tasty smoked-salmon, cream cheese and capers sandwiches on fresh-baked bread. The after-lunch clean-up had just been completed, when a small dinghy puttered up to us with a man and woman aboard.

'Oh, look,' said Helene, 'here's Mum and Dad. Can they come aboard?'

'Of course,' I replied, hastening down to take their mooring rope. They were a striking couple; Yvette was tall, dark and slender, while Anton was short, dark and stocky. Yvette wore a wrap-around piece of filmy material as a brief skirt and a brief bikini top; Anton was wearing an oversize shirt with an eye-watering display of many colours and designs. He appeared to be wearing little else under that, although to my relief, I caught a glimpse of what appeared to be a very brief pair of bikini pants that were trying to contain a part-erection.

I tried not to stare as I welcomed them aboard, but it was difficult as apart from Anton's bizarre attire, Yvette was very attractive and it would seem that she had forgotten to put panties on before she came to visit. Regardless of their attire, they turned out to be totally charming people and we spent the rest of the afternoon happily swapping tales of cat sailing, storms and funny moments. We had to be careful when talking about our last few weeks of island and port hopping, in case they talked to the wrong persons, but I think we successfully avoided rousing suspicions.

Although Yvette was very pretty, Anton spent a lot of time looking at Janice and Sandy and didn't mind checking out the twins either, since they hadn't bothered to put their tops back on since the morning's swim. Yvette seemed very tolerant of Anton's wandering eye, regarding him fondly when he seemed to be getting overly close to either Janice or Sandy.

The four teens had quickly returned to the bow once Yvette and Anton were settled and it looked like they were going to stay for a while.

'You are a very fortunate men to have such beautiful and sexy companions, M. Harry.' Anton commented.

'Thank you, Anton. I am indeed truly lucky. But, as you can imagine, it does take a lot to keep up with them.'

That earned me a look from both ladies to see if I was being facetious, but I controlled my facial muscles and avoided a whack or two.

'Ah, yes. Of course, but if you had this treatment that I am currently testing, you would have the stamina of five men, and they would be the ones trying to keep up with you.'

The ladies giggled and Yvette leant over and patted Anton on the leg. 'Yes, my darling, but maybe Harry doesn't want to walk around with an erection most of the day. He does, I believe, wish to behave correctly in front of their young ladies.'

Anton nodded, 'But of course. I forget myself. Our own young adults are familiar with our sexual behaviour, but perhaps yours aren't?'

Janice answered that one, 'In some ways the twins are, Anton, but although I have always encouraged nudity, I have tried to avoid them watching live sex.'

'Ah. The moderating voice of the Mother and I cannot argue with that. What works for us may not be to your taste. No problem.'

The Bernard family stayed for the 17:00 drinks session but declined the offer of dinner and took their leave. Angie asked if Dom and Helene could return in the morning and Janice gave the OK. We'd all had an interesting day and the evening was filled with little stories about our new friends, although discussion about Anton took up a lot of the time. Everyone had a giggle or two about Yvette's lack of underwear, which had been noticed by all, but in favourable terms, as her personality and sense of humour had been a real delight.

CHAPTER 61

Since I'd missed out on yesterday's planned trip through to the beach to try some surf fishing, I told the crew at breakfast that we would go this morning.

'Can we drop you guys ashore and then get Dom and Helene?' Angie asked after breakfast.

'It's okay by me,' I answered, smiling at her, while Janice agreed and added, 'you all seem to be getting on very well.'

'Oh, yes. We are. They're really fun and interesting to talk to.'

'Are you going to join us over on the ocean beach, or go do your own thing?'

She gave a little grin, 'If you don't mind, we might go and explore along the arm. It seems to go a long way back toward Lakes Entrance.'

I smiled, 'No problem, but you might like to fill the outboard tank before you go. If we come back early, we can almost wade out to *Firebird*, but otherwise, if you can be back by midday, that'll be fine. Just keep an eye out for those tattooed characters. I reckon they'd cause trouble if they find you four alone.'

She nodded seriously, 'Good thinking. We'll be careful and thanks, Harry.'

So the girls dropped us off on the beach, Jasper included, and puttered away happily toward the far side of the anchorage. We walked the short distance along a well-defined track through the coastal sand dunes to the vast open and un-spoiled stretches of Ninety Mile Beach. To our surprise, there were more people on the surfside than at the anchorage. Some were swimming, some surfing, some fishing and others in large family groups setting up BBQ's or just laying around. There were even a few tents set up back in the dunes for some protection from the sea breezes, although that wasn't a problem for now as the next cold front was still a day or two away.

The ladies had packed a small hamper for morning tea along with a blanket to sit on, so we set up camp on the edge of the dunes, away from the main crowd. I told Jasper that he had to behave and stay away from other people so he didn't scare them. I guess he understood because he huffed loudly at me, before bounding off to chase an errant seagull that had dared to land on the sand nearby. With those domestic chores out of the way, I set about rigging my 15 ft surf rod.

There was a nicely defined gutter beyond the shore break that looked as if it might have some predatory fish travelling through looking for small prey, so I started casting a slice lure in there. It took about 30 minutes for the first couple of hits, but then I picked up a nice Jewfish that weighed about 4kg. Two smaller ones followed, one of which Jasper pinched and sat chewing it just out of reach, growling at me every time I tried to take it off him. The ladies thought that was very amusing and wandered along the beach a way before going in for a swim. In their bikinis, they attracted their fair share of admirers, although most stayed away from the cranky old fisherman with the big, black dog with the very long tail.

Morning tea on the beach was very civilised with my two lovely ladies and my beautiful big, black cat who had got over his earlier hissy fit. Two young kids wandered over to pat the 'dog' and were innocent enough to be utterly delighted to find that he was a cat. They stayed for quite a while playing with Jasper who was very excited to have little people to play with. He even let them sit on his back, one at a time and have a ride, until one of the parents came over to collect them expressing horror that I dared to bring a vicious, wild animal onto a public beach.

'Yes, I can see your point about the danger of having a vicious wild animal in a public area, but perhaps you need to ask your daughter about how dangerous the creature is that's letting her ride around on his back. Or perhaps you should get your son's opinion once he's finished getting dragged around the beach by hanging onto that vicious animal's tail. It's also a pity you weren't here earlier when your daughter was pulling on Jasper's tongue, amongst all those razor-sharp teeth.'

She was a bit taken back by my mild, but heavily sarcastic response, but thankfully had the sense to hear what I said and think about it. Fortunately, Jasper and the daughter co-operated by walking past with the girl on his back, the little girl squealing with delight as the little boy pulled his tail. Jasper looked up at the Mother with a dopey grin on his face, then continued on, moving carefully so as not to spill the little girl off even though she was bouncing up and down with excitement.

'Ah, yes. I do see your point, but what sort of cat is he to be as big as that, if he's not the cub of one of the big jungle cats?'

So, I launched into my set speech about Jasper's origins and slightly obscure bloodline and managed to turn her indignation and fear into interest and then finally delight when Jasper came over, sans child, to be patted and scratched.

'I must admit that he certainly behaves just like a normal domestic cat. We have two cats at home so we're used to feline habits.'

'That's it,' I replied, 'apart from his size, he is a normal cat.' I left out the part about him mauling then partly eating a man recently in defence of his family.

I left Jasper playing with the kids and their mother and went back to fishing. With a large and a small jewie in the bag already, another few somethings would be great for a couple of fresh fish meals. Since we'd left Erith Island, the girls had been a bit slack in the fishing department, so we needed to re-stock. Another half hour and I had three more fish, a 3 kg salmon and another two jewfish. Figuring that was enough, as it seemed that there would be no problem getting more, I packed up the rod and helped the ladies with the rest of the gear.

Jasper said goodbye to his new playmates and we trekked back over the dunes to the inner beach, where Zoe was waiting with the dinghy.

'Did you catch anything?' she asked, then ooh'ed and aahh'ed over the bucket full of big fish.

'Did you guys have fun?' Janice asked in turn.

'Oh, yes. We picked up Helene and Dom and went quite a long way up Bunga Arm. There's good water almost right to the end; certainly plenty for *Firebird*, if you wanted to go there, and there are lots of little beaches and coves. There seem to be several camping grounds on the ocean side and clusters of people with boats, but not as busy as here.'

By the time she'd told us all that, we were tied up at the stern platform and unloading our gear. Angie, Helene and Dom came aft to help, with Angie being very appreciative of the fish, and started to plan a menu around them already. I noticed that they were all happy, but Angie looked particularly pleased with herself.

Dom and Helene stayed for lunch, but asked to be taken back home soon after, saying that they'd see us tomorrow, as their parents wanted them to join in visiting some other boaties they'd just met. Soon after they returned, Angie came up to me with a strange expression on her face and handed me a mobile phone.

'This is Helene's. There's a video on it that I'd like you to download onto a flash drive for me, if you don't mind. Don't worry about the photos, just the video.'

'Ok. I'll do it shortly.'

'That's good, thanks Harry. And I don't mind if you look at it, if you want.'

I raised my eyebrows, but said nothing, as she joined Zoe up on the foredeck. My curiosity aroused, I sat down at the chart table and made the appropriate connections. There were a bunch of photos on there, most of Helene and Dom's friends, but tucked in amongst them, with today's date, was a video file that I commenced to transfer to a 8GB flash drive.

As the transfer started, I selected monitor and immediately saw that, as expected, it was of the morning's excursion. It started with a small beach, then panned around to show Angie and Dom cuddling up together on a blanket spread on the sand.

The quality was extremely good and after clothes were shed, it showed in graphic detail Angie losing her virginity with Dom. He appeared to be a careful and considerate lover and Angie looked very happy throughout. High resolution made it obvious that he didn't use a condom and equally obvious that Angie placed total faith in her birth-control measures.

I didn't save a copy, but completed the transfer, verified that it wasn't corrupted and took the flash drive and phone to her on the foredeck.

'Here you are,' I said with a smile, 'all done. Nice bit of work that,' I added cryptically, 'but I didn't save a copy and I've not said anything to your mum or Sandy.'

She jumped up and hugged me. 'Thanks, Harry. It was actually pretty terrific, and I can understand now what everyone else has been enjoying.'

I smiled at her enthusiasm and went aft.

We had a quiet afternoon and at some point, Angie told Janice and Sandy who came to see me soon afterwards.

'Angie says that there's a video of ah…the event,' Janice asked with a grin.

'Yep. I transferred it off Helene's phone onto a flash drive, deleted it from the phone and gave Angie the drive. What she chooses to do with it is her business, but it solves one problem for us.'

'What's that?' asked Janice.

Sandy chuckled, 'I know what you're going to say. There's now video evidence that she's no longer a virgin and therefore the big deal that Luke planned for them is null and void.'

'Oh, yes. Of course,' Janice remembered, 'but what about Zoe!'

I chuckled evilly, 'Ah yes, however there's still tomorrow. And Dom and Helene have planned to come over in the morning again. Excuse the pun.'

Sandy kicked me in the shin, 'Smart arse!'

Janice didn't know whether to look concerned or cool, so I jumped in early.

'Now before you become Mrs Righteous Mum, just remember what they told you a few days ago. They're old enough to make up their own minds, and Dom and Helene are too. I suggest that you say nothing, sit back and let nature take its course.'

She thought about that and finally nodded, 'You're right. I don't have to do anything and things will work out alright.'

'Well said,' Sandy offered, 'that's exactly the right thing.'

Angie and Zoe were in high spirits and Angie grilled some of the fresh fish with a lime butter sauce and salad for dinner.

After dinner, as some sort of celebration, I did the NQ tea routine, even allowing the girls one strong one each and we drunkenly played board games until realising that we were all tired and retired to bed quite early. Sandy had only just joined Janice and I, when I heard a subdued, very deep rumbling that sounded like another boat had just arrived, but as Sandy was doing things that demanded my attention, I pushed the incident aside to concentrate on the matters in hand. So to speak!

CHAPTER 62

They had arrived after dark, the radar helping them avoid running over any anchored boats, although the lights from them showed the way. Dave allowed the big boat to idle slowly into the crowded little anchorage, then decided to drop anchor well out from the rest. Cheerful, drunken voices echoed across the water as dinghies buzzed to and fro, transferring one drunken party to yet more booze and another drunken party.

'This looks like fun,' commented Jackie as she stood up on a cockpit seat to see the festivities, while Dave picked a clear spot to anchor.

'Yes. It usually is when a bunch of boaties gets together. That's part of the attraction of boating; everyone just wants to have fun! Therefore, no arguments, no fights, and few dramas.'

'Can we go meet some of these people and maybe join in?' she asked.

'Sure, we can and we will, but not tonight. There's nothing worse than walking into a party where everybody's pissed except you! Tonight, we'll have a few drinks and a feed on-board.'

'Oh, okay. We'd better go organise dinner then.'

'That'd be great, thanks. I'll be down shortly to ply the chefs with strong liquor and lots of encouragement.'

'Lovely man. We'll be waiting.'

Corrine poked him in the ribs; 'Much more of that soppy bullshit and you'll be sharing your bed with two very randy girls tonight.'

'Oh, really?'

'Yes, really! Of course, you could always allow your immediate boss to join you in that oversized bed and that might keep the desperate maidens at bay.'

'Oh,' he said, eyeing her off speculatively, 'is that so?'

She smiled smugly, 'That's so. Unless you want the nympho twins to do the honours.'

'Hmmm. Perhaps not. You're on.'

'Good choice,' she purred, 'now, let's get this thing bedded down and join the cooks for a drink or three. We can't do much else tonight.'

Dave stood up where Jackie had been, peering around trying to see what boats were there, but it was too dark and crowded, so he reluctantly gave up and went below to help Corrine and the girls put a dent in Xavier's booze supply. Allie and Jackie whipped up a lovely meal of rib-eye fillet steak in a red wine sauce, peas and corn and baby potatoes. They found an apple pie in the freezer and served that hot for dessert with ice cream melting over the top. Dave kept them well supplied with wine and they quickly became pissed. It probably was an after-effect of the drugs from the night before so he kept their glasses topped in the hope that they'd crash early.

In the event, that was what happened and after they all helped with the clean-up, Allie and Jackie almost fell asleep over coffees and disappeared into their cabin straight after.

Dave eyed Corrine as they finished off their coffees. 'Now they've crashed, you don't have to protect me. I don't think they'll stir until morning.'

She glared back, 'Are you rejecting me?'

'Ahh...No. But I thought that if you were just being nice before, you don't have to go through with it.'

She patted him on the arm, kissed his cheek and said, 'Silly man. Come on. I feel like lots of loving tonight.'

FIREBIRD...BUNGA ARM, GIPPSLAND LAKES, WEDNESDAY AM
I took my time getting up, as both the bed and the company were way too inviting for any foolishness like pre-dawn deck washing.

Consequently, it was Zoe who arrived bearing steaming mugs of tea, after loudly announcing herself in case she was interrupting something.

'Come on, sleepy heads,' she chanted, 'it's a lovely day, the sun's shining and the warm north wind doth blow!'

Her mother poked her head up from the doona, 'You're in disgustingly high spirits this morning, but thanks for the tea.'

'No problem. Brekkie will be on in 15 minutes if you can drag your bodies out of bed.'

'OK. We'll be there.'

We went aft one at a time to pee and wash, then joined the girls in the cockpit where they'd laid out a full cooked breakfast of bacon, sausages, scrambled eggs and tomatoes. I wasn't so sleepy that I couldn't have a look around and spotted the source of the rumbling I'd heard last night.

'That's a very nice boat,' I commented, 'it looks like an Italian AB 68. It's a pretty rare beast in Australia.'

'Sure looks fast,' Sandy mumbled around a mouthful of bacon.

'They are. At least it's a proper boat, not another top-heavy gin palace,' I grumbled, sitting down to eat.

'Get off your soapbox, dear, and eat up. You need to get your strength back,' suggested Janice.

'Ha, ha,' I poked my tongue out at her, before getting stuck into the excellent food.

With breakfast disposed of, I asked the girls what they were doing for the day.

Zoe busied herself clearing plates away, leaving Angie to answer, 'We'll go and pickup Helene and Dom soon and head back up the Arm, if you don't need the dinghy.'

I nodded, 'That's okay. I need to do an oil change on the starboard engine, that'll keep me busy.'

'I'm in the middle of a great book,' said Janice.

'And I'll swim ashore and go for a run on the ocean beach,' Sandy said, 'so no problem for us.'

'Great, thanks guys.'

With almost indecent haste, they cleaned up, packed their gear and buzzed off in the dinghy. I was still in the cockpit a few minutes later, when I spotted them heading east up the arm, but taking a detour out around the anchored mass of slowly stirring boats, presumably to check out the sleek new arrival that was dominating the anchorage with its slightly menacing presence.

I grinned at the ladies, 'I guess I'll have another video to transfer later.'

Janice looked sad, 'I know I shouldn't, but I can't help feeling that our lives over the last few weeks have been in so much in turmoil that the girls have lost their relatively young innocence. I mean the mental thing, not the physical. I'm not worried about that anymore.'

Sandy nodded agreement, 'I can understand that, but from what I see, they're coping just fine. They're treating it as one big adventure so far.'

Janice thought, then finally agreed and let her misgivings float away astern with the dropping tide.

We all got on with our activities, or inactivity in Janice's case. The oil change went well and I was finished in 40 minutes, joining Janice in the cockpit in time to line up for a fresh mug of tea. Sandy was still ashore, although I thought I saw her trotting back up from the beach. I also saw the AB 68 up-anchor and slowly rumble its way east up the Arm, although the tinted windows were too dark to see how many were on board. It gave me a slightly funny feeling watching the long, low red boat rumbling quietly along in the same direction the teens had gone, and I decided to discuss it with our Security Chief. I'd barely finished that thought and my tea, when Sandy hauled herself up onto the stern platform, attracting everyone's attention when she unconcernedly stripped down completely to wash off.

SEEKER — BUNGA ARM, GIPPSLAND LAKES, WEDNESDAY
The *Seeker* crew all slept in for one reason or another and the sun was well up before Dave reluctantly dragged himself out of Corrine's

sleepy embrace. He was feeling very pleased with himself and happy that he'd met Corrine and that they got along so well.

Unless a very good actress, she had enjoyed last night and this morning just as much as he did. He was still curious about the ugly scar he'd felt, then seen, along her right side, but she wouldn't say how or why.

Dave surveyed the new day in solitude from the cockpit as he sipped his tea. The anchorage was only just starting to stir, with just a few dinghies shuttling sleepy crew back and forth. One dinghy caught his eye since it was really zipping through the cluster of boats. There were two girls in it so he tracked them to a pretty 40-odd foot cat on the western side of the anchorage. They picked up two persons then accelerated away, curving in an arc to pass close by *Seeker*. He stood to get a clear view and almost spilled his coffee when he saw who was in the dinghy.

He was almost certain that two girls were the ones he and Corrine were looking for! Despite their dark tans and sun-bleached hair, he saw their faces clearly as they whizzed past just metres away, giving a cheery wave as they went.

A well-built boy and another pretty, dark-haired girl were the other passengers.

'*Holy shit!*' Dave muttered to himself. '*How about that! Jagged the targets on the first try.*'

He hadn't seen where the dinghy came from, but that didn't matter for now as he headed for the main cabin to wake his new bedmate with the news. That was where he learned that Corrine wasn't a morning person, and that it would take more than a tender whisper in her ear to stir her into action. Stripping the bedclothes off just provoked threats of violence directed at his tender bits. Finally, she sat up after he restored the bedclothes, the jiggling of her breasts as she yawned and stretched holding his attention while it stirred his loins yet again.

'What the fuck's wrong with you, waking me up in the middle of the night?' she snarled.

'It's not the middle of the night, it's 09:30 in the morning and I've just spotted the targets!'

That shut her up as she stared in disbelief, then flung the covers aside and swung out of bed.

'Well, why the hell didn't you say so at the start?' she asked, dragging on shorts and a T-shirt without bothering about underwear.

Dave shrugged, enjoying the view until it was covered up, then walked out, saying over his shoulder, 'I've got a hot mug of coffee ready for you.'

'Bloody hell man. You could've told me that a bit earlier too!' She followed him out of the main stateroom and then kissed him tenderly as he handed over the fragrant, steaming mug.

'Thanks for last night. I've not enjoyed myself so much in a long time. And in case you're wondering, I want to do it again tonight.'

Slightly taken aback by her shift of moods, Dave was nevertheless very pleased to hear that. With mugs in hand, and Corrine revived by the caffeine, they finally started planning.

'So where did they go?' Corrine asked.

'I didn't see exactly. After they picked up the other two young people, they swung past here and went up the Arm, but they can't go too far since it's a dead end. They must be at one of the little beaches along the shore.'

'There was just the four of them?'

'Yep. The two girls plus the two from the cat on the west side of the anchorage.'

Corrine thought a moment. 'I reckon we should go and grab them now. There should only be the other two as witnesses, and we can bring them all back here.'

It was Dave's turn to think. 'If we bring them back here in the dinghy, everyone will see us. That's way too much exposure in a public anchorage. How about we take *Seeker* up the Arm so we can put them straight on board without any other eyes on us?'

Corrine smiled approvingly, 'Great idea. Will it take long to get this thing moving?'

'Nah! Just a few minutes since we'll only be idling up there.'

'Do it!'

Five minutes later, the anchor clunked up into the stowed position and *Seeker* slowly eased away, the engines note not changing from their deep, rumbling idle as the jet drive buckets hissed hydraulically into the full-up position. Dave steered well clear of the other boats, although he looked over at the two boats he thought were where the girls had come from. There was a naked woman towelling herself dry in the cockpit of a big catamaran that was distracting, except that Corrine grabbed his nuts in one slim little hand and squeezed gently.

'Focus, big fella! Watch where we're going.'

The noise of the engines starting and the rattle of the anchor chain had finally roused their two passengers, who emerged full of questions, so Corrine filled them in.

The news galvanised them into immediate action and a few minutes later, they were back in the wheelhouse, dressed about as well as Corrine.

Once clear of the other boats, Dave edged over to the right side of the Arm, sure that the kids had gone to a beach on the opposite side, away from the frequent campsites spread along the ocean-side shore. They had to go nearly 5km before Dave spotted a RIB dinghy pulled up on a patch of sandy beach tucked away behind a small spit of scrubby sand poking out into the Arm. It was the first really secluded spot they'd come across and the dinghy was the only one on that side of the Arm.

'I bet that's them,' Dave announced confidently, 'so how close do you want *Seeker*?'

'How about right on the outside of that little point,' Corrine replied, looking carefully at the figures laying out on the sand, one of whom was now sitting up, no doubt cursing the thoughtless arseholes who were parking right on top of their little hideaway.

'If you cut the engines and drop the anchor quickly, we can run ashore and grab them.'

'How are you going to convince them to come with you?' Jackie asked seriously.

By way of answer, Corrine lifted the hem of her shirt and showed the intimidating black shape of a PMR-30 pistol shoved into her waistband.

'Yep,' said Jackie, 'I reckon that'll do it. I guess we should stay here?'

'Yes please. You might like to open the crew cabin hatch. We'll stow them all there for now. I checked it the other day for possible weapons and you cleaned it yesterday.'

Jackie nodded as Dave reversed briefly, then cut the engines and immediately dropped the anchor with just enough chain to stop them drifting. Both were in the dinghy a minute later and motoring slowly into the bay. As they approached, the other three sat up and Dave noted that all were naked and didn't bother rushing to get dressed.

Parking their dinghy beside the other, they walked up to the group as the boy, who Corrine noted with interest was very well built, challenged them.

'Surely you can find your own quiet beach, without having to crowd onto ours?'

Smiling disarmingly at him, Corrine replied, 'Normally yes, and I apologise for the intrusion, but I'm afraid that you have something we need.'

'And what might that be?' the boy asked, a note of alarm sounding in his voice.

'We know!' One of the pretty blonde girls said in a disgusted voice, 'These arseholes want Zoe and me. There's a contract been put out on us by our dear, paedophile father and these mercenary scum, who don't give a shit about us, are here to collect their reward.'

By now they had all scrambled to their feet, but the action of Corrine drawing her gun out of her waistband abruptly halted any thought of resistance.

'That's better,' she said, 'Dave is going to check your clothes for phones and weapons, then we'd like all of you to get dressed and come with us. Right now! I really don't want to hurt anyone, but I will if I have to.'

She looked at the dark-haired girl and the boy, 'You're not part of the deal and we're sorry you've become involved, but unfortunately, you'll have to come along for now. We'll get you safely back to your parents as soon as we can.'

Dave could see that although shock was setting in, Corrine's reasonable tone kept them calm as they quickly dressed. Dave found a phone, but that was all they had on them.

'Please get aboard your dinghy. Leave the motor tilted and definitely don't attempt to start it. We'll tow you out to our boat and I'll have the gun on you at all times.'

'You won't shoot,' one of the twins said, 'you need us in one piece!'

'That's correct. But your two friends are a little more expendable and I won't hesitate to shoot. Nothing fatal, mind, but a nasty little leg or arm wound is extremely unpleasant, I can assure you. So please behave.'

Although all four looked sullen, it seemed that resistance had been quashed for the moment, as they boarded the dinghy without further protest. Dave took their bow rope, pulled it up short and with Corrine pointing the pistol at Helene, they slowly motored the short distance to *Seeker*.

Jackie and Allie were waiting to help the four captives out of their dinghy, while Corrine kept her gun in plain sight as she herded them forward.

'Up for'rard, please, right up to the bow and down through the open hatch into the crew's cabin. You have water and a toilet, but this hatch is the only way out and will be secured. If you try to scream, we'll come and hurt someone, so please don't do anything stupid.'

'You really don't know what you're doing or what's involved,' one of the twins said, 'I wish you'd let me explain the full situation.'

'For now, dear girl, I'm afraid that the only situation you must understand is that I need you down in that cabin and being very quiet. Maybe you'll get a chance to have your say later, or maybe not. But in the meantime, please behave or it's hurt time. However, I do have one question and it's in your interest to answer it truthfully. Which boat did you come off?'

The twins looked at each other, until one nodded slightly. 'The big cat, *Firebird*.'

Corrine nodded, 'Thank you. I presume that your mother is on board?'

'Yes.'

'Good. In that case we will be informing her directly of developments, so she won't start making a fuss because you haven't returned from your boating trip. Now, get down below and behave or else.'

With that threat hanging over them, they filed down below and the hatch was secured from outside.

Dave looked carefully around and couldn't see that anybody was interested in them, so they moved aft. 'What now?' he asked Corrine when they were all back in the cockpit.

'I think that before we do anything else, we need to send those other two kids back to their parents.'

'Fair enough, but aren't they going to raise the alarm?'

'Sure they will. But if we stop briefly at the big cat to tell the mother first, can we then head straight for Melbourne?'

'Yes, we can. The tanks are full, so we just have to drop Jackie and Allie off in Lakes Entrance, then head out.' He looked at the two ladies, 'Sorry about the shortened Lakes' cruise, girls, but our work here is almost done.'

Jackie shrugged, 'I suppose we can't complain. You didn't have to bring us in the first place, so we can go back into the Motel. It won't be as exciting as kidnapping people at gunpoint, but we'll manage.'

Dave gave her a strained look then left them to get *Seeker* underway.

CHAPTER 63

I told Sandy and Janice about the curious sight of the AB 68 motoring slowly east up the Arm, including my feelings of unease. It wasn't time to expect the teens back from their excursion, so we didn't really have anything to be worried about. That was until I saw the long, lean red shape coming back down the Arm, two dinghies towing astern and aiming straight for us.

'Sandy. We might have trouble; load up please. Quickly.'

As she dropped the towel and dashed below, I released the hidden latch I'd recently installed on the helm seat base, lifted the cushion and fished out the little Mini-Uzi we'd acquired two attacks ago. Slipping a magazine into it, I held it down beside my leg, as Sandy reappeared in the cockpit in a pair of shorts, her Glock 22 in a Police-issue holster around her waist. By that time, the AB 68 was curving slowly around, the driver apparently aiming for our stern. They even had a fender already hung over their bow. What appeared to be a small girl was standing in the bow of the AB ready to jump down, a pistol in one hand pointing down by her side, so Sandy and I stepped back to the top of the stern steps, lifting our weapons as well. As the big boat came to rest with its pointed bow gently kissing our stern, the small girl who jumped lightly down onto our deck, turned out to be a short, adult female whom I instantly recognised.

'Corrine? What the hell are you doing here?'

She stared then cried, 'Harry! Fucking hell, Harry! I can't believe it. Is it really you?' She hurriedly stuffed the PMR-30 into her waistband, before rushing forward to grab me in a tight embrace. 'Oh, Harry, you darling man. It's so good to see you again.'

Sandy had already raised her Glock, ready to repel an attack, but backed off when she saw Corrine with tears of happiness streaming down her cheeks, still hugging me.

'Ahh...I gather that you two know each other,' she said dryly.

I nodded over Corrine's head, which was still jammed against my chest, while prying her off me was like getting a limpet off a rock. 'Yes, we do know each other, but perhaps we'd better secure that overgrown speedboat to a stern cleat first and get the driver to shut the engines down before he does something stupid. There would appear to be some explaining to do!'

Corrine finally let me go, scrambled back aboard and talked to the driver who shut down the engines but remained out of sight. I was pleased that when she re-appeared, she'd left the pistol behind, but presumed that the driver was armed and watching. After appraising the situation, Sandy holstered her Glock, and took the time to throw a shirt on. We sat around the cockpit table and it was Sandy who kicked the ball into play.

'Ok, Harry. First up, you'd better explain how you know this lady who boards us with a gun in hand. Regardless of it being the 21st Century, I think it's still called piracy!'

I made basic introductions, 'cause names are always better than calling each other something else.

'Corrine joined up with my squad in Afghanistan when we got into a bit of a mess.'

Corrine butted in, 'I'll tell this bit, 'cause Harry always leaves stuff out. But it's still just the short version. I was part of a squad tracking down some Taliban top-level bad guys, when we were ambushed and their bodyguards opened up with a well-sited heavy machine gun in good cover that quickly chewed away at our really crappy cover of a dry-stone wall.

So dear Harry, who'd arrived with another small squad to bail us out, jumped up and ran back and forth in the open, firing at them. That drew their fire so most of the guys could fall back to better cover so they could lay down suppressing fire. Luckily the bad guys were mostly rotten shots, but Harry still got hit.

I couldn't move since I'd already copped a bullet through my side, so Harry came by, casual as you like, asked me if I was comfortable, or would I like to join my squad mates. When I explained that I had a bit of a problem moving, he slung me over his shoulder and we managed to get clear with the help of covering fire from our guys. It turned out that the couple of hits Harry took meant he wasn't as healthy as he pretended to be either, but our guys were able to call in air support who wiped out the rest of the bad guys before we copped any more aggro.

We also found out later that while he was prancing around drawing enemy fire, Harry had topped two top-level bad guys, so our 'brass' were rather impressed.

I was too, after the medics told me that I wouldn't have lasted much longer without getting the hole in my side plugged up, so I reckon Harry saved my life. I sort of owe him for that.'

Sandy and Janice looked at me a bit wide-eyed. 'Is that how it went down?' Janice asked.

'Yeah. I guess so. Pretty much,' I mumbled, feeling rather uncomfortable about being made out to be a hero, 'but I'm not sure about the 'prancing around' bit!'

That was good for a chuckle to lighten the mood slightly, but there was a long way to go to sort out this clusterfuck.

'Ok,' Sandy said, assuming the role of moderator, 'that covers the who's who bit. Now we need to know what you guys are doing running around with guns, and maybe you can explain where our four young people are, seeing as you're towing our RIB behind that red Italian sex symbol!'

Corrine grimaced, 'Without anybody getting excited, and remember that my driver is armed, we have the four teens and they are safe and well.'

Janice shot to her feet, eyes blazing and would have attacked Corrine across the table if I hadn't held her back. Her fit of coughing made me belatedly realise that I was still holding the Mini-Uzi and had held Janice back with the barrel tip in her throat.

'Oops, sorry about that. But please sit down and let's hear the whole story before we take any action.' I still kept a hold of the Uzi, despite my words.

Corrine resumed, 'As I was saying, they are all safe and well, but I need to hear a lot more from you guys, before I tell our story. All I have so far is that one of the twins said something about us 'not knowing the full story' and 'paedophile father'.

Janice sat, but still glared a torrent of pure venom across the table at Corrine as she growled,

'If you've harmed just one hair on their heads, I'll track you down and kill you if it's the last thing I ever do!'

'Oh, cut the melodramatic threats, for Christ's sake,' Corrine said wearily, 'I've already said they're in perfect health, so please, can we move on?'

Janice muttered a few more very rude things before sitting back, her mouth tightly clamped in full-on chook's bum mode.

My quick assessment of the situation was that Corrine would be amenable to reason, as long as she got the truth, so without consulting the others, I told the condensed version of the story, but made sure she got all the information on Luke, the paedophile ring, the Melbourne mansion and the involvement by the top levels of ACP, various police, politicians and celebrities. I included a brief account of each of the three attacks leading up to today, as well as the demise of the two Steel Associates operatives.

'So that's what happened to them. Stupid pricks. Bloody Peter always was an idiot, but it's been driving Xavier nuts not knowing what happened, and he's been copping a heap of grief from the Tassie coppers over the pilot-drugging thing in Wynyard and the missing seaplane. I'm guessing that you snagged that Mini-Uzi from one of those turkeys. It used to give them a hard-on just waving that thing around.'

I smiled at her, 'So you're full-time with Xavier at Steel Associates. I always wondered where you'd ended up.'

She sighed, 'You know how it is, Harry. In the Service, the guys treated me as an equal and respected my skills, not just because I had a standard fit out of tits and pussy. Out of uniform, I've got a set of skills that aren't highly regarded on any CV. Sniper and wet job specialist doesn't translate into a comfortable office environment. Therefore, I was regarded as a freak! I'm also supposed to lie down for every swinging dick that thinks he's a tough guy, so I've got to be better than the best, and even then, I'm at the bottom of the pecking order, so where do I go?'

'Yeah, yeah. I know where you're coming from, but kidnapping is a bit of a stretch.'

She looked a bit uncomfortable, 'I know. Up to now, it's just been basic stuff like finding people and at first it was just taking orders and doing the job better than the rest, but this one raised a few red flags with me from the start. Dave's a good guy boat-driver who hasn't been on operations before and we were hoping that we couldn't find any trace of you and could report failure, although that usually sends Xavier into fits.'

'So how did you get on our trail in this area?' I asked.

'One of Xavier's clowns spotted you and Janice in the Lakes supermarket and followed you back to the dinghy. That was enough to get him fired up and send Dave and me out here in Xavier's personal Italian pussy catcher!'

I looked at Janice and Sandy and shrugged. 'Sorry guys. My bad. I thought we could duck in and out and not pick up a tail, but Xavier seems to be on the ball.'

'Oh yeah, he is. He might be a Pommy thug, but he's a smart little prick, so don't underestimate him.'

'Yeah, I'm starting to appreciate that. So, what's your position now you've heard what's really behind the operation?'

Corrine looked pensive. 'I believe you and this incredible story, so as far as I'm concerned, we haven't found you. We'll just cruise around the Lakes for a week or so, enjoying the sun and Xavier's food and booze, then return to base.'

Sandy made a noise that could have been a stifled cough, but sounded more like, 'Bullshit!' 'Do you really trust her word, Harry? What's to stop them calling down the whole Steel Associate mob on us as soon as we let her go?'

I looked at Corrine, then at Sandy. 'Sorry guys, but I do trust her. Implicitly! If she says she's on our side, that's good enough for me.'

Sandy sat back, clearly not happy, but prepared to see how things shook down.

'OK, Corrine. I just said I trust you, but Janice and Sandy aren't so sure, so what can you do to win them over?'

'Will you give me a few minutes to explain things to the others? Then I'll try to clear the air.'

'OK.'

'Are you going to let her get back on that boat without producing the girls?' Janice demanded, glaring with renewed intensity at Corrine. 'There's nothing to stop her from taking off!'

'Yes, I am going to do just that,' I replied mildly, then turned to Corrine.

'Maybe it would be better if you called your crew to come forward to the bow, without any weapons, so we can hear you tell them what we've told you.'

Corrine nodded, 'No problem, that'll work for me.'

She walked to the stern and called out, 'Dave. Will you all come forward, please? No weapons, no tricks. Everything is fine and there's a way out of this mess if we all do the right thing.'

Moments later, three people appeared; a tall, well-built guy, a blonde woman and a dark-haired woman, both pretty and shapely. When they stopped near the tip of the bow, Sandy stepped forward and flashed her Police badge. 'I'm Sergeant Thomson. Please behave, as I'd prefer not to have to arrest you, since it'd take me half an hour to work out the long list of charges, but for now, please lift your shirts up so I can see that there are no weapons tucked away.'

As a weapon search, it was well short of a proper frisk, but better than nothing and in the circumstances, probably quite sufficient. The guy complied, happily pulling his shirt up to show a six-pack and a half and did a 360° turn. The ladies looked rather intimidated by the Uzi that I still waved around and somewhat over-enthusiastically pulled their shirts up to show a lot of tanned skin, nice boobs, but no guns or knives. They didn't look like Steel Associates people to me and I was keen to hear the 'who and how'.

'OK,' Sandy said, 'that's enough. Now Corrine has a few things to say to you. It is very much in your interest to listen carefully, since we don't want any misunderstandings.' She nodded at the wicked Mini-Uzi to make the point.

Corrine stepped up and gave a brief rundown on what I'd told her about the situation with the girls and the paedophile ring. The other three didn't say anything until she finished.

'You obviously believe what you've heard, so what's your suggestion?' Dave asked.

'We haven't found them,' she replied simply, 'I suggest that we bum around this lovely Lakes' area for a while, enjoying free food and booze, then go home when Xavier gets sick of the lack of action and paying the fuel bills.'

Dave grinned, 'Suits me. This kidnapping of girls isn't right; especially now we've heard the full story. I'd prefer not to lose my perfect job, but I won't go along with Xavier's orders any longer.'

Jackie spoke for Allie as well. 'We're just along for the ride and a bit of fun, so now things have been explained, we're all in favour of doing the right thing. We can see that things weren't right, so we'll help in any way we can, or you can just dump us ashore if that's what you want.'

'Good,' I took over again, 'I'm glad that we have agreement on that, and ladies, we would appreciate it if you would stick around a little longer, since there are bigger plans in motion that shouldn't be interrupted. However, there still remains the vital question of, 'Where are the teens'?'

Corrine looked a bit ashamed, 'Oh shit. I'm sorry. With all the standoff stuff, I forgot. They're right here,' pointing at the bow of *Seeker.* 'Dave, would you do the honours please?'

Janice jumped to her feet as Dave unlatched the crew hatch and called the teens out. Angie and Zoe were first up the ladder, followed by Helene and Dom. They jumped down onto *Firebird's* stern and the girls embraced their mother, tears flowing. Dom shook hands with me and I scored a big hug and double kisses from Helene. I invited the crew from *Seeker* to come aboard as well and had Dave let out some line so that *Seeker* lay back a bit from our stern. Dave sheepishly handed over the folded blanket and the phone, and I was amused when Zoe immediately handed it over to me.

'You know what to do,' she said quietly, leaving the others looking mystified.

I grinned as I tucked it away in my pocket, 'Yep! I sure do.'

I called the group to order and had them sit down where they could around the cockpit.

'We have a final piece of business that's very important and is vital if our agreement is to hold up.' I looked at Helene and Dom. 'You guys are totally innocent bystanders in this mess and I think that you're owed a very big apology by the four *Seeker* crew. However, more to the point, do you want to make a formal complaint? You have, after all, been kidnapped at gunpoint and held against your will.'

They had a quick conversation in very rapid French that nobody was able to follow, before Helene said, 'We were able to hear everything that was said and it explained a great deal. We understand why you couldn't tell us the full story earlier, but we have become very fond of all of you for your hospitality and kindness. As there has been no harm done to any of us and we can see that the consequences for the twins would be considerable if we laid charges or even told our parents, we think it best if we say nothing and regard the incident as part of our great Australian adventure.'

'That's very gracious, Helene,' I said gravely, 'thank you very much. Now we should hear from Corrine and Dave.'

They stammered their way through a series of awkward, but seemingly heart-felt apologies to the four teens, who heard them out, then accepted graciously.

At that point, Helene said, 'I think that we should return to our parents for now, please Harry. We will abide by our agreement not to say anything, but you have much to discuss and need to settle in with your new friends. However, we would like to visit again tomorrow if we may?'

'Of course, Helene. Forgive me for not thinking of you sooner, but you are very welcome anytime and tomorrow is fine.'

They said their goodbyes and Angie elected to run them back.

Corrine looked at me, 'Okay, Harry. That's one more step, so where do we go from here?'

I looked around the group, but mainly addressed the *Seeker* crew, 'Under the circumstances, I'm prepared to let bygones be bygones if everyone else is willing to as well.' There were a thoughtful series of nods all around, even a slightly reluctant one from Janice, so I continued, 'In that case you are welcome to stay in company with us and enjoy the delights of the marvellous Lakes. We usually move every few days to keep the scenery fresh.

Although we can't stop you if you want to head off on your own, in light of what's brewing with all the pending prosecutions, it might be safest if you did stay close and keep your heads down. We may need your help if any other Steel Associates' people or bounty hunters come this way and as long as we can all accept that this morning's happenings didn't take place, then you are all blameless with nothing to fear from being swept up in the net.'

I figured that it wouldn't hurt to remind them that they were potentially looking at a capital crime charge that could only be averted by playing the game our way, but fortunately, Corrine said it for the rest. 'No problem from us, Harry, now we understand how things really are. We're very grateful that charges won't be pressed and that we have the chance to make things right. We'll stick around and help in any way you say.'

The others nodded, even Jackie and Allie. 'Wouldn't miss this for the world,' added Allie, 'bugger the shop for now! Mum and Dad can look after it for a bit longer.'

'Thanks, Corrine. We've been looking over our shoulders for a bit too long. I thought I was done with all that, but not so.'

She smiled, 'You and I need to have a chat about that sometime soon. There's a lot you're not saying.'

I just grinned back and left it alone for now. 'You'll need to make contact with Xavier sometime soon, I presume?'

'Yes, but not for at least another day or two. We spoke yesterday afternoon when we handed over the dickhead who'd spotted you and Janice to another Operative and got the latest set of updates on your position. Which reminds me, I'll just go get them so you know what Xavier knows.'

She went to pull *Seeker* back up to our stern, but I said the Dave, 'How about you fire up that thing and run it forward enough to drop the anchor, then lay back so we can raft up. It'll make transfer between boats a lot easier.'

He agreed and did so and I went along to help, getting a tour of *Seeker* at the same time. It was a beautiful boat, built for a totally different purpose than *Firebird*, but still a lovely sea boat. I was just glad I didn't have to pay the fuel bills or overhaul one of those V12 diesels. It didn't take long to set the rafting up and with plenty of fenders out we were soon secure. I felt better having them physically attached to us, because with the alliance in its infancy, I intended to keep them close until I was sure that everybody was firmly on the same page.

Dave stayed aboard to check a few things and Allie and Jackie took advantage of the new arrangement to go pee or something, while Corrine handed over the briefing notes from Xavier. I had just set down to read them with Sandy and Janice, when Zoe came up and said quietly, 'Jasper's getting a bit worried about what's happening. Can I bring him out?'

I laughed, 'Oh shit! I clean forgot about him in all the fuss. Yes, please do. I'll have to apologise for leaving him out of things.' I turned to Corrine and said, 'Please don't be alarmed, but it's time you met the boat cat.'

She raised one eyebrow, a neat trick of hers I'd always admired, and said, 'Oh, that's good. I like kitties.' Then she saw the long, black shape slinking out behind Zoe, his great amber eyes fixed unwaveringly on hers.

'Holy shit, Harry. What the hell's that?'

'That is my kitty. His name is Jasper. Jasper, this is Corrine; she's a friend.'

For once, my big cat didn't take my introduction very well as he slowly paced up to her and sniffed cautiously. He then sat back and huffed loudly.

Zoe and I laughed as Corrine asked, 'What just happened?'

'Don't be offended, but there are apparently some things about you he doesn't like. He's very sensitive.'

'I'm not sure I like the idea of a cat that big not liking me!' she retorted. 'That could be unhealthy.'

I looked at her seriously, 'Yes it could be, and it was very unhealthy for that bloke with the seaplane who called himself Mr Peter. I didn't tell you earlier as I didn't want to alarm everybody, but when Peter and the pilot tried to take the girls at gunpoint, Jasper helped defend us. He attacked him and pretty well tore him apart, literally. It made a fearsome mess all over the port landing platform.'

Despite her training in close-quarters killing, Corrine turned a bit white at the thought of a person being ripped to pieces by this big, black cat sitting quietly, but staring intently at her from two paces away. 'He really did that?'

'Yep! Chewed his gun arm off first, tore his throat out then ripped open his belly! Spilled his guts everywhere. Like I said, it made a fearsome mess and he didn't die too quickly either. Particularly nasty way to go.' I leaned over and scratched Jasper's ears, so he immediately closed his eyes and started purring, sounding like the auxiliary generator kicking in. Corrine didn't know whether to freeze or try to get away, so I said, 'Try scratching him under the chin. He likes that.'

So she did, very tentatively, but with growing confidence when she realised Jasper wasn't going to chew her hand off and that he really did like it. Finally, he shuffled forward until he could rest his head on her knees so she could scratch his ears and neck properly. She looked up with a strange expression on her face, 'He really likes it! He's just like a normal cat.'

'He is a normal cat,' I replied, 'just a lot bigger and with rather strong protective instincts for those in his family. Sandy, Janice and the girls are included in that family,' I added pointedly.

She didn't miss it. 'Got it! So where was he when I came aboard waving my gun around?'

'Just inside the saloon door, about one leap away,' I said with a straight face.

Corrine went quiet for a moment. 'Oh! So it was nearly a repeat of the Peter incident?'

I nodded, straight-faced, 'Yep. He's like that, best guard cat I've ever had.'

Corrine laughed weakly, but still looked oddly at the sleek, black purring head she was scratching.

FIREBIRD & SEEKER – BUNGA ARM, GIPPSLAND LAKES, THURSDAY

We'd spent the remainder of Wednesday traipsing back and forth between the two boats, had several discussions and sorted out who was to do what and when. After Corrine explained in private what she'd learned from Jackie and Allie while they were drugged with her cocktail, I endorsed her idea to keep them close until everything was wrapped up. I also explained to Corrine, in detail, just what was being planned to strike at all the paedophiles at once, to reinforce the point that it wouldn't be in her best interest to go talking to Xavier or anyone else at this point.

There would be one exception, as I'd called Hilary to let her know, as promised, that we were within range again if she and Debbie wanted to visit. As brief as my phone call had been, it was like I'd poked her with a cattle prod since I received a call back early this morning to say that they would be at the Public boat ramp on the Esplanade at Paynesville at 11:00 looking for a pick-up.

Accordingly, I'd asked Dave if he fancied a quick run over to Paynesville to collect a couple of very interesting ladies.

'No problem,' he replied, 'how far is it?'

'About 5 nautical,' I said.

He grinned, 'At 60 knots, that'll take all of 5 minutes! The engines will hardly get warm!'

'That'll be fun, then. You'll enjoy talking to these ladies. They're great people.'

Wednesday night, Dave had invited us all to dinner aboard *Seeker*, and ably assisted by Jackie and Allie, served a beautiful Beef Wellington with all the trimmings. Angie, all previous animosity forgotten, had pounced on him and was busy getting recipes and cooking ideas. The girls' natural charm quickly won over the whole *Seeker* crew and that went a long way toward melding us into one big, happy family united against Xavier and the paedophile ring. Perhaps having Jasper prowl over both boats throughout the night helped the mood swing toward peace and harmony.

Thursday breakfast was served on *Firebird* with Angie and Zoe trying to outdo Dave's beautiful feed of the night before. Dave and I talked about the run to Paynesville, but as there was no shopping either boat needed, it was only the ladies to be picked up. Naturally, Sandy, Janice and the girls would stay, with Jackie and Allie opting to join them. Surprisingly, Jasper made noises about wanting to join the quick run across Lake Victoria, so he was included.

We separated from the raft, hauled anchor and fenders and due to the shallow-draft jet drives, Dave took the overgrown speedboat up to near full speed straight away. I'd been on fast boats before, but not on one nearly 70 feet long doing 115 km/h in knee-deep water. Dave cut corners with reckless abandon, but he obviously knew the boat very well and it was an eye-opening experience to be travelling at that speed only a couple of metres from dry land. Jasper pretended to be a dog and sat up for'rard, his ears flattened and mouth open with the wind puffing out his cheeks. Every so often, he'd turn and grin stupidly back at us, staying there even when we hit some choppy water halfway across.

As predicted, 5 minutes after Dave opened the throttles in Bunga Arm, he throttled back to a sedate 5 knots as we approached the two little L-shaped jetties beside the Public boat ramp. Both were crowded, so Dave showed off the shallow-water capability of the big boat by nosing up almost to the beach at the end of one jetty where I could tie up to a bollard. We hadn't been there long before the familiar figures of Hilary and Debbie strode briskly across the car park and up to our parking spot. They didn't recognise the boat, of course, but the sight of Jasper bounding down the jetty to greet them, to the alarm of several locals, brought cries of recognition.

Debbie, the frustrated boatie, cast a critical eye over *Seeker's* lines and said severely, 'I do hope, Harry, that you haven't swapped your beautiful catamaran for this...thing!'

I chuckled, 'Hello, my dear Debbie. No, I haven't done anything silly like that. We're going to take you to *Firebird* right now, but there's a long story behind the presence of this boat, and we'll tell you later.'

Mollified, she gave me a big hug then passed me on to Hilary who gave me a kiss and a harder hug then stood back and patted my cheek.

'Dear boy! What have you been up to this time?'

'Oh, just the usual, Hilary — boats, bad guys, bullets and old friends. You're going to love this one!'

'I do already, but please introduce me to that lovely, handsome young man and those darling girls.'

'What? Aren't I good enough for you anymore?' I demanded with a grin.

'Always, Harry, always! But he's younger, they're prettier, and I have to keep all my options open in case Debbie ever kicks me out.'

Debbie rolled her eyes and smiled indulgently. So I made the introductions to Dave, Corrine, Jackie and Allie, then we loaded our visitors aboard for the brief run back to Bunga Arm, where we rafted up again and the girls, Janice and Sandy, greeted Hilary and Debbie warmly.

I let Janice and Corrine tell the latest story to Hilary and Debbie, while Sandy updated her boss, Bob Casey, and I made contact firstly with Rob and then Annette to fill them in on the latest situation and its quite astonishing outcome. Both were a little sceptical about the turnaround of attitude by the *Seeker* crew, but finally conceded that it sounded all right, especially if Hilary's investigative nose was firmly buried in the case. Rob was appalled yet again that we had been assaulted, but amazed that we had escaped with the latest opposing force defecting to our side.

It was Annette who dropped the big bombshell. 'Things are

finally progressing with a co-ordinated move planned to seize their headquarters — the mansion in Melbourne, while everyone who has been identified in photos and videos will be arrested simultaneously.'

'That's great news!' I said, 'When should this happen?'

'Probably on Saturday evening, which we think is best for the mansion raid, but there's still a lot of work being done to trace the movements of all the other identified persons so that they can all be grabbed at the same time wherever they are. We expect that they will have an emergency communication system set up, so it's essential to act simultaneously to stop a warning getting out.'

I sagged against the chart table with relief, 'Oh, Annette! That's fantastic! So, by Sunday morning, the heat should be off us?'

'Basically, you should be in the clear by then. That Xavier character who's been giving you grief is on the pick-up list as well, even though he's not actually a suspect in the paedophile side of things. But he's done so many very dodgy jobs for various members of the Ring, that the task force has included him on the shit list now there's good evidence against him from that Tasmanian mess. So he and some of his key operatives will be scooped up, and that Company of his, Steel Associates, shut down and all Company records and assets seized.'

'May I tell the two ex-employees we have with us that they should go very low profile for a while, or are they on the list as well?'

She chuckled, 'They're on our database, but based on what you've said, you probably owe them one, so go ahead, warn them off. But tell them from me that they'd better seek a different line of work immediately or some very large feet will descend on them from a great height. We will be keeping an eye on them.'

'Thanks Annette, there'll be some very relieved people here shortly, but especially after Saturday night.'

'I'm glad to be giving you good news for a change and I know what you've gone through but remember that you've still got to stay quiet for two and a half more days, so don't pop too many

Champagne corks just yet. Make sure you get the Sunday papers however!'

'It's a good thing that Hilary isn't concerned with breaking the story, but she'll be very pleased to do the follow-up stuff.'

'Cheers, Harry. I'll be in touch.'

'Thanks Annette, for everything.... '

I called a round table conference that we had to hold in *Seeker's* much larger main saloon, given that we had eleven people to seat. When all were comfortable, I told them of the simultaneous raids scheduled for Saturday night, which caused an immediate outbreak of chatter and questioning. Holding my hand up, I said, 'Hold on and back up the bus. It's only almost over, not completely finished! We still have to avoid any Steel Associates' operatives or bounty hunters until Sunday, so that means business as usual, but at least we do have a very close target date and can relax a little.' After the fresh outbreak chatter had died down a little, I looked at Jackie and Allie. 'You ladies will be free to resume your normal lives from Sunday on, and *Firebird* or *Seeker* will run you back to Lakes Entrance where you can re-start your holiday. If you feel the desire to talk about this afterwards, please remember that some people know that your involvement hasn't been entirely innocent.'

'Ahh. What do you mean?' Jackie asked, a tremble in her voice.

'To put it bluntly, we know all about the plans you made with James to track down the girls yourselves for Luke's reward. That makes you as bad as the clowns who tried to bust us on Erith Island and I remind you what happened to them — one dead and one locked up.'

They looked utterly stricken. 'But how do you know? We didn't say anything.'

'Let's just say that we got the information from the horse's mouth, in fine detail and it's all recorded. Court admissible, if necessary.'

Allie burst into tears, while Jackie shut up and appeared to find the carpet pattern fascinating.

I looked at Corrine and Dave. 'Your boss is being scooped up too. Not because he's a paedophile, but because he's done a lot of very dodgy work for members of the Ring over the years, so now that there's strong evidence tying him to the Tasmanian debacle, the ACP want to take him out permanently. Steel Associates will be shut down and all Company assets seized.'

Corrine looked worried, 'So where does that leave us?'

'I'm authorised to tell you that although you're known Xavier associates, because of your change of heart yesterday, you won't be prosecuted with the rest. Provided of course, you keep your heads down and don't get involved in this sort of business again. That's the official word from the ACP!'

They both looked very relieved, but Dave asked, 'What about the boat? Is it going to be seized along with everything else?'

'Is it company property or Xavier's private toy?'

Dave thought a moment, 'I'm not sure.'

Corrine chipped in, 'I know. When Xavier called me to come on this trip, he said that he normally wouldn't use the boat on a job, as it's his personal toy, not company property. But as time was pressing, he approved its use. So it shouldn't be included in any company asset seizure.'

I looked at both of them, 'I guess you're trying to say that you'd like to hang onto the *Seeker* for yourselves.'

They nodded in unison. 'Not my concern, but I'll put in a good word to the proper people for you. Do what you want with it, but I strongly recommend that you do something very legitimate, like executive charter or something like that.'

They looked at each other, 'Great idea! Thanks.'

'For the rest of us, we'll have to wait to see what the fallout of all the arrests are, but we should know how that's going within a few weeks. I imagine the trials will take a lot longer than that to come about.'

As there were no more questions that seemed as good a reason as any to break out Xavier's booze. Animated conversations broke out around the table, but all I could see of my future was with my lovely boat and my beautiful, mystical cat.

EPILOGUE

#...Two nights later, on Saturday night, as a cold front swept its cleansing blast across much of South-Eastern Australia, Officers from three State Police Forces and the ACP, made a series of raids on the homes or other locations of suspected or identified paedophiles.

#...A Mansion in Melbourne yielded the greatest prizes — the most vocal being a selection of Melbourne's upper echelon of government, politics, high society and celebrities, along with a number of young children, most of whom were illegally in the country. The kids all showed signs of abuse of one form or another. An office on the ground floor held an astonishing collection of paper and digital records listing all the members of the Ring, their tastes, preferences and contact details. As International addresses were listed, Interpol was supplied with the details and promptly passed them on to the various Police Forces of the countries concerned for action

#...Many social gatherings, both large and small were disrupted that evening, when uniformed Police officers came knocking on doors, regardless of the name or status of who those doors belonged to. The results of that sweep filled the holding cells of nearly every Police Station to capacity with the most astonishing variety of men, as well as a few women, all yelling for lawyers. Due to an unprecedented co-operative agreement reached between judges and magistrates within the judicial system of all four involved States, massive legal fees were racked up in vain by lawyers, all making attempts to get their clients out on bail that were repeatedly refused.

#...In a number of private homes in each State, the echo of a single gunshot rendered an arrest pointless, although the stunned families affected were then subjected to the most intense house searches and witnessed the removal of masses of records and computer drives.

#...Although some guests thought it an arranged part of the evening's entertainment, Mr Xavier, aka Terry Johnson, was removed in handcuffs from a very fashionable party in St Kilda. That was after the guests were treated to the reading of a long list of charges which started with murder, extortion and kidnapping, worked down through tax evasion, before ending with failure to pay parking fines. A fellow guest was heard to comment facetiously that, 'I do believe that he's been a very naughty boy!'

#...Miss Julie was roused out of her bed and taken, still in her nightie and dressing gown, to the Steel Associates office to open every locked drawer and safe, as well as booting up and un-protecting all computers. A three-tonne truck had to be hurriedly hired to cart away the files and hardware from that office alone. She would receive a suspended sentence in return for her co-operation in telling the entire story about the company's dark dealings and showing the Police literally where the bodies were buried.

#...On Sunday morning, a large and very fast powerboat crossed the rough Lake Victoria from the Bunga Arm to Paynesville, in strong winds and pouring rain. It nosed up to a small jetty beside the Esplanade, just around the corner from the Public boat ramp, but opposite a Newsagency. A pretty, blonde girl leapt ashore and ran the short distance across the road, heedless of the rain and emerged minutes later with an armful of local and inter-State newspapers. After she scrambled aboard, it departed to the south at a highly illegal and anti-social speed. If there had been any curious onlookers on that cold, wet and windy morning, they might have heard the sound of clapping, cheering and laughter drifting back from the sleek red craft as it thundered away into the murk.

#...In a ceremony that puzzled the *Seeker* crew, Angie and Zoe were solemnly presented with a mobile phone each.

#...Over the following weeks and months, most of the detainees from that fateful Saturday night roundup were processed through the legal system, which in an Australian first, functioned without delay to convict an unprecedented 93% of all those originally arrested. Incontrovertible picture and video evidence were cited as the main reason for such a high percentage of convictions.

#...An astonishing who's who of Australian notables figured prominently in the trial reports, and as a wise man predicted, it had the potential to bring down a ruling Government. However, in what was described afterwards as a 'close re-run of the 1975 Australian Constitutional Crisis', it was the cream that rose to the top this time with a Prime Minister who actually acted Prime Ministerial for a change, and made the strong decisions that were needed to flush out the undesirables and saved the Australian people from having to elect, at hideous expense, another bunch of over-paid, low-achieving, no-hopers. Since the opposition party weren't immune to the fallout, with many of their inner circle caught up in the net, they made no objections to a more thorough flushing-out of paedophiles in positions of trust and power. The long-term savings in Senior Executive Service salaries alone nearly paid for the whole operation.

#...For his prominent part in the purchase of the Headquarters and functioning of the Ring, Luke Emery received a 25-year jail sentence, although his lawyer cheerfully told him that he'd be out in 18 years if he behaved himself. Unfortunately for Mr Emery and for most of the other convicted persons, the inmates of Australian prisons don't hold paedophiles in very high esteem. Therefore, Luke

Emery survived just three months after being elected prime bitch for a group of ex-bikie club members, before he was found naked in the showers one morning in a decidedly deceased condition, a lump of soap having rendered further intake of air impossible.

#...Janice, Angie and Zoe tearfully departed *Firebird* a week after the raids, with the girls returning to University, while Janice arranged to sell the lovely old house and made the move to a charming rural area with supportive and influential friends close by. As promised, they planned to join *Firebird* whenever possible during Uni holidays.

#...In a gala presentation by the National Press Club, Hilary Jones was awarded the Gold Walkley for her series of articles on the rise and fall of the largest paedophile ring in Australia's history. A book was rumoured to be under way.

#...The law enforcement sections of various overseas governments were quietly effusive with their praise for the assistance given in clearing up a large chunk of the kiddie porn market in their own countries. Rumours of awards for the operatives involved were quietly squashed.

#...To Janice's delight, Rob and Annette got together permanently, with Rob moving to Canberra to live with her. They saw no need to formalise the arrangement any further than that. She received a big promotion as a reward for her part in tracking down the culprits and more importantly, a great deal more status and credibility from her peers. Oddly, Rob declined any recognition and refused to take any part in the prosecution process. He continued to practice law as a Barrister in Queanbeyan.

#...At the urging of her boss, Sandy took a bunch of accumulated leave and after she and Harry gave a series of notarised formal interviews, *Firebird* departed the area and within the week, was wandering aimlessly around the Whitsunday Islands. Selected persons received invitations and made the flight to Hamilton Island airport where they were met by a tanned couple on a catamaran with a large black cat.

#...Less than a year later, Annette, Janice and the girls were devastated to receive notification that Rob had been involved in a head-on car accident with a drugged driver and did not survive. When clearing out his effects, Annette came across a key to a long-term storage locker with a Melbourne address, so she sent it to Janice along with a few other items she didn't want to keep. When they found the locker, they saw that it contained many items from the old family home, souvenirs and memorabilia, most of which Janice threw away or donated to Charity. There was one curious item that Zoe found that she decided to keep. It was a HytechToyz voice changer box, which still had batteries fitted and flashed lots of lights when she flicked the switch. A perfect re-production of Darth Vader's voice came out of the speaker when she talked into the microphone plugged into the box.

'I wonder what Pops had this for?'

'Probably was going to give it to you or Angie as a present,' her mother suggested, 'are you going to keep it?'

'Yeah. Might as well. These are pretty cool things and it'll be fun making a phone call to our friends using that weird voice. No one will know who it is!'

#...Harry's standing with the ACP had also increased dramatically with the success of the operation. He was retained as a deep undercover operative, with the brief of just blending into the boating community as an eccentric, wealthy boat bum, but his discrete funding was increased. He and Sandy made no particular personal plans, but she received a double-jump promotion to Inspector that required her to attend management courses, even though she'd already done most of the training modules. Her boss, Bob Casey, let her keep her undercover role, but until another investigation came up, she had to return to station life for a while which included relieving duties in several remote area stations.

#...After hanging around the Whitsunday's for a while, Harry moved the *Firebird* to the Gold Coast and leased a permanent mooring off the yacht club so he could be close to Sandy, although she was frequently away on various courses or gaining experience in her new inspector position as a relieving officer.

#...Harry needed to use his pull with both the ACP and the Queensland Police to keep Jasper after several people complained about the presence of a 'dangerous animal' in their midst. No further action was taken.

#...Corrine and Dave remained together and were allowed, by various un-official paperwork fiddles, to keep *Seeker*. They set up an Executive Charter service and made it flourish.

#...Hilary and Debbie flew to the Gold Coast to present Jasper with an 8-week old female black kitten, from the one litter that their Domestic Shorthair house cat had been allowed to produce. She had round amber eyes like an owl and an unusual scattering of pretty silver speckles throughout her fur. In a display of indignation at being confined in a pet carrier for the 2-hour flight from Melbourne, the tiny, feisty bundle of bristling black fur darted out of the carrier, bit Hilary's finger and swiped at Debbie's bare toes with her needle-sharp claws, before scampering up Jasper's foreleg to crouch on his head, claws extended for stability and mouth open, loudly voicing her disgust with all humans. Jasper closed his eyes and started purring contentedly which seemed to indicate that he was happy and the situation was as expected with his new companion.

End of Hitch Hikers